THE NEWCASTLE FORGOTTEN FANTASY LIBRARY
VOLUME XIII

SHY LEOPARDESS

THE NEUSTRIAN CYCLE, BOOK THREE

SHY LEOPARDESS

BY

LESLIE BARRINGER

npc

NEWCASTLE PUBLISHING COMPANY, INC.
NORTH HOLLYWOOD, CALIFORNIA

1977

FIRST AMERICAN EDITION

A NEWCASTLE BOOK
FIRST PRINTING OCTOBER 1977
PRINTED IN THE UNITED STATES OF AMERICA

INTRODUCTION

With the publication of this first American edition of *Shy Leopardess*, we bring to a close Leslie Barringer's Neustrian trilogy, which began with *Gerfalcon* and *Joris of the Rock* (both still available in Newcastle editions). We are delighted that so many of you have enjoyed discovering the excitement of these books, as you have indicated in your many letters. Barringer was truly a "forgotten fantasist," and although the first two books were not impossible to obtain, they had become difficult over the years. Indeed, few of today's fantasy fans have ever had a chance to read them.

But his third book, *Shy Leopardess*, is far rarer than the others. We had no idea what a hard time we would have finding a copy to print from when we decided to revive the Neustrian Cycle for today's readers. We had almost every book search service in this country and England on the lookout for a copy, but none turned up in well over a year.

Finally, an old friend of ours from the days when we were publishing *Forgotten Fantasy* magazine came to our rescue: Al Germeshausen, a veteran collector and a very generous gentleman, offered to sacrifice his own copy for the cause. In order for us to bring the book to you now, rather than who knows how long from now, he agreed to let us remove the binding for reprinting. (Our printer's machinery requires removal of the binding; some others' do not). All of us who enjoyed the first two Barringer books and have been eagerly waiting to read the third owe Mr. Germeshausen a debt of gratitude. Even though we can have the book rebound in its original binding, not many collectors would make such a sacrifice.

This isn't the first time Al has come to our rescue: back in 1970, when we were serializing the rare inner-world novel, *The Goddess of Atvatabar*, in *Forgotten Fantasy* magazine, someone broke into the typesetter's office and stole my personal copy of the book, which we were using to set from. Needless to say, we were panic-stricken—we had a printer's deadline staring us in the face and the magazine unfinished, and the book was not an easy one to obtain in a hurry! But Al stepped forward and lent us his copy and we were able to finish up on time. So once again, we say thanks a million, Al Germeshausen!

We also owe a debt of gratitude to a thoughtful fan from Australia, Keith Curtis, who sent us some biographical information on Leslie Barringer. Such information has been almost impossible to find in the United States; Barringer seems to be completely unknown to compilers of literary biographical material in this country, even those who specialize in historical romances. Even L. Sprague de Camp, in his excellent essay in *The Conan Reader* (Mirage, 1968), slightly revised to appear in *Literary Swordsmen and Sorcerers* (Arkham House, 1976), was able to offer only the sketchiest of biographical information. But finally, we can now share with you a fuller picture of this writer of extraordinary romantic fantasy.

Leslie Barringer was born in 1895 at the Friends' School, Rawdon, in Yorkshire, England. His father was headmaster of the institution, and young Barringer later attended Ackworth. While still in school, he met his future wife, Dorothy, but they were not able to marry until 1922 because of financial difficulties and the war.

In 1914 World War I was declared, and Barringer, then 19, joined the Friends' Ambulance Unit and went to France. Two years later, he decided he wanted to be more directly involved in the fighting and enlisted in the Second Infantry Battalion of the Honourable Artillery Company. He was wounded in action and honorably discharged in 1917.

In 1918 Barringer decided to take up a literary career and joined the staff of Thomas Nelson & Sons, publishers. He remained with them as editor and educational representative for the next 18 years.

During this time, two important things happened in his life. The first was his marriage to Dorothy, who eventually gave him four daughters. The second was his growing passion for the study of world history, which culminated in the writing of his first novel, *Gerfalcon*. It was published by Heinemann in 1927 and in the U.S. by Doubleday, Page the same year. Although the book was well received by critics on both sides of the Atlantic, it was not a popular success.

Undaunted, in 1928 Barringer published the closely-interwoven sequel, *Joris of the Rock* (Heinemann, London; Doubleday, Doran, New York, 1929). (Plot synopses of both these books and *Shy Leopardess* can be found in my introduction to the Newcastle edition of *Gerfalcon*.) Like the previous book, *Joris* was also critically acclaimed but popularly ignored.

The two novels were set in a mythical medieval France called Neustria. Barringer invented a clever and detailed analogue of the real country, peopling it with a vivid and imaginative cast of characters engaged in exciting, colorful battles and intrigues. To this heady brew, he added a pinch of real witchcraft and the supernatural, particularly in *Joris*. The result was two of the finest fantasy-adventure romances of the 1920s. But the public was not receptive, and the books remained unknown to all but a few fantasy collectors for almost 50 years.

Perhaps discouraged by this dim reception, Barringer turned back to a more prosaic career. The two novels stand as a cohesive whole; perhaps he had said all he wished to say at that time.

A new world war brought another change for Barringer; in 1942 he became a writer and editor for the weekly British magazine *Radio Times*. This was a popular periodical published by the BBC, featuring illustrated articles on radio personalities and listing all BBC radio programs. He remained with the magazine until 1946, then entered the British Civil Service as Senior Information Officer at the Central Office of Information.

But his love of writing and world history made him restless for other things. Twenty years after the failure of his first two novels, Barringer returned to his mythical world of Neustria to write the final volume in its history, *Shy Leopardess*. His writing skills sharpened by 20 years of literary work, he produced what many consider to be the best of the three books. His colorful powers of description, his excellent use of dialogue, and his gift for believable, well-rounded characterization all came to fruition in this exciting novel of betrayal, intrigue, struggle, and vengeance. Young Yolande, orphaned daughter of the Duke of Baraine and the "shy leopardess" of the book's title, is one of the most intriguing and sympathetic female characters in all fantasy fiction.

But if the previous novels had been neglected by the public, *Shy Leopardess* was completely ignored! Published in a small edition by Methuen in 1948, it was not even reviewed and was never published in the United States. The British people were still recovering from the turmoil and trauma of the war and apparently had little time for mythical romance.

Barringer left the C.O.I. in 1954. Later, he went to work for the Amalgamated Press, where he became an editor in the Encyclopedia Department. Here, he was again able to utilize his broad historical knowledge, to contribute an outline of world history for a new edition of the Amalgamated Children's Encyclopedia.

Still, later, Barringer again turned his hand to writing novels, but this time without the tinge of fantasy. *Kay the Lefthanded* takes place in the England of King John, and both *Know Ye Not Agincourt* and *The Rose in Splendour* are rooted in other periods of English history. These "straight" historical novels were no more successful than his fantasies, and today are even more obscure.

And so, after a full but disappointing literary career, Leslie Barringer retired to Ilkley in Yorkshire, where he died in 1968 at the age of 73.

We hope you enjoy this third and rarest Neustrian romance, the story of Yolande, the Shy Leopardess, and her two loyal pages, Lioncel and Diomede, as they are pitted against the ruthless and sadistic Balthasar.

And let us hear from you.

> Douglas Menville
> Joint Editor,
> Newcastle Forgotten
> Fantasy Library

Los Angeles, California
August, 1977

TO
GORDON AND MILLICENT STOWELL

CONTENTS

ENCOUNTERS AT PARDELIN

'FROM here,' said Yolande of Baraine, 'you can see why it's called Lake Falchion.'

Balthasar, Viscount of Montguiscard, gave a little grunt of agreement. They stood together on the keep of Pardelin, and the westward-reaching water beneath them had indeed the rough shape of a sword—a heavy curved sword whose blade widened and returned to a point amid the wild hills.

It was the time of afterglow, and no wind stirred the iron-grey and silver-grey, the rose and blue and saffron of the lake. Clouds were high and still; mountains lifted rocky summits towards the first stars. A confusion of crags and screes, of heather and bracken and gorse and pine, stooped sombrely to greenwood along the twilit shore.

'Falchions,' mused Balthasar aloud. 'You should see the falchions of the bodyguard of the Archduke Adalbert. Heavier than any of our swords, except two-handed ones. He has them specially made, at Antioch, I believe. When my father and I were at Brelstein the Archduke promised a Muscovite prisoner his life if he could beat three of the guards, he on horseback and they on foot. They carved him and his horse in pieces before you could have said an *Ave*.'

Yolande watched the day's last dragonfly whirl over the battlements and vanish against the tree-tops.

'I should not *much* like,' she said, 'to see the falchions of the bodyguard of the Archduke Adalbert.'

Balthasar glanced aside at her, and his shapely mouth twitched. He was sixteen years old, blue-eyed, golden-haired, lovely as the morning; Yolande, two years younger, was dark and thin and shy, with no more than comeliness in her smooth high-cheekboned face. She resented the presence of strangers at Pardelin, where she was used to having her father to herself. Even this dazzling cousin, first seen today, was not to be easily admitted to confidence or liking.

'This is a desolate place,' went on Balthasar. 'What do you do all day when there is no hunting?'

'Ride and swim and . . .'

'*Swim?*'

'Yes. Or sail or row along the lake, and take our fruit and wine there on the island. And sometimes I make drawings on paper or wood. The Dame de Chevronel helps me to paint them. Or we climb the hills, and practise archery. One year we built a hut in a tree.'

'You . . . and *my lord duke?*'

'Yes, and the pages. It is lonely, and we like it. Each summer we stay for a while. This year earlier than most, because the plague's spreading. You know what the peasants say: *April dry, beware July.*'

'Is that what peasants say?' asked Balthasar with mock innocence.

'Yes. Peasants can talk, you know. There was only a hunting-lodge here before Duke Pelleas came. And we have no tourneys.'

'If you did they would have to be water-tourneys. Even the little cornfields slope.'

'You like water-tourneys?' enquired Yolande, recalling her *rôle* of hostess.

'Yes, they're great sport. Last year at Hautarroy . . . but tell me, was that Pelleas the first duke of Baraine?'

'Yes. After him was Faramond, and then came three more, and then my grandfather, and now my father.'

'And there is only . . . er . . .'

'Yes. There is only I to follow. My brothers died when they were babies.'

'But you are betrothed to the Duke of Boqueron.'

'Yes.'

'Then when . . . then some time you will be the greatest lady in Neustria after the queen herself.'

'So it is said.'

'Duke Drogo is tremendous in the lists. I saw him unhorse the Constable at the king's birthday jousting. His father was one of the two dukes who stood by the king in the great rebellion and at the battle of Pont-de-Foy.'

'Yes. *My* father was ill. Our men were there, in the king's own division.'

'My own father would have been there too, but he was besieged in Ferisgar, in the service of the emperor.'

Yolande stood silent, catching at her six-year-old memory of the hawk-faced young man who glittered out of the blur of sound and colour and fatigue that was her betrothal-day. He had smiled kindly at her, put a ring on her finger, kissed her hand twice and her lips once, patted her on the head, and left her clutching a bracelet studded with rubies and sapphires. . . .

This year she was to have seen him again, but the spice ships had brought plague to the western seaboard of Neustria, and death and confusion were stalking through three provinces. Here, on the eastern *massif* called the Casque of Baraine, that trouble seemed far away. . . .

Yolande came to herself with a start, and made another effort of courtesy.

'Why, yes, of course,' she said. 'My lord your father and you have travelled over most of Europe. This must seem to you a very quiet country. There's been no fighting here since Pelleas cleared the hills of outlaws.'

'He built this hold?'

'Yes, and named the mountains. Of those three on the south side, the first is called Siege Perilous, after the magic chair at King Arthur's Round Table, and also because it's hard to reach the top. The middle one is Siege Orgulous; that's the tallest. The far one is Siege Fabulous; it has a ring of standing stones in a hollow on this side of the crest, which must have been a temple of the old religion.'

'Do they use it now—the peasants, I mean?'

'I don't think so. My father says it's too windy even for wizards, and too far for witches who must be home by milking-time.'

'And that great pile on the northern side?'

'Siege Gracious, which we see oftenest in full sunshine.'

'And this grim one behind us, blocking the end of the valley?'

Yolande turned and looked up the frowning slopes.

'Siege Umbrous. We live in its morning shadow until the hour of terce. When the Prior Gilomar of Sanctlamine visited us last year he never saw the top at all, for it was clouded for a whole week. He said it should be called Siege Ombrous, *ombros* being the Greek word for rain.'

'I knew a Greek once,' said Balthasar. 'He was a famous poisoner, and I saw him broken on the wheel.'

Yolande folded her hands behind her and frowned a little, wondering how to make this experienced guest feel more at home. A distant shape on the mountain-side came to her rescue.

'You see that great hawthorn beyond the turn of the black cleft, above the topmost waterfall?' she asked him.

'Yes.'

'It's called Faramond's Tree, because the Duke Faramond had a mercenary captain hanged from it for some discourtesy to a lady.'

'A long way to go for a hanging,' commented Balthasar drily. 'This great oak here by the hamlet would have been just as useful.'

'They were up there hunting wildcat,' explained Yolande. 'There are still great wildcat hereabouts. The shepherds killed one a month ago.'

She glanced up at the purple banner hanging stiffly from its gilded spar above the highest turret of the keep. There ramped the greatest wildest cat of all—the Golden Leopard of Baraine, black-spotted, with crimson coronet and eye and tongue and male member, gathering to himself the last light, threatening with a furious frozen gesture the mountains and the sky.

'Sorry I'm only a girl, Gold Puss,' she told him silently. 'If I were a boy I'd take this paladin up on the tops, and hope a wildcat or a wolf would come along and make him jump.'

Aloud she said only: 'Here come my lords our fathers.' The boy turned beside her to face the nearest turret stair.

Engelbert Duke of Baraine led Azo Count of Montguiscard out on to the keep ramparts.

The duke was dark and slender, with melancholy face and pointed black beard; his black-and-violet gown was brightened only by a jewelled girdle. The count, two inches taller than his host, was gorgeous in vermilion, with the golden collar of a foreign order upon his broad shoulders; his face was pastily good-looking, with a long pinkish nose, shaven cheeks, and a square-cut greying beard. His eyes were blue and fine and a little staring.

Yolande curtseyed, Balthasar bowed, and the two elder lords inclined their heads.

'Azo should have bowed to *me*,' thought Yolande as she stood erect. 'Just because he married mother's sister he thinks . . . what does he think? Now he's Seneschal of Jarapt, but for years and years he was just another mercenary captain.'

'And now, Azo,' said the duke, 'you can see why Pelleas called it Lake Falchion.'

Count Azo in his turn made a sound of assent. The duke began to name the mountains, and Yolande ventured to interrupt him.

'Look, my lords,' she exclaimed. 'A boat with a lantern, coming along the lake.'

The group of them stood still for an instant. Behind, on the tallest turret, an archer moved sharply and shattered the evening hush with the howl of a war-horn. Voices jarred, doors banged, steel began to clink and rattle along the ramparts of Pardelin. The far black shape with its spark of light now visibly furrowed the surface of the water.

'We're to have some sauce with our supper,' the duke told his guests. 'There's a tower called Quatrelances at the far end of the lake, with no road beyond. Any news coming that way must be brought over the high ranges.'

'God sent it be no evil news, my lord duke,' said Azo gravely.

Half an hour later, in the castle hall, Yolande sat staring in front of her, conscious of discreet glances that slid away if she turned her head. A shocked glumness reigned on the dais; the sauce was sharp, the news was evil, Drogo Duke of Boqueron was dead of the black plague.

Yolande was sorry for him, sorry for herself, but sorriest for her father, who had taken such care to find for her a husband whose rank and fortune were matched by his fair fame. She wondered if Gold Puss were sorry, up there in the windless darkness; he must have grown used to the thought of sharing a blazon with the red scallop-shells of Boqueron. And she was touched by mutttered words from the household, by tears on the grim cheeks of her governess, the old Dame de Chevronel.

Nevertheless Yolande enjoyed the dish called mortruse, which tonight was of pork, finely ground, boiled with crushed almonds and rice flour, salted and sugared and strewn with powdered ginger. And for the first time in her life a second goblet of wine appeared beside her platter; true, it was well-watered, but the gesture had been made.

'I wish the Montguiscards away,' she found herself thinking. 'I hate to have anyone not of the household to share this news with father.'

Opposite the duke sat the lean, freckled squire who had come from Quatrelances. Engelbert let him eat his fill, and then leaned forward.

'Hugo,' he said clearly in the hush, 'tell this company how you dealt with the messenger from Boqueron.'

Hugo swallowed and spoke.

'My lord duke, the messenger is a chevalier of discretion. He reined in a score of paces from me, and wouldn't come closer, shouting his tidings. We prepared a hut on the hillside, with a fire of wormwood blowing smoke into and around it. Also we kindled another fire, and in it he burned his clothes and saddle, and went into the hut naked, with blankets and straw to keep him warm. I've sent back vinegar, so that he may heat it and bathe himself each day. After ten days we'll give him new clothes, and burn the hut with all he has had in it.'

'What about his horse?' asked the Count Azo.

'We dug a pit, my lord count, and he slew his horse so that it fell into the pit, and covered it with lime, and buried it himself.'

'That was well done,' said the duke. 'There's peril in the sweat and slaver of beasts. Take heed, all, and fear nothing from Quatrelances.'

Then there was a buzz of talk, and Yolande sat silent, listening. King Thorismund and his queen had fled with half their court to Hastain, the royal demesne in Basse Honoy. The other half, dispersing, had not altogether avoided infection. A duke was dead, and a dowager duchess with her three daughters. At the capital the old Archbishop was stricken on the steps of the high altar of Saint Andreas. The Provost of Hautarroy died in a room over one of the city gates. Nobles, clergy, merchants, townsfolk, soldiers, peasants and beggars were falling to the deadly sickness. Yolande's betrothed had been smitten down in a little wayside inn a league from his own principal castle. . . .

Dutifully, for six years, Yolande had put him next to her father in her prayers; and now nothing remained but to pray for his soul.

'I must sleep a little and change my gown before our midnight Mass,' she thought. 'And Azo there will have to shed his vermilion for something less glorious.'

Suddenly she was terrified, wishing that what had to be said to God could have been said before supper; but the duke had chosen not to let guests wait upon business of the duchy. Fat Dom Piers, the castle chaplain, seemed also to be enjoying the mortruse; but Dom Piers was used to looking beyond the things of this world. . . .

Never since the day of her mother's death had Yolande trusted in God; never since her first motherless night had she accepted all she was told about his allmightiness and wisdom and mercy. Sometimes the Sieur Jesus seemed the only part of God you could hope to understand; but God-the-Father had treated the Sieur Jesus very badly. Now he—God-the-Father— seemed to be at it again, smiting people for the sins and sinful thoughts he let the devil put into their hearts. Great texts flew far on golden wings: *In the fear of God is the beginning of wisdom . . . there is no fear in love, but perfect love casteth out fear . . . God is love . . . the Father sent the Son to be the Saviour of the world . . . and the whole world lieth in wickedness.* The great texts dodged each other among the burning stars. The voice of the Sieur Jesus gave terrible advice: *Estote ergo vos perfecti . . . be ye therefore perfect, even as your Father in heaven is perfect.*

It simply couldn't be done. Yolande would have liked to put a hand on her earthly father's velvet gown, but on her other side was the silent, observant Balthasar. Pride kept her hands in sight, her back straight, and her eyes steady.

Also it allowed her to notice a newcomer serving at the board. This morning there had been one page, Lioncel de Forne— Lioncel, very fair and trim, with white-gold hair and violet tunic bearing the Golden Leopard on its breast. Tonight there was another beside him, a dark, sullen-looking boy with black hair and brown eyes that held her own for a shocked instant and then were veiled by long, black lashes.

When next Lioncel passed behind her Yolande spoke over her shoulder.

' Lioncel.'

' Yes, my lady? '

' What's the name of the new page? '

' Diomede de Torre, my lady. He came from Sanctlamine today. He's my lord prior's nephew.'

' Bring him to me next time his hands are empty.'

Lioncel bowed and went about his tasks of carving meat and pouring wine and changing silver dishes. Presently the dark boy was standing at her elbow. Stiff-faced with her own shyness, Yolande turned to look up at him, ignoring the curious sideways glance of Balthasar.

' Diomede.'

' My lady.'

' I bid you welcome here. I hope you'll be happy.'

' Gramercy, my lady, and God have you in his keeping,' whispered dark Diomede. He seemed to find this greeting kind and unexpected.

So too did Balthasar, who waited until Diomede had bowed and moved away. Then he looked down his shapely nose and shifted his gleaming wine-cup a little.

'Fair cousin,' he said, 'I hope your pages won't prove too ladylike.'

'My father finds that one, the fair one I mean, skilful in the mysteries of wood and rivers,' Yolande replied in her best grown-up manner. 'He's a good archer and swimmer.'

'Does he swim with *you*?' murmured Balthasar, his blue eyes wide with polite interest.

'It's not a Neustrian custom,' said Yolande, as though Balthasar were really a foreigner.

'The other one looks soft,' he went on, a little sulky at the snub.

'We'll transmute him into iron,' she promised, and again remembered her place as hostess. 'That's a splendid ring,' she murmured, looking down at his near hand.

The ring was a signet of gold and onyx, bearing the Thunderbolt of Montguiscard beneath Balthasar's label of cadency. Balthasar brightened up at once, spreading his fine brown fingers on the damask tablecloth.

'It was given to me by the Archduke himself,' he said, confidentially.

'Tell me some of the things,' she bade him, 'that happened to you in Franconia.'

Balthasar's beautiful face grew angelic with wine and reminiscence. Yolande sat half-listening, hoping the Montguiscards would soon go away, wondering why the sudden terror had faded out of her heart.

'Asleep?' whispered Diomede, leaning forward on his oars.

'Fast asleep,' replied Lioncel, just above his breath. 'We'll put in here under the willows. There should be wild strawberries up in the old quarry.'

Yolande was not asleep, but too drowsy to speak or open her eyes. She lay on cushions in the stern of her blue-and-silver hunting barge. Diomede was in the bows, and Lioncel

next to him. Between the feet of Lioncel and Yolande dozed
a great staghound named Alcor.

It was high noon on the lake, and Yolande's first escape in
a week of castled melancholy. Duke Engelbert sent his blazon
and Yolande's to the funeral of Duke Drogo, but kept the
rest of their mourning within his own frontiers. The last
part of Pardelin to be seen as the pages rowed her down the
lake was the black streamer floating above the banner on the
keep; and this banner was now Yolande's own, the Golden
Leopard in a purple *lozenge*—a square shape set diamondwise
on a white silken field.

Duke Engelbert had ridden away to Bargreant, capital of
the duchy, taking the Montguiscards part of the way with him.
From Roclatour on Lake Targe, which lay twelve leagues
beyond Siege Umbrous, Azo could strike through deep forest
to his frontier hold at Jarapt.

Yolande had parted with some relief from her cousin
Balthasar; she had tired of the mockery in his eyes, a mockery
which only dissolved when he was talking about himself. Also
he had grinned at some of her little sketches; she had put them
away, ashamed, and since then had done no more drawing.
And now, after days of wind and rain, the skies were blue
again. The old governess was in bed, upset by the week's
repeated fasts; the seneschal—the Sieur de Forne, who was
Lioncel's grand-uncle—could never resist Yolande when she
set herself to cajole him.

' You must take your repast on Isle of Cats,' had been his
only condition. Isle of Cats lay like a jewel at the crossing of
the hilt of the falchion; the barge was already well beyond,
and soon it would be time to turn round again.

Meanwhile Yolande lay in luxurious ease, wearing instead
of a horned head-dress a little hunting-cap of gilded leather,
tied on by a ribbon beneath her chin, with her black hair most
unmodishly bound in two long plaits. The red-brown colour
behind her eyelids flickered to bronze-brown and grey as the
barge slid into shade; its bottom grated softly on pebbles, and
Diomede reached out with the painter and made fast to the
bough of a willow.

'I won't be long,' muttered Lioncel, carefully shipping his oars. 'Keep Alcor on the leash. If you should see anyone it will most likely be a forester. The peasants mayn't land without leave at this time of year, but they may be out in boats cutting reeds.'

The barge trembled as he stepped ashore.

'Cut me a long stalk of bracken,' Diomede bade him.

'What for?'

'Flies.'

'Right . . . phoo, I must sharpen my dagger. Here you are.'

'Gramercy, captain of the barge.'

'And don't go to sleep.'

'You ganderhead, as if I should.'

Lioncel chuckled, and was gone into the thickets. Diomede changed his place quietly. Yolande felt a faint stir of air as the bracken waved over her head. The growing hum of insects receded and kept its distance; Diomede sighed, and his shoe squeaked in some slight shift of balance.

Yolande caught her breath and moved, to see what would happen. She was rewarded by dead silence. Then the hound, Alcor, moved too, yawned with a whistling note, and gave a mighty sneeze. Yolande opened her eyes; behind the willow was an oak, with fragments of sky, deep blue as stained glass, amid its sunlit and shadowed greens.

When she squinted along at him Diomede was holding his fly-whisk out across the gunwale, sulkily watching its reflection in the green-brown water.

'Diomede,' she said softly.

'Yes, my lady?'

His dark eyes and face came round as though he had forgotten she was there.

'Why do you look so cross?'

Diomede put down his stalk of bracken, reached behind him, took up a small loaded crossbow, pointed its wicked steel-tipped quarrel at the sky, and looked at himself in the bright little silver plate screwed into the ebony butt.

'It's the shape of my face,' he explained, forgetting to

entitle her. 'It gets me into trouble for not looking pleased
when I should ... although at Sanctlamine it sometimes works,
I mean worked, the other way.'

'How? Tell me.'

'The sub-prior ... but my lady, you know the sub-prior.'

'I've seen him. But go on. I don't tell tales.'

'I ... I'm sure of that,' muttered Diomede as he put down
the crossbow. Then he frowned out across the lake, and again
seemed to lose all trace of embarrassment.

'The sub-prior,' he went on simply, 'is very worried sometimes by fear of his own damnation. Why, nobody knows ...
he's good and kind and gentle. But sometimes at meals he
puts his spoon into his bowl and gets up and goes out without
saying anything. And then the brother who's reading the
Scriptures looks sad or ashamed because he hasn't kept the
black fear away for long enough to let the sub-prior get his
dinner ...

'And he, the sub-prior I mean, sometimes stops as he walks
round the cloister, and stares in front of him as if he could
see a fiend. You want to shout "It's all right, Father, there's
nothing there and you aren't damned!" Except, of course,
that you aren't sure there isn't, *are* you?'

'No, I suppose you aren't,' admitted Yolande, rather taken
aback at being whisked into the story.

'Well, then he goes on in a misery, and sometimes before
he has done the round he remembers that the Sieur Jesu died
on Tree for him too. Then he shakes himself and looks
better and goes on again. But now and again the boys are
playing in the garth ... it isn't a graveyard at Sanctlamine ...
and the noise offends him, and he shouts at them to stop, and
forbids them their raisins at supper. ...

'And often I sit, I mean sat, in a corner, looking glum as
usual, I expect, although I might be drawing ... er, drawing
with charcoal on the pavement. And when the rest were
laughing and yelling, and the black fear came down on the
sub-prior, he's seen me there like an owl among the jackdaws,
and he'd call across and tell me to attend him to the church
with candles. And after he had done praying he would give

me sweetmeats and ginger. And he never came across to see what I was drawing.'

'And what was it?'

'Oh, fat brethren, fatter than life, and those with long noses with longer noses, and that sort of silly thing.'

'And were you frightened too?'

'Yes, of course. Kneeling alone with the sub-prior, I could feel devils grinning in at the clere-story. I used to think one little devil came and sat on my shoulder. . . .'

'Why? Go on!'

'Saying that the Sieur God was very unreasonable to let the good sub-prior be tormented like that. But I carry a little ivory image of Saint Michael stamping on a dragon. My mother gave it me before she died, and I know she intercedes for me. So I used to kiss the image and feel safe again.'

'And your father, Diomede?'

'He was killed at Pont-de-Foy. I can hardly remember him.'

'Which side was he on?'

'The king's.'

'Lioncel's father was killed too.'

'I know. He was with the rebels. Lioncel asked me never to speak of it before the Sieur his grand-uncle.'

'That battle was won in the end by a trick of the Count of Ger.'

'Yes. Did you ever see *him*, my lady?'

'He was at my betrothal, but I don't remember him.'

'They say he very seldom goes to Hautarroy.'

'That's because he's Warden of the Coast March.'

'Yes . . . yes, of course,' went on Diomede, suddenly conscious that he was talking about one of the Peers of Neustria to the daughter of another. It was also gossip that the king found gratitude irksome, and shunned the group of great lords who had helped him to his throne. . . .

Then Diomede remembered something else about the Count of Ger.

'He is a poet as well as a soldier. Do you know his song in triolets about King Arthur's sword?'

'No. Can you sing it? Is the little harp there?'
'Lioncel put it somewhere.'
'You like Lioncel, don't you, Diomede?'
'Yes.'

Diomede rummaged behind him again, and pulled the harp from its canvas case. He took it carefully on his knee, and an elfin succession of chords awoke beneath his fingers.

'This is a good song to sing here,' he said.

Yolande crossed her hands behind her head and lay listening, enchanted by the drowsy heat, the cool shade, the far gleam of a waterfall on the sunlit bulk of Siege Gracious. Diomede's voice was a little unsteady, but he was neither shy nor clumsy.

> '*When Merlin brought him to the lake*
> *To take the brand Excalibur,*
> *Pendragon seem'd but half awake*
> *When Merlin brought him to the lake*
> *The brand Excalibur to take;*
> *But lo! The shining steel astir*
> *When Merlin brought him to the lake*
> *To take the brand Excalibur!*

> '*But little thought had Arthur then*
> *Of Gwendolen or Guinevere.*
> *He heard the thunder of his men,*
> *And little thought had Arthur then*
> *Of Guinevere or Gwendolen.*
> *The witch-prow cleft the haunted mere,*
> *And little thought had Arthur then*
> *Of Gwendolen or Guinevere!*'

'Gramercy, Diomede,' whispered Yolande. 'That is as you say a good song.'

'I sang it better before my voice broke.'

'I liked it. Now if a hand came up out there, holding a great glittering sword, what would you do?'

'Row and get it, I suppose, unless the boat were enchanted like King Arthur's, and went gliding out by itself.'

'And what then?'

'Ask leave of the Lady Yolande to take the sword to King Thorismund.'

'M'm. Yes. That would be proper.'

'There *might* come a magic voice booming out of the mountain. . . .'

'Which said: "*First conquer Franconia!*"'

'That would be more in Lioncel's line.'

'But you would help him?'

'Of course.'

Yolande laughed, and at last Diomede smiled. His withdrawn expression vanished for an instant, and Yolande felt much older than he, although she was nearly two years younger.

'Wasn't Launcelot's brother called Lioncel?' she asked.

'No, Lionel. One of them. The other was Lamorak.'

'Learned Diomede. Sing another song.'

Diomede pondered, flaking delicate sounds into the June air. Presently he began to sing again.

'*Shadow of leaves on moonlit eaves*
Beside the churchyard pale;
Elms three, and a cypress tree
Where sang the nightingale.
Over my head the stars were spread,
And all was calm and fine
Except my fear to meet my dear
Dead Eglantine.

'"*Our gentle vow is honour'd now,*"
I told the empty air;
But on my word a shadow stirr'd,
And Eglantine was there.
"*The serpent lied who said I died,*
And now by yonder shrine
I'd hate it most to be a ghost,"
Said Eglantine.'

'Did ever you see a ghost, Diomede?' asked Yolande when he had done.

'No, my lady. I thought once I had met an elemental.'

'What was it?'

'A great old tortoise broken out of an abbey garden.'

'What did you do?'

'Climbed a tree.'

'What did the tortoise do?'

'Ate grass and took no notice.'

'What happened then?'

'A rabbit came out of the wood and watched the tortoise.'

'And then?'

'I learned valour from the rabbit, and got down and gave the tortoise a chestnut or two. They were still white, in the burr, and the tortoise seemed to like them. I was about seven then, and I sat down on the tortoise's back and he gave me a ride. Never since have I felt so much like Alexander the Great.'

'Diomede, I'm glad you came to Pardelin,' said Yolande.

Diomede cleared his throat, opened his lips, and closed them again. For a while they lazed in silence, until Lioncel's rapid returning footfall swished in the long grass. Lioncel had taken a basket with him, and now it hung laden on his arm. Sunlight patterned his violet tunic as he trod between the oaks and willows.

'Did you hear Diomede singing?' Yolande asked him.

'Yes, my lady, it was debonair. *Diomede, cast off quickly.*'

Lioncel stepped into the barge and reached across the hound Alcor to lay the strawberries at Yolande's feet. His face was rather grim.

'Gramercy, Lioncel . . . what's the matter?'

'Pull away,' said Lioncel over his shoulder, as he lifted an oar and pushed off into deeper water. When he was seated and rowing he spoke to them both again.

'I stood still a moment up there,' he explained. 'And I saw a man sitting watching you in a tree across the deep ravine. I only noticed him because he was eating something, and his knife-blade flashed in the shadow. I don't think he saw me; he never looked my way. He had a longish pointed sandy beard, and a black patch instead of a left ear. He looked like a soldier.'

'You're sure he wasn't one of our people?' asked Yolande, trying to remember long beards among the foresters and shepherds.

'Yes, quite sure.'

'Watching us?' growled Diomede. '*Where* did you say he was?'

'Sitting in a tree—the left-hand oak of those three under the first pines. Hey, what are you at?'

Lioncel half-turned, for Diomede had stopped rowing. Yolande saw the tilt of the crossbow and Diomede's dark face flushed with anger.

Spang! said the crossbow, its bolt ripping through foliage to slap into wood fifty or sixty yards upslope.

As though he knew it for an act of war, the great hound let out a growl, and his hackles went up. Then there was nothing but oar-splash, insect-hum, and the light stir of wind in the wood.

'Temper!' exclaimed Yolande, amused, but Lioncel leaned to his oars and snapped back at the crossbowman.

'Row, you idiot! Suppose *he* shoots! Lie down, my lady, and get Alcor on the seat behind you.'

'Sorry, I never thought of that,' gasped Diomede, pulling mightily. The barge lurched away from shore, and no sound or movement attested the presence of the hidden watcher.

'We must go back,' said Lioncel, 'and tell my lord seneschal.'

'Pass me the bow to reload,' commanded Yolande, sliding from her seat and pushing Alcor into it. If any open danger threatened her, Lioncel and Diomede might be greatly blamed and perhaps heavily punished.

With the staghound's bulk between herself and the three oak-trees, she wound at the weapon and set another bolt in chase.

'Shift over, Alcor,' she muttered, and pushed at the brindled shoulder. Cumbrously Alcor obeyed, flinching at the second note of the bow so close beside his ear.

This time the bolt rustled into silence.

'My lady!' groaned Lioncel, and suddenly chuckled and

went on. 'Whosoever that knave may be, he'll begin to think we don't like him.'

Again nothing else happened. The reach of water astern widened; the bow-ripple splintered the mirrored shapes of wood and mountain-side. When he judged it safe, Lioncel gave an order, and Diomede helped him swing the barge head-on to Pardelin.

'Isle of Cats another day,' said Yolande, still scanning the thickets around the three oaks.

'They won't let you come another day,' Lioncel promised her, 'What if that soldier's the first of many fleeing from the plague?'

The ghastly word, forgotten for an hour, fell like a shadow over the glowing afternoon. Yolande sat up and shook her plaits back over her shoulders.

'I suppose you're right,' she said, and clutched at what was left of enjoyment of the spoilt expedition. 'We'll dish our strawberries with cream up in the rampart garden. Lioncel should really eat them all, because Diomede and I have both been naughty.'

Lioncel's blue eyes, tender and amused, told her that he understood how she had screened his fellow-page's indiscretion. As they passed the slumbering Isle of Cats she watched Lioncel glance aside up the arm of the lake that formed the northern half of the falchion crossbar. Then his gaze came back and levelly sought her own.

'He won't tell if I don't,' she thought contentedly. 'But he won't mind if I *do* tell . . . and Diomede's unhappy.'

'Diomede,' she began clearly, 'there's an old hermitage hidden along there, half-way up one of those steep crags. Lioncel discovered it; nobody lives there now. We've set signs to tell us if anyone else goes, and so far none of them has ever been disturbed. Some time we must show you . . . or Lioncel will, if I can't come.'

'I should like to see it, my lady,' said Diomede, very subdued. 'That is, if Lioncel doesn't mind my knowing about it, too.'

'I don't mind,' said Lioncel, 'but I hope that soldier doesn't come across it.'

'He's on the other side of the lake,' Yolande pointed out.

'But who knows how long he's been prowling about? This is demesne land, Diomede, and he could be hunted off it.'

'Perhaps one of us winged him, or . . .' suggested Diomede.

'Someone else can find that out,' said Lioncel grimly. 'A blight upon him for spoiling our fine afternoon.'

A barge-load of archers went along to search the shore, but nothing more was seen of the one-eared watcher, and as the weeks went by the Pardelin household forgot him. Duke Engelbert did not come back; news of the plague slackened in bouts of cooler weather, but there was other trouble to the north and south of Baraine. A league of Franconian robber-barons launched a series of raids upon the Coast March of Nordanay; within the frontiers of Queranay a rogue called Turlequin assembled a thieving company and sacked two great abbeys before retiring into hill country where only an army could hope to catch him.

'It's believed he learned his outlaw craft with Joris of the Rock,' the old seneschal told Yolande.

'At which name I cross myself,' said Dom Piers, who was listening, 'even though that dreadful knave has burnt these ten years in hell.'

'Saints be praised there's nothing to bring this Turlequin here,' said the Dame de Chevronel.

'Also the Count of Montguiscard and the hold of Jarapt are placed most happily in the way,' the seneschal reminded her.

Yolande pictured cousin Balthasar pursuing fleeing outlaws over hill and dale, pausing from time to time to complain: 'This is nothing like the sport we had hunting basilisks with the Doge of Venice and the Khan or Tartary at Furenburenhabengrafstein, where the river runs pink and I broke my second-best mangonel.'

'My lord duke will come when he can,' the governess said when Yolande fretted. 'The chancellor's ill with the gout . . . and my lord duke sends you a present by *every* messenger.'

Mention of the chancellor made Yolande uncomfortable; she did not like that dignitary, who was elderly and morose and kept advising her father to marry again. Now that the Boqueron alliance was broken—for Duke Drogo's successor was his cousin, a boy aged three—it might be that the chancellor's counsels would prevail. . . .

Sometimes at Bargreant one ornamental lady or another was lodged for a while in the Serpent Tower—so-called because of the carving over its main doorway—but Yolande had somehow discovered that no step-mother would arrive that way. Those ladies were always very polite to her, and several of them she liked and admired, but the Dame de Chevronel discouraged close acquaintance with them; and none of them was ever invited to Pardelin beside Lake Falchion.

II

AZO'S WAY

WHEN at length the duke's trumpet sounded in the pass on the northern shoulder of Siege Umbrous it was already August, and heather was purple beside that high winding track. Yolande counted no more than six riders behind Sanglier, her father's great white stallion; and her heart sank a little, for that meant a short visit.

Summoning Alys, her fat young tirewoman, she went to her bedchamber. Even at windy Pardelin it was too hot for furs and velvet; Yolande was gowned in crimson silk before the Dame de Chevronel could come upon the scene. A horned headdress of red and white presently hid Yolande's black hair.

Being a girl at all was sometimes bad enough; being a dark girl was a slight upon nature. Roses and snow, and eyes like sapphires in sunlight, and golden hair like Cousin Balthasar's, were what the court minstrels most liked to sing about.

' T'ch! T'ch! ' exclaimed her governess, sailing into the chamber. ' Why not the violet and tawny, child? '

' It makes me look the colour of mud. Please, dame, he'll be here before I can change.'

' Well, you're a great cozener, but have it your way this time. Down to the hall steps with you, and remember to keep your chin up.'

' When I've put Amarand to bed,' promised Yolande.

Amarand was a sturdy wooden doll who stood nearly a foot high. He was delicately carved and painted and silvered to represent a chevalier in the chain armour of bygone days. Being named after the soldier-saint who was patron of Baraine, he bore that saint's blue cross-potent on a yellow silken surcoat. His closed helm was of real silver, crested with a leopard rampant; it could be taken off to show his cheerful mail-coiffed

21

face and blue enamel eyes. His silver sword could be drawn, too, and set in his right fist; his sword-arm moved up and down, and there was a keyhole in the armpit. A diminutive key swung as ornament on the strap of the swordbelt; Amarand's body was hollow, so that when his surcoat was removed his back swung open on hinges. Inside him lived certain of Yolande's most treasured possessions, and he had a bed of his own on a shelf in the great cupboard where Yolande's gowns were hung. Only Yolande herself was ever allowed to touch him.

'Make haste, then,' said the dame, and waited until the chevalier lay like a recumbent effigy under his purple leopard-embroidered coverlet.

The castle trumpets awoke as Yolande left her bedside. The portcullis was still grinding aloft as she went out on the hall steps. The seneschal came and stood beside her, with the governess and the two pages in silent attendance. Afternoon sunshine gilded half the courtyard; above the keep Yolande's own banner began sedately to sink and make room for the larger leopard folded below.

Horsehoofs thundered on the drawbridge, and Sanglier trampled into sight again. Engelbert of Baraine was armoured except for his head: a hunting-hat shaded his tired face, and even as he smiled at her Yolande thought he looked ill. Lioncel moved to the stallion's head; Diomede waited in the doorway with a goblet of spiced wine.

'Here's one place at peace, by Our Lady,' said the duke, and swung himself out of the saddle. He kissed Yolande, and his steel-girt arm was heavy across her shoulders as they walked together into the hall.

'Pardelin seems to agree with you, boy,' he said to the blushing Diomede. Then he lifted the goblet and spoke softly so that only the youth and the girl heard him.

'Here's to my lady Yolande of Baraine . . . my shy leopardess!'

Later, at ease in the painted solar, he explained why he must very shortly ride away again. The freebooting raids into Nordanay seemed mysteriously well-planned and well-directed;

the Count of Ger, Warden of the Coast March, not wanting troops from western holds to bring the danger of plague among his own forces, had sent southward for help, and before letting him have it Duke Engelbert summoned a council at Bargreant. Azo, Count of Montguiscard, now his foremost captain, pled that the incursions be dealt with while the King of Franconia still disowned them.

'A third of each garrison goes north,' said the duke to the old Sieur de Forne. 'Another third goes east. That will strengthen Azo at Jarapt against any threat of real war. I shall join him there next week with my own bodyguard. All's ready to raise the town levies if the need arise.'

'Do you want any of my men?' the seneschal asked him.

'No. You've only thirty here, with half a dozen at Quatre-lances. If the damned plague would abate I'd send Yolande to Hautarroy, but now she must stay here until these troubles are over.'

'Why not Bargreant?'

'Two friars died of it there three days ago.'

'Ah! They were the first?'

'Yes.'

'That's bad news, my lord duke . . . except that it might dissuade Franconia from pushing matters further.'

'Yes.'

'You're tired, and should rest," said the old soldier. 'It seems to me you have a fever.'

'A migraine,' confessed the duke. 'I shall sup and go to bed.'

After the meal Yolande walked in the little rampart garden with the privileged hound Alcor beside her, and watched the sun go down amid a smother of stormclouds. The wind was rising, the mountains grew grim, the lake was swept clear of reflections; the great oak-tree by the hamlet began to roar as if it fought back the powers of air. High over Yolande's head the duke's banner flapped on a creaking spar. . . .

Sixty feet below, beyond the deep moat and the narrow plank bridge which slid out beneath the postern gate, she saw three figures standing close to the boathouse tower. They were those of Lioncel, Diomede, and the huge fat castle cook, a veteran of the duke's wars, who seemed to be demonstrating some strange new weapon. His great arm and hand swung up to discharge a flash of flat steel at an ancient tree-stump twenty yards away from him above the pebbled beach. The steel stuck in the stump, and Yolande saw that it was one of the kitchen meat-choppers.

'That's bad for the joints he carves,' thought Yolande, and then herself grew fascinated. Another and another chopper flew; the stump looked gruesomely set-upon and ill-used. The whirl of steel reminded her of the falchions of the bodyguard of the Archduke Adalbert, and she composed a rejoinder in Balthasar's own vein.

'Ah, but you should see the choppers of our fat cook at Pardelin.'

The boys were obviously enchanted at the cook's dexterity. Diomede's arm was around Lioncel's shoulders. A faint jealousy twisted in Yolande's heart. Those two could talk to each other, be with each other, in ways from which a girl was utterly shut out. . . .

A large wet lick on her hand reminded her that she was not altogether alone.

'That's all very well, Alcor,' she said, 'but they can take you hunting, and I can't, unless half the garrison comes too.'

Her glance rose to the second pass from which a track ran down to the lake—the southward nick between the shoulders of Sieges Umbrous and Perilous. That track came through an upland waste from the lonely priory of Sanctlamine, where Diomede had been brought up by his uncle, the Prior of Gilomar.

A last gleam of sunlight lay along the southern heights, and into it, over the distant crest, charged a solitary horseman, his helm sparkling, his tabard a tiny blot of moving blackness.

Again the war-horn bellowed; the cook and the pages clawed the choppers out of their tree-stump and made for the postern, where a grumbling archer waited to slide back the bridge.

'Oh, curse the wars and tumults,' said Yolande. 'What is it *this* time?'

This time it was the Sieur de Caherne, a cadaverous chevalier who had been at Pardelin with the Montguiscards. In deepening dusk, on a jaded horse, he reached the castle again. He came from Azo, and his news was grim; the outlaw rogue Turlequin had evidently learnt of the movements of soldiery in Baraine and had pushed up out of Queranay into country new to his raids. He and his company had been sighted in the wild hills south of Sanctlamine. Azo, starting out from Jarapt to head him off from the priory, had sent word to Roclatour, and now appealed to Pardelin. Could even a handful of men be spared to come down from northward? They might at least reach the priory in time to help trap Turlequin.

Duke Engelbert sat up in bed and groaned and swore at his migraine. He bade the Sieur de Caherne borrow one of his own horses, take twenty-five of his men, and ride by torchlight. A skiff was sent along the lake to recall all but a couple of archers from the tower of Quatrelances. For an hour the hold of Pardelin hummed like a hive, and then fell silent. The wild glow of blown torches streamed through the narrow woods at the eastern edge of the lake; the watchers saw it begin to scale the heights above tree-level; and finally the last orange spark slid into the pass and vanished.

Yolande knelt beside her bed and prayed for the safety of the Prior Gilomar and his monks and servants, and for the Count Azo, whom at last she thought of as her uncle. Also she prayed for Balthasar, who might be riding with him. Even Balthasar might find something to boast about in the overthrow of so cunning a rogue as Turlequin.

At about midnight Yolande awoke and heard rain dashing against the shutters of her chamber. In the wavering light of a tall candle already one-third burnt away she watched embroidered figures shift and tremble on the wall-hangings. Deborah and her hammer and nail, Ruth with her sickle, Judith with her sharp falchion, seemed joined in the paces of a just perceptible dance. Yolande watched them and was glad of her soft bed and guarded state. . . .

It was better after all to be a girl in a castle rather than a man who must ride out with clenched teeth and sopping clothes,

getting ready to slam and rip and stab at crafty armoured
enemies. If you were a man, and downed your opponent, there
was always the whistling arrow to reckon with . . . how men
could enjoy fighting puzzled her beyond measure.

Well, there they were, the swordsmen and archers who smiled
at her and touched their steel caps when she came near them.
Our Lady be praised that Lioncel and Diomede were rather too
young . . . yet . . . to plunge into that welter of strange male
strength and cunning and beastliness.

Lioncel and Diomede . . . two or three nights ago she had
dreamed about them both. Lioncel was standing beside her in
the rampart garden, and she asked him: ' Where is Diomede? '
He laughed, and she looked round at him, and it was Diomede
himself who stood there.

' But where's Lioncel? ' she demanded, suspecting a trick,
even in the dream.

' Turn round,' Diomede advised, and she turned, and there
was no one there.

' No, right round,' he went on, and when she had done so
he was Lioncel again.

Then she was not astonished but angry, and burst out crying.
She awoke and found tears on her face, and felt a very strange
horror, as if she had herself injured the two boys who were her
friends. Dreams often entertained her, but she had prayed that
she might never have that particular dream again.

In waking hours the pair of them helped to fill much of her
day. Tomorrow . . . today, for it was probably already morning
. . . Diomede was going to climb the great oak-tree beside the
hamlet on the shore. From there he would shoot into the lake
two bolts from a crossbow; to one of these he had fastened a
stick having parchment wings. These wings were whitewashed
to be more easily seen; it was Diomede's idea that they would
prolong the flight of the bolt. Lioncel said that the extra weight
would check the flight and lessen the range. Lioncel was going
to take her out on the lake in a skiff to watch what happened.

At Bargreant there was always a crowd of women about her;
pages hovered on its edges, and were ordered about and blamed.
Some of them were unpleasantly clumsy, or greedy, or spiteful.

Lioncel was never any of these things; and now by a sort of miracle he had been joined by Diomede. . . .

Yolande liked to watch them engrossed in a game of chess. Then she could sit at her embroidery, patterning with the silks she loved, and look up and see the fair head and the dark bent over the inlaid board with its beautiful red and white pieces. The way Lioncel wrinkled his nose, the way Diomede pouted, the way their hands moved, the unconscious grace of their bodies, all combined in a picture which somehow belonged to her alone.

They never quarrelled; Diomede accepted without question Lioncel's good-natured lead. Yolande wondered how Diomede would fit in at Bargreant. She had seen him floor Lioncel once when they wrestled on the shore. That had been queer, too, for she wanted them both to win. . . .

Faintly through the wind and rain the sentinels of Pardelin told each other that all was well. Yolande took their word for it and went to sleep again.

In the morning the wind still blew hard, but gleams of brilliant sunlight passed along the lake and silvered the little waves that broke on sand and pebbles. After Mass and breakfast the duke rode out around the eastern end of the water. With him went Yolande, as she had hoped; Alcor paced beside her palfrey, Lioncel and Diomedes came abreast behind, and six mounted archers brought up the rear.

There, in the strip of dense woodland, pheasants ran across the path; shock-haired children peeped from the thickets below the edges of the heather. One small sturdy boy, caught in a glade with his single garment held up to make a pouch for blackberries, squealed as his little brown legs twinkled away in front of the horses.

Duke Engelbert laughed aloud; he never grudged his serfs good pickings. This morning his migraine had left him; he eyed with approval the trim new haystacks, the heavy-laden walnut trees, the little fields of ripening corn. The priest, the miller, the smith in his forge, the goose-girl and the swineherd, looked out of doorways or under their hands at the trotting

cavalcade. Foresters and woodcutters and all those whose duties
took them away from the hamlet had been told to stay close that
day. Only a shepherd or two had gone up on the heights.

Halted in her saddle on the hillside beyond the two inlets
that formed a split pommel for Lake Falchion, Yolande gazed
at the sunlit castle, the thatched cots, and the oak-tree standing
between them.

'Sieur God, keep the plague away,' she begged in her heart,
and crossed herself.

'Amen,' said her father, as if he guessed the prayer. 'With
God's help and Our Lady's, Yolande, we'll weather this unhappy time. And then I must turn to again and find you a
proper husband.'

'Not too soon, father,' she begged him.

On their return they found at the castle gates two sturdy
packmen and a white-haired Franciscan waiting for admission.
One of the packmen was bowlegged, with a drooping eyelid
and light lashes; the other, a square dark creature, fixed Yolande
with bright beseeching eyes, pulling off his cap with one hand
and tapping his great slung tray with the other.

'Where have *you* been? Which way did you come?' demanded the duke sternly.

'We come from Roclatour, my lord,' growled Bowlegs, very
humbly. 'You passed us yesterday while we ate in the forest
edge.'

'Where were you before that?'

'Jarapt, my lord duke. We're men of the duchy. We heard
you kept state in this castle.'

'It's true, my lord duke,' said the friar, leaning on his staff.
'I knew both of them in Jarapt.'

'Have you been near Bargreant?'

'Not this year, my lord duke,' declared Bowlegs, crossing
himself.

'And you, friar?'

'I am from Roclatour itself. My friary is at Jarapt. These
honest traders overtook me, and I've been glad of their company.
I've not been near Bargreant since the autumn. I'm on my
way to Hautarroy, my lord duke.'

'Very well. Packmen, you may stand in the courtyard until sunset. Friar, you will hear no confessions in the castle. What you do among the huts is between you and the priest.'

'The Sieur God and all his Saints requite you, my good lord duke,' said Bowlegs, bowing low.

Later, as she passed along a rampart walk, Yolande saw the packmen at work in the shadow of the hawksheds, close to the postern. A groom was counting out pennies for some difficult purchase. Two of the kitchen women were giggling over a tray which stood open on the cobbles. The friar was outside the castle, wandering rather forlornly near the boathouse tower. As Yolande watched, he sat down on the tree-stump lately carved by the cook; he drew up his hood against the sun, shut his eyes and began to tell his beads. . . .

The wind dropped, and the day grew sultry. Yolande took off her headdress and lay down on her bed. Lioncel would let Alys know when he was free for the testing of Diomede's winged bolt. She picked up a book of the lives of the Nine Worthies, and presently began to drowse over the exploits of Judas Maccabæus.

A wild scream shook her awake. The horn roared on the keep turret, hounds began to bay in the courtyard, somebody shouted orders above the stamp of running feet. Yolande sat up, blinking, as Alys burst into the room.

'My lady, dear my lady!' gabbled Alys. 'Get up, come quickly . . . the outlaws are in the castle . . . those packmen blocked the postern open . . . that friar had a hatchet under his frock . . . hurry, hurry, your shoes and this scarf for your head . . . oh, dear God!'

She shod Yolande, and hooked her from the bed with a sweep of her strong arm. They ran out of the chamber into a world gone mad. There was a scuffling, a slamming of doors, the rasp and rattle of weapons; Yolande found herself in the solar, where the old seneschal, white with rage, was swearing as Lioncel buckled him into a corselet. Up the kitchen stairway came tumbling some of the servants; from the ground floor below rose confused sounds of battle.

The chaplain waddled in, unclerically armed with a crossbow. The Dame de Chevronel appeared, calm, but fingering a dagger. Then the duke strode half-armed out of his bedchamber; his voice cut coldly through near and distant tumult.

'Seneschal, they're in the keep. This is my fault and no one else's. Hugo is holding them in the armoury passage. Take the Lady Yolande and the women and Dom Piers out on the lake. The grooms and kitchen lads can row you; a couple of archers can come, too, to beat off any attack from shore. The rest of us will contain them until I put my chest of papers into another barge. Get out of bowshot and then make for Quatrelances. Off with you now, women first . . . one moment, Yolande.'

Yolande had made no movement to go, and now she was gathered in a tight embrace. Her father's hands pressed a ring on to her left thumb. Her father's voice came quietly in her ear.

'God keep you, darling child, and forgive me this blunder. See, here's my privy signet . . . give it me later if you can. If you can't, it's yours, for you will be Baraine. Be brave and just, and keep faith, and guard your own counsel . . . trust few men and fewer women . . . *and never trust a Montguiscard*!'

They kissed each other blindly; Yolande's breasts were bruised by the steel. Then her father thrust her into the arms of dame and seneschal, smiled at her, and turned away. She heard his sword ring as he tore it out of the scabbard.

Lioncel stood girlish-grim by the door of the passage down which the rest had crowded; as Yolande passed him she remembered something, and caught at his hand that gripped a lancegay.

'Lioncel—Amarand—if you can!' she gasped. His white-gold head jerked down so that his lips brushed her fingers; then she was hustled away. Through a window opening on the courtyard she caught a last glimpse of Alcor; he was tearing the throat out of an outlaw, while another swung an axe high over his brindled head. . . .

Yolande gave a sobbing groan. Stairs, first straight and then spiral, enveloped her in dark gloom. At their foot was the slit-windowed basement of the boathouse-tower, with barges and skiffs afloat in the half-darkness. Beyond them, between splayed protecting screens of masonry, the lake lay placid and pale green in the shadow of a passing cloud.

Then came a bumping, a clatter of chains, and the echoing voice of the Sieur de Forne.

'Two who can row hard, into this skiff and out oars quickly. Gavin, you, too, with your bow. Now, Dame, you and my lady. Alys, no room for you . . . into the barge there. I'll take the steering-oar. We go first. The rest of you follow. Dom Piers, keep between us and the shore. Leave the other big barge ready for my lord duke's party to cast off.'

. Aside to Yolande, he said: 'Sit in the bows, child. We'll win away in good order, and my lord duke'll soon be here.'

'Yes,' was all Yolande could say, as the skiff began to move. Then she sat erect, staring at the dark stair-foot, aghast at what she had asked Lioncel to do for her. Suppose in attempting it he was cut off and . . .

Under the stony arch, past the great iron-studded doors whose spiked feet were green and slimy under the muddy water, she was borne into the open air. Just as the stair-foot was passing from her range of vision, Lioncel darted out of it and leaped down among the others huddled in the following barge. A wallet was slung around his neck; Yolande swallowed a cry of relief and remorse.

Then she shut her eyes, hearing the sounds that rose shrilly from castle and hamlet. There was a smell of burning; a haystack was on fire near the church. Cattle bellowed far off.

'Sieur Jesu!' prayed the Dame de Chevronel. 'Send the Count of Montguiscard quickly!'

'He'll be on his way,' said the seneschal. 'They can't reach my lady now. My lord duke and the others will bar the stair approach as they fall back. Three men could hold an army in that passage.'

Suddenly Yolande flung up her hand, biting on the heavy signet-ring.

'What is it, my pet?' cried her governess, peering into her horrified face.

' *Diomede!* '

'Why, isn't he in the barge?'

'No! I've just remembered . . . he went out to climb the
oak . . . he must . . . they must have . . .'

She choked and was silent, with tears streaming down her
cheeks. Castle and shore and scurrying figures blurred before
her gaze. She wiped her eyes on her sleeve, and stared at the
following barge and the black entry of the boathouse tower.
Surely her father would be coming too . . .

'Look there, my lord,' said the archer Gavin. The seneschal
swore and leaned on the steering-oar. The Dame de Chevronel
called out again on the Saviour of mankind. Yolande turned to
see a long boat, laden with armed men, driven with flashing
oars from a cove on the wooded northern shore.

'Who are these?' said the seneschal aloud to himself.
'Where in hell did they get the boat?' And to the grooms who
were rowing he said: 'Pull your hardest, boys; the duke and
his men will be out soon.'

He turned the skiff away still further, so that Dom Piers
could more easily bring the barge between; but the long boat
carried six oars a side, and came swiftly on a curving course to
defeat the seneschal's manœuvre.

'Give the word, my lord,' said Gavin, with an arrow nocked
on his string, 'and I'll drop the oarsmen one by one if they
come any nearer.'

'Who are you?' roared old de Forne, standing up with a
hand on the archer's shoulder.

'Stop, both of you!' came in a screeched hail over the water.
The helmsman of the long boat was standing up too; Yolande
saw that he had a beard, and a feather stuck on his steel cap.

'Who are you?' thundered the seneschal again.

'My name is Turlequin!' the other yelled cheerfully, and the
boatload of ruffians with him sent up a rattle of laughter.

'Let fly, lad,' said the Sieur de Forne, and Gavin's longbow
spat and hummed. It seemed to Yolande that her eyeballs
bulged; the arrow streaked whitely into the armoured group,
and one of the oars sprang up as its handler collapsed on it.

'Yield yourselves, de Forne!' came the yelling voice again.
'We want the girl for ransom, with the rest of you thrown in!'

Yolande felt her spine go chill. Surely, surely her father's barge should by now ... no, there was nothing there yet. Everything *could* go wrong, then; prayers and trust and the might of Baraine need make no difference. The privy signet was clumsy on her thumb, and she groped for her purse, but it was not at her belt. Alys must have it—kind, fat Alys, a rigid shape in the barge steered by Dom Piers, whose oarsmen were making frantic efforts to head the long boat off ...

Now she could see Turlequin more clearly. His longish sandy beard flowed down over his plain buff jerkin. At a turn of his head she saw a black patch on its left side. ...

As though in a dream she perceived that the long boat must overtake them. Both the larger craft were closing rapidly on the skiff; Dom Piers and his archer were shooting at short range; men in the long boat were screening their rowers with bucklers, and suddenly they returned the bowshot. A volley of bolts and arrows leaped, and Yolande's dream became a nightmare.

'Alys!' she whispered. 'Lioncel! Dom Piers!'

Dom Piers disappeared behind the huddle of screaming women. One of the grooms toppled into the water with his hands up to his face. A girl in the prow fell prone like a broken figurehead, her kerchief bobbing, her arms dangling one on either side of the stem-post. ...

In the skiff Gavin was whispering and snarling, planting his arrows with deadly skill. When the barge fell away, the long boat itself was checked for a moment; two rowers on the port side were out of action at once. Then it lunged forward again, riding up to starboard. Yolande saw the green water lessen and lessen; oars swung, crossing and clicking, and a great guisarme flashed out, its hook engaging the skiff gunwale close to the swearing Gavin. ...

She saw grinning faces, rusty bucklers, a gleam of scarred skin across the bridge of the helmsman's nose, a dreadful wink from a red-haired ruffian who leaned out and grabbed at her ... then his grimy hand on the thwart, his grimace as the Dame de Chevronel nailed it with her dagger, the dame's own silent collapse as a mace thumped down on her head. ...

She saw the Sieur de Forne, sword in hand, hewing like a madman, beaten to his knees, dead ... Gavin slumped across him, the grooms sprawling this way and that. Then came a great heave of the skiff and hands on her arms, neck, ankles. . . .

She was swung aloft and bundled into the bottom of the long boat. A cheer went up around her; one man pinched her buttock. Two or three were still holding her when a cloak came down on her head and shoulders, blocking her last glimpse of the skiff as oars and weapons overturned it. The bodies of her faithful friends were rolling into the water . . . Gavin's teeth were bared in a dead grin of rage . . . then for a moment she saw no more.

'Now the other lot,' said someone. There was a reaching and leaning across her, an impatient thrust from a bony knee, the rasp of rowlocks and grunt of men bending to the oars. Yolande was left with only one pair of hands to hold her; she sat quite still, sick with horror, sustained by rage, hardly frightened at all now.

The long boat had come about, and leaped forward again. There was a jarring crash as it rammed the barge amidships. One of the gripping hands left Yolande's shoulder. She flicked up the edge of the cloak and saw the rest of her household battered with oars and stabbed with spears, hurled into the lake, gasping, crying, splashing as they drowned. Kind fat Alys turned a helpless face and gulping mouth up to the August sky; an oarblade drove her head under the frothing bloodied surface. The boy who had groomed Yolande's palfrey, the girl who had swept her bedchamber, vanished amid their fellows. The second archer fought to the last with his sword; and from the stern, where Dom Piers lay dead, Lioncel poised his lancegay and flung it as a javelin. Then, as the barge in its turn was tilted to capsize, he dived overboard and disappeared.

'With the rest of you thrown in, I said!' whinnied the bearded helmsman, and again a roar of laughter went up from his crew.

Yolande shot a last despairing glance at the empty reach of water between herself and the castle. A ghastly certainty crowned the horror; her father and the rest of his men must have been killed too.

She pulled the cloak over her face and wondered if she could manage to follow Lioncel's example. Probably Lioncel was hurt, and meant to drown instead of being battered to pieces. If she herself jumped in she knew she would swim; she would not be able to help swimming. That would mean being hauled out again . . . better sit tight . . . *shy leopardess* . . . take off the signet of Baraine, *her* signet now, and stuff it down between her breasts, where her corset would hold it. . . .

'Hey!' yelled someone in the sudden quiet that marked the end of the massacre. 'That little white-haired bastard dived under our keel! He's swimming out behind there . . . wind your bows . . . get after him!'

Again there was a shoving about her, again the rowlocks rasped and rattled. Yolande hesitated, and then twisted herself about. The grip of a fist on one arm tightened, but again she shaped the edge of the cloak—it was rough frieze and smelt of horse-dung—into a tunnel through which she could see the fair head cleaving the water. An arrow feathered the surface beyond; the head straightway vanished.

Yolande could neither pray nor scream, but her convulsive movement was noticed.

'That's not for you to watch, my pretty,' said the man who held her. His other hand came down on the bunched-up frieze, restoring Yolande's darkness. Longbows and crossbows twanged and thrummed; voices jarred as oarsmen and bowmen cursed and mocked each other.

'He's swimming under water.'

'He can swim, too, the rat!'

'That was a mangy shot, Marcel.'

'I'd like to see you do better, with the bloody boat rocking like a see-saw!'

'There he goes again . . . bah, just past his ear.'

'Steady all . . . wup! Got him!'

'Got him, by God!'

The last cheer of triumph seemed to spin a wheel in Yolande's head.

'I'm going to faint,' she told herself. 'Lioncel's dead, and . . . Amarand's . . . lost.'

She herself was lost, too, twirling endlessly down into black night and silence.

'There, there, child,' said a quiet deep voice she knew.

Struggling back to awareness, she fought off for a few seconds the knowledge of catastrophe. She *might* be in bed, coming up out of an evil dream . . . but hideous murder and sacrilege could not be dismissed as phantoms. She had to think of them now, because there was no one else left, and because she was Baraine. She opened her eyes and found herself looking into the deep blue eyes of Azo de Montguiscard. In the shadow of his lifted vizor the long pink nose bore a transverse smear, as though its owner had wiped a dirty glove across his face. Between his helmed head and the far summit of Siege Gracious was a slow drift of blue-white smoke. The smell of burning was stronger than before; near at hand there was shouting and screaming.

'You are safe now,' said Azo. 'Here, drink this wine.'

The rim of a metal goblet came against Yolande's lips. A vintage strange to her assailed her palate and sweetened her gullet. She swallowed, licked her lips, and gasped as memory gashed her mind awake.

She was propped on cushions in a horse-litter which stood on the ground outside the castle gate. The curtains of the litter were open only on the castle side. Lowered drawbridge and raised portcullis showed her men in Azo's black tabards carrying ragged-looking corpses, leading horses out of the stables, stacking weapons against a wall. On the highest keep turret someone was lowering the banner of the Leopard.

Yolande blinked and pushed up her hair, which was falling over her face. The back of her hand was grazed and bleeding.

'My father?' she demanded, in a croak beyond her control.

Azo de Montguiscard crossed himself, his eyes bright and sombre together.

'He died fighting in the keep,' said Azo gently. 'God rest his soul and the souls of those with him. They made a great stand and nearly won away . . . they stayed to bring a chest of papers . . . it's safe now with me. . . .'

'Hugo . . . the others . . . all dead, too?'

Azo nodded and crossed himself again.

' And the outlaws? '

' We surprised them. I don't think any escaped.'

' The village people? '

' Fallen or fled, poor souls.'

' What . . . why are the women screaming? '

' Those are men, child. Men can scream when they're wounded and going to be hanged.'

' Oh . . . my lord count! '

' Yes? '

' That one with the beard . . . Turlequin . . . ? '

' He's dead also.'

' I'm glad of that,' said Yolande more strongly, hearing her own teeth snap shut.

' Drink again. You'll feel better.'

' Yes. My head's spinning again. I want to see my father's body.'

' Not just now.'

' I want to see him now.'

' No. The castle is a shambles.'

' What does that matter after what I saw on the lake? '

There came an alteration in Azo's eyes; they went somehow blank, and as Yolande drank a second time they began to wait for something.

' Child,' said Azo gently, ' I am in command here. Your father wouldn't wish you to see what is in there. Besides, you couldn't stand, let alone walk.'

That was true enough. The second draught of wine seemed to darken the sunlight. A curious purple-brown mist began to surround the scene, spreading inwards from her eyelids. Azo's armour, glittering so close, assailed her with sliding shapes of dazzle.

' Did no one else escape? ' she asked, finding her querulous voice sound silly.

' The sentinel on the keep was wounded by an arrow. We found him dying in the hall gallery. He had managed to get so far, and saw some of the fighting below, but not the end of it. He died as my men tended him.'

' I wonder who that was . . . oh, couldn't you have come just a little sooner? '

' We nearly killed our horses,' said Azo mildly. ' Ten of my men are dead, and a dozen more wounded. Only by the grace of God did we learn that Turlequin's company had passed Sanctlamine without going near it. One of my scouts overshot the priory and saw them beyond.'

' And your gentleman and the archers who went from here last night? '

' They must have reached the priory and waited for an onset. I sent to tell the prior we had turned aside. They should be here again by now.'

' It's all so hard to understand . . . how did Turlequin get that boat on to the lake? '

' That we don't know . . . yet.'

' Have you sent along to Quatrelances? The men there should be visited by a skiff each day.'

' That has been done, my lady duchess.'

The ghost of a smile appeared above Azo's bever.

' Duchess? Oh, yes, I am that now, I suppose. My lord, did Balthasar come with you? '

' No. He was at a frontier post when the news of Turlequin's raid reached me.'

' Tell me . . . oh, I'm going to faint again.'

The purple-brown was spreading and thickening. Azo and his polished steel wavered in the midst of it. Yolande drew a long breath, meaning to ask if Diomede had been found among the dead people in the hamlet; but her voice refused the task. She let the breath go, and seemed to float away on it. The wail of a trumpet reached her, thinning into soundlessness as the purple-brown closed and grew black.

That trumpet was Azo's own, mustering his black coats from oak-tree and hamlet, from hillside and shore, to the food and wine prepared for them by their comrades in the recaptured castle.

After its sounding a silence reigned for a while around the great oak. Then the first hooded crow swept into the shade. By twos and three his kindred gathered, and kites and ravens followed to discuss with them the banquet. Twenty-seven outlaws had been hanged from the lower boughs.

When Azo's column formed up outside the castle gate—with Duke Engelbert dead in one litter, Yolande drugged in another, and the chest of papers topped by sacks of recovered jewellery, plate, and clothing in a third—men well-used to warfare did not look too often at the fury of beak and claw two hundred yards away. And when the column moved slowly off, the squire and score of archers left in charge at Pardelin kept their distance.

So it was that no one, from noon till darkness, noticed Diomede sitting in a great fork forty feet from the ground.

Hunched and flattened, shadowed and screened amid dense foliage, lashed by his belt to a crossing branch in case he were to faint from fright or exhaustion, Diomede alone of the castle household saw the first and last of the attack upon Pardelin.

It was his custom to begin that climb by reaching a first low limb as the ancient Greeks mounted their horses—namely, by using a thonged lance. Diomede's lance improved upon Xenophon's by having two thongs; those were near the sharp end, which could thus be deeply earthed and used as a scaling-ladder. But today Diomede was hampered by his crossbow and bolts, including the special winged bolt with which he hoped to confound Lioncel; so he persuaded a groom to let him ride a led destrier under the bough. From the monster's bare back he scrambled into the tree; and if the outlaws were already watching from the thickets, none of them marked, or afterwards remembered, the vanishing of a boy among the lowest leaves.

Ascending by well-tried footholds, Diomede found his chosen perch, which commanded a good view of the lake, but only gave him narrow glimpses of castle and fields and hamlet. There he settled himself to wait for the appearance of the blue-and-silver barge containing Yolande and Lioncel; and there he day-dreamed until the first shouts and screams and the sudden bray of the war-horn shattered the peace of the summer afternoon. . . .

The bushes on the moorward side of the hamlet had been allowed to sprout and thicken; even near to the castle they were not usually cut back until the autumn brought word of wolves. And so the outlaws were able to creep close before their concerted rush. They were well-provided with bows of both kinds; the few serfs who reached the church were mostly wounded as they ran. There seemed to be hundreds of the attackers; in the shade of the oak itself they caught and slew a dozen peasants.

In a turmoil of anger, shame and terror Diomede watched the priest brained on the vicarage threshold. The foliage which protected him also baffled his aim; again and again he tried to bring his weapon to bear on some leather-jerkined shape which slid or danced or raced out of sight before his hands were steadied for a shot. There was a great shouting at the forge; the blacksmith and his sons made a stand, and when they were overpowered a smother of smoke began to drift and hang around the tree. Diomede sat still and wondered whether his duty did in fact lie in slithering down to get perhaps one of the outlaws before his own throat was slit. . . .

That they had rushed the castle itself did not at first occur to him. The postern was on the far side; by craning his neck Diomede could see the main gateway, with drawbridge up and no attacker showing near it. Then the near uproar lessened, and he took the stab of realisation; howls and yells drifted over the ramparts, and a glance at the boathouse-tower froze him in his place. . . .

The skiff slid out, the barge followed, the mysterious long boat appeared beyond, converging to bloody encounter less than a quarter of a mile away. Sunlight showed him Yolande's blue gown whisked from one craft to another—showed him the sword-flashes and sinkings, and Lioncel's white-gold head in the water. Diomede gasped and began to pray; his stomach seemed to twist and collapse as the shining speck heaved up and disappeared for the second time. There was driftwood near, and the watcher strained his eyes, knowing how far and well his friend could swim under water; but there was no further sign of the swimmer, and Diomede pressed his face against the oaken bark, and his tears runnelled away and were lost, and when he looked out again the long boat rode solitary and unhurried in the sunshine.

At this point Diomede belted himself to the tree, and so saved his neck; for a drumming of hoofs swelled in the southward woods and meadows, and he squealed with excitement as the first black-tabarded horsemen rushed their badge of the Red Thunderbolt through the hamlet and up to the castle.

The drawbridge had been lowered now, and the portcullis was up. The outlaws were not so quick at the chains and ropes as garrison men would have been; a rider leaped his charger on to the bridge as it began to move again. Another followed, and the bridge dropped back; a fresh tumult broke out as the newcomers stormed in.

Diomede wriggled back into the balance he had lost, and sat praising God and his Saints until he remembered the long boat. That, no doubt, would have turned and headed away with its precious booty . . . was the duke prisoner too, he wondered? No, by Saint Amarand of Baraine! The long boat was very slowly aiming for the shore midway between the castle mound and the oak tree. Scores of horsemen had thundered past below; half a dozen of them turned aside and cantered their mounts down to the lake-side, where they halted and waited for the crew to land.

Diomede, very puzzled, was suddenly aware that confused fighting was still going on in the hamlet. He saw two outlaws cut down in the yellowing corn. A third broke out of a hut and ran straight on to a poised lance; behind him, pursuing him with upraised axe, the sturdy swineherd of Pardelin pounded to a halt and laughed. Then Diomede added a scream to the din, for a second Montguiscard man-at-arms reined in near his fellow with the lance, and split the swineherd's skull from behind.

Smoke drifted across Diomede's view of the lake. A woman carrying a child scuttled past below, making for the church. Another Montguiscard horseman swung round the corner of the vicarage, and all but severed her neck with his sword. Leaning out of his saddle, he swung the sword again. Diomede heard himself make a kind of mooing noise. The swineherd might have been killed by mistake, but no one could pretend a woman with a baby was one of Turlequin's horde.

C

Diomede hung his crossbow up, and carefully cut the winged
stick from the bolt to which he had fastened it. That gave him
four bolts . . . the long boat was beached now, and Yolande
drooping in a man's arms, was handed up to one of the riders
Others of the crew busied themselves helping wounded com
rades ashore. No conflict, no disorder even; no sign of the
duke or anyone else out of the castle . . . but in the church
there was a new outburst of clamour. They must be making
an end there, too.

Diomede hugged himself in his place and tried to make
sense of it all. A near smother of smoke was growing, and
presently he was glad of this fact, for the uproar in the castle
was ended, and a long file of captured outlaws was led down
from the gate and along the shore towards him. Beneath the
oak itself a group of Montguiscard archers began sorting a
tangle of rope. Diomede's blood prickled in his veins, and he
cowered as if frozen to his perch. They were tossing the
lengths of rope over the spreading lower limbs; the prisoners
were lined up, and nooses were going over their heads. Some
were stoical, some struggled, others whined and screeched and
blubbered; and now the group who had manned the long boat
were moving off towards the castle, whither the horsemen
guarding Yolande had preceded them.

'They're *his* men, then,' thought Diomede, wincing at the
sounds from below. 'Oh, just and holy saints, don't let them
see me! It's a plot, it's a bloody villainy, Azo must have been
in league with the outlaws . . . and then turned on them when
the mischief was accomplished. If my lord duke's alive . . .
no, he'll not be . . . *but what are they at with my little lady?*
Hullo, here's the leader of them . . . ay, it's Azo himself.'

The Count of Montguiscard rode slowly down to inspect his
improvised gallows; and at his stirrup walked a tall man with
a longish sandy beard flowing to a point on his plain buff
tabard. He turned his face up to the Count, and Diomede saw
plainly that he wore a black patch where his left ear should
have been.

'It's you, is it?' flashed through Diomede's mind. 'And
now, what's to do with the miller?'

The frightened miller of Pardelin was brought up to the Count, who checked his horse and sat questioning him for a moment. The miller began counting on his fingers; the two men who guarded him stood impassively by. There had been perhaps forty serfs in the hamlet that noontide; as the priest was dead, none would number them more readily than the miller. . . .

Azo tightened his rein and moved forward again. When he had gone a few yards, one of the guards stepped behind the miller, flicked out his dagger, and cut the miller's throat.

Azo and his bearded captain watched the hangings for a while, and then turned back towards the castle. Diomede. could just see the horse-litters being lined up by the gate. Smoke drove quickly through the foliage about him, he nearly burst himself trying not to cough, although the hideous noise below must cover any he might make himself. . . .

At length, as the last prisoner joined the dance of death, the trumpets sounded from the keep, and the executioners bustled away.

Diomede sat still, and the turn of the birds began. He drew his own dagger, ready for a jab if flapping wing or clashing beak came too near him; and so waiting, saw the procession of horsemen and litters start away towards the northern pass.

No use descending in daylight, he told himself; but already the sun was sinking behind Siege Fabulous, and the lake was yellow and steel-grey under a half-clouded sky.

Diomede said a *Paternoster*, an *Ave*, and his usual evening prayer. Then he carefully unfastened the belt which secured him in his place, and as carefully girded himself with it, fishing the spare bolts out of his hose and securing them close to the belt buckle. The winged stick he had cut loose and wedged securely, so that its fall might not betray him; he looked at it glumly, marvelling at the peace and fun and friendship of which it had been a token and was now only a silly ghost. . . .

And when the Sieur de Caherne and the party he had led to Sanctlamine came galloping back in the last daylight, Diomede stayed where he was.

'That Caherne is Montguiscard's man,' he told himself.

' He must have been sent to draw away as many Pardelin men as he could. The next person I talk to must be my Uncle Gilomar . . . I wish I had a horse, for he's ten leagues away across wild country.'

Dusk came down, and lights appeared in the castle. The intermittent bellowing of cattle grew continuous, and then died away as someone began milking them. Haystacks were still burning, and here and there a cottage was alight. The crash of a falling roof-tree resounded as Diomede began his slithering descent. Once he had to kick out at two tugging crows which barred his way. When he reached the lowest bough there was nothing for it but to jostle two of the sweaty disfigured corpses. He swung himself down by his hands, and jumped and rocked on his feet for an instant, and swung his crossbow up to the ready.

But there was no one to see him there in the gathering gloom. He stumbled away to skirt the hamlet on its moorward side, pausing irresolute when he found himself desperately hungry. Summoning courage to risk seeing dead people sprawling about inside, he entered a hut and found black bread and cheese and an onion. Outside again, he jumped and was nearly sick with fright; a wandering pig whistled and grunted and turned to scuttle away from him.

He stole into the lakeside fields, along a hedgerow that reached towards the enclosing woods. It was still not quite dark as he cut across the neck of land that split the pommel of Lake Falchion. Reaching the shore again, he began the first climb that led to the pass. An owl hooted so close to him that he shuddered and pushed out the bow. Then he pulled himself together and went on, munching his food.

Somewhere ahead, on the right of the winding track, was a slope covered with silver birches, and beyond them a great tangle of hollies where he could wait for moonrise. Lioncel and he had sheltered there when a sudden rainstorm overtook them on their last ride in that direction. . . .

The night grew dark, and the wind was stirring again. It hissed in the leaves, and began to gather sounds a long way off. Moorland smells blew into the coverts, the track became hard to see, the end of the lake and the glow and smother of the hamlet dropped beyond the first edge of hillside. Then the lights of the castle were hidden for a time, and still Diomede toiled upwards in a kind of nervous daze that was least oppressive while he kept moving.

He had never before been benighted in waste country. Evil spirits and wild beasts might, for all he knew, be dogging him; he hugged the powerful weapon against him and was glad of the murderous spike at its tip, for apart from that he had only his dagger if once he shot without time to reload. . . .

Now and again he crossed himself, shying away in his mind from the blasphemous accusations that hovered on its threshold. Simple ashamed relief that he himself had so far escaped, and black fury at what had befallen Lioncel and all their friends except Yolande, occupied as much of his attention as could be spared from outward stress. Then a numbness of reaction joined with growing fatigue to drag at his limbs; and when at length he reached the birchwood and wove a stumbling way between the slender boles, he had attained a whimpering recklessness.

He halted among the hollies, poked about in the blackness, and lay down on his stomach with protecting masses of prickled leaves above and almost all around. He thrust the crossbow out in front of him, tucked the spare bolts up his sleeve, and lay for some time with his chin in his hands, miserably taking stock of the gruesome afternoon.

He had come to love Lioncel dearly; and now perhaps the guzzling pike were already at work on Lioncel's still face and graceful body. Before going to Pardelin he had scarcely seen a girl since he was eight years old, and there he had fallen in a worshipful love of Yolande; now Yolande was taken away as though she were a prisoner, and never again would he hand her into the blue-and-silver barge, or hold the gilt basin for her to rinse her slim brown fingers at table. The duke, so grave and mighty, had commanded his awed loyalty; and the duke was no doubt savagely slain, so that the whole duchy was suddenly headless, strange, and grim. . . .

Uncle Gilomar was approachable, but even he might think

Diomede had failed in his duty. And what would he do with a nephew returned in such a way? Send him to Bargreant, saying: *Here is the lad who can tell you what really happened at Pardelin?* Diomede found himself glad of that impossibility; he had accepted the past three months as an interlude extra-ordinary. Perhaps the prior would keep him in his own household . . . but even that could easily be awkward, yes, and dangerous.

And, first of all, he must reach Sanctlamine as soon as might be. The precious sacred relic there was the battered bronze helmet of Saint Longinus; Diomede felt he knew the good Saint sufficiently well to have a sharp word with him about the divine wisdom as exemplified in the day's work just ended. . . .

The waning moon came shouldering up over the eastward confines of the pass. Diomede was nearly asleep when its first horn threw glare in his face. Silvery light began to spill into the track, and he knew that he should be moving on.

He rose to his knees, and said his prayers all over again. Then, opening his eyes, he made to stand up, and was stricken to stillness by a sudden glitter of metal at a turn of the way below.

Someone else was coming up the road behind him.

Out of light into shadow, out of shadow into light again, plodded a tall man holding a drawn sword. He carried a longbow over one shoulder, and a buckler swung beside it. Over the other shoulder seemed slung a bulging sack. Beneath his steel cap a bandage came down to one eyebrow. He walked with a slight stoop which gave a prowling, purposeful air to his advance.

Diomede, on one knee in deep shadow, had plenty of time to decide what he must do.

'It must be one of the outlaws,' he reflected, shivering a little. 'If I let him pass he can ambush me . . . Jesu, Lady Mary, Saint Michael, I've got to shoot him down, I've *got* to.'

He crossed himself and raised the bow. Nearer and nearer came the tall figure, the moonlight revealing a black beard, a rolled cloak, a plated belt that carried scabbard, dagger, quiver, and swollen wallet.

'The last of his tribe,' thought Diomede. 'Full of plunder and plots and wickedness . . . he's talking to himself.'

Indeed, the man was grumbling and growling as he marched steadily uphill. When he glanced aside at the moon his face was that of a gilded image of rapine; the wilderness needed no demon other than this survivor of Turlequin's menie.

'Is it murder to murder a murderer?' Diomede asked himself silently as he aimed at the outlaw's middle. Somehow he had stopped shivering; he drew in a breath and held it as he curled his trigger-finger.

The note of the crossbow was almost a clink in the wind. The bolt vanished in the moonlit shape, which trod forward one astonished pace and collapsed prone with a groan and multiple bump and clatter. The long sword flew free, the legs sprawled wide, one great empty hand clawed at the grass and was still.

'Because if it is,' gabbled Diomede aloud, 'I've just done it.'

Before rising he wound and reloaded his weapon, watching the fallen shape in terror lest it humped itself up and came for him. Then he crossed himself again, got to his feet, stole forward with finger on the trigger, and snatched up the sword whose corded grip was still warm.

'I ought to behead you in case you're shamming,' he muttered severely.

But now he could see the point of his bolt, stuck upright through the body. After a second's hesitation Diomede stood the sword in the soil and bent to draw the long dagger.

'We'll see what's in your sack,' he said. 'I doubt you've no right to any of it.'

Squatting in the moonlit track, with an occasional glance around him, he turned out the plunder. It consisted of a silver platter, a silver spur, a bent copper candlestick, a sweetmeat-box of carven horn, a pair of parti-coloured hose, an empty leathern bottle, a little embroidered pillow, half a cooked chicken, a black pudding, an apple, and a bronze armorial pendant from the trappings of a destrier.

'Some of this comes on with me,' said Diomede to himself. 'And now for the wallet.'

In the wallet were a wooden dice-box with three ivory dice in it; a chevalier and a pawn of the chessmen Diomede and Lioncel had used; a flint and steel; and a purse containing a gold bezant, two Franconian crowns, a Styrian silver penny, and several coins strange to Diomede. Tipping the wallet up to empty it, he also found a bronze pilgrim's sign of Saint Andreas of Hautarroy, a gold and enamelled brooch that had belonged to the Dame de Chevronel, a file, a stub of beeswax, a lump of deer's suet, two bowstrings, three leathern laces, and, last of all, two queer objects at which he stared in turn.

The first he dropped as if it were on fire; it was a woman's finger with a silver ring on it.

'Too tight to pull off, I suppose,' said Diomede to the dead man. 'It was time somebody killed you.'

The second object was the little silver leopard-crested helm of Yolande's doll Amarand. Diomede gave a quiet groan, and his eyes filled with tears, one of which splashed on the dainty leopard. Diomede rubbed the toy on his sleeve, kissed it, and dropped it into the lean purse at his own belt.

'I'll give you back if I can,' he told it, 'Saint Michael helping me, amen.'

He looked up and around with a sudden new defiance. The pass ahead was bathed in moonlight; behind and below a flaming cresset marked the keep of Pardelin.

'Come on now,' said Diomede, and set about dividing the spoil. The food, the silver, the sword and buckler, the dagger and cloak and wallet he retained, filling the latter with the things of any value. The longbow he hacked in two, the arrows he threw into the thickets; everything else he left where it lay, except the poor ringed finger, which he buried carefully at the foot of a silver birch. On the birch-bole he hastily scratched a cross, and knelt to say a prayer for a maimed woman whether she were alive or dead.

Then he got up for the last time in that strange windy place, and arranged his new burdens, wishing that the sword did not make him feel small. Presently he was climbing again, this time more slowly.

Once he turned to look at the lake, at the still-burning hamlet and the castle with its point of fire, at the track with the woods thinning beside it, and the hollies black above the glimmering birches. The dead man was just visible, a blur at the wayside.

' Saints send no one treats me the same way,' said Diomede. ' And now once I'm over the top I'll find somewhere to eat and sleep.'

Later, in the cleft of a rock, with his hunger appeased and his body wrapped in the good cloak, he fumbled in his purse and drew out the miniature helmet.

' If I were a wizard,' he told it, ' I'd pile a great charm on you and send you flying to comfort and protect her. As I'm not, you can listen while I pray for her safety. . . .'

After a while he thought again of Lioncel, and then, being exhausted with behaving like a man, he buried his face in the crook of one arm and cried himself to sleep in the shadow of Siege Perilous.

III

ROCLATOUR AND SANCTLAMINE

AT the same hour moonlight and torchlight made bright as
day the cobbled square beside the gateway of the Abbey of
Saint Marthe in the little walled town of Roclatour. Azo de
Montguiscard had sent to tell the abbess to expect a guest about
midnight, and rumour had run in the narrow streets, rousing
the shocked and wondering burghers, to whom Duke
Engelbert had proved a just and careful ruler.

Thus Yolande, coming to herself in the swaying horse-litter,
found the newly-risen wind blowing aside the curtains to show
her moon-glitter wide on the crinkled midnight surface of
Lake Targe. Ahead and below was the castled rock with its
silvered and shadowed towers; beyond again, a jumble of
silvered roofs fell to the little curved quay and the handful of
lake craft moored beside it.

Yolande knew where she was, and guessed her immediate
destination. There were no women in the Castle of Roclatour,
and she was accustomed to pausing at the abbey on journeys
between Bargreant and Pardelin. She parted the curtains to
see more clearly, and pressed her hands to her head, which was
aching; the strange taste of the drugged wine lingered on her
lips and palate. Also she found herself·shivering, in spite of
a bearskin tucked around her body.

Leaving the curtains flapping, she joined her hands to pray,
and then let them fall apart again as angry little fists. Her
heart filled with a slow scalding rage; she gasped, and blinked
at the wild flame of cressets brightening the western gateway
of Roclatour. The column of armed and mounted men
wound down to enter there; at a turn of the way Yolande
caught a glimpse of the black-draped litter in front of her
own.

A church bell began to toll; that would be Saint Michael's, close to the castle. Beyond the gateway the streets were lit and thronged; the crowd was all but silent as the litters lurched through it. Yolande did not try to hide; she sat erect, confronting the glow of lantern, torch, and taper.

'Poor lamb,' said one weeping woman, and another: 'God ease her.' A third said: 'God be praised they saved the sweet little duchess.'

Yolande felt nothing like a lamb, or a sweet little duchess either. Nor would she praise God for life which cost the lives of her father and all her friends at Pardelin. Two phrases wove in and out of her heartsick fury: *shy leopardess* was one, and the other: *never trust a Montguiscard*. What her father had meant by that she could not imagine, but it recurred again and again as the hoof-beats clashed in the windy alleys; and now invisible swirls of fever shook across her vision, beginning to distort everything she saw.

When the convent gateway loomed up, when lances, bright helmets, and tossing horses' heads were aligned across the little square, Yolande gripped the side of the litter and looked at the great chestnut tree that stood up behind the convent wall. The litter was halted, and the vast white headdress of the old abbess appeared under the archway. Azo de Montguiscard came glimmering up to help her step to the ground.

'Diomede fed the tortoise with chestnuts,' she told him with some intensity.

The tall bland count stool still, one hand bared and extended, the other mailed and clutching the mail glove he had drawn off. He gazed at Yolande for a second or two, and made some movement which brought the abbess and one of her nuns surging forward to replace him.

'He thought the tortoise was an elemental,' Yolande told them.

'Holy Mary have pity,' said the abbess, putting a warm dry hand on Yolande's.

'She may, when the Sieur God isn't looking,' muttered Yolande darkly.

The abbess said something to her companion, a tall, middle-aged nun, who made an impatient sound and reached into the litter. Scooping Yolande up in strong arms, she swung her as though she were a baby.

'The foul fiend's been at work,' the tall nun said, gruffly, to anyone who could hear her. Then she sailed with her burden under the archway, up two steps, and into a passage where long candles burned. Yolande, with starched linen cool against her hot forehead, smelt scoured stone and scrubbed wood, incense, ferns, roses, boiled milk, wine and cooking, and finally clean bedclothes and lavender, perfumed soap and oil. . . .

She was laid down on a truckle bed, stripped and bathed and towelled, given a silken coat for warmth, and popped into the great bed she had slept in three months before. Another nun brought broth and a cordial, and the tall sister fed Yolande with an elegant ivory spoon. The abbess had watched her for a while and then vanished; the bedchamber was half-lit, and the nun's shadow slid enormous over dim hangings and painted ceiling.

'Zoster Adela,' her colleague had called Yolande's attendant; Yolande found comfort in her ruddy cheeks, placid forehead, square jaw, and steady brown eyes.

'Why does she call you Zoster?' she asked.

'She comes from Ostercamp in the Coast March,' said the tall nun.

'May I call you Zoster Adela?'

'Yes, child, of course you may.'

'Thank you for tending me so kindly, Zoster Adela.'

'God have mercy, dear child, it's only my Christian duty.'

'God has no mercy, but I know you have. The trouble with God is, he isn't a Christian.'

'No, no, child, of course he isn't . . . eh? What did you say? No matter, come, have another sup. Don't talk any more. My lady abbess will come back, and you'll frighten her into thinking you're ill.'

'Is that the signet ring you took out of my clothes? Put it

on my thumb again, please. Thank you, Zoster. I mustn't lose it . . . I feel dizzy and stupid. If I look at the shadows there in the corner I can see the lake and the servants drowning . . . they upset the boats . . . Lioncel dived in and swam, but they shot him with arrows. He saved my doll Amarand for me, and now I've lost them both for ever.'

Zoster Adela got up, lit more candles, and set them in corners to dispel the deadly shadows. Then she came back and gathered Yolande against her massive shoulder.

Thus propped, Yolande regarded somewhat glassily her benefactress and rescuer, for the abbess brought the count with her into the bedchamber. Azo had taken off his helmet and sword-belt; also he had washed his face, and now looked grave, kind, alert and wise, as became a loyal soldier and devout servant of Holy Church.

' Good even, my lord count,' said Yolande, a little pompously. ' It was a pity you came so late. Did they catch the rogues who dressed up as packmen? I never liked men with bow legs . . . the peasants say they're no good for stopping a pig in an alley . . . the pigs were squealing, too . . . you can hear sounds more easily when they come across the water . . . I'll have justice on everyone who hurts my father's peasants. . . .

' Zoster Adela says I'm not to talk, but the Dame de Chevronel always told me to set people at their ease by talking a little about what interests them . . . next time you come to Pardelin, my lord count, let it be in the hawking season. Have you seen my beautiful hound, Alcor? He's named after a star in the Great Bear. Al Cor, the Heart of the Bear. There are bears in the deep forest beyond Siege Umbrous. The Count of Ger gave us good mention in his famous ballade . . . you know it? *In high Baraine are skilful spears for boar and bear that fume at bay.* The Dame de Chevronel says that the vowels there are cunningly placed. Chevaliers wrote poems for her, too, when she was young. But one of the outlaws hit her on the head . . . I wanted to scream, but you mustn't scream when you are Baraine. Gold Puss wouldn't like it. Gold Puss would snarl. *I* can snarl, too. . . .'

Yolande gave a very creditable snarl, and the abbess and the count disappeared together, leaving Zoster Adela to wipe away the sweat that had begun to trickle into the eyes of Baraine.

Next the bedchamber dissolved, and curious scenes assembled and faded for Yolande's admiration. . . .

She stood near the black edge of a precipice; fires burned out of sight below, and a shape of dull fire rose up and became a horned and bearded head, sad and stately rather than devilish. It looked at her with eyes that were nothing but black pits; the beard spread over the cliff top in six trickling points of flame which presently stopped and swelled at their tips into glowing orange-coloured pearls. The beard now looked like King Solomon's crown in Yolande's painted Book of Hours at Bargreant; only, of course, the crown seemed upside down. Head and beard sank and disappeared, pearls and all, with one ironic flicker of light in each of the eye-holes. . . .

The edge of the precipice ruffled itself up and became distant twilit mountains; the slow strokes of Saint Michael's bell pushed into the vision as rosettes of green and gold and pink which floated up like clouds in inexorable procession, tilting in turn to vanish edgeways among the angry stars. . . .

Gold Puss appeared, enormous, climbing the mountain skyline; his progress took him through a recurring sequence of heraldic postures, *rampant, salient, passant, statant, rampant* again. Suddenly he was *rampant gardant*, looking at her with his tongue hanging out. It waved like the tongue of Alcor after a gallop in the heather.

' No, no! ' cried Yolande, not knowing why. Gold Puss drooped and crumpled as if made of paper, having just life enough to slither down the mountain-side and shuffle off into the shadows, looking now like a rather shabby clay-coloured sheepdog.

' He'll have to wait,' said a kind remembered voice nearby. Buildings had grown up, and the voice came from Dom Piers, who stood in front of a great iron-studded door.

' Why? ' asked Yolande, sorry for Dom Piers because he had been killed in the barge.

' It's time to rickle the ramkins.'

'How do they do that?' asked Yolande, who thought of ramkins as little balls of cheese toasted in breadcrumbs.

Dom Piers made an amiable gesture, and vanished. Crossbows began to throb and thrum, shooting black birds the size of larks past Yolande at the iron-studded door. *Plock, plang, plack* went the birds, splashing into square red patterns like painted bosses on a carven ceiling. A different bell chimed faintly, and its sound was a curling blue cloud that leaped and skeined among the red shapes, dissolving the door and leaving only a grille beyond which a barren landscape stretched away into the distance.

The vegetation there consisted of clumps of guisarmes and pennoned lances; a river wound between them, with the long boat forging slowly nearer over its leaden surface.

'Keep that away!' cried Yolande, looking up over housetops at the summit of Siege Gracious.

'I'll keep it away, my pet,' said the mountain, ruddy in dawnlight. For a moment the high crest was the head of Zoster Adela, now no longer hugely coiffed in stiff white linen, but bare, with thick iron-grey hair cut short below the ears like a page's, and kind brown eyes reflecting the gleam of candles.

'*Ave Maria, gratia plena,*' began Zoster Adela quietly. Presently Yolande saw her father standing alone on the keep at Pardelin. In a minute he would turn and smile at her as he had so often done . . . but this time he went on staring at the lake as if he had forgotten her. His unheeding face and melancholy figure vanished in all-devouring blackness.

When next Yolande became properly conscious it was late afternoon. Sunlight poured in at two lancet windows; beyond them the top of the chestnut-tree showed beneath blue sky. A thrush sang, and poultry clucked, and Zoster Adela's coif came floating past the plain blue wall-hangings. A trumpet wailed far off, and Yolande stirred and mumbled.

'What's happening? How long have I been here?'

Zoster Adela rustled to the bedside.

'You're to lie still, my pet,' she said. 'This is the second evening since you came.'

'I should go on to Bargreant. Where's the Count of Mont-guiscard?'

'Ridden off about his business and yours. They say a Franconian army is marching towards the River Malvaine. The townsmen are mustering to join the count at Jarapt.'

'More fighting, then?'

'Maybe, but nowhere near here.'

'The Dame de Chevronel said that at Pardelin. My father's funeral . . .'

'They buried him yesterday in Saint Michael's until the troubles are over.'

'That will be a long time,' said Yolande sullenly, and began to cry without troubling to screw up her face. Zoster Adela wiped away the tears and brought a drink of mulberry wine, which stung Yolande's senses awake. Yolande's body began to belong to herself again; feeling it under the bedclothes, she found a great bruise on one hip. Her hand was bandaged where it had bled.

'I have no friends now except you,' she told Zoster Adela.

'Nay, nay, child,' said the big nun, 'don't talk like that. We're all your friends here. Reverend Mother Abbess will take good care of you. My lord count and all your men will guard you and honour you.'

'My father said . . .' began Yolande, and then remembered more of what he had said, and let her words die away unfinished. Zoster Adela was kind, but she was under the orders of the abbess. The abbess was kind, but she was under the orders of the Bishop of Bargreant. The bishop was kind, but young and tense, and Yolande mistrusted him. The chancellor would now be shaking his head because she was to rule. There was no one to whom she could turn with the frightening problem of her father's last advice to her. . . .

Each time she made confession at Bargreant, mild old Dom Blaise, who was Dom Piers' elder brother, would somewhere during his admonition tell her to think no evil. The precept of her father in God clashed sadly with the precept of her father in the flesh.

Yolande remembered how a year ago she had been too shy to

tell the priest that her body had come under the dominion of the moon. Now, it seemed, the dominion of Mars had reached into her life. God who created moon and planet would have to sort it out for himself; here was something else with which she would not trouble old Dom Blaise.

Nevertheless, it was very confusing. In fact it was horrible. 'Zoster Adela,' she whispered. 'Say an *Ave* with me.'

Zoster Adela knelt down on the cushioned step beside the bed. Distantly the trumpets of Roclatour began to wail again.

At that same hour Diomede was pouring out his tale to his uncle, the Prior of Sanctlamine. Dom Gilomar sat beneath the copper beech which shaded a corner of his private garden, and stared under bushy grey eyebrows at this dirty, exhausted refugee. With them was the sub-prior, whose troubled eyes slewed from one to the other of them; it was he who had found Diomede stumbling through the woods towards the priory gate-way. When someone else was in trouble the sub-prior forgot his fear of damnation.

'This boat . . h'm!' growled the prior at length. 'You will swear to all that you have told me?'

'Yes, my lord uncle,' said Diomede, scarcely hearing his own voice through the ringing in his ears. The nails of his fingers which clutched a goblet were still blackened with oak-bark; the contents of the wallet and sack were spread on a table at the prior's elbow.

'Well, you were always a truthful boy. Reverend father sub-prior, here's my key to the shrine. Will you now secretly bring me the blessed relic?'

'Yes, my lord and father in God,' said the sub-prior, trembling with anxious goodwill.

'This bearded man with the black patch . . . h'm!' went on the prior. 'Only your friend Lioncel—God rest his soul and comfort *you*, dear lad—only Lioncel saw him that day beside the lake?'

'Only he, my lord. Shall I . . . shall I have to bear witness elsewhere?'

Dom Gilomar reflected, frowning and sucking a tooth. A

wave of fright began to rear up somewhere in Diomede's middle.

'I think not,' said the prior at length. 'I do not see what . . . h'm . . . h'm.'

The wave paused, sank, receded. Diomede was ashamed and glad. The sub-prior came gliding back into the garden. In his arms he bore a burden wrapped in white-and-gold samite. Diomede got shakily to his feet and crossed himself.

'Here,' said the prior, touching the table. The sub-prior laid the heavy reliquary tenderly down, and removed its silken covering. Diamonds, emeralds and sapphires flashed upon gold and enamel; through the bars showed green bronze that once was bright on Calvary. On the lid a little gold replica of the saint's spear leaned against a crystal rood, whereon hung an ivory Christ whose blood was tiny rubies.

Diomede knelt and laid a grubby hand on the glittering splendour, swearing in words given to him that he had told the truth about Pardelin.

'Now bring the porter on duty,' Dom Gilomar commanded his subordinate.

The surprised porter appeared, and was sworn to secrecy concerning the return of Diomede. The reliquary was covered up, and the sub-prior took it away. The evening wind rustled in the leaves of the copper beech, which turned crimson where the light pierced them, and filled Diomede with the sadness of a known place revisited and found utterly strange.

He drank up his wine and ventured another question.

'What will you do, my lord?'

'Hide you,' said Dom Gilomar.

'Hide me? Are the count's men still here?'

Messengers had come from Pardelin, passing Diomede while he broke his fast in the rocky cleft before setting out again.

'No, they left yesterday, with orders to report to Jarapt. The King of Franconia has sent an army against Baraine. The raids into Nordanay were a feint, to draw our men away.'

'Will they come here, my lord?'

'I pray they will not, but . . . h'm. The Count of Montguiscard is a famous captain.'

'I . . . I thank you, my lord.'

'For what? You have attempted a great service to our lady the duchess.'

'Our lady the duchess!' whispered Diomede, finding the title as strange as Yolande herself had found it.

'Yes. But whether or when we can use that service remains to be seen.'

'My lord, that reminds me . . . before I sleep . . .'

'Well?'

'I told you . . . I killed a man in the pass!'

'So you did. Kneel down again.'

Diomede knelt, and received a brisk absolution. Then he had a bath and a meal, and was given a truckle-bed on the floor of the prior's bedchamber. The lay brother who was bodyservant to the prior left the flagon of wine out when he should have cupboarded it. Diomede grinned his thanks but was asleep the moment after; the bells of Sanctlamine, which once had ruled his life there, now failed even to rouse him through a night and most of the following day.

By the time he next awoke more messengers had reached the prior, bearing the full details of Azo's version of the doings at Pardelin. Dom Gilomar came to Diomede's bedside with a written account in his hand.

'There's an oddity here,' he began, 'which argues against invention. Boy, did you know the castle cook yonder?'

'Yes, my lord. I liked him. He was an old soldier, and he could hurl his kitchen choppers like an angel . . . that is . . .'

'That is, if angels were given to hurling kitchen choppers. Yes. Well, it seems the archer who was sentinel on the keep turret blew his horn and was hit by an arrow before he could do anything else. He was badly hurt, and could only move as far as the hall gallery. There he dragged himself in on hands and knees, and lay watching the fighting below, unable even to lift his bow to help. The count's men found him there, but he died after telling what he had seen. . . .'

The archer saw the duke and his half-dozen men drive one group of attackers out of the keep and into the hall by a door-

way at one side of the dais. There was a pause there, for
Turlequin himself appeared and shouted for a parley.

' I don't want your castle, man,' he told the duke calmly.
' I want your live carcass for a ducal ransom, and then I'll
forswear entry to your duchy for life.'

Before the duke could reply a shout of laughter went up
from the outlaws. Everyone glanced aside—to see, at the end
of the dais screen, where a doorway led from the kitchen, the
unwieldy figure of the castle cook, steel-capped, and wearing
over his white apron a demi-plastron too small for him. In one
hand he grasped a chopper, and in the other the lid of an iron
cauldron. Several more choppers hung from the hooks of his
great-belt.

' What are *you* doing here? ' asked Engelbert of Baraine.

' Come to clean out a few more tripes, my lord duke,'
wheezed the cook.

' You should be in the barge with the others.'

' Too fat. I might upset it.'

' God bless you, then, old friend . . . gut me that forest hog
there.'

' Duke Engelbert, you are a fool! ' yelled Turlequin,
dropping on hands and knees as the chopper flew. It flashed
over his back and split the stomach of the man behind him.
Tumult of battle roared out again, and the watching archer saw
three other choppers go home before the defenders were pushed
back into the fatal passage. . . .'

According to Azo, the duke's serfs were wiped out, and the
Lady Yolande brought ashore, before her rescuers galloped in.
Yolande was torn senseless from the arms of an escaping outlaw.
She was the only living survivor; and for this much mercy
(wrote Azo) the prior would join him in humble thanks to God
on behalf of the stricken duchy.

' So that's what will be told and known,' said the prior, looking down at his nephew. ' You must hold your tongue now,
and perhaps for always.'

' I'd like to return my lady Yolande her doll's helmet,' said
Diomede.

' H'm. I'll try to do that later. There's peril for *you* anywhere near her . . . that is, if Azo, or his son, or any of his men, should see you and remember you, or even hear that you had been of her household before the massacre. So now I must find some distant friend in need of a page . . . a page who must forget that he was ever at Pardelin.'

Diomede said nothing to that; he wished for a moment that he could stay at Sanctlamine for the rest of his life. But that could only be done by entering Holy Church, and Diomede knew he had no vocation; nor did it occur to him to begin to pretend to have one.

The sub-prior's footfall sounded in the passage; the sub-prior poked his head around the arras which covered the door.

'My lord prior,' he said, 'one of the foresters is here, with a half-dead lad on his saddlebow. He picked him up in the hills this morning . . . in the hills toward the pass. A gentle-looking lad it is, with very fair hair.'

Diomede gasped and bounced up on one elbow, his eyes wide and shining, his naked body curled to spring. Dom Gilomar got to his feet and shook a finger at him.

'Get dressed and wait here, my sanctuary knave,' he growled, and banged the door behind him.

Diomede plunged into his clothes, and hurled himself on his knees to pray.

A few minutes later the sub-prior came quietly back and looked in at him.

'Diomede, boy, get up,' he said. 'We think it's your friend . . . wounded, but not gravely.'

In the prior's parlour five seconds later Diomede's tears were raining down on Lioncel's still face. Dom Gilomar took the forester by the arm and steered him out in the direction of the priory church and the blessed relic of Saint Longinus. Sub-prior and lay brother left them alone for a moment; Diomede hugged his friend and sobbed in helpless joy and thankfulness.

Lioncel opened his eyes, blinked twice, and stared. Then he stirred and pouted his mouth to meet Diomede's reassuring kiss.

'You're *not* dead!' he whispered.

'No, but I'm nearly drowning you again,' gulped Diomede.

'Am I hurting you? Where's your wound? How did you escape? How did you get here?'

'I was shot in the behind,' murmured Lioncel ruefully. 'I shall never be able to boast about my first battle. I dived out of the boat . . .'

'I saw you.'

'Where were *you*, then?'

'In the oak-tree, as we arranged.'

'Ah! Well, I dived again and swam sideways to that drift-wood . . . I came up among it and floated with my face above water until the boat had gone. An arrow was stuck right through one buttock. . . . Saints be praised it wasn't a thick square bolt. After a while I swam ashore, and crawled into the bushes, and broke the arrow and pulled it out, and spent the night on the hillside, and then started to walk here, dodging anyone I saw on the road.'

'You knew it was treachery, then, between the count and the outlaws? You didn't go to the castle?'

'I saw the Montguiscard men-at-arms hunting the serfs along the shore. And those men in the boat were soldiers, not outlaws. That damned helmsman was the soldier who watched us that afternoon when I gathered the strawberries. But chiefly I stayed hidden, because I was most horribly afraid.'

'So was I,' said Diomede.

'Come on now, boys,' said the sub-prior, bursting in again with the servant. 'We'll set up another bed in yonder and get him washed and tended.'

Dom Gilomar came back and sat by his great bed, watching them. He creased his forehead and fingered his cross of gold and turquoise, and when they had done, bade them leave him alone with Lioncel.

Diomede waited in the parlour, staring at the gilded leather hangings, feeling rather than thinking that now life could be good again. When the prior called him he paused, astonished, on the threshold of the bedchamber. Bright in the evening sunlight that flickered through the foliage of the copper beech, Yolande's doll, Amarand, stood on the painted wooden chest beside Lioncel's bed.

'The worst of it is,' whispered Lioncel, 'I only just got away in time. His helmet must have fallen off as I pushed him into my wallet.'

The prior smiled at Diomede, who laughed and fumbled in his purse. He found what he sought, and helmed the gallant Amarand with a flourish. Lioncel's eyes grew wider and wider in his tired, thin face.

'I'll tell you how I got it,' promised Diomede, placating their astonishment.

'Two of you to hide now,' growled Dom Gilomar. 'When I can I shall send you away, out of this province. But remember, your two necks are not much thicker than one.'

Diomede suddenly turned on his uncle.

'My lord,' he said, 'are we putting you and Sanctlamine in danger, too? Hadn't we better take ourselves off as soon as Lioncel's wound is healed?'

Dom Gilomar sat still for a moment, looking out into his garden.

'*Et catuli leonis dissipati sunt,*' he said. 'Diomede, can you translate?'

'*Et catuli leonis* . . . and the lion's cubs . . . *dissipati sunt* . . . are, er, scattered abroad.'

'Yes. But not at once. Sanctlamine must take the risk of harbouring such creatures. I shall be sorry to lose you, boys, for I think Baraine could do with both of you.'

Yolande was of the prior's opinion. When at length she was reckoned strong enough to visit her father's temporary tomb, she made a prayer for each of their souls next after the soul of Duke Engelbert. And then, as she walked back from the church of Saint Michael, she saw a ghost from Pardelin.

Pacing slowly beside the abbess across the little cobbled square, with Zoster Adela and the six abbey men-at-arms following behind, and hushed townsfolk doffing their caps and curtseying as she passed, she happened to glance at the abbey wall where the great chestnut overhung it. An alley-mouth opened there at the tree-shadowed corner; three tall soldiers paused in it to watch her little procession.

They saluted in unison; over the bald head of a bowing
burgher Yolande saw that the middle soldier of the three had a
longish sandy beard flowing down on his tabard. Also he had a
faint scar across the bridge of his nose, and a black patch where
his left ear should have been.

Yolande stood still and clutched at the arm of the abbess.
Black horror struck into the sunshine; a shriek was torn from
her breast, and her pointing finger rose as if of its own will.

' *Turlequin!* ' she cried, in a sudden startled silence. ' *God
blast you, evil spectre! Back to hell where you belong!* '

Covering her eyes with the hand she had lifted, she leaned
back on the horrified abbess. Zoster Adela caught her from
behind, the men-at-arms leaped to surround her with a rasping-
out of swords, women screamed, men stood gaping . . . and
when Yolande looked again there were only two tall soldiers
standing at the mouth of the alley.

' There were three! ' she gasped. ' There were three, and one
of them was Turlequin! '

' Our Lady help her,' groaned the abbess. ' I feared it was too
soon to let her go to the church.'

' There are only two men there, my precious,' said Zoster
Adela, steering Yolande towards the abbey gateway. ' They're
two of my lord count's captains . . . I've seen them about in
the town before.'

' I tell you there were three! ' wailed Yolande, and suddenly
became aware of a watching face in the crowd. It was a man's
face, strange to her, but full of pleased curiosity; its owner—
greasy, unkempt, gap-toothed—was triumphing over a duchess
in distress. The gleam of his little piggish eyes shocked her like
a douche of water; she turned away and let herself be shep-
herded under cover.

' Grief has broken her intellects,' said an awestruck voice
outside the gate.

' Get back there, or something else will break your skull,' said
one of the men-at-arms angrily.

The great gates clashed behind them; Yolande drew a
shuddering breath and stood still in the passage.

' Reverend Mother in God,' she said, ' and you, Zoster Adela,

... was that wraith a warning to me? Or was it a warning to Roclatour, or to the soldiers of Baraine? Don't ... Reverend Mother in God, don't tell my lord count!'

'You must go back to bed, my child,' said the old abbess crisply. 'Your health is not sufficiently recovered ... don't worry any more about this apparition.'

But she did not promise not to tell the Count of Montguiscard about it, as Yolande realised when she lay once more between cool sheets.

'Zoster Adela,' she whispered, as the big nun gathered up scattered clothing. 'Zoster Adela, do you think I'm going crazy?'

Zoster Adela smiled at her, and seemed to ponder for an instant. Then she glanced at the door and came to the bedside.

'When I said there were two men there,' she whispered in return, 'there *were* only two. But *I* saw three before you cried out.'

'Then the other was real ... and hid himself. But the count told me Turlequin was killed ... and what could he be doing here with the count's captains? What can I believe now?'

'Believe that I am here to help you,' said Zoster Adela quietly.

'Yes, I do believe that,' Yolande told her.

Later in that same afternoon Yolande asked for a game of chess. Only two or three of the nuns could play the game; and instead of going at once to fetch one of them for her, Zoster Adela stood again considering her charge. She herself understood chess, but it was time for her to go to supper.

'My precious,' she said, and paused.

'Yes?' replied Yolande, suddenly alert.

'I'm only your nurse here, but my father was one of your father's captains. If you should wish or think it wise to stay in this place, don't recover too soon from the shock of that apparition. Don't play chess yet awhile ... my lady abbess doesn't greatly esteem it, finding it too warlike and crafty a game. Rather ask to be read to by Sister Marcelle. That will please my lady abbess ... and Sister Marcelle, who's much with her.'

Yolande lay thinking for a moment.

'Gramercy, Zoster Adela,' she said in a small voice. 'Would you ask Sister Marcelle to be so kind as to read to me out of the *Gesta Romanorum?*'

Zoster Adela and she exchanged a faint smile. When next the abbess came in she found Sister Marcelle embarking on the last of a series of short tales, and sat down to listen. The tale was of equity; Sister Marcelle's voice was agreeably soft and deep.

'"The Emperor Heraclius, amongst many other virtues, was remarkable for his inflexible justice. It happened that one chevalier accused another of murder, in this form: *That chevalier went out, in company with another, to war; but no battle was fought. He, however, returned without his companion: and therefore we believe that he murdered him.* The emperor appeared satisfied with the inference, and ordered the prisoner to be executed. But as they approached the place of execution, they beheld the lost chevalier advancing towards them, alive and well. The emperor, angry at this interruption of the sentence, said to the accused: *I order you to be put to death, because you are already condemned.* Then, turning to the accuser: *And you also, because you are the cause of his death.* And then, addressing the returned chevalier: *And you, too, because you were sent to kill the first, and did not.*"

'The application of this tale is: my beloved, the emperor is God. The first two chevaliers are body and soul. The third chevalier is any prelate.'

Yolande was nearly asleep, but this more than usually strained conclusion hooked her back for a moment's reflection. Why did the body and the prelate go off and leave the soul behind? Why did God support the soul in accusing the body of murdering the prelate, and also condemn the prelate for not having murdered the body?

'Gramercy, Sister Marcelle,' she murmured. 'God give you a good night.'

'And you, dear lady duchess,' said the gratified Sister Marcelle.

'He's just as likely,' thought Yolande crossly, 'to send you a great murdering prelate to cut off your head . . . but you wouldn't notice.'

Then she turned dark appealing eyes on the old abbess, who smiled at her.

' Are you at rest now, child? '

' Yes, Reverend Mother in God. I feel safe here with you.'

Lioncel and Diomede lived for nearly a week in the prior's house, and then were roused in the small hours to go with the forester to his summer hut miles away in the hills. Their pages' tunics and hose they had to leave behind; there were a dozen boys at school in the priory, and the sub-prior found old clothes enough for the fugitives to wear.

The doll Amarand was wrapped up and placed with the other valuables from Pardelin in one of the prior's strong-boxes. Diomede's spoils of ambush were laid aside for him, except the dagger, which he found more impressive than his own, and the money, for which Dom Gilomar gave him Neustrian coins in exchange. Diomede halved these with Lioncel, and they each gave a silver penny to the friendly lay brother, who wished them godspeed as they crept away at moondawn from the prior's postern gate.

' Look after the young masters,' he bade the forester. The forester only grunted, and set a swinging pace through the woods. When they reached the drystone hut in the curve of a lonely ravine Lioncel exclaimed and pointed to where a gap in the uptossed hills showed them a rose-flushed mountain thirty and more miles to the northward. It was Siege Orgulous breaking the banner of morning over Lake Falchion.

The forester, whose name was Gothard, served them with oatmeal porridge and smoked trout and apples. Silent from obedience and custom of solitude, he asked no questions about Pardelin, and only gradually began to talk to them at all. His main trouble in life concerned the iron-smelters with licence to work itinerant forges in the forest, who regularly abused their permission to gather fuel.

' They steal my lord prior's wood,' said Gothard, ' rootfall and windfall both. And if there's neither about they cut green

wood, blast them. There are stone quarries beyond '—h(
gestured vaguely to the southward—' but you can keep an ey(
on *them*, for they don't get up and go off in the night.'

Lioncel and Diomede took lessons in cutting and stacking
peats, and studied the rudiments of thatching with heather.
They lived half-naked, and swam each day in a brown moorland pool; they collected antlers in the woodland glades, and
heard the barking challenge of the roe-deer in rut, and
watched the flight of buzzard and kestrel, heron and wild
duck. Sometimes the great red deer dignified a skyline, and
once a mud-caked wild boar grunted a challenge from his
wallowing-pool and put the wanderers to headlong flight.

Gothard usually went to the priory once in a week; his
tidings of plague and war were scanty, and sometimes Diomede
awoke in the night and felt it wrong to have dodged so neatly
out of danger and perplexity. Several times he had ghastly
dreams recalling the massacre. Once or twice he lost his
waking nerve and listened for the footfall of the man he had
killed; then the quiet breathing of Gothard and Lioncel, and
the fact that he himself lay furthest from the bolted door of
the hut, gradually restored his peace of mind.

Then, one night, a need of nature forced him barefoot and
unwilling out into the bushes. The sky was clear; before
returning he compelled himself to pause and look up and
about. Denep was nearest the zenith, with Vega blazing blue
hard by. The Plough was swinging under Polaris, Arcturus
had set, Aldebaran was rising; and under Aldebaran a new
red star quivered in the night wind from the hill-crest over
Sanctlamine.

Ice seemed to explode between Diomede's shoulder-blades;
he stood staring for a long second, and then padded back to
the hut.

' Wake up! ' he cried, fisting the open door. ' The beacon's
burning over the priory! Gothard, Lioncel, wake up! '

They followed him out into the darkness, and stood awhile
talking in low voices.

' Means we're beaten beyond Jarapt, I reckon,' said Gothard
glumly. ' Now we must all turn out . . . except you two.'

'Steady on!' protested Lioncel. 'Remember we're both handy bowmen!'

'My lord prior's orders . . . you're not to go to the priory until he sends for you. I'm off straight away. I put you on your honour to stay here.'

Diomede listened, torn between excited curiosity and the desire to be left alone in this delectable corner of the province, and not yet quite sure enough of Lioncel to confess to so mixed a sensation.

'My war-gear's at Sanctlamine,' said Gothard more cheerfully. 'I haven't worn my brigandine since we came back from Pont-de-Foy.'

Diomede clutched Lioncel's arm under cover of the darkness. Because their fathers had fought on opposite sides he could not let that name pass without a shameless display of affection.

'There goes another,' said Lioncel, pressing the clutching hand gaily against his bare ribs. A second point of fire had appeared to the south-east; presently a third sparkled beyond it, and Diomede thought of clashing bells, of torchlight at street corners, and of men grumbling and women crying from end to end of Baraine.

'That's what comes of murdering the duke,' he told himself dourly. 'I warrant that pink-nosed Montguiscard has made a mess of a real battle.'

Diomede's certainty could not have been worse founded. Azo de Montguiscard had retreated before superior force, drawn the Franconian army into the Gorge of Arionbel, and there smashed it to pieces. Its general, the Count of Harksburg, fled almost alone; his subordinate commanders were killed or captured with thirty thousand of their fifty thousand men; Harksburg's banner and tent and treasure, his baggage and cannon and siege-train, were taken entire. A ten-mile pursuit and slaughter completed the victory; two frightened Franconian towns gave up their keys at blast of trumpet; Azo de Montguiscard stood revealed as the saviour of Baraine and Neustria. The beacons, prepared to rouse a desperate resistance, were fired to celebrate a victory such as no Neustrian army had won for two hundred years.

'The count's son, this Balthasar, has taken the banners and treasure to the king at Hastain,' said Gothard, after one of the silences which fortified him against the strain of narrative.

'Balthasar?' muttered Lioncel, who was not often spiteful. 'A gilded image of self-conceit, only good to carry banners.'

'Nay, nay,' objected Gothard. 'They say he fought like a tiger and captured a baron all by himself.'

Lioncel snorted and parried the blow.

'Well, after all his big talk it was time he did something.'

Diomede nodded, remembering the little movement under Yolande's smooth brown chin as she swallowed yawn after yawn while listening to Balthasar.

Blue sky and brilliant sunshine, pale green rowans ablaze with berries orange-red, roll and dip of purple heather rising to blue-grey rocks or sinking to blue-green pinewoods . . . blue gleam of a tarn, yellow of distant cornfields seen through a gap of green oak-forest . . . Lioncel, sunburnt, graceful as a god, more beautiful than Balthasar because his fun was gentle and his pride unselfish . . . the great wineskin which Gothard had brought as a gift from the prior, the red wine glinting in old-fashioned drinking horns . . . Diomede's own brown contented body, sticky here and there with sweat, dusty with peat and sand, and stained with bilberry-juice . . . all these realities were suddenly a little clouded and saddened.

With wine-distended awareness Diomede perceived that henceforth Baraine was likely to be the pasture of Montguiscard, and that it was quite unlikely that he, Diomede, would ever see Yolande again.

A fortnight passed, and Gothard brought the prior's command that Lioncel and Diomede should present themselves before him.

'There's a great chevalier come to visit my lord,' said Gothard in his halting manner. 'Very old friend of his, they tell me. His blazon's the oddest I ever laid eyes on . . . it's no blazon at all.'

'How d'you mean?' asked Lioncel.

'It's plain silver. Nothing on it.'

'Oh, I've heard of *him*,' exclaimed Lioncel. 'That's the Chevalier Janus de Largire—Janus of the Silver Shield.'

'Ay, that's the name.'

'He's enormously strong, and rides between court and court like one of the old chevaliers errant, looking for people to joust with him, or waiting about for tournaments. He wins the prizes, too. It was he who captured the great banner at the Battle of Pont-de-Foy. He owns a castle and a rich silver-mine in Elquitaine, and visits them every year or two to collect more money for his journeys.'

'Sounds crazy to me,' said Diomede.

'I think he is a bit crazy. They say he carries a silver harp and a silver coffin around with him.'

'In case he dies and goes to heaven?'

'Yes, I suppose so. I hope he's still there when we get back tonight.'

He was, and they were not disappointed in expectation of oddity. The Chevalier Janus de Largire was tall and broad, with a handsome ruddy face and curious water-grey eyes. His thick brown hair came down to his shoulders; it and his short pointed beard were themselves shot with silver. The sub-prior said that except for the gilt spurs of chivalry, no touch of gold appeared in the chevalier's arms and equipment.

'Shadow and shine, eh?' said the chevalier in a flexible bass voice when the pair of them made their bow to him in Dom Gilomar's parlour. 'I have the three best servants in Europe; but to serve you, my Gilomar, I'll gladly go back on my custom and sport a couple of pages for a time.'

'Boys,' growled the prior, 'my old friend here has greatly obliged me by promising to take you with him into Elquitaine. He is fresh from the great battle in the gorge at Arionbel . . .'

'A well-omened day,' broke in the Chevalier Janus. 'I saw three shooting-stars on the right as I rode in the forest the night before. Nevertheless, the count should have masked the side-ravines, and then even Harksburg would not have escaped.'

'The Chevalier de Largire led the left horn of the ambush,' went on the prior, evidently used to the conversational habits of his guest.

'It was a near thing,' said the visitor. 'I reached the count's camp only an hour before he held his council of war.'

'God be praised you did so,' added Dom Gilomar, turning upon him a glance of approval that lapsed into speculation as it came back to the attentive faces of the boys. 'Diomede, the Chevalier will most courteously step aside from his own road to deliver you and Lioncel, together with a letter which I have already begun, to my brother, your uncle Dagobert, at Gax.'

Diomede bowed again.

'For reasons we have already discussed,' went on Dom Gilomar to his guest, 'these boys will need re-clothing in the first sizeable town you come to.'

'Rougefontaine,' murmured Janus, making the word a poem crooned by doves in silvery twilight.

'Rougefontaine,' agreed the prior, his workaday voice rebuilding the town in stone and timber. 'And as for horses, I have two jennets which will not disgrace your train.'

'We shall rest at the Sign of the Archer,' said Janus, smiling at his new followers. 'Can either or both of you sing?'

'Both of us, sir,' said Lioncel with great respect.

'Good. My squire Scipio reads like a bishop, but sings like a corncrake. As for my three serving-men—I call them Rosso, Verde and Nero, their surname being Colore—they sing simple songs on the road, but are not adept in hall or parlour. Their mother is quite dumb, poor soul ... and yet an Apulian beauty, a face from a Greek coin, Artemis or Persephone ... Gilomar, may these lads sing for me?'

'No, old friend, they may not. You forget they are in hiding.'

'By God's Monday, I've already banished their antecedents from memory, as you bade me. Boys, I believe we shall journey well together. My lord prior tells me you can handle bows of both kinds ... not that I anticipate calling on you to do so. I mostly travel in company, and seek no quarrels on the road.

I fight at times and in places of my own choosing. Also my three Apulians are very deadly archers . . . in the Danube forests I and Scipio and they fought off a pack of wolves that had terrorised a bailiwick and closed an ice fair.'

'You two will sup with us,' said the prior. 'Maybe the Chevalier Janus will sing before we go to bed.'

'What did I tell you?' whispered Lioncel, as Diomede and he washed their faces.

'It seems to me,' replied Diomede, 'that here we have the real victor of Arionbel. But I like him . . . and did you see? Even his eyes are silver when the light falls sideways through them.'

'I believe it's going to be fun,' said Lioncel.

After supper Janus sent for his magnificent harp. Diomede gasped at its glitter, at the slim high-breasted nymph whose silver nakedness shaped the fore-edge of the frame.

'First time they've had a lady like this at Sanctlamine,' he reflected. 'No, it isn't. He's been here before. She's very grave and sweet and pure; having no clothes on doesn't matter.'

Dom Gilomar did not seem to notice the silver lady, but the sub-prior came in, and the sub-prior's eyes goggled into a squint of horror. Lioncel and Diomede averted their gaze from the nymph, the sub-prior, and each other.

Janus gave no sign of having breached the priory wall at the head of the hosts of hell. His cheerful sensual face took on a strange intentness; his great brown hands were gentle as he tightened and tuned the harp-strings. Gusts of magical sound began to bewitch Diomede; he turned so that he could see Lioncel's still profile.

Janus sat motionless for a moment, staring across the candle-lit parlour; his wonderful sword-belt gleamed on a carpet-covered chest beside the door, each massive link a different creature's head of beaten silver. Gryphon, wyvern, lion, eagle, stallion, ram and bull lay heaped between the silver hilts of the long sword and the broad dagger. The dagger hung upright, and Janus sang to it in a muted but powerful and melodious voice.

D

' Misericord, sweet blade peculiar,
Deadliest friend, bright brother of the sword,
Who sped the Duke Philemon at the ford,
And by the mere the Marquis Berengar:
I cannot use you when the foe stands far,
But in the stumbling mellay you are lord,
Misericord!

' At Gondarem, beneath the evening star,
When through our failing flank the Crescent gor'd,
One stroke the fortune of the field restor'd;
You nail'd an emir to his gilded car,
Misericord!'

This, as the boys were to discover, was a trick of the Chevalier Janus. He never praised himself in his songs, but he frequently praised his weapons, his horses, his armour, attributing to them his successes in war and tournament. . . .

The candlelight, the singing, and the silver wove a fantasy in Diomede's head. Immense and glittering figures gathered against a sunset. Charlemagne, iron-crowned, was there; beside the crown four golden casques were crested with a sphinx, a dragon, a six-winged cherub, and a wolf, and Diomede knew that those lords were Alexander, Arthur of Britain, Judas Maccabæus, and Julius Cæsar.

'Are they all here?' rumbled Charlemagne to the dark captain standing behind him.

The captain turned to look at the host whose banners mirrored the coloured sky, and Diomede saw the mighty horn, the elephant's tusk ablaze with gems, hanging beside the sword Durandal.

'All here save one, my lord,' said Roland. 'He will be coming soon.'

'His name?'

'Paladin Janus of the Silver Shield.'

'Good. We will wait for him.'

In the morning that sense of fantasy still hung in the air. While the canons were at chapter, and Diomede's former schoolfellows bent over their books, Diomede received a command from the sub-prior.

'Bring Lioncel across the prior's garden and up the back stairs of the guesthouse. The chevalier's out riding with my lord prior; he said you should see his gear. None like it in Neustria.'

The guest-chamber into which they were bidden seemed half-full of silver and steel. Sunshine poured through window-glass; painted ceiling and tapestried walls were spangled with points and bars of reflected glitter. One of the three Apulian brothers met them at the door, and gravely lifted coverings of velvet and leather and canvas. His dark handsome face puzzled Diomede with a resemblance not at once to be recognised.

'It's seeing him with his brothers last night,' Diomede decided.

This one must be Rosso, for the little silver escutcheon on his tunic was set in a square of red silk. Verde had green, and Nero black, according to their names; they were all three big young men, supple-jointed and easy-tempered.

'The casque was made in Milan,' said Rosso softly, and both boys drew a long breath and stood silent. Availing himself of the fact that his baptismal name was also the name of a two-faced heathen god, Janus had entrusted the idea and its execution to Luca della Riola. The movable visor was a beautiful steel-and-silver mask of Mars; its void eye-sockets were elongated for Janus to see through, and the elongation produced an effect of merciless pride and power. The back of the helmet was shaped into an equally beautiful steel-and-silver mask of Pan, with amethysts set in white enamelled eyeballs, and a graven curly beard cascading to the rim of the neckpiece. The crest was itself a miracle of silversmiths' work; out of the torse, or twisted wreath, rose a gauntleted forearm and hand with wrist bent forward. On the wrist was perched, like a hawk, a little gleaming eagle with wings displayed and head turned to the dexter side.

'But that's the imperial eagle,' whispered Lioncel.

'Yes,' said Rosso, showing white teeth in a sudden grin.

' The chevalier saved the emperor's life at Trohacs in Hungary. He refused a county, and the emperor said he was ashamed to grant nothing, so he chose a crest, the eagle *argent*. He has the right to bear an augmentation, the eagle *sable* as the emperor uses it, but small, in dexter chief. He never does bear it, though. He'll never put any charge on *this*. . . .'

' This ' was the famous shield itself, its tall convexity minutely roughened so that it reflected nothing but light; no one could ever boast of seeing himself in its surface. Even so, it lit the observers' faces as though they were looking at sunlit snow.

The almost equally famous coffin stood with its emblazoned lid leaning against the wall beside it. A spare suit of armour lay within, as if keeping the space warm for the Chevalier Janus. The various shining pieces were wrapped and disposed among rich clothing, soft riding-boots, gifts of chased cups and caskets and coloured stuffs, and parchments of commendation bright with the scarlet seals of reigning kings and princes.

' Saints, what a load to carry about,' said Lioncel aloud to himself.

' There's a four-horse litter,' Rosso explained. ' It's made like an ark, too, and caulked, so that it floats; and it has iron runners for snow or steep places.'

Diomede began to feel that the Chevalier Janus would require a lot of living up to, but no doubt or hesitation shadowed the pleasure of Lioncel.

' It's the sort of adventure I've dreamed about sometimes,' he muttered shyly. ' Something fresh to see each day and evening . . . and always riding on again.'

Here, too, was the standard of Janus, a chaste magnificence of black silk and cloth of silver, with the motto *Splendeo* slanted between the embroidered crests—one the eagle-on-fist of the emperor's grant, the other the white wolf *passant* of the ancient house of Largire.

Beside the banner stood a silver trumpet, wrapped in its plain silvery streamer; and a canvas sack, partly unlaced, revealed a horse-panoply of white Cordovan leather and delicately-chased silver bells smothered in pinkish powder.

Most of the armour Janus had worn at Arionbel was in evidence, but not the corselet, which he had on him; he made it a practice never to go twenty-four hours without at least that much weight of steel. A dented helm of ordinary shape, with the stub of a shorn ostrich feather still standing in its steel comb, presided over the heap, which included a pierced cuisse and a badly-battered vambrace. Shrewd blows had been exchanged at the head of the left horn of the ambush.

'Were you in the battle?' Lioncel asked.

Rosso shook his head gravely.

'We diced for one to go and two to stay,' he explained. 'Nero won. He got a great crack on the knee that still makes him limp, but he came back with a fat purse and a sackful of good weapons. Verde and I had to look after the baggage.'

'What bad luck!' exclaimed Lioncel.

'I've been in plenty of battles, thank you,' said Rosso with a good-natured grin. 'Nero shared his keep-sakes out. The chevalier believes in guarding what he's got.'

'Quite right, quite right,' murmured the sub-prior. 'When you're away from home three years at a time, with gear as precious as all this, it's well not to leave it unattended.'

'Especially good pack-horses in a camp,' said Rosso. 'I watched them, and Verde watched all this stuff.'

The lean squire Scipio came in, knitting his brows; he was the least tranquil of this convoy-errant.

'Ah, it's you, reverend father,' he said to the sub-prior, and nodded civilly enough at Lioncel and Diomede. 'We shall be riding soon after dawn tomorrow. These lads, I take it, will leave before us and wait at the wayside. Pity there's no time to fit them out properly, but we'll see to all that at Rougefontaine.'

'This is what it's like to be the fifth leg of a chair,' thought Diomede, but he sympathised with the guardian of so much celebrated spendour.

Also he sympathised with the sub-prior, who was now worried beyond measure about the patches on Lioncel's elbows.

'Page and equipage, eh?' chuckled Janus, when the problem was laid before him. 'Gilomar, let the good sub-prior borrow some of the Sunday best of the lads you have at school here. No need to tell *them*. Give the whole lot a crown apiece from me in token of our victory in the gorge at Arionbel. Send your lay brother with us to bring the clothes back.'

'It's not strictly in accordance . . .' began the scrupulous sub-prior, but Dom Gilomar silenced him with a smile and a gesture.

'It's our best way out, reverend father in God. Janus, a great general was lost when you eschewed more than occasional service in the field.'

'I'm half-inclined to agree with you,' said Janus, so solemnly that Diomede decided he meant it.

When the boys were alone together before the prior came to his bed, Lioncel suddenly spoke so oddly that Diomede was startled.

'Diomede!'

'Yes?'

'There's just one thing I'm ashamed of in all this.'

'What d'you mean?'

'My lady Yolande . . . it's like deserting her. We're really nobody's servants but hers now.'

'I know. It bothers me, too. But we've both . . . er . . . run away once already.'

'Yes. But so long as we mean to go back some day. . . .'

'How can we do that? She thinks we're both dead. We both *ought* to be dead, I suppose, like all the others. At least I ought. You did risk your life to get Amarand away. And in the boat you fought, and then you were wounded. I did nothing at all.'

'You put paid to one of the enemy, and that's more than I did.'

'Don't talk about that. I hate remembering it.'

'Sorry.'

'Roland and Oliver, eh? Roland shot in the backside, and Oliver tree'd throughout the battle.'

'M'm. And if I'd turned up here alone . . .'

'Lioncel, if you *hadn't* turned up I don't think my lord prior would really have believed what I told him.'

'Certainly no one else will ever believe either of us now. The great Count of Montguiscard, who rode to protect the abbey, and ridded the province of the worst rogue who's ever been in it, and then saved the kingdom in a tremendous battle! Well, no matter what anyone else says or thinks, and no matter how he did that treachery, I'll always know him and hate him for a villain.'

'So shall I. And that means we shall have to go on, always ashamed of ourselves for . . . for not doing something more about it.'

'I suppose my lord your uncle knows best. Perhaps as time passes on you forget how you felt . . . or the excuses seem better and more sensible.'

'Our excuses will only be good, ever, if we *can* find something to do.'

'Yes, I suppose so. Diomede . . . do you realise? She'll be more like a kind of prisoner now. You know how princesses are tied up in ceremony. No one will ever let her live again as she lived at Pardelin.'

'No. No, of course. And she'll never want to see Pardelin again. Neither do I, for that matter. It's all spoilt for ever. But I shall always remember what you've just said, about our really being nobody's servants but hers.'

'Other people won't think so. My lord prior, naturally. And your other uncle too. And Chevalier Janus himself. And Scipio . . . certainly Scipio. You just watch *him* when we get going tomorrow. All that steel and silver to polish. . . .'

'I know. Our loyalty must be so secret it might not be there at all.'

'Yes. But now I know *you* know it makes it much more real.'

Diomede said nothing more, wanting the talk to end there. He lay half-happy in the darkness, wishing he were as brave as Lioncel, vowing that never, never, would he betray Lioncel's trust in him. When the prior came in with his candle Diomede watched him through half-closed eyelids, appalled at the thought of what would have happened had there been no such refuge and rallying-point as Sanctlamine.

The priory had been his home for six years and more, yet Pardelin for three months had been a more homelike place. Yolande and Lioncel had made the difference; Diomede philosophized concerning their relationships.

'Of course she liked him better than she liked me,' he reflected. 'But I don't think I should think so much of her if she hadn't.'

IV

A SILVER SHIELD AND A GREY KITTEN

BY sunrise two days later Lioncel and Diomede were a league away from the priory, riding in borrowed suits which Diomede remembered. The lay brother was with them, yawning in the cool air; the dew sparkled, the birds sang in the woods, the mists climbed and dissolved along the flanks of great heather-clad hills.

' This is where we wait,' said Diomede, indicating a clump of pines on the left hand of the way. And so they first saw a progress of the Chevalier Janus.

The sunbeams slanted between the trees and flashed on the black-and-silver standard. Verde rode first, steel-capped and corseleted, with trumpet corded to his shoulder and buckler slung behind him. The steel spike of the banner-staff was sheathed in a little scabbard welded to his off stirrup-iron.

Janus himself rode next, on a huge grey destrier called Castor. Janus wore a white tabard over full armour, and a new white ostrich-feather nodded on the battle-dented helm. A white-painted shield hung at his back, and his lance and saddle and horse-trappings were coloured leaden-grey. Today the silver glitter came only from the hilts of his sword and dagger, from the wonderful belt, the exquisite bit, the studded bridle, and the rosette on Castor's broad forehead. The long spurs gained a peculiar dignity from their solitary golden gleam. Janus looked like the King of Winter himself, riding forth out of season.

' Of course . . . *January*! ' said Diomede to himself.

Scipio, also splendidly armed, came next behind his chief. Scipio's destrier was a chestnut, with Castor's black brother Pollux pacing beside him. Pollux was fully harnessed, but carried only the great helm and the shield of parade in their white leathern cases.

Nero, following in his turn, canted a loaded crossbow whose strap went over his shoulder. A halter passed from his saddle-bow to the head of the off-leader of the team which carried the painted litter. The famous coffin was quite enclosed; the ark, as Rosso had called it, was painted chiefly in black and white, but bright small flecks of colour gave it a startling richness. The pictures were of hunting-scenes, against a conventional background of patterned leaves and flowers; the roof curved to a ridge surmounted by a little wolf of *cuirbouilli* silvered over except for its red snarling mouth.

A second halter, tied to the litter-pole, secured the first of the six pack-horses following after. These carried the harp and the spare weapons, the gear of Scipio and the Apulians, and such gifts or spoils as overflowed from the coffin.

Last of all came Rosso, with longbow strung and quiver under his hand, his watchful gaze quartering the rearward aspects of the way. . . . Lioncel laughed in admiration of this polished unit of chivalry. Diomede, too, felt a pang of pleasure at sight of such planned and steeled perfection. They doffed their caps as Verde came level, and Janus gave them a boyish grin over his glimmering bever.

' Give you good day, youngsters,' he boomed. ' Fall in behind Scipio. Your fellow can ride at Nero's left hand. Examine the country as you go; the day may come when you have to guide an army along this track. I'd not been in the Gorge of Arionbel for ten years before the night of the battle, but I knew it better than most of the captains gathered at the council of war.'

Lioncel, Diomede and the lay brother wheeled their horses into the column. Rattle and creak and clink of equipment, thudding irregular rhythm of hoof-beats on grass and rock and sand, set up a pattern of sound that lasted the secret servants of Yolande through the late summer and into the fall of the year.

By noon of the day of their departure they were out of the foot-hills of the Casque of Baraine and into fertile country

to south of it. The road led through villages, with oats and
rye and flax in the valleys, and vineyards on the low hills.
The Chevalier Janus drew rein at an inn door, and at his
gesture Verde earthed the spike of the standard among the
cobblestones beside the doorway.

The innkeeper and his family scurried about with food and
wine for the riders and fodder and water for their horses; even
here it was plain that Janus was known and remembered.

'Three years since you sat there, sir,' said the innkeeper,
beaming across the board from which cold veal and oatcakes
and cheese were vanishing apace. 'And now you'll be straight
from the great battle?'

'Yes,' replied Janus, eyeing him over a drinking-horn. 'Tell
me, host, does your son prosper—the one you apprenticed to
an armourer in Rougefontaine?'

'God in heaven, sir,' exclaimed the innkeeper, 'who would
have believed you would remember that? You let him ride
in your train that day, and grateful we all were . . I thank
you, he does very well.'

'Did they march him out with the muster?'

'Nay, he was at the forge three days and nights, asleep on
his feet by the end, I reckon.'

'It's like that every time a town stands to arms. Did they
lose many men?'

'No more than half a dozen, sir, out of two hundred and
more. They'll not be saying *that* the other side of the frontier.
I never heard tell of this great captain, the Count of Montguiscard, till less than a year ago. It's well for us the good
duke—God rest his soul and damn the souls of all who helped
slay him—it's well for us he appointed so stout a captain. Is
there more news of the plague, sir?'

'None from the priory. None from Jarapt that I heard.'

'God be praised.'

'Amen. Bring me another wineskin.'

Diomede, witness of these courtesies, reflected that it was
really not easy to hide in the company of the Chevalier Janus.
He said as much to Lioncel when they were on their way again.

'It'll feel safer when we're in his livery,' said Lioncel.

In the late afternoon they came into a red-earthed plain where suddenly, beyond a wood, the towers and spires of Rougefontaine stood up across a curving river. Scipio handed over to Verde the halter of the spare charger, and hastened ahead to bespeak the night's lodging. His beautiful chestnut mount and fine bright armour vanished in a cloud of dust round the bend of the way, and the pages closed up to ride immediately behind Janus.

They began to overtake people travelling to reach the gate of the town before sunset. Diomede felt suddenly nervous and inexperienced, and blinked when a girl on a farm cart put out her tongue at him. No use pretending he hadn't seen her. Perhaps the way you looked at people made them want to put their tongues out.

The worst of it was that if three people stuck out tongues at him one after the other, he, Diomede, wanted to ignore the first two but to get hold of the tongue of the third, cut it right out, and throw it to be eaten by the nearest dog. This was a habit of mind not understood by good people, or quarrelsome people, or mischievous people either; God be thanked for people too dull or self-absorbed to stick their tongues out at all.

When Verde came within a hundred yards of the barbican which defended the red stone bridge, he lifted the silver trumpet and blew an intricate blast timed in anapæsts and spondees. A war-horn made a hoarse uncultured monosyllabic reply from the battlements. When the cavalcade arrived at the gateway a small crowd had gathered; the burgher guard grounded six halberds in honour of Janus, and their captain saluted him.

Janus responded with a superb dip and flourish of his lance. The square pennon of cloth of silver flapped an inch from the ground and rose again; the heel of the lance rang sweetly home in its little steel bucket. Janus handled every weapon as skilfully as he handled his harp. A few children cheered; Diomede stared straight ahead, and heard somebody say that he looked like a pug-nosed Turk.

At the Sign of the Archer there was bowing and fuss, steam and uproar and a wonderful smell of spiced gravy. Diomede watched wide-eyed while Nero and Lioncel plucked Janus of his armour with hardly a clink or rattle. A master-armourer and two of his men were in attendance; they wrapped and stuffed in a sack what pieces required repair, and whisked them away before Janus was in his bath-tub. Two tailors, a hatter, a shoemaker, and a glover were in attendance also; Diomede had hardly time to wash before he was gripped and trussed with a tape. Then he was crowned with paper like a heretic, and made to stand shoeless on a board while his feet were drawn round with a stick of charcoal.

'Lost your livery at the battle, young master?' grunted the friendly old hatter.

'No, before that,' said Diomede.

'Ah, there's always pilferers in an army,' said the hatter.

'Ay, there are,' agreed Diomede darkly, as if he had found it so in every one of his long campaigns.

Outside the windows the sunset-light gilded the red tiles of the town. The inn yard rang with the tumult of stabling the eighteen horses of the train of the Chevalier Janus. The lay brother from Sanctlamine was carefully tending his own gelding; Diomede saw him gather up the harness and give the animal a goodnight pat. A peeping servant-girl turned away at sight of the lay brother's frock, preferring to stare at the chiselled profile of dark bare-headed Rosso, who was leading sable Pollux into place beside his great grey brother Castor.

Turning from the window, Diomede saw the profile of the Chevalier de Largire, also bare-headed, at exactly the same angle. It was suddenly evident to him that the three Apulian brothers were the sons of warrior Janus.

For three nights the little company rested at Rougefontaine; on the third morning the new clothing and mended armour were ready. Lioncel and Diomede stood forth in tall black brimless hats, black tunics and hose with silver braid at neck and wrists and hems, and silver shields on the left breasts. Their new black shoes had silver rosettes on the insteps. Lioncel, with hair of white gold, carried this livery off to perfection; but Janus pulled a wry lip at sight of Diomede.

' My funeral is not yet,' he announced, and ordered Diomede
a white hat instead.

The black riding-cloaks of the pages had white hoods and
borders. Their belts and gloves were white, and their black
thigh-boots had white tops. Diomede approved of this
splendour, but felt a twinge of homesickness for the purple and
gold of Baraine.

At Rougefontaine and elsewhere throughout that journey the
talk was mostly of the Gorge of Arionbel; tidings of victory had
overtaken and largely quenched excitement concerning Turlequin's raid and the death of Duke Engelbert. To the nearer
towns the burgher levies had already brought home their
triumphant banners; later, the cavalcade sometimes overtook a
column marching at ease with fife and kettledrum. Then
Janus and his colours got a cheer from men who remembered
them.

On church steps, at street corners, in courtyards and on
rampart walks, the same things came to the ears of Lioncel and
Diomede; this was the kind of warfare that everyone admired.
Plunder of the Franconian army and camp was selling freely;
Lioncel bought a *chalumeau*, or little hautboy, getting it cheap
because of blood-stains on the ivory. Lioncel's pursed lips,
inflated cheeks, and desperate eyes, together with the cautious
liquid wobbling notes of the hautboy, gave Diomede comical
pleasure many times when they were alone.

' God and His Saints be praised for so mighty and devout a
captain,' said priests, hearing of Azo's rich offering at the shrine
of Saint Amarand in Bargreant.

' Safety on the roads again,' said merchants and packmen in
the taverns.

' You can sleep quiet in your beds these days,' said women
among the market-stalls.

' You can plough and know you'll reap your own,' said the
folk with the farm carts that streamed in and out of the town
gates.

' There's one count that earns his keep, at least,' said cynical
apprentices, spitting absently rather near the shoes of a passing
page.

' There's one count unites great skill with the luck of the foul fiend himself,' thought Diomede many times. ' I wonder what they'd say if . . . but now it will never be known. Thus we escape with dignity . . . we who ought to be dead.'

It proved an education to ride with this Herculean soldier-poet through the southern parts of Baraine, the northern edges of Queranay and Trevence, and the eastern half of Elquitaine. In the private rooms of inns Lioncel and Diomede learned songs from him, read to Kim, and tried to answer his question about the rules of chivalry and blazonry. In the guesthouses of abbeys they observed his austere courtesy, his tact, his wealth of anecdote chosen to suit the company, and his generous bestowal of praise on others at Arionbel and far beyond the frontiers of the kingdom.

In castle solars, as the journey proceeded, the manners of the Chevalier Janus underwent a change, expanding with the scope and freedom of his stories. It was as though Janus began to turn his grotesque helmet back to front, welcoming the drier sunshine with features Panic rather than Martian. He drank more deeply, and his songs developed a different flavour. One of them sprouted an additional ending which much impressed Diomede. It was called *Green Mounds*, and Janus first sang it in the hearing of the boys on an evening when afterglow fringed the great oak-forest of Queranay.

The group of listeners in a castle garden was largely middle-aged; the lady of the castle was a cousin of Janus, who presented her with an elegant box of some red wood, with lid carven to represent a little palmer trudging among low humped hills towards a hermit's hut. The silver harp commanded silence, and Diomede sat on a bench and listened in the warm twilight.

> ' *Stranger than all strange sounds*
> *Is the song of the men of the green mounds,*
> *Tingling far in trembling noon,*
> *Eldritch under a horn'd moon,*
> *Tearing the forest trance asunder,*
> *Summoning weight of wind and thunder.*

Checks your palfrey in his stride,
Chills your blood on the mountain-side;
Flinch the hawks, and shiver the hounds,
At the song of the men of the green mounds.'

' Chevalier, on your forest rounds
Have you seen the girls of the green mounds?'

' Yes, they are brown and shy and swift,
And sudden death waits in their gift.
It is a brisk uncomely thing
To hear their flint-tipt arrows sing.'

' Chevalier, it is said you caught one,
But never to your castle brought one.'

' Damsel, kitchen chatter abounds
Concerning the girls of the green mounds.'

' Fool, do you know what fame resounds
From your midnight rides to the green mounds?
Why do you feign to fear their flint
When the brown flesh carries your seed within't?
How will you guard that stinking rout
When the king's word comes to smoke it out?'

' Damsel, forget what you have said,
And take this thought in your narrow head:
Our sovereign lord himself compounds
My crimes concerning the green mounds.
For it fell on a day of summer weather
The king and I fared forth together,
Climb'd at noon to the bleak mid-wild,
And watch'd a brown girl suckle her child.
The mound-folk sang, and the shadows crept,
And the children play'd, and the king wept,
And gave me strictest charge of them
For the sake of the Child of Bethlehem.

And now they have learnt there is no need
To shoot at me and my trotting steed.
From the thunderstone to the ruin'd bridge,
Up to the cairn on the topmost ridge,
Down to the oak that stands alone,
And round again to the thunderstone,
The king has fee'd his hunting-grounds
For a song of the men of the green mounds.'

A fortnight later Janus sang that song again, but this time it
was in Trevence, in the castle of an old companion-at-arms;
several young and merry ladies were there, outnumbering the
menfolk. That night Diomede encountered a new alarm; one
tall fair-haired girl smiled at him again and again, twisting her
pretty painted mouth as if she perfectly understood he was
afraid she might eat him.

Standing among the pages of the household, Diomede con-
fined his gaze to Janus, the harp, and the arras by the door, on
which Perseus curveted from the sky to sabre a black dragon.
He had determined to escape, and at mention of the thunderstone he began to edge past his neighbours; but Janus went on
to a new and brutal conclusion.

' *The king has fee'd his hunting-grounds*
For a song of the men of the green mounds.'

' *Chevalier, they are heathen still,*
And yours are not the sheep they kill.'

' *And what do you mean by that, my pigeon?* '

' *I think you are bound to the old religion.'*

' *And what else do you think, my pet?* '

' *I'll see you burn at the stake yet.'*

' *What then, when you see me dead?'*

‘ I'll laugh out of my narrow head
To know the body you love so well
Will burn beside your own in hell
When some sharp sword of God confounds
The damn'd folk of the green mounds.’

‘ Damsel, I know Dom Cupid sighs
At your fat hands and your flabby thighs;
But I warrant he finds a worse disgrace
In your mean soul and your cruel face.
Watch your mirror: you grow older:
Watch the shadow beyond your shoulder.
Summon the sight you would admire:
The vermeil glow of a peat fire,
And the riot of love that knows no bounds
In the depth of the midst of the green mounds.
What, you are fall'n in one of your swounds?
Sing hey, for the folk of the green mounds! ’

‘ Fie upon you, Janus,’ called the ladies cheerfully, and Diomede saw a handsome priest lean his chin on a white shoulder to whisper something into a jewel-hung ear.

‘ This is the idle dissolute south,’ he thought uncomfortably. ‘ The Chevalier Janus belongs here. I wonder if his castle is full of loose ladies waiting round corners.’

Janus, however, as they were to find, was too good a soldier to allow his pages to be seduced before they were old enough to wear armour. His rules and errands defended them without causing them embarrassment. He sent them to their bedroom before taking a lady to his own, and one of the Apulian brothers was always on duty there in the morning.

The famous silver panoply was never cleaned by Lioncel and Diomede. In castles and abbeys Verde polished it; in towns a chosen armourer was sent for to undertake so delicate an office. And having lately hewn his way clean through the Franconian host, Janus felt in no immediate need of military exercise; his one resort to arms on the journey was occasioned by Diomede himself.

That was in a town of Queranay, where the yard of the best inn was adorned with blazons of several noblemen and chevaliers. These blazons were small shields of parade mounted on seven-foot staves, so that they could be seen over the heads of a crowd. Placed by the entry, they served to advise the armigerous of guests of their own sort within; when Janus and his troop arrived the devices assembled were those of a bell, a lynx, a ship, and several others more complex.

Janus did not expect his pages to know many coats-of-arms beyond those of the northern provinces; while in his bath that night he instructed them as to the bearings displayed below. The bell was Anglou, the lynx Luzarne, and so on; and on the following morning Diomede slipped through a group of pages more brightly-coated than himself to gain the courtyard gateway and the street beyond. He was sent to collect a liripipe—the long scarf wound round a fashionable brimmed hat—which Janus had purchased the night before; the raised voices of the other youths meant nothing to him.

When he came back, however, a row was in progress. An Anglou page, white bell on green tunic, was threatening a Luzarne page, red lynx on yellow. The Luzarne page, obviously a cocky imp, held a ripe plum in his hand, and suddenly let fly. The Anglou boy, who was the taller, dodged aside; the plum splashed to red ruin full on the silver shield of Largire. Part of it fell; the rest stuck in dexter chief, just where the Chevalier Janus was entitled to set the augmentation he never used. A yellow drop slid swiftly down to the nombril or mid-shield: and while it slid the inn courtyard grew very quiet indeed.

'*Argent, a plum eclatée,*' said somebody shakily. Everyone laughed except Diomede, who knew he must give himself no more time to consider.

'Hey, you!' he roared, bursting through the onlookers and catching the smaller boy by the neck of his tunic.

'Let go!' squealed his prisoner. 'I didn't mean to do it! Let go! It was *his* fault!'

'Yes, let him go,' urged the Anglou page. 'It *was* my fault—'ll wipe it clean.'

Diomede felt the moral wind going out of his sails. The

liripipe hung over his arm; the abominable plum affronted the silver shield in sight of all the grinning world.

'Very well, you clean it off,' he told the Anglou page. 'But I won't let go until you do.'

'I won't clean it till you let go,' said the other calmly. He was rather taller than Diomede, good-looking, with auburn hair and pleasant grey eyes.

'Clean it, and I'll let go,' repeated Diomede grimly.

'No. I've told you. Let go first.'

'*I've* told *you*.'

'Hold on,' said Lioncel miraculously in Diomede's ear; and to the Anglou page he said: 'Be quick, or I'll do it, with your cap or your ginger hair, or both.'

The Anglou page hit out at once, and Lioncel hit back. The Luzarne page writhed in Diomede's grip and fisted him in the stomach. Diomede gasped but held on; his right arm, swung for a mighty blow, was flicked as if with red-hot iron, so that he gasped again and did let go, spinning round to confront the young Sieur de Luzarne himself.

Other pages had flung themselves on Lioncel and his opponent. Again the inn yard was suddenly very quiet. The lash of the Sieur de Luzarne's whip trailed on the cobbles; his dark blunt-featured face was stiff with disdain.

'Leave smaller boys than yourself alone,' he advised coldly.

'Sieur de Luzarne!' said a great voice from somewhere above their heads, and everyone looked up. The Chevalier Janus stood in the gallery which ran round the courtyard and gave entry to upper rooms. He was smiling a little, with his great hands folded on the railing in front of him. Diomede glanced at the Sieur de Luzarne, whose black eyebrows rose a little.

'Sieur de Luzarne,' said Janus again, 'I have seen this affair from the start. Will you be good enough to observe how your page has ornamented my shield?'

The nobleman glanced over his shoulder, and his face remained quite wooden.

'I will come down,' said Janus, and nobody else moved

except the Sieur de Luzarne. He took two or three paces towards the doorway where Janus must appear.

Janus appeared, still smiling a little, overtopping the other by perhaps two inches.

' It would have been better,' he said, ' to have left it at page level.'

' My boys will clean your shield,' said the Sieur de Luzarne stiffly.

' I do not allow my page to be struck when carrying out his duty,' said Janus, ' without apology to me, or such satisfaction as may be given by arms.'

' Damn your page and you too,' was the nobleman's crisp rejoinder. ' Clean your shield yourself, and I will meet you and break it where and when you like, with three strokes of a sharp lance and what swordplay you like after.'

' I hoped you would,' said Janus. ' There is a smooth convenient glade a mile from the west gate, beside the wishing-well. We will foregather there at nones tomorrow. I shall have my coffin with me, but you will have more need of yours. Meanwhile . . . there is this to attend to.'

Leisurely the Chevalier Janus approached the line of shield-hung staves. Plucking out his own, he handed it to Lioncel. Then, plucking out the stave of Luzarne, he pitched it upon the dunghill in the middle of the courtyard, and walked calmly through the silent crowd without looking again at his morrow's opponent.

' You did quite rightly, Diomede,' he said when he had the boys in his bedchamber. ' These affairs do not arise so neatly as writers of romaunts would sometimes have us believe.'

Diomede's hands shook as he wiped and polished the silver surface.

At the hour of nones on the following day it was drizzling a little. The sombre oak-glade was brightened by the white caparison of Largire and the yellow caparison of Luzarne. Hundreds of hushed and hooded townsfolk sat in their saddles or stood in sopping grass to watch the joust à l'outrance.

The two chevaliers and their destriers waited like images of steel nearly a hundred yards apart. Half-way between them a tall nobleman, a fellow-guest at the inn, sat grimly holding a white truncheon up over his horse's head. Lioncel and Diomede stood by the litter, which had been set on the ground with the horses tethered nearby. Scipio had very exact instructions as to procedure should Janus come presently to occupy the coffin. Diomede felt his knees knock in their fine black riding-boots.

'Don't worry,' whispered Lioncel. 'He's done this oftener than the other has.'

The lances were feutred, the bridles gathered, the armoured bodies tilted slightly forward. The white baton fell, the spurs winked, Castor and his rival went stamping ahead, gathering speed, rushing with caparisons blown back, rearing to the smack-clang-crash of impact. The Sieur de Luzarne was torn from his saddle and hurled clattering against the roots of the nearest oak tree. The Chevalier Janus tilted the stump of his smashed lance and reined round to watch him.

The fallen man lay still, and when they took off his helmet they found that he was dead.

A quarter of an hour later Janus led his little procession away into the thickening drizzle. Diomede felt sorry and a little sick, and wondered how the Luzarne page would look at his next ripe plum.

'I don't see what else *I* could have done,' he told himself dourly.

That night Lioncel and he noticed the Chevalier Janus sunk in a grim reverie unlike any mood he had yet shown them. They were allowed to use his chessmen, and in an oppressive silence they set out and began a game. It seemed as if even Janus could regret killing a man.

After a while the chevalier took out his inkhorn with paper and a pen, and began scratching away on his knee with occasional glances at their game.

'Boys,' he said sadly at length, 'I've lost a word, three syllables, a dactyl. It's the name of a Spanish shrub, and I want to remember it. It's something like coracle, caracole, calliper, caravel . . . galingale, gallipot, Ganymede, gaberdine, God damn!'

Lioncel and Diomede were dumb and dismayed, knowing
no names of Spanish shrubs. The chevalier stared glassily at
the first fire of their journey; they were high in the hills then,
and the evening wind was chilly. Soon his lips began moving
• soundlessly; several times he checked himself and wrote and
frowned and sucked at his beard, ploughing unhappily through
what seemed a covert of unrewarding dactyls.

At length he spoke aloud again, as though the tail of the
elusive word had flickered in the undergrowth.

'Mangonel, marigold, amaranth, amethyst, avalanche,
asphodel, anchorite . . . by God's Monday, I've got it . . .
alkanet! Something like henna. Boys, bring your wine-horns
here and fill up. I thought I should never sleep tonight. A
health to you both. Another three weeks and we're at Gax.
I shall be sorry to lose you.'

'Did you need the word for a new song, sir?' Lioncel
enquired with great respect.

'No, no. Looking back, I remembered tipping a friend of
mine into a vat of it. They use it as a dye in Spain. He came
out looking like the Red Chevalier who plagued the Table
Round until Gareth overthrew him. Another of these boastful
pippins. . . .'

That was all they ever heard Janus say which might have
related to the death of the Sieur de Luzarne.

As the cavalcade advanced into the native province of the
Chevalier Janus, Diomede recognised a kind of country which
had sometimes appeared behind the figures of saints and kings
and bishops in painted manuscripts at Sanctlamine. Rivers
wound between hills that rose abruptly out of the plain;
flattened roofs of red tiles glowed beyond orchards and olive
groves and vineyards; poplar, cypress, and cedar lanced and
barred the sloping meadows. Now Janus sometimes wore his
grotesque double-faced helm; it was queer, and at first a little
gruesome, to ride for a day under scrutiny of the amethystine
eyes in the steel-and-silver mask of Pan.

In Elquitaine everyone seemed to know who Janus was; the
ogress was less of a freak to beholders, and more of a family

affair. People gathered at crossroads and wells to watch him pass. Word of his share in the victory of the gorge had evidently preceded him.

Smoke of the first autumn burnings began to spire from farmyards and fields into evening skies of tourmaline; the scent of the cypress groves floated up to windows and balconies of cream-coloured stone. At noon, in the blue-shadowed streets, you saw through round-arched entries the flash of fountains whose waters spouted from the mouths of stone beasts and monsters, or from vases poised in the hands of nymphs and fauns and tritons. People sang more, and sang better, than in Baraine or Queranay; innumerable stringed instruments reclined on coloured cloths in the shops, or resounded to the antics of brown-ringed fingers in scented gardens and shadowed taverns.

Sometimes a group of giggling girls threw down, from wall or lattice, roses or savagely-coloured flowers whose names Diomede did not know. And Diomede learned to smile straight into the eyes of strangers, and to dance steps unknown beyond the pale granite mountains which ridged the northern skyline.

At length Lioncel and he dismounted in the guesthouse courtyard of the great abbey of Gax, only to hear that the treasurer, Diomede's younger uncle, Dom Dagobert, was away on the abbot's business, having gone to the coast a week before and taken ship for Rome. While they waited with the chevalier for the coming of his cousin the abbot, Janus smiled at sight of their troubled faces.

'You must winter with me at Largire,' he told them. 'I will write to Dom Gilomar of this mischance. His letter I hold until I can give it Dom Dagobert himself.'

'But, sir,' Diomede pointed out, 'this is to trouble you far beyond my lord prior's intention.'

'Sir, you are your uncle's nephew,' replied Janus with mock hauteur. 'It is long since I had a pupil at the harp. And you, Lioncel, make foul noises on that hautboy of yours when you think I cannot hear them. That must be remedied; I play the hautboy too. We shall have plenty of time when we are not hunting over those pleasant hills that lie ahead.'

When the abbot came he had recent news from Hautarroy and Hastain. Azo, Count of Montguiscard, was created a marquis and appointed Grand Seneschal of Baraine.

'And guardian of the little Duchess Yolande,' added the abbot, refilling with his own hands the crystal goblet which stood before his kinsman. 'Of course, he's her uncle by marriage and next-of-kin.'

'Her non-inheriting next-of-kin,' amended Janus thoughtfully.

'Yes, yes, naturally. Now, who is heir-presumptive of Baraine?'

Janus pondered genealogies complicated by laws of inheritance Salic or Ripuarian, and slashed across by the ten-year-old slaughter on the field of Pont-de-Foy.

'Engelbert had one Baraine great-aunt,' he murmured into the goblet. 'She married Lestembourg . . . now extinct in the legitimate line. Take it back a generation. There was only one daughter there too . . . not prolific, that family. *She* married a younger son of Boqueron and had only a daughter, who married Gerard of Ger, father of Bors, father of Lothair, father of the Count Raoul. The heir-at-law of the little duchess is her fourth cousin, Raoul of Ger.'

'So,' said the abbot, and seemed about to say something else, but looked at Lioncel and Diomede and then into his own wine-cup.

Diomede's Pardclin-pangs were renewed; Yolande was becoming a great name farther and farther removed from him.

In becoming a great name Yolande nearly ceased to be anything else. A week after she saw the captain who had once called himself Turlequin, she turned faint at the top of a stair and fell half-way down it. For the second time Zoster Adela was summoned to carry her to bed.

Thereafter Yolande had no need to stress her dependence on the abbess. She was made a fuss of, and even allowed to discourage Sister Marcelle from too frequent readings out of the Lives of the Saints and the *Gesta Romanorum*.

'I'm tired, Reverend Mother,' she would say. 'I should go

to sleep during the reading, and that would seem discourteous to Sister Marcelle.'

'Sleep as much as you can, child,' the abbess would reply. 'Sister Marcelle will pray for you instead.'

At that Yolande's conscience would nip her, but often she really felt too ill or depressed to change her mind.

When the news of Arionbel came in she tried to encompass emotions proper to the occasion. Gratitude to God, to Uncle Azo and to all the soldiers of Baraine; pride in the conquering rush of Gold Puss along the valley of rout, with the Thunderbolt of Montguiscard in close attendance upon him; sorrow for men, mostly young and strong, killed in their task of killing; triumph over a crafty enemy, who had taken advantage of the plague to attack a peaceable province: all these were suggested to Yolande by the abbess and the half-dozen nuns who shared the care of her. . . .

Yolande felt them all, but without sharpness or satisfaction. White-haired Dom Cyril, a canon of Saint Michael's and castle chaplain, came to hear her confession, and talked to her of the dangers of the sin of acedia, or slothfulness in acceptance of belief and performance of religious duty. Yolande listened to him, and counted the hundred-and-fifty-three subdivisions of the sin as a main branch of the Tree of Evil in a book he lent her.

Then she locked up her doubts in her heart, as her treasures were locked up in poor Amarand. When Dom Cyril had left her she linked her hands around her knees and stared into vacancy, summoning the images of those lost trifles. One was a gold ring set with a diamond, which should have been kept in a treasure-chest; but now there was no one to reproach her with taking insufficient care of it. There were other jewels, too, and a small crystal box with a lock of her mother's hair in it. There was half of a pebble, whose flint core showed pallid marks like a misted sun and crescent moon in a blue-grey sky. A little ivory horseman smiled under his drooping moustache; he had come out of Cathay, and was given to her by her father when he had been to Venice on an embassy. There were a seashore shell or two, a jet hand and an amber heart. Tucked in with all these, to prevent their rattling, was a kerchief of purple silk with her name embroidered in gold thread upon it.

There they were . . . and it felt safer to mourn for them than for her father. Why, Yolande did not know, except that sometimes, when crying for him as she lay alone at night, she wanted to jump out of bed and run naked and screaming down the long corridors, where tapers flickered in the draughts, through doors which her fiery grief would dissolve, down the dark silent streets and over the low wall of the harbour, to splash into the black waters of Lake Targe.

But if you dodged out of senseless suffering in this life, you were said to be very thoroughly punished to all eternity. . . .

There were always Our Lady and the Sieur Jesu, but Yolande felt that those two kind friends could do very little with the Sieur God when he had a smiting mood on him.

With the help of the abbess she composed a letter to the Count Azo, thanking him and her army, and a letter to the chancellor at Bargreant, explaining that her delicate health detained her at Roclatour. And when the chancellor sent word that the king had given her person and her duchy into Azo's keeping—'as no doubt my lord, your father, would have wished'—she asked to see the nobleman who brought the chancellor's letter.

He was one of Azo's own men, a bulky morose-looking middle-aged captain called Odard, Sieur de Xantroy; and as he came to her across the floor of the principal parlour a curious expression flickered in his deep-set, almost yellow, eyes.

He fell on one knee by her chair and kissed the hand she held out.

'God send Your Grace a swift recovery,' he said first of all.

'I thank you, my lord,' she replied, composed and prim and secretly glad that he was not the Sieur de Caherne. 'My lord the Marquis . . . the Grand Seneschal . . . I trust he is well.'

'He is, Your Grace, and bids me say he hopes to be with you very soon.'

'Where is he now?'

'Gone to meet our lord the king at Belsaunt in Nordanay
There's no news of plague there.'

'And my cousin, the Viscount Balthasar?'

'He's still with the king, and very well regarded. It's saic
he rode hawking with him every day for a week.'

'That would please him. I am glad. I pray you, my lord
be seated and tell me about the battle.'

Odard de Xantroy embarked on a rapid account of the
campaign. When he had finished she enquired about the
plague at Bargreant.

'It was only in a suburb, Your Grace. They cut it off with
a wooden fence, and drove the people into the woods, and
burned all the houses.'

On a golden afternoon a fortnight later Yolande sat in the
abbey garden, embroidering a girdle of soft leather. From
time to time, Zoster Adela passed along the half-walled
passage behind her, pausing to admire the blue and silver
flowers which grew in the wake of Yolande's needle. Then
the abbess came out of a doorway, carrying a gilded basket.
Yolande made to rise, but the abbess motioned to her to sit
still.

'Here's a cargo of mischief,' said the abbess, and put the
basket into Yolande's lap.

Yolande drew the fastening-pin and threw back the lid,
gasping with delight as a kitten looked up at her. He was
smoke-grey, with yellow eyes; his first pink luxurious yawn
seemed to swallow Yolande's heart entire. Lifting a tiny paw,
he patted her gold thimble; she gathered him carefully against
her breast and looked up at the abbess.

'Reverend Mother,' she whispered, 'how can I thank you
for such a present?'

'By looking more often as you do at this moment,' said the
abbess rather gruffly. Her hard old finger came gently against
Yolande's flushed cheek.

'God bless you, child,' she growled, when Yolande caught
the finger to her lips. 'I had him from Master Philastrius, the
apothecary down by the quay. He buys herbs from our garden

and makes up physics for us. There were four kittens in the litter. Master Philastrius had the basket woven on purpose.'

'I must go and thank him,' said Yolande, who hitherto had only left the abbey to attend Mass or pray at her father's temporary tomb in Saint Michael's.

The abbess nodded and sat down beside her. Doves cooed, and late butterflies danced in the September sunshine. Yolande laughed as she circumscribed the scrambles of the kitten, and bent her energies to the task of finding a name for him.

She consulted her companion, and pondered history, legend, and romance. Names of other animals and flowers and jewels marched through her head—but not the names of stars, because of the hound Alcor, who died fighting at Pardelin. Finally she decided on Topaz, and dubbed the kitten with a stroke of a feather out of her work-box. Topaz grabbed the feather and rolled on his back; then he climbed Yolande's sleeve and mountaineered around her neck. All that evening she was almost happy because of him.

In the morning Zoster Adela and two of the abbey men-at-arms escorted her down to the apothecary's shop. This was the first time many of the townsfolk had seen her since the morning encounter with the bearded captain; they stood silent and respectful and very attentive as she passed. Zoster Adela's high cheekbones were redder than usual by the time she reached the shop door, over which a gilded pestle stood in a gilded mortar.

'What is it?' whispered Yolande, looking up into her friend's face. 'Why are you angry?'

'It's nothing, child, and I'm not angry,' said Zoster Adela between clenched teeth.

Philastrius, a tall lean sad-faced man, with a good fur cap on his greying hair, and a trim green gown very handsomely belted, stood bowing to Yolande beneath his painted statue of Saint Damian. His grey-green eyes were friendly, and his dark shop was fascinating.

It contained a shelved array of pots and flasks and jars marked with symbols and initials; a furnace of blackened

bricks with a bronze gallipot gleaming on it; an open fireplace
where a cauldron simmered over the logs; a convex mirror,
swung high and slanted, which made an almost magical
picture of everything before it; and a half-delightful, half-
sinister compound of mysterious odours.

'Master Philastrius,' said Yolande, 'I came to give you
gramercy for the beautiful basket. I've named the kitten
Topaz; may I see his family?'

'I'm honoured, my lady duchess,' said the apothecary.
'And first I would say that all of us, your loyal people of
Roclatour, are glad you should be here, though bitterly grieved
at the cause of your late coming.'

'I thank you again . . . Zoster Adela, let the men-at-arms
wait by the door. I shall ask Master Philastrius to show me
round his shop.'

Zoster Adela seated herself on the settle appointed for
patients; Philastrius brought a stool so that Yolande could
kneel by the box where Topaz's mother lay at ease with the
remainder of her kittens. One of them had black markings,
among them a black left ear; Yolande looked at it for a second
or two, picked it up, edged a little away from Zoster Adela,
and leaned over one of the counters to examine a great silver-
capped ram's horn with black peppercorns in it.

'Master Philastrius,' she said softly. 'What do you use
those for? And what's the name of the Grand Seneschal's
captain who has a black patch instead of an ear?'

'I burn them to mix in pills,' said the apothecary, almost in
a whisper. 'And I grind them for sneezing-powders, and for
use in hot baths against cramps and pains in the back. The
captain's name is Radomar.'

Yolande lifted the kitten, and Philastrius saw what she
meant, and smiled.

'Alas, Your Grace, that one is a lady,' he said.

'There, my pet,' murmured Yolande, replacing the sister of
Topaz. 'You have perhaps escaped a villainous-sounding
foreign name.'

Philastrius showed her his beautiful brass scales, his marble
slabs for the rolling of pills, the skull on which patients could

chalk the sites of their migraines, the sealed glass jars of clear honey for herb potions, the pumice-stone from Mount Vesuvius, and the oils and aromatic gums from Arabia. On one table were boxes and pots containing aloes and musk and myrrh, with great flagons of vinegar and a tray of lily-roots.

'God and Saints Cosmas and Damian send I don't need those all together,' said the apothecary. He gestured with a stained and bony hand, and then raised it to cross himself.

'Why?' asked Yolande.

'They are gathered in case the plague reaches Roclatour.'

Yolande crossed herself too, and moved away to admire bowls of heaped berries. Philastrius lit a taper and brought an incense-burner for her to set going; a glorious fragrance crossed and began to conquer the rest.

'What is it?' she asked.

'My own secret, my lady. May I send you a jar and name it "Loyalty of Roclatour"?'

'Yes . . . yes!' cried Yolande. 'Zoster Adela, have you any money?'

'No need for that,' said the apothecary, seeing the bleakness which had not left Zoster Adela's face.

The jar was duly wrapped in linen and handed to one of the men-at-arms. Yolande took a last look around her, and drew a last appreciative sniff, before she said good-bye to Philastrius.

'I shall come to see how the kittens thrive,' she promised the mother cat, and went out of the door to confront an interested crowd. Once more there seemed a quiet intentness in their respectful salutations; Yolande knew how to show and maintain a mask of public courtesy. She noticed the little greasy man who had enjoyed her distress beside the abbey gate. This time he could not sustain her steady gaze; she perceived that he was afraid she had remembered him.

'Perhaps it is not going to be so bad here,' she told herself cautiously. 'But I wonder why Zoster Adela is cross . . . and I wish Uncle Azo were not Grand Seneschal of Baraine.'

She had lived for two months in the abbey before Uncle Azo came to visit her. The abbess and Zoster Adela and Topaz

between them were restoring her to the outward seeming of
the Yolande who had first greeted him at Pardelin. His blue
eyes beamed approval when she answered his salutation with a
perfect curtsey.

'My dear child,' he said quietly. 'My dear lady duchess
and niece, we have much to discuss, you and I. Reverend
Mother in God, will you be pleased to excuse us?'

When he had bowed the abbess out of her principal parlour,
Azo came and sat down beside Yolande in the wide window-
seat, smiling as she collected Topaz and held him in her lap.
Azo's fine crimson robe glowed against the dull cushions; his
thick greying hair and square-cut beard were very slightly
perfumed, and there seemed to be a dust of powder on his
smoothly-shaven cheeks. The gold hounds'-heads on his shoe-
straps caught Yolande's glance as she looked modestly at the
floor.

'Is my cousin Balthasar with you, my lord?' she enquired
politely.

'No. Would you have liked to see him?'

'Of course.'

'Before long you shall. He is still with the king. The king
has been very graciously pleased to make him a chevalier and
a gentleman of his bedchamber. In a week's time he will be
created Count of Jarapt.'

'My felicitations, my lord, to Balthasar and yourself. That
is a very high favour . . . although no more than deserved.'

'You are kind to say so. It is true he stands very well with
our lord the king. And also, I am proud to say, with our lady
the queen. The Duke of Honoy, too, is apt to command him
closely.'

Azo smiled again, for the Duke of Honoy was Réné, King
Thorismund's six-year-old son and heir. And then Azo went
on.

'I am especially happy that Balthasar is also in favour with
my lady and his, the Duchess of Baraine.'

This was spoken so deliberately that Yolande wanted to say,
I don't mean I like him so much as all that. Instead she
said nothing, but linked her hands in her lap and looked across

the room to where a brass tray held a heap of painted beads. When Azo went on again his deep voice had become caressing.

'You know . . . or soon will know . . . what anger and distress was felt by the king when my lord, your father, was . . .'

'Murdered.'

'Yes, murdered. The king's letters of condolence you shall presently read. The chancellor has answered them, you being disabled by the grief natural to a very grim occasion. There are other letters, too, from kings and princes, and from the Peers of Neustria, as was to be expected.'

Azo paused and crossed one knee over the other. The gold hound's-head on his fore-swung instep seemed to grin hungrily towards the tray of beads. Topaz was quite still; he had gone to sleep. Azo's voice sank a little as he continued.

'The king was also filled with distress at your own situation . . . afflicted as you were by two such blows in succession. Two of his foremost friends removed . . . both famed for their many estimable qualities. Recognising the honour your father did me in appointing me to command at Jarapt, and considering the near relationship between us, the king was moved to appoint me your guardian.'

This was the place for at least an approving murmur, if not for a reference to the Gorge of Arionbel, but Yolande sat still and silent, conscious that Azo was staring steadily at her. She felt a sudden desire to jump up and run away.

'This signal trust I have taken upon me with prayer, but also with great pride. It has pleased God to let me carry your banner to a great victory. I honoured your father more than any man, more even than the king himself, and it is my dearest wish to see his daughter secure and happy in the seat of her great ancestors. . . .'

'I am sure of that, my lord,' said Yolande, suddenly looking up into the intent blue eyes. She could not hold their purposeful regard for more than a second or two; it confused and frightened her, and belied the careful kindness of Uncle Azo's voice.

'The king took long counsel with me concerning a matter of great concern to him, and to yourself, and to me who am his

E

servant and your own. It is expedient that I presently bestow
your hand in marriage.'

Yolande looked up again, this time at the red flame of the
taper burning before the painted image of Saint Marthe in its
niche beside the chamber doorway. A cold and shadowy axe-
blade seemed to divide her across the middle. Above it she was
blankly surprised, below it helpless and afraid.

Of course this had to happen some time, but they seemed to
be in a great hurry. Holy Mary, please, please, let them find
someone not too old, ugly, rough, stupid . . . not too fond of
his wine . . . not too fond of other women, either, although
that was said to be sometimes a blessing for young wives. . . .

And of course it would get rid of Uncle Azo . . . that is,
unless he, the new *he*, were too near her own age. Part of
Yolande's mind broke away in a darting flight amid names
and persons of the heirs of the Peers of Neustria. Her uncle
was still watching her, and it was time to say something. She
was blushing now, and annoyed with herself for blushing, and
explaining to herself that it was natural, and hating Azo for
not looking away.

' How soon, my lord? ' she asked grimly.

' At Christmas.'

' At Christmas! Then you have already chosen. . . .'

' Yes, we have chosen your husband. He is my dear son,
the king's friend, Balthasar.'

' *Balthasar*,' repeated Yolande, and felt her world spin dizzily
round to come to rest with the splendid golden-haired blue-
eyed figure standing haughtily in the middle of it. . . .

Not too old, certainly not ugly . . . don't know about rough,
not stupid in some ways . . . but, but, Holy Mary, I don't like
him at all, and now I shall *never* get rid of Uncle Azo. . . .

' What are you thinking? ' asked Azo gently and with great
good humour. ' The king and I . . . and Balthasar . . . hoped
you would be pleased.'

Never trust a Montguiscard. But you couldn't very well
say that, or: *Before Arionbel you and he were nobodies.* Find
something quickly. . . .

' Balthasar and I are cousins.'

'The Bishop of Bargreant is on his way to Rome to obtain a dispensation from the Holy Father.'

'He *would* be,' thought Yolande dully.

'And Balthasar will be Duke of Baraine,' she said aloud but as if to herself.

'Yes. He will be joined with you in possession of the duchy.'

'Balthasar will like being a duke.'

It sounded a childish thing to say. Better go on being childish.

'Yes,' returned Azo simply. 'Balthasar will like it. He will be very proud to marry you, and he will take great care of you.'

'I'm sure of that,' said Yolande. It was her first lie so far; she improved it with another. 'If the king and you have decided it is best for Baraine and for me, I shall be content to marry Balthasar, and I shall try to be a . . . a good and obedient wife. What does the chancellor say about it?'

Azo seemed to have his mouth open to breathe fatherly reassurance, but shut it again for a second, as though he found this ending not so childish.

'The chancellor,' he said at length. 'He joins his loyal prayers and hopes with the bishop's and my own. Why do you ask?'

'Because he was always wanting my father to marry again and have a son. When shall I be Balthasar's wife?'

'As I have told you . . . at Christmas.'

'I mean . . . really his wife.'

'When you are sixteen.'

Yolande looked again at the golden hound's-head, which was grinning across the room at her beads as though he were going to gobble them up . . . just as the Montguiscards were going to gobble up Yolande.

'Drogo . . . the Duke of Boqueron . . . said I should be . . . er . . . should be left alone until I was seventeen. But then, of course, Drogo was already a duke himself.'

This innocent piece of reasoning had the effect of pushing Azo's hand into his gold-embroidered purse. It came out

holding a resplendent ring, on which a delicate gold thunderbolt set with diamonds and rubies curved to contain the
gold-mounted splendour of a great black pearl.

'This is your betrothal ring,' said Azo, and slid it on to
Yolande's finger.

'It is very magnificent,' said Yolande politely. 'Will there
be a betrothal ceremony, like my other at Hautarroy?'

'No. We will let ceremony wait until your wedding. That
will be at Bargreant. The plague is still moving eastwards in
Arroy and Beltany.'

Yolande sat silent for a few seconds, inspecting the symbol
of her new order of life. The cold axe-blade had gone; the
melting fright below her middle had curdled into a kind of
despairing rage at this calm disposal of herself and her
dignity.

'My lord Grand Seneschal,' she said suddenly.

'My lady duchess?' enquired Azo, with half-humorous
deference.

'Tell me, please, just what you know of how my father and
his men were killed.'

Azo repeated the tale of the archer who had watched from
the gallery of the hall at Pardelin.

'Then,' said Yolande, when he had done, 'if Turlequin
was in the hall so soon, the man who steered the boat against
us was not really Turlequin.'

'No, he was not. You say they all laughed when he claimed
the name.'

'Yes. I suppose he was making game of us. You know I
thought I saw him again?'

'Outside the abbey wall here? Yes, I was told you mistook
one of my captains for the man you thought was Turlequin.
He . . . removed himself when he realised your mistake. He
wears a black patch over one ear, like the rogue you saw in
the boat. That rogue was slain on the shore while you were
unconscious.'

'Oh. Yes. It was that patch which made me think your
captain a ghost. That and his beard. Did you find out how
they got their boat on to the lake?'

'No. The Sieur de Caherne reported having seen a trail on the hillside where they must have dragged it on wheels and runners across the moors from the south.'

'It is queer that they had so much time . . . it seemed a chance raid. Only, of course, *we* had seen that man with the patch before.'

'Where was that?' asked Azo, gravely attentive.

Yolande told him about the afternoon in the barge.

'Turlequin's right-hand man, no doubt,' commented Azo. 'There is no one left now to set a name to him. And when you say that it seemed a chance raid, remember that there is nothing in men so compelling as their vanity. Turlequin may have dreamed for years of just such a cunning stroke which would raise him to power. I think he aimed to capture my lord your father as well as yourself. I have heard it said he was with Joris of the Rock, when Joris made prisoner the king . . . of course, *before* he was the king . . . and held him for a time in the wilds of Honoy. What you have told me shows he could plan with patience.'

Azo rose and stood for a moment gazing down at Yolande, with one hand on his jewelled belt, and the other fondling the jewelled cross hanging on his gold neck-chain. His next words came in what was almost a purr of contentment.

'I had my lord your father's utmost confidence,' he said. 'He would be glad to know what provision I make for your state and your safety.'

Yolande looked up into the fine blue eyes, and then looked down again at Topaz, feeling powerless and frightened in face of that bland all-smothering lie.

'The letters I spoke of are up in the castle,' went on Azo, suddenly brisk. 'Tomorrow I will have them brought down for you to read.'

'I give you gramercy, my lord Grand Seneschal,' said Yolande of Baraine.

When he had gone she sat awhile staring at the splendid ring. Topaz woke up and pawed it experimentally. Yolande gathered him against her breast, and rose to go to her bed-chamber. There she took off the ring and put it in an ivory

box given her by the abbess; the only other thing in the box
was the privy signet of Baraine, the lordly Leopard rampant,
intaglio in green chalcedony.

'I should tell Uncle Azo that I have this,' she reflected,
looking at the signet. 'Or I should give it into his keeping.
But only Zoster Adela knows I have it, and I will do neither.
Gold Puss, you must get acquainted with your new shield-
mate. Queer that both the outlaw and the captain had a
scarred nose. I was afraid to tell Azo that.'

Feeling that she had not altogether ignored her father's last
injunction, she took Topaz again upon her knee, and sat for
a long time staring into the future.

Saint-Marthe at Roclatour was proven a violable sanctuary.
Perhaps Balthasar would turn out to be kind when they were
alone together.

Before the autumn roads grew all but impassable Yolande
had to be at Bargreant, capital of her duchy. The abbess was
insistent that she prepare herself for the journey; Azo had
sent two palfreys so that she might ride in the woods and along
the shore of Lake Targe. Zoster Adela rode with her on a
war-horse, and a squire with half a dozen archers followed as
escort. The squires were experienced soldiers, Azo's own men;
none of the former ducal household appeared at Roclatour.
The seneschal of the castle was promoted away from it;
Yolande heard that the Sieur de Xantroy was coming to take
his place.

Fine horse-litters appeared in the abbey stables; men-at-arms
and grooms multiplied in the streets between abbey and castle.
Leaves began to shower down from the chestnut tree that overhung the abbey wall, and the time came to say good-bye to it.

On the afternoon before her departure, Yolande went down
to the apothecary's shop to take leave of her kitten's family.
Philastrius showed her a cup made from an ostrich egg, with
a plaque of unicorn's horn set in the bottom. This plaque, so
Philastrius had been told, would infallibly strike rainbow
hues into any poison served in the cup.

'Have you tried it?' asked Yolande.

'I do not deal in poisons,' said the apothecary drily.

'Of course you do not,' Yolande was quick to agree. 'I only meant . . . you must know how to make them.'

'Yes, I know how,' Philastrius admitted, putting the cup into a cupboard and turning the key on it.

Then he showed her a talisman, a disc of agate curiously patterned in yellow, brown, and blue-grey. The markings made a dim little picture; a cave-mouth frowned from a rocky hillside, with a tree standing above it against a cloudy sky.

'I pray you will keep this, my lady duchess,' said Philastrius, with sober insistence. 'Your birthday falls in June.'

'Yes,' said Yolande, holding the agate on her palm.

'This is a good stone for vigour and success, especially for the June-born. I have read that the Sieur Aeneas escaped from Troy by virtue of such a talisman. It averts tempests, meteors, and thunderbolts . . .'

Yolande closed her hand on the stone and opened it again. Philastrius, unused to thinking in terms of blazonry, went on without noticing his blunder.

'. . . and if strung on a hair from the tail of a lion it brings success in love and friendship.'

'You have no lions' tails in the shop,' she asserted rather than asked.

'Alas, no, my lady.'

Yolande laughed, and looked at a casserole tightly packed with little bundles of vine-twigs.

'What are these for?' she asked.

'I make charcoal with them, for drawing.'

'Are you a limner too?'

Philastrius reached into a cupboard and pulled out a number of small planed boards. Yolande exclaimed with delight; some of the drawing were pictures of the wife of Philastrius, a quiet, beautiful young woman called Blanche, who hovered shyly in the background and blushed at praise of her portraits.

'Master Philastrius is lucky to have someone so lovely to help him,' said Yolande.

'I only have to sit still, Your Grace,' murmured the grey-eyed Blanche.

' There is more in it than that, as Your Grace has perceived,'
said Philastrius. 'Here are some drawings of the street, and
the harbour, and the castle.'

Yolande would have asked him for one, but did not want to
appear greedy.

' I shall sometimes wear your talisman, Master Philastrius,'
she promised. ' And I shall remember you for your kindness and
loyalty, and for the marvellous perfume and the drawings . . .
and the kittens.'

She smiled at the curtseying Blanche, and went out into the
windy autumn sunshine. Lake Targe, much broader than Lake
Falchion, and set among hills rather than mountains, was
beginning to be friendly; and now she must leave it. At a street
corner she paused and looked down the cobbled incline at brown
and white sails gliding in and out of the harbour; Zoster Adela
stood beside her, with the soldiers a pace or two behind. There
were few people about, but here and there a woman's head had
appeared at a window; the invisible goodwife whose voice
crackled out must have thought the four of them gone well past
her.

' Well, they may say she's mournful-crazy, but I say she's a
trim piece and as right in the head as any of us.'

There were gasps and squawks from those who heard and
could see Yolande standing within earshot. Wimpled shapes
vanished as though beneath the headsman's axe. With a clatter
of wooden shoes one bystander whisked her two children away
up an alley. A man-at-arms growled something; Zoster Adela,
crimson-faced, caught her charge by the arm and propelled her
forward.

' So that's what they say,' murmured Yolande, looking up
with a rueful smile. ' I suppose it's because I saw the ghost of
Turlequin . . . don't be angry, Zoster Adela. Now I know why
they stare so. I thought they were *sorry* for me.'

' So they are, the besoms,' said Zoster Adela. ' But they go
stretching their silly necks to gossip instead of tidying their
houses.'

' At least I have one champion among them,' said Yolande,
and suddenly found a real laugh stirring under her ribs.

That evening she took Topaz into the abbey garden and watched the sun go down behind the heights which hid Siege Umbrous. A dreadful desolation possessed her; in fancy her spirit soared over the ranges and stooped to lonely Pardelin. There the late sunshine would still be gilding the head of the valley, boring into narrow castle windows, flecking the stony gloom of corridors and chambers where only an occasional archer passed on his way to rampart duty.

'I want to go back there,' Yolande told herself. 'But if I did I should hate it. I should be afraid of meeting their ghosts . . . yet just now I'm a ghost myself, more there than here at Roclatour. Saint Amarand be praised the abbess and Zoster Adela are coming to Bargreant. Without them I should really be lost, and go mournful-crazy, as that woman called it.'

The kitten licked her finger, and she looked down at him.

'Of course there is always you to comfort me, bless your pink nose,' she said. 'But for the rest, I feel very shy, more like a frightened rabbit than a stately leopardess.'

V

BALTHASAR'S WAY

BY the time the first snow had whitened the tower-tops and roofs of Bargreant, Yolande felt that she hardly belonged to herself any more. Balthasar she had not yet seen, for he was still with the king at Hastain, but the shadow of Uncle Azo lay everywhere about her.

Most of her fourteen winters had been spent in the huge grey castle which sat squarely at one corner of the capital city of her duchy. Four times the size of the holds of Pardelin or Roclatour, it sprawled with two sides darkening the streets, a third frowning above the swift-flowing River Malvaine, and the fourth confronting the hills that rolled towards the Franconian frontier.

There Yolande had been accustomed to keep to one range of buildings surrounding an inner courtyard. The ducal apartments had their own chapel and hall and garden and archery-butts, and now she found herself unable to move beyond them; there was still a danger of plague in the city, explained a blushing young squire when Yolande took it into her head to look at preparations in the great stables.

' None of Your Grace's personal household may come out this way,' said the squire.

' It's only for your safety and ours, child,' the abbess told her when she complained. And when she remarked that former servants were being replaced by strangers, the abbess said that the Grand Seneschal had found the duke's retainers lazy and unfitted to cope with the coming invasion of wedding guests.

The harbinger of that invasion appeared in the person of the old Duchess of Queranay, herself a Montguiscard, who six months earlier would have regarded Azo as a poor relation of her own. She had agreed to steer Yolande through the maze of wedding ceremonial; she looked like a parrot coiffed with yellow and bottled up in green velvet, and she at once began to cast about for a new governess for Yolande.

Grim dowagers loomed up and closed in on all sides; Yolande's heart sank, and again she spoke to the abbess.

'My lord Grand Seneschal has not asked the Duchess to concern herself in that matter,' said the abbess very bleakly, and Yolande realised that private war had broken out between the two redoubtable old women. The abbess herself came of the ducal house of Ahun; her abbey was small, but she stood in no awe of the Queranay, and Azo continued to rely upon her in Yolande's private affairs. Sister Marcelle was of the party, and she and Zoster Adela sometimes exchanged remarks not intended for Yolande's ears; but Yolande's ears were keener than most, and once or twice she overheard them.

'He wants none of her old folk about her,' said Zoster Adela.

'The king is using them, father and son, to build up his own faction,' said Sister Marcelle. 'He's letting the Grand Seneschal rush this marriage through because he's afraid the great lords would want them to marry her to the Viscount of Ger.'

So that was it, reflected Yolande. She was given to Balthasar to keep Baraine out of the hands of the Count Warden, whose own loyal and famous exploits ten years gone by were now quite put in the shade by the achievements of Uncle Azo.

Her father had liked and admired the Count Raoul of Ger; the Viscount Lothair was two years younger than herself, and marriage between them would have made Count Raoul supreme in the north and east of the kingdom.

So Yolande, a pawn in her sovereign's game, was condemned to stand for hours in the midst of kneeling and absorbed tire-women who wrapped and folded and pinned and scissored to make of her a suitable shape at altar and board and tourney-side.

'Remember not to lean forward,' said the old Duchess of Queranay, as a weight of ermine was loaded on to Yolande's slim shoulders. 'Remember to look up at about the level of the Saviour's knees, so that the light from the east window will fall full upon your face. . . .

' Remember not to wince when the trumpeters blow on the steps . . . remember not to curtsey any more to anyone when once you appear in your coronet. . . .

' Remember when you throw largesse to scatter it widely as if you were feeding pigeons. . . .

' Remember to laugh a little at all the tumblers and joculators . . .

' Remember that your wine will be twice watered. We don't want a scene like that when Maude Camors began hiccoughing at her father's second wedding. . . .'

' There's a devil of a lot to remember,' said Yolande crossly to Zoster Adela.

The nun ignored her turn of speech, and put across her shoulders an arm more welcome than the ermine.

' Remember one thing more,' she said. ' I shall be praying to Our Lady for you from the first minute to the last.'

Strange sights began to appear in the streets and suburbs of Bargreant. Yolande, escorted abroad for fresh air, drew rein when she found a camel looking scornfully at her across the low wall of a paddock. Negroes were in charge of it; their rolling eyes and flashing teeth and pink palms fascinated her and recurred in her dreams.

An infinity of queer folk, full of strange talents, was gathering together around the east gate of the city. From them the Grand Seneschal's officers chose balanced teams for the entertainment of his guests in the castle hall and the courtyards assigned to their retinues. There were men and girls who juggled and contorted themselves and worked many kinds of puppets; there were sword-swallowers and fire-breathers and people who ate nails and broken glass; and there were scores of minstrels, some in company with dancers and dwarfs and acrobats, some solitary, or in pairs, with long swords and pretensions to gentility.

There, too, were performing bears and horses and dogs, a squirrel which ran in a wheel and by so doing played tunes on little bells, a monkey which carried a shield and spear and rode on a caparisoned pig. And there was Nestor, the wonderful ape

who sat on his master's knee and talked, while his master's wife
went round in the crowd with little wooden carvings of him.
Nestor's booth ran on wheels and was drawn by a cream-
coloured mule; the squire in attendance on Yolande pointed it
out to her as their archers made way for them through the crowd
after they had seen the camel.

'Why are you going off like that?' roared somebody to
Nestor's owner; for the ape's equipage was headed away from
the gate.

The haggard, clever-looking man who held the mule's bit-
chain looked over his shoulder and replied with mechanical
gaiety.

'Nestor's cut his thumb, and he's sulking,' he shouted.
'We've still four days to go, so we're taking him for a cure along
the river.'

Yolande was generally too sorry for entertainers to enjoy the
bulk of their tricks and arts; the jokes and contortions, the paint
and finery, never concealed from her the strain and grime and
greed behind them. But she liked the look of Nestor's owners;
the man's trim head and grave face as he doffed his cap to her,
the thin young wife's bob of respect and shy curious smile, made
her look after them as they threaded the throng on the river-
bank. Before they were out of Yolande's sight the man put his
arm round the girl's shoulders; no doubt if trouble came they
would face it valiantly together.

The four days went in a whirl of preparation. The streets
between castle and cathedral were roofed with three hundred
yards of canvas striped purple and yellow; the castle wards and
courts filled with daylong and nightlong noise. Ermine and
velvet, samite and brocade, cascaded in frozen splendour over
clothes-horses and trestles in the apartments of the duchess.
Yolande's baths grew oppressive with perfume; her hair was
washed for one whole afternoon, and she lay on a couch with
her head to a brazier, half-stupefied, while the women spread
the tresses wide and combed them and sprinkled them with
rosewater. Six great rings made her hands feel clumsy; the
monstrous headdress she must wear was further weighted by a

coronet of pierced gold with a noble pearl on each of its twelve little spikes.

Balthasar, when at length he came and was admitted to her presence, bowed very politely and hoped that she was well.

' My lord, I am glad to greet you,' said Yolande as he kissed her hand. ' What kind of journey had you from the court? '

' Fair, I thank you, but it looks like more snow tonight.'

He seemed so proud and lovely that all the women's hearts were melted; his sixteen-year-old cousin, Melania de Montguiscard, who was to carry the tail of Yolande's train in procession, chuckled in Yolande's ear when the brief meeting was ended.

' Aren't you sorry it isn't a real wedding? ' she whispered.

' It is a real wedding,' said Yolande, pretending to misunderstand.

' It isn't. It can still be dissolved until . . . you know. Wouldn't you *like* to go to bed with Cousin Balthasar? '

' No, I would not! '

' Well, you're about the only woman under forty in Bargreant who can say that.'

' Shall I put in a word for you? ' asked Yolande, who disliked Melania at sight.

' You'll change your mind in a year or two,' said Melania loftily.

To Balthasar, Yolande had perceived, she was just one of the properties of this great occasion.

' At any rate,' she told herself, ' he can't say they did things better the last time he was married.'

People smiled at her a great deal, and she made a smiling face at them. But several times during those days she saw what she was not meant to see; not everybody was as happy as he was supposed to be.

Thus, when Uncle Azo escorted her with Balthasar to examine their wedding-presents in the Serpent Tower, she saw out of the gallery window three archers driving along a prisoner with a black eye and a bleeding mouth and hands tied behind him.

'What has happened?' she asked, halting her little procession.

'It's nothing, Your Grace,' said someone. 'Only a thief who tried to make off with some candles.'

'What are they going to do to him?'

'Hang him, Your Grace.'

'My lord Grand Seneschal!' she exclaimed, so that everyone grew quite quiet around them. 'I pray you, let the poor wretch go.'

Uncle Azo smiled at her with his mouth, but not with his eyes.

'Impossible, dear child,' he said. 'It would encourage other would-be thieves, and rascals of all kinds.'

'Can I not pardon whom I please in my own castle?' Yolande demanded.

'You can forgive him,' said Azo smoothly, 'but our lord the king has entrusted to me the matter of pardons in Baraine.'

'Will you please grant me the pardon, then?'

'No, my lady, in the name of law and order . . . your law and order.'

Yolande looked at him for a second, and sought for an unyielding phrase to seal her defeat.

'That is a pity,' she said simply, and left it to her audience to judge where the pity lay.

'Come along, cousin,' said Balthasar, amused. He took her by the hand and led her into the next gallery, where men-at-arms with drawn swords guarded the glittering gifts. Yolande swallowed her rage, but afterwards found it very hard to remember what she had seen there.

Another uncomfortable glimpse, again out of a window, showed her a fight between overdriven kitchen folk, who caught up stools and loaves and joints of meat and wooden platters and screamed with rage as they flung them at each other and at the archers who came with staves to thump them into submission.

A third scene, beyond a balustrade, revealed a pretty serving-girl carrying a great dish, piled high with fruit, across a greasy reach of cobbles. A young nobleman came up behind her and

slid his hand into her bosom. She made no movement to
escape, but stood wearily balancing her load, afraid of spilling
the pears and peaches. Her face sagged, and she began to cry,
turning her head aside so that plebeian tears should not even
wet them.

'Zoster Adela!' gasped Yolande, and started forward, but
the nun was before her. Leaning over the balustrade, she
dropped a scalding sentence on the young man's self-esteem.

'The duchess bids you mend your manners, beastly little
knave!'

The young nobleman whipped out his hand and slapped it
to his sword-hilt; the white fury was chased from his face by a
crimson confusion. For a second or two he stood staring like a
fool, and then took off his hat and bowed himself away
backwards.

'Come here,' called Yolande to the astonished girl, who
obeyed as if fascinated. 'Rest the edge of the dish on the stone.
Now, take this and hide it, and use it as you please.'

Yolande had money in her purse; the gold coin disappeared
where the brutal hand had been. The wet-eyed girl stammered
something, and Yolande leaned over and patted her red cheek.

'I'm sorry that happened to you in my castle,' she said.

Bells pealed in the darkness beyond the great shutters. Zoster
Adela stood by the fire, warming a beautiful silken chemise.
Behind the steaming bath-tent the great coroneted headdress
shone like the horns of a heathen god. Women gathered as if
to make a sacrifice to it.

Wearing a rich furred gown, Yolande went to Mass in the
blue dusk of morning. In the crowded ducal chapel everyone
bowed to her, and she made no curtseys except for one to the
Rood. Then she returned to her bedchamber for a collation of
pasties and wine; and after that she was loaded with her pro-
cessional robe of purple velvet trimmed with ermine.

She trod long corridors filled with jarring colours and gleaming steel, and a staircase where torches blew and smoked in the
cold dry wind. She passed through archways while rows of
guisarmes clashed and flashed in salute. In front of her strutted

the Captain of the Ducal Guard, with a sash of cloth of gold over his glimmering armour; behind her Gold Puss coiled and curled under the awnings. Waiting for her, four young noblemen held aloft the silken pall under which she must walk.

The silver poles of the pall were hung with silver bells. Yolande moved forward in a sweet tingling mist of sound, with her two pages and Melania de Montguiscard pacing sedately behind her. Red carpet crossed the courtyard, the gateway, the bridge, and ran under the twin arches of the bannered barbican to lead her to the west porch of Saint Amarand-in-Bargreant. Archers blocked the ends of alleys where the crowd yelled and struggled to see her. The booming of all the bells of the city vibrated in the ground she trod.

Inside the cathedral a rustling crowd, coloured like the rainbow, like butterflies and flowers and autumn leaves; two dukes, three duchesses, Balthasar in purple and gold, Azo in vermilion and sable coming to lead her to where the mitre of the Bishop of Bargreant gave back the light of the altar-candles in flashes of ruby, sapphire, and emerald.

Half-deafened by the roaring of the organs, Yolande made her genuflection. The morning sun had found the east window; Uncle Azo's face, pleased but serious, was green and crimson and blue by turns as his cold hand guided her up the nave. . . .

There was the Sieur de Caherne, with Balthasar's coronet on a cushion. The train of Balthasar's robe was held half-way along, like her own, by two pages, and at the end by Camus de Caherne, a younger edition of his blackavised father, and Balthasar's best friend.

Balthasar, composed and gorgeous, stepped out to stand beside her. The bishop handed his crystal-headed pastoral staff to his chaplain; the choir burst into full song; and the marriage service of Yolande and Balthasar began.

Nearly two hours later the coroneted pair walked back to the castle, hand-in-hand under the pall, with the Thunderbolt and Gold Puss impaled on a great banner before them. Behind, leading the procession of notables, came the Sieur de Caherne, carrying over his shoulder a magnificent silver mace.

' Did you see the Count of Ger? ' asked Balthasar under the
tumult of cheers, not forgetting as he spoke to smile graciously
into the crowd.

' No . . . what is he like? '

' Not tall, violet and silver, pale brown foreign-looking face,
short pointed beard. I didn't think he would come at all . . .
you know he's your heir? '

' Yes, of course, but I don't suppose he ever expected to be
Duke of Baraine.'

' If he did he's disappointed today . . . but he might have
liked to marry you to his son. Instead of that you're married
to *me.*'

' *Your* father's son,' said Yolande, not without malice.
Couldn't this paladin even wait to exult until he was back in
the castle?

' A pity the king stayed away,' she went on as if piqued.

' Ah, you mustn't think of it like that. He wanted my father
to have the chief place . . . so that it should be plain who is
master here.'

' I see,' said Yolande, feeling suddenly very much like a
dummy dangled from the hand of this resplendent monument
of self-satisfaction. ' And now do you think, my lord, we shall
be allowed something more to eat? '

' You little greedy-guts,' said Balthasar affably. ' You'd do
better to stay empty until the banquet tonight.'

During the afternoon Yolande found time to view the
Christmas presents provided for her to give away three days
later. There was a jewelled sword for Balthasar, with jewelled
dagger and belt to match; and a gold and chrysoprase cup for
Uncle Azo; and two branched candlesticks of gold and
turquoise for the old Duchess of Queranay. Uncle Azo had
thought of everything; for the Convent of Saint Marthe in
Roclatour there was a reliquary of gold, jade, lapis lazuli,
mother-of-pearl, and ivory, in which to keep the good saint's
battered thimble of silver. For the abbess there was a splendid
Book of Hours, and two little Books of Our Lady for Yolande's
friends the nuns, with plaques of gold and enamel and patterns
of seed-pearls on their perfumed leather bindings. And there

was a cornucopia of gilded bronze full to the brim with florins, for Yolande to take under her arm when she threw largesse to the crowd from the steps of the cathedral.

'I begin to feel glitter-sick,' she said to Melania, whose dark eyes rolled in her dark face as she tried to guess which of these sumptuous presents was likely to come her own way.

'You would do well to take a cordial,' advised Melania, envisaging cordials for two.

The banquet was a magnificence of colour and sound and scent and taste and movement. Drums and fifes beside the door, trumpets on the dais, viols and flutes and harps in the minstrels' gallery, played the guests to their seats. A mounted marshal in full armour controlled the company of archers who kept order in the third of the hall where the commonalty was crowded to watch. Great tables in the courtyards had already been picked clean, and many of that loyal audience could only stand upright because they had no room to fall; but even those who still saw singly found the heat and pressure worth while.

Curtains and hangings of tapestry, tall shields of parade and devices of the cities of the duchy, half-hid the clean grey stone of the walls and glowed in the light of the swung chandeliers, in which the candles were big as torches. Behind the side tables were cupboards decked with gold-ringed elephants' tusks, antelopes' horns tipped with silver, and gilded antlers of deer. The light from the branched candle-sticks was doubled by reflection in huge silver plates and dishes ranged behind them. The serving-men were all in red and white, the perfumed tablecloths were white embroidered with fishes and birds and dragons in pale colours; the rushes were dusted with powdered herbs and damped with hot water that stirred their fragrance, and no hounds ran loose between the long tables.

Yolande, in white and emerald-green, had got over her glitter-sickness. Balthasar, in gold and crimson, was a nonpareil of beauty, and when he raised her to her feet to acknowledge the roars of the assembly she inclined her head and waved and smiled with real pleasure and gratitude.

In front of each guest at the chief table was a little silken pavilion with a sugar chevalier on guard. The golden salt-cellars were ships and castles, the golden handles of knives and spoons were angels with down-folded wings.

The food poured in with a riot of odours; pages whose boyish faces were grim with responsibility bowed and dodged and bent the knee and held their breath as they served Yolande. One of them was Berel de Forne, younger cousin of Lioncel; his features and hair and blue eyes were very like Lioncel's, and a great pang of distress shore through Yolande's excitement and took half her fun with it.

'Good even to you, Berel,' she said. 'You stand to it like an old soldier.'

She could not bear the delighted grin with which he received this praise. The abbess was at the top table, seven places away from her. Sisters Marcelle and Adela were with the ladies of the household at the head of a side table. Their white coifs and black habits made an island of custom and sanity amid the blaze and hullaballoo.

The first course was of swans and cygnets, roasted and sewn back into their feathered skins. The leading swan had a twist of parchment caught in his gilded beak, and this she must read and admire and show to Balthasar on her right and to the Duke of Elquitaine or her left.

> ' God guard our duke, brave Balthasar,
> So young in years, so skilled in war.
> God bless our duchess, sweet Yolande,
> And grant her joy on every hand.
> God speed our wise Grand Seneschal,
> And every loyal blade withal
> That helped him smite our foes to hell
> In the dread Gorge of Arionbel.'

'The Muse's wings are clipped on this occasion,' said the Duke of Elquitaine, passing the effusion on to the old Duchess of Queranay.

'What's that, what's that, my lord?' she snapped, not being sure of what he had said.

'Mars is still at the zenith, and Venus not yet risen above

the horizon,' particularised the duke in a shriller key. He was Italian, a brother of the queen, and Yolande found him oily but disdainful; she realised what he meant, and that he was airing the culture of the sunny south.

But a bearded nobleman beyond the old duchess was a match for Elquitaine; he leaned forward and tossed at him a phrase from one of the sonnets of Messer Francesco Petrarca. His voice rang pleasantly in the half-hush; the carvers were flashing their steel under the noses of the servers.

' *O fortunato, che si chiara tromba trovasti!* '

' What the devil's all that about? ' boomed the fat Duke of Trevence from somewhere on Balthasar's right.

' Ger showing off in Italian,' replied Balthasar with his mouth full.

' Let me show off too,' put in Yolande, ' and tell you what he said. Alexander came to the tomb of Achilles, and sighed: *O fortunate one, who found so clear a trumpet.* He meant Homer. My lord of Ger was being polite to the minstrel who wrote the verses, and to you, and to the Duke of Elquitaine, who didn't deserve it.'

' You understand Italian? ' demanded Balthasar accusingly.

' A little. Don't you? '

' No, by Saint Andreas. Neustrian and Franconian are good enough for me.'

' What would the queen say if she heard you? '

Balthasar's beautiful eyes sparkled with amusement, and every woman who was watching envied the young duchess.

' The queen speaks very good Neustrian,' he said.

After the roasted swans came beef and mutton, venison with frumenty, capons, herons, partridges, larks, crabs, pike, salmon, peacocks in pride, a boar's head with little baskets swung from each gilded tusk—in one basket sapphire earrings, in the other a gold toothpick for Balthasar—and after all these were served wonderful fritters and fruits in compôte, custards royal, subtleties in shapes of saints and ladies, of fighting-men and unicorns and galleys beset by dolphins, and a great sugar shield patterned with tinted leopards and thunderbolts.

The chief subtlety of all was a sugar garden, topped by three

statues of saints in solid gold; in the middle Saint Amarand of
Baraine took his axe to a Franconian writhing beneath his feet,
on the left Saint Michael beheaded a fiend, and on the right
Saint Joris speared a dragon.

Yolande sipped at each goblet that came to her hand, but the
grey-haired serving-man behind her whipped them away before
she could drink twice. When the healths were called, and the
whole company got to its feet to pledge bride and bridegroom,
the same serving-man took a grip on the arm of the Duke of
Elquitaine and prevented his collapsing sideways over the arm
of Yolande's chair. Balthasar was very flushed, and the pasty
cheeks of Uncle Azo had grown as pink as his long nose.

But the stately old duchess was quite sober, and her nod of
approval told Yolande that she, Yolande, was demeaning herself
as befitted a good young duchess.

Then began the mumming and the miming, the dancing and
tumbling and joculation. The bulk of the noble guests had
drunk enough by now to laugh at any kind of foolery. A
notable show was a game of chess played to music by living
pieces; men and boys and two lovely girls, accoutred in red or
white linen, danced and glided to make their moves on a huge
chequered cloth of the same colours. More popular were the
girl dancers flung about by their male partners, or walking on
their hands so that their coloured gowns fell back and showed
them naked except for spangled loincloths.

There was a bear which danced with a woman, and jesters
who talked so quickly that no one could hear what they said;
but so long as they banged each other with bladders, nobody
minded that.

Yolande picked sweetmeats from a golden dish, pretended
not to notice the drunken handclap of Balthasar and the plump
Duchess of Trevence on his other side, and wished she could
hear what the old duchess and the Count of Ger were saying.
But they were talking quietly under the tumult, and their words
were slurred by the snores of the Duke of Elquitaine.

In the morning, for the first time, she met her husband alone;
and he was not kind. He looked tired and a little less radiant

than usual, if still able to hold his own with all but the top flight of angels. His eyelids were slightly puffed, and he took no trouble to smile at her.

With Topaz in her arms she had come for a second look at the great array of wedding gifts in the gallery nearest her own apartments. Balthasar, in dove-grey satin, had two magnificent staghounds—one white, the other black—pacing behind him. She tightened her grasp on the growing kitten and stood waiting for her lord to approach.

Something in her watchful aloofness seemed to find a crack in the glaze of his self-satisfaction. He bowed stiffly, and advanced not quite in a straight line.

'I hope you're rested, my lord,' she told him. 'Will you take a glass of wine?'

'Rested? Oh, I'm rested. No, I don't want any wine. What have you got there?'

'This? He's my kitten Topaz. He came from Roclatour. Isn't he beautiful?'

'No, I hate cats. They're good for nothing but catching mice, and they won't learn to obey. Do you know how the Wends use cats to work magic?'

'No.'

'Oh, Well, I'll tell you. They put a live cat on a spit and roast him; and they believe that his yowls and yells will summon a great spirit cat, which will answer any question they ask about the future; and a man sits in a cow's hide . . .'

'I hope the spirit cat claws their eyes out.'

'Eh? You hard-hearted little creature! I thought you were kind to peasants. Don't interrupt your wedded husband. A man sits in a cow's hide . . . hey, where are you going?'

'Back to my own rooms.'

'That's dis . . . disrespectful. And they aren't your rooms any longer. They're mine. You're mine too . . . remember that. You belong to me, like this castle and this duchy . . . don't stand staring at me like . . . like . . . like an owl.'

'Go away and come back when you're sober,' said Yolande desperately, for he had lounged between her and the door by which she had entered.

'Do you understand?' he drawled, and now his eyes were glad and searching. His nostrils had dilated, and his mouth was a little twisted. 'You *don't* understand . . . but you will. You belong to *me*. It wouldn't be any fun to sleep with you yet . . . but don't think you can ever escape doing anything I want you to do. Women should be tamed straight away . . . stand still, I'm not going to hurt you.'

'I am standing still,' said Yolande, and then screamed at the top of her voice, for his strong hand tore Topaz from her clasp and flung him mewing into the air.

The black and white staghounds had stood like statues, but now they came alive in a whirl. Clash, snap, and the little furry body was torn asunder in mid-air. A gout of blood slanted to splash on the lid of a sandalwood chest; the great hounds grinned and chewed and swallowed. Balthasar, too, was grinning, in much the same way; Yolande had backed to the arras, and stood with her clenched fists scratched and bleeding where Topaz had tried to hold to them. To Yolande her husband's golden hair and blue eyes seemed to swim in a mist of fury.

'You foul beast,' she whispered. 'You miserable, murdering fiend.'

'Do I go on my knees and ask to be forgiven?' asked Balthasar, collecting himself and watching her curiously. 'You shouldn't try to cross me, you see. Don't be such a fool, Yolande. I'll send you a hound instead of that wretched thing.'

'Send me a hound and I'll poison him.'

'Will you? That's how you take it, is it? You'll learn better some day, and it may be fun to teach you. Here come your loyal people to bring the smelling-salts. I'll see you at the banquet tonight . . . and mind you're in a better temper.'

Zoster Adela and Melania had both heard the scream; each appeared in time to meet a steady stare from the young duke.

'Attend your lady the duchess,' he told them, and swung away with his hounds stalking happily behind him.

'It was to show he is master,' explained Yolande with an effort. 'He threw Topaz to his hounds. He hates cats . . . and I hate *him*.'

'He's been drinking,' said Melania, and Zoster Adela rounded upon her.

'If a man cuts his mother's throat, there's always some wise bloody fool to say *he's had a drop too much* and then go home to supper. Your hands, my sweet . . . let me see. Blood on your wedding-ring! Jesu have mercy!'

'You ought to be ashamed of yourself for talking like that,' said Melania. 'And *I* see no reason for such a fuss about a kitten.'

'Then go away,' commanded Yolande, and turned her back until Melania had sailed from the room. Then she looked up at Zoster Adela.

'I'm going to be sick,' she announced; and a little later she asked: 'What does Holy Church teach about animals going to heaven?'

That afternoon, exhausted by her rage, Yolande slept for an hour in her shift and stockings and furred bedgown. When she awoke a small box sewn up in canvas was standing on the table by her bed.

'Reverend Mother Abbess brought it,' explained Zoster Adela. 'It's a gift sent to you through her from the lord prior of Sanctlamine. He has the winter cramps and couldn't come to the wedding.'

'Another gift,' said Yolande wearily. 'Will you please open it, Zoster Adela?'

Two minutes later she reared herself up on her hands and stared at her doll Amarand, who regarded her stolidly through the occularium of his now slightly tarnished helmet. For the death of Topaz she had cried only with rage, but the return of this beloved toy cracked the stony carapace forming round her heart. She unhelmed him, cradled him in her arms, and baptised him anew in a torrent of tears.

Zoster Adela lifted out the prior's own present—a little ivory group of Our Lady and Child, attended by Saint Michael with sword and banner.

'There's a letter, too,' said Zoster Adela, and presently Yolande asked her to read it.

*' To my gracious lady duchess and beloved daughter in God,
Yolande of Baraine: health, duty, and greeting. God and Our
Lady give you for your late grievous sorrow, healing; in your
exalted marriage, joy; and in all that may come hereafter, peace
and blessing and comfort of your friends. That I am one of
them, let the little gift bear witness. With it receive a valiant
image of your own, brought to my hand by a chance recovery; I
doubt not that you will welcome it again. That the Holy Trinity
may have you in guard is the prayer of God's humble servant
and your own.* Gilomar, *Sanctae Laminae Prior.*

Yolande collected herself, wiped away her tears, and inspected
the dainty ivory figures. Then she pushed Amarand's arm up
and unlocked his inside, to the admiration of Zoster Adela.
Turning her treasures out on the bed, she called a roll and
found them all there; she kissed and caressed especially the little
crystal box with the lock of hair in it. But something else was
there too, something that she had never seen before. It was
a scrap of paper, with three short verses on it, entitled *Amarand
Sings of the Elves.* Yolande read them with deepening astonishment.

> *Diotree and Liolake*
> *Must needs flee the realm.*
> *Priokin hid them*
> *Under the helm.*
>
> *Lio from the lake,*
> *Dio from the tree,*
> *Prio knows what they know,*
> *And where they be.*
>
> *Diotree and Liolake*
> *Have pledged themselves*
> *Some day to serve again*
> *The Queen of the Elves.*

She sat very still, re-reading, puzzling, telling herself at first
that they must be nonsense. But the words and phrases caught
at her breath and hammered in her heart. She stirred, pinched

her thigh under the tumbled purple kerchief, and ground the diamond of her ring into the flesh of her wrist; no, she was not still asleep. The little ivory warrior from Cathay fell out of her lap, and she picked him up and set him beside the sacred figures of the prior's gift; he and they regarded her benignly, and Zoster Adela looked a little anxious.

'What's amiss, dear heart?' she asked.

'Nothing,' answered Yolande, 'It's only a piece of nonsense I had forgotten.'

Her heart smote her that she should lie to Zoster Adela; but this was something that needed care and thought. The writing was Lioncel's, and only Diomede or he could have made the verses. *Priokin* was the prior, Diomede's kinsman; *the helm* was Sanctlamine. Diomede had escaped from the tree, Lioncel from the lake . . . why must they be banished and write her a cryptic message? *Why* did not the prior say anything about them? *Why* did he have his cramps just now? *How* could she reach him and find out what only he and the exiles knew?

Lioncel and Diomede, alive and safe . . . no, not safe, but alive, and pledged to find her again. . . .

The morning's fantastic outrage burned redly in her mind; the afternoon's fantastic tidings lit a different flame, a sun-gold radiance of hope and courage. Yolande found to her surprise that she could contain these different energies without their interfering with each other. She supposed it was part of growing up.

When she replaced her treasures she added to them the privy signet of Baraine. Amarand, with his arm lowered, presented to the world an inscrutable cheerfulness. Yolande helmed him with satisfaction.

'Now I can meet Balthasar again without spitting at him,' she thought. 'I don't know where *they* are, but *they* know where *I* am. Before I dress for tonight's banquet I shall write to Dom Gilomar. Reverend Mother Abbess will send the letter for me. Queen of the Elves . . . I'm caught, and I must be stealthy. Blood on my wedding-ring. I don't want *ever* to be the wife of Balthasar. I must be meek and obedient and win all hearts. And I have two years before I must start breeding the next duke. Two years in which to seem shy, and to become a leopardess.'

The second banquet of that sequence proved even more memorable than the first. Yolande wrote her letter to the prior, and begged from the abbess a finger's-breadth of mulberry wine, with fennel in it, before she emerged in blue and silver to meet Balthasar in bronze and orange and head the formal procession into the hall.

When the guests mustered the Duke of Elquitaine was found to be missing; enquiry confirmed the whispered rumour that he was dead drunk in his bed. This discourtesy pleased Yolande, for it brought to her left hand her distant kinsman and heir-presumptive, Raoul Count of Ger. She remembered to thank him for the two white palfreys which were his wedding-gift to her.

The noise and glitter and surfeit proceeded as before; Balthasar and she were civil with each other, neither of them referring to their morning's encounter. The Duchess of Trevence was in great good humour; the new Duke of Baraine had tired himself out in her service the previous night.

There were more poems of a sort to be read, more clinking of crystal goblets, and very many good things to be eaten. Yolande made an excellent meal, smiling aside each time she caught the solicitous eye of Zoster Adela.

'What have you done to your hands, my lady?' murmured the bearded count.

Yolande glanced at him; he was very handsome in a queer, slightly devilish way, with high cheekbones, an ivory-brown skin, an aquiline nose, and a pointed chin-beard under a strong full-lipped mouth. His eyes were grey-green with little amber flecks in them; their gaze was steady and friendly, and Yolande much preferred it to that of the Duke of Elquitaine.

'My kitten scratched me,' she said simply. 'My lord my husband was teaching me a first lesson in obedience. . . .'

She found that she could tell the tale without wanting to cry. The smile went out of the count's eyes before he looked down at his plate.

'And now,' finished Yolande, 'he is trying to make me drunk to show that he bears no grudge.'

She nodded at the grey-haired serving-man, who tonight was behind the old duchess.

'Pass your cups to me,' said Raoul of Ger softly, and turned to say something in the ear of a squire who stepped forward from the screen.

'Is this someone else I can trust?' Yolande wondered, and did as he advised, keeping her lips tight shut against three out of four of the drinks Balthasar pressed her to take. Estragon, Malvoisie, Chian enough to have kept a soldier happy for a day passed under her nose into the count's care; the squire conjured with the goblets, and Yolande saw them no more.

'Enough, my lord,' she said gaily to Balthasar. 'I must keep my wits to add up to fifteen.'

'Why fifteen?' demanded Balthasar solemnly.

'My lord of Ger is showing me how to make a magic square.'

'Eh? Oh, that nonsense; have you never seen it before?'

'No, I was never at the Archduke's court. My lord, your other duchess would have a word with you.'

Balthasar turned again towards the marvellous white shoulder and painted red lips of Ermengarde of Trevence, leaving Yolande to watch the tablets of the Count Raoul. He had pulled them, with a style, from his purse, and was making the square of points numbered from one to nine in such a way that however she added them in threes they totalled fifteen.

Then he joined the points in numerical sequence, making a symmetrical figure in the wax.

'This is the Square of Saturn,' he said. 'Remember that shape, and you can always place the numbers.'

'It's like an orderly flash of lightning,' said Yolande. 'Very useful, my lord, for one who must live with a thunderbolt.'

Raoul of Ger glanced at her and smiled, and they both looked up at the first of the evening's pageants.

Satyrs, woodhouses, dwarfs and mummers hauled on the ropes of a gilded car shaped as a Ship of Fortune. Under the prow sat a beautiful girl naked to the loins and then sheathed in a mermaid's tail of thin leathern scales painted in metallic colours.

She herself was painted blue-green; from her gilt-metal head-dress flowed a frizz of gilded wire, and she had gilded eyebrows and lips and nipples and finger-nails. She plucked at a lyre or pulled a cord which shut a lid over one of the great eyes painted beside the ship's stem-post. This lid flew back of its own accord, producing a gigantic wink which delighted the beholders.

In the vessel above her was Fortune herself, gorgeously dressed, and nursing a winged wheel; with her were two maidens crowned with laurel and carrying cornucopias. The inevitable jester flailed his bladder from the stern.

The mermaid waved at Balthasar and Yolande, and Fortune saluted them. The maidens raised their horns in greeting, the jester shook his combed crest and cackled a couplet in which the goddess was called the *marraine* of Baraine. When they reached the far end of the hall the girls showered coins into the crowd; even the full green breasts of the mermaid were forgotten in the ensuing scrimmage.

Then the monkey rode his pig at a quintain, and tumblers built human pyramids, and dancers staged a mock battle, beating out a tune with bells on their quarterstaves. A dwarf on stilts fenced with a dwarf on a pony; a juggler balanced cups and swords, and a tightrope walker waggled a pole with a pasteboard leopard at one end of it and a pasteboard thunderbolt at the other.

'A delicate process indeed,' said the Count of Ger, as if to himself.

Yolande looked down again at the cedarwood tablets beside her dish.

'My lord, may I take these and copy the square and let you have them again?' she asked.

'Take them, cousin,' said the count, for the first time acknowledging their distant kinship. 'But don't trouble to send them back.'

'But I must send them back,' she told him, closing the delicate hinged lid with its enamelled yellow shield charged with a black gerfalcon.

Then she put a ringed finger on one of the bright sable wings, and changed her mind.

'No my lord, I must not send them back,' she murmured. 'I must keep them to bring *me* fortune.'

'Why should they do that?'

'Because they are given to a girl, not to a duchess. As a duchess I have great good fortune; as a girl, very little.'

That must sound silly, she thought, and did not care.

Raoul of Ger put a finger of his own against the side of the tablets and pushed them towards her.

'If ever you should send them again,' he promised, 'I shall know I may be of some service to you. Then I will do what a kinsman may to help his kinswoman. Remember, I have lands in Queranay. If I should happen to visit them my way can lie through Bargreant, or Roclatour, or . . . Pardelin.'

'I shall never forget that, my lord,' said Yolande, slipping the shaped cedarwood into her own girdle-purse. 'And now, see what comes; the famous Nestor must have recovered from his cut thumb and his sulks.'

The tall wheeled booth had appeared in the doorway, trundled by the sad-looking man as if it were a wheelbarrow. His wife was nowhere to be seen, and he made no response to the buzz of recognition, advancing carefully until he could halt opposite the centre of the top table. Then he swept off his hat and bowed to Balthasar and Yolande, to the Grand Seneschal, and again to the Bishop; and when he pushed back his hood his eyes were bright and staring and unfamiliar. An almost wolfish grin suddenly creased his haggard face.

'Have you seen him before?' asked Yolande of her new friend.

'Yes,' replied Raoul of Ger, bending forward with his elbows on the table, and then leaning back to speak to his squire.

'Go and tell my lord Grand Seneschal,' he commanded, 'that this fellow is either very sick, or drunk, or both together.'

Nestor's owner was now standing motionless, as if waiting for silence. One of his hands still held his hat; the other was on the bar of the booth door. The din in the hall lessened and died to a murmur; pages and serving-men stood still; guests broke off their chatter and craned their necks or turned in their places. The marshal of the feast reined in his pacing charger;

his bridle was hung with little bells, and their sweet jingling outlasted any other sound.

Of course he must have silence for the ape to be heard, Yolande told herself. Then she saw the glisten of sweat on the man's pale forehead; and at the same instant he broke into a loud rasping rigmarole.

'Great lords and beautiful ladies, and all here present, you have heard how King Solomon of old had a fleet which every three years brought from Tarshish gold and silver, elephants' tusks, apes and peacocks. Here is a leader wise as Solomon, skilful in war as Joshua, and here with our brave duke and our lovely duchess are the gold, the ivory, the peacocks . . . but, lords and ladies, *there is no ape!*'

'Many of you have seen and heard of my Nestor, and have listened to him talking sense like a Christian. Nestor said to me three days ago: *Never disappoint the good folk by whom we get our modest living.* Having said this, he, being grievously sick, died . . . and my wife and I buried him in the woods along the river. . . .'

A buzzing murmur arose in the hall, and the man waited until it had passed.

'Having no longer Nestor to advise me, I took counsel with my wife as to how we should entertain you on this most auspicious occasion, and she, being the best of wives, offered to look back upon this city, so that if God were minded to work a miracle for our salvation, she might become a pillar of salt, and so take Nestor's place as a wonder among the fairs and markets. . . .

'So, lords and ladies all, my gentle wife turned her about and raised an arm in supplication, and the Sieur God was very merciful, and here in my booth she stands, safely tied up, a marvel for all to see!'

'By Our Lady, he's mad,' said Raoul of Ger, as the showman twitched open the door of the booth.

Already many people were laughing, expecting cause for laughter; others grinned in expectation as they saw the sheeted figure with one arm held up and forward. Then the sheet was torn away, and a long *a-a-a-ah!* of astonishment rose to break in a chorus of shouts and screams and a crash of overset chairs and servers' benches.

The showman's wife stood stark and dead; her eyes were shut, her face was bandaged under the chin, her upflung arm was naked. Naked, too, were her left breast and side; and around the smudge of hair in the armpit were half a dozen blackish swellings, two of them bearded with a filthy dried exudation.

The showman's face was now an appalling mask of glee; he howled with laughter, and caught up a canvas bag, and began throwing the little wooden images of Nestor this way and that at the backing, huddling figures about him.

'*Shoot him!*' thundered Azo, with no change of expression in his bland flushed face. Three archers flung up their bows, the long shafts whizzed into the lean body, and the showman's howl was cut short as he collapsed like a sack at the foot of his gruesome show.

Yolande had reached round and caught at the count's arm; the arm came about her body and drew her to her feet. Balthasar was dragging up the screeching Duchess of Trevence; Yolande glanced aside and reflected that Ermengarde would not screech if she knew how absurd she looked. Further down the table a woman had fainted, her horned headdress upsetting cups and goblets as it banged down on the board. The hall was full of panic din, the doorways were blocked with struggling people, and around the grotesque central figures was left a wide empty space. No one, in fact, was nearer to them than were bridegroom and bride and principal guests; calmly the Grand Seneschal motioned them all towards the ends of the great screen, remaining with the Bishop and three captains, who presently broke away from him and began to shout at the chevaliers and archers on duty. The marshal steered his charger clear of the rout and came up to the dais, making a wide detour round the canvas booth. Before Raoul of Ger had got Yolande past the end of the screen, servants and soldiers were throwing benches and faggots and straw to make a pyre about the corpses. Oil was splashed on it, and Yolande saw the Sieur de Caherne fling a first torch into the heap. Great

F

smoke-wreaths puffed up, and some of those who had laughed
when others laughed now screamed anew because others
screamed. Yolande's last glimpse of that feast showed her a
page vomiting on one of the tables, while another page tried
to drag him away, and a third picked up a flagon and drank
with none to rebuke him.

Then she was in the antechamber, where nobles and
chevaliers were snatching at cloaks and swordbelts, and cursing
their attendants. The abbess and the two nuns struggled
through the crowd to where she stood, still with the count's
arm around her; Berel de Forne, whitefaced and shaky, got to
the curtain which covered the passage leading to the ducal
apartments in time to draw it aside for the party to pass.

The count would have let go Yolande's waist, but she caught
his hand and held it.

' Please come with us,' she said.

So Raoul of Ger escorted them along a cloister walk where
thin snow was blowing in across the low wall. All horrors
notwithstanding, Yolande found a pleasure in that change
from glare and uproar to silence and darkness lit only by an
occasional wall-torch. These four older people were all she
cared about in the castle; for already the count had taken a
place with Zoster Adela in her heart. When he bent to kiss
her hand in farewell she put her other hand boldly on his
crimson velvet shoulder.

'My lord, we are cousins,' she reminded him, and lifted her
mouth for another kiss.

' God prosper you, Cousin Yolande,' he said, and bowed to
the abbess, and was gone.

Tumult eddied through the castle; orders came that Yolande
must be ready at dawn for instant return to Roclatour. The
ground was hard with a three days' frost, and from a tower
window Yolande saw the opening of the east gate and the first
sparkle of torches over snow as flight from the city began.
None of these alarms could altogether destroy the satisfaction
of knowing that no matter which way she added them up, the
figures scratched in wax by her kinsman would come to fifteen.

VI

JEHANE'S WAY

'THERE was no help for it,' gabbled Jehane de Xantroy.
'I said to my husband, I said, we've no more than three hours
to pack, we shall have to leave a mort of gear to be sent on,
especially my prie-dieu, it was given me by my brother, you
know him, the Duke of Camors, he was to have come to the
wedding but three of his gentlemen are dead of the plague,
God have mercy on us, so we got no sleep at all, the pack-
horses were out in the street before my plate was chested, my
lord Grand Seneschal had hardly left us, my husband had to
muster his men, you never know where the rogues have got to,
and I had to send for the damsels, you've not met them, that
is you only saw them get into the litters. . . .'

'Yes, my lady,' said Yolande.

'. . . Aurania is my cousin's daughter, not on the Camors
side, she's a Medrincourt from Honoy, Douce I've only seen
twice, no, three times, she's a Verville, my sister's husband's
cousin, she was at the christening of my niece Maude, she's
a quiet little thing, she wanted to bring a great basket, I said
what's in that. . . .'

'Dear blessed Virgin Mary,' said Yolande silently, 'you
know what was in the basket, please help me to keep awake,
please help me mind my manners, please guide me through
this dreadful Christmastide, for your pity to all virgins and
for the sake of the First Christmas, amen.'

Yolande was hooded and cloaked and gauntleted and
muffled in furs over the ears; at her left side the curtain-straps
of the four-horse litter creaked as the north wind battered at
the canvas. On her right the curtain was laced back a little,
giving her a narrow view of towers and ramparts of Bargreant,
and on the sunrise that pushed their blue shadows over the

frozen fields. The column of horses and litters had left the castle by the eastern gate to avoid traversing the city, and so had to skirt the suburbs to gain the westward road.

And here, opposite her, so that their knees nearly touched, was Dame Jehane, whom Uncle Azo had suddenly produced like an apparition popped up through the floor of the stage in a Shrovetide mystery. . . .

Azo had visited Yolande before she went to bed; his only concession to the occasion was that he carried an elegant pomander which surrounded him with a scent of cloves. Once or twice he had made as if to carry this gaud up to his nose; then he had lowered it again, absolving Yolande's apartments of any suspicion of infection. And with him had appeared glum Odard, leading by the hand a tall dark woman whose long glowering face seemed ravaged with grief and disappointment.

'I am providing that Your Grace shall at once take up residence at Roclatour,' said Azo, without more ado. 'My lord of Xantroy, the castellan, is already known to you. His wife, my lady Jehane, will be your governess. Your tutor will follow; he is Dom Ursus Campestris, lately returned from the University of Padua. He will conduct your studies for the next two years.'

Yolande forgot the admonition of the old Duchess of Queranay, and dropped a polite curtsey to the pair who were to guard and guide her. The Sieur Odard bowed grimly; Dame Jehane's visage suffered a lateral softening, and Dame Jehane's long limbs responded with a curtsey more prolonged and magnificent than Yolande's own.

'Reverend Mother Abbess, I pray you will excuse us,' said Azo with something less than his customary deliberation. 'You and these ladies must have some sleep; and for all your care of this dear child, the Sieur God will reward you.'

'And you for yours, my lord Grand Seneschal,' returned the abbess grimly. 'We shall be happy to see her often at the convent.'

'That will be as my lady of Xantroy decides,' said Azo, and bowed himself and his companions out.

What took six tirewomen hours to arrange was stripped off

by Zoster Adela in something over ten minutes. Shaking her hair loose, Yolande glanced up at the nun's forbidding frown.

'Did Reverend Mother Abbess know about Dame Jehane?' she asked.

'I think not,' growled Zoster Adela, her hands suddenly tightening on the towel she had placed around Yolande's body. 'You'll have to be careful with that one, my sweet. She was getting ready to hate you if you'd waited for her to curtsey first.'

'Was *that* what was the matter with her?'

'That and more, I'll warrant. She looks to me like a born grudger. But speak her fair, speak her very fair.'

'I wish *you* were coming to the castle with me.'

'Dear Saint Marthe be witness, so do I, sweetheart.'

Yolande stood up, half-naked, and flung her arms around the broad linen-encumbered shoulders.

'Without you, dear Zoster,' she said, 'I should have been crushed into a . . . a pudding of misery.'

Zoster Adela's broad forehead grew thunderous in the candle-light; blessing and healing seemed to flow from her strong hand into Yolande's spine. . . .

But now Zoster Adela was four litters away, and the ghostly shape of a misery pudding was forming under Yolande's ribs. *Yes, my lady,* and *no, my lady,* and *indeed, my lady,* escaped her lips at intervals, but they were barely needed to oil the clattering tongue of Jehane. . . .

'. . . not only that, it was the anniversary of my daughter's death, her name was Yolande, no one knows what it's like to lose a child unless they have lost one themselves, and even then it's not like losing three . . . none of my own family, cousins included, has had such sorrow, I don't like to talk about it, I never say a word to strangers, one of my sisters lost a boy and Saints know she made enough fuss, these things are in the hands of the Sieur God, He is our only refuge, sometimes you find a priest who knows how to bring consolation, half of them are just men taught to play a part, consolation isn't in them, they don't know how to comfort a woman, they're like all men in that, men forget more easily, God forgive them, they're often very stupid, I remember my own father, I was his favourite daughter, my father gave me a chestnut palfrey and promised me golden bells for the bridle when he came back from Hautarroy, and he forgot, and I cried all night, and he sent for the bells, and I was very glad to have them, but every time I looked at them I remembered the grief, there's nothing so grievous as presents gone awry, I saw your great array of presents, it reminded me of my brother's wedding, but that was in the summer, we danced on the grass by torch-light. . . .'

' I wish. . . .'

' Uh? What did you say, child? '

' I wish my wedding could have been in summer,' said Yolande softly, already beginning to realise how to please Jehane.

' Yes, it was very splendid, the king was there, old King Réné I mean, whom God hold in keeping, he was very kind to me when I was a child . . . Hautarroy was a happy place in those days, have you been there often? '

' Three times, my lady.'

' I had lived there for years when I was your age, merry winters they were, do you know the Hotel de Camors? '

' I think I remember it, my lady.'

' You must remember it, it's the finest of all the noble houses in the great square by the cathedral. Four wind-vanes on the towers, great copper stags of Camors, the gardens reach down to the river, I never saw finer gardens, even the king's or the archbishop's, the old archbishop was my mother's cousin, his herbarium was the best this side of the Alps, I learned the properties of herbs from his apothecary, he was a very learned man from Constantinople, do you know how to prepare remedies against the pestilence, or against cramps, or fluxes, or fevers? '

' No, my lady.'

' Then I'll teach you, I know these things, the apothecary said he had never had such an apt pupil as I was, there's a room in the castle next to the armoury, with a well-chain going through the floor, and a wide chimney, that'll serve. My mother used to say I'd the deftest hands in the whole family . . . these two damsels, I wonder if they'll prove willing, girls nowadays are not well grounded in household tasks, if they can sing to a lute that's all they think of. I never took much heed of a lute, I'm not swayed by music as so many are, I was always for binding up wounds in my dolls, my aunt of Beltany used to call me her little wise-woman, I learned to read very early, not that I think a girl should read so much that she gives herself a frown and a stoop and won't sew when she should, but I believe in the quiet wisdom of women, the kind that's handed on when men aren't there to listen, of course I mean women of rank and dignity, there's nothing more absurd than the airs the burghers' wives give themselves these days, wearing furs and girdles as if they had coat-armour, where would their rich husbands be if the nobles didn't beat back the foreigners and stamp out thieves and outlaws, like my lord Grand Seneschal? '

' Where indeed, my lady? '

' When this accursed plague has abated we'll have tourneys at Roclatour, perhaps in the spring, at first we must keep the castle clear of all but our own people, no friars and packmen sniffing round the gate, Saints be praised, there's no need nów of a great rabble of soldiers, it's they who eat up the stores and stick greedy heads in at the kitchen windows, at Camors we never had less than five hundred to feed, counting in the boat-men and masons, they were building all the time I was young, now a tower and now a rampart, and new stables and a new chapel, I used to climb the ladders and frighten my nurses, Reckless Jehane, the steward called me, I was a great one for liberty, I say children should grow up to be bold and hardy, not, of course, forward or beyond control, they should always be obedient to anyone set over them. . . .'

' Anyone like yourself,' remarked Yolande in her own mind, that already had begun to rear defences against this tide of egotism. She missed a turn of the discourse, and found it had gone on to the matter of omens.

'. . . I pray there are no ravens at Roclatour, at any rate that none of them nest in the castle, I cannot abide ravens, especially in the winter season, or indeed any birds at all, when they come close for food they look at you like departed souls, I say that in jest of course, it would be wickedness else, I was always known for my jesting, Merry Jehane, the old archbishop used to call me, God rest his soul, not knowing what bitterness was to be mine, and always there were ravens at hand when sorrow was to befall me, or if not ravens, then crows or rooks, or sometimes it was just magpies. When my daughter was taken to God there were owls crying all night in the woods, and when my younger son fell ill a hart of ten was found dying, his antlers locked in a hawthorn bush, so that he couldn't release himself and had starved there at the edge of the forest. He was lucky no wolf had found him thus. . . .'

'Was he?' asked Yolande, fascinated.

'Uh? What d'you say? Was he what?'

'Lucky to starve instead of being killed by a wolf.'

'I was never one for splitting hairs of subtlety like the schoolmen, for nights together I had no sleep, it was spring-time and the stock of fruits and berries was exhausted, I had a sovereign remedy that lacked only one ingredient of eighteen, I should have saved him had I had it, it was the white wort of Saint Hiltrude, my lord my husband was hunting outlaws, and had no time to attend to it, at least he left it too late, his servant had failed to find it, I was desperate, I pledged my gold cross to buy the worts, those who have always had what they want can never understand how glad I was to give up a treasure to save a dear life, the child died as my husband rode in at the city gate with a basket of the worts. . . .'

'Oh, my lady, how dreadful for him!'

'Uh? Dreadful for *him*? More dreadful for *me*, badly served as I was, and very ill myself, I who when I was young had a maid and two lackeys of my own . . . I took the worts and threw them in the fire, and the apothecary mumbled that he would gladly have bought them, but I said no, I could never have taken money for that basket of herbs, and my husband's sister, and she a nun, had the hardihood to blame me, saying the worts might have been given as alms at the town spital, but how could she understand the sorrows of a mother, never having been one?'

'She could not,' said Yolande.

'I never believe in masking my humours, the lineage of Camors is famous for its hasty generous temper, quick to blame and quick to forgive, I can't understand these brooding slow revengeful minds, it's foreign to my nature, my brothers were both like that as boys, they fought up and down stairs all day but wouldn't sleep apart at night, and when my elder brother was slain the other took no food for days, and I all but lost him too. . . .'

'It was happy you did not, my lady,' said Yolande.

'Happy? Perhaps, yes, or so it seemed. He was held a prisoner after the war between the king and his cousin. . . .'

'You mean the rebellion,' thought Yolande.

'. . . and when one is restored to high rank and another has married boldly but rashly according to natural inclination it's not always easy to hold a family together. Nor to forget cruel slights and selfishness that darken the colour of kinship . . . I was the youngest and too much given to admiration of the others, my sisters are the Countesses of Muron and Verville, but I don't think I need ask them to visit us at Roclatour. . . .'

The dolorous spate of self-praise and self-justification went on. The white hills grew steadily out of the white plain, the noses of the mounted escort turned red and blue in the icy wind, and Yolande ceased to interject an occasional remark; her courtesy gradually crumpled before the assault of weariness.

'. . . but I'm like that, I must have things in order, I remember once at Camors, I should be about your age, we were out in the woods at Lammas-tide gathering elecampane roots, although to be sure it was rather early, I generally leave them now till October, it's a marvellous remedy for malignant fevers, and some even use it against the black plague itself, and the old story is that Dame Helen had her hands full of the flowers when the Sieur Paris came and carried her off to Troy, and my niece Alys, fell in a stream, she was always a tedious bawling child, and being so near in age we hated each other like sisters—he, he!—and one of the squires hauled her out.

and I hung a wreath of elecampane round his neck, I never
liked him, he had a long horse-face and it looked like a horse-
collar. . . .'

'She *can* laugh, then,' thought Yolande, who now even for
politeness' sake could not summon any answering sound.
The muscles around her eyes were contracting; the edge of her
hood concealed their drooping lids. She never learned the
connection between the gathering of elecampane roots and the
orderliness of Dame Jehane. The jarring voice became word-
less as the croaking of a chorus of frogs; it slowly receded
behind a curtain of sleep.

The halting of the litter jolted her awake. The lifted visor
of Odard de Xantroy gleamed against the gateway of a fortified
inn.

'Here's a mean-looking tavern,' exclaimed Dame Jehane,
as though the lonely moorland village had at least three taverns
better than this one chosen by her husband.

Odard said nothing, but held out a hand to help Yolande
descend.

'I pray you will go first, my lady,' said Yolande quickly,
wondering how long the morning's monologue had gone on
unheeded.

With a groan, as of suffering heroically controlled, the tall
daughter of Camors levered herself up and out. Yolande
followed, and presently her new damsels were brought to kiss
her hand. Aurania was plump and blonde and shy, Douce
pale and very composed. Dame Jehane began to order them
about before they were out of masculine earshot.

'Remember, both of you,' she bade them, 'that Her Grace
is accustomed to very skilful service. Aurania, don't fumble
with your cloak; I'm as cold as you are or colder, keep your
hands folded as I do when you are in attendance . . . be quick,
hold the curtain aside for Reverend Mother Abbess. . . .'

'If she keeps her hands folded she will need to use her
teeth,' said the abbess, smiling at the flustered eighteen-year-
old Aurania.

Dame Jehane's face stiffened with bitter amusement. Was

this jealous old churchwoman—only second cousin to a duke—trying to slight the authority of Jehane de Xantroy?

'Our own servants will wait on us here,' she said abruptly. 'My lord Grand Seneschal will have no one approach Your Grace save those of the household.'

No one had anything to say to that. Later, as they sat down to a meal, Yolande caught Zoster Adela's hand and squeezed it hard in passing.

After the wine Dame Jehane's mood changed to one of distant dignity. The Sieur Odard found that Douce was a cousin, not only of his wife's brother-in-law, but also of his own sister's husband. Mention of the shrine of Saint-Maur-by-Dunsberghe brought the abbess into the desultory conversation. Yolande ate well and drank all that was offered her, wearing her bright company face in front of desolation.

At length she took advantage of a pause to address herself to Odard.

'My lord, do you know Dom Ursus Campestris?'

The castellan's impassive face came round towards her.

'No, Your Grace, I do not,' he said. 'Dom Ursus is a Dominican and learned; that is all, I have heard of him. We shall do our best to make him very welcome at Roclatour.'

Yolande inclined her head and widened her mouth a little, hoping the extension would be taken for a smile.

Christmas in the castle of Roclatour with the Sieur and Dame de Xantroy . . . a shapeless but formidable tutor bulking below the horizon . . . the thought of Lioncel and Diomede like a dream slipping beyond recall . . . the ghastly banquet still less than twenty-four hours away . . . the friendly Count of Ger, by now no doubt riding northward to his wife and children and Coast March, leaving only the cedarwood tablets to mock a huge loneliness. . . .

'Aurania and Douce will be Dame Jehane's ladies-in-waiting, not mine,' she told herself sourly. 'And now I must be a good girl, or at least, look like one. Hide away my distrust and fear and hatred. Grow claws, but not show them.'

That night, in an abbey guesthouse, she slept with Aurania

and Douce. The three of them had little to say to each other; Aurania seemed overawed and depressed, and the one remark she ventured was not a success.

'My lady duchess,' she began after a pause, 'I saw you at a window the other evening holding a most beautiful kitten. Have you brought it with you?'

'No,' said Yolande stonily. 'It . . . he . . . was killed yesterday morning by two of my lord duke's hounds.'

'Oh . . . oh, my lady, I am sorry . . . what a dreadful mischance on such a day. . . .'

'A not unseemly beginning, remembering what came after,' said Yolande, and wondered if it seemed callous or pompous to talk like that. Listening to Jehane made you critical of your own speech. The grave considering gaze of Douce was going to be useful, too; it would restrain you from candour or mockery or open anger.

Before she fell asleep Yolande was aware of a steady sound from the next room; it went on and on, being the voice of Dame Jehane. It was punctuated by short and shorter remarks in the deeper tones of the Sieur Odard.

'Saint Amarand be praised she's married, so that I don't have to sleep in her room,' thought Yolande. 'No wonder the Sieur de Xantroy looks as if he drank marsh-water. Even so, he must be made of iron.'

At twilight two days later she bade a subdued farewell to the abbess and the two nuns. At midnight Mass in the church of Saint Michael she would presently see them again, but by then it would be different; the castle walls would already have stood for a while between them and herself.

Those walls duly engulfed her; women she had never seen before timidly took her heavy cloak and opened her clothes-chests to find her a lighter one for indoor wear. On her way to the solar for supper she found Jehane gabbling to the Sieur Odard by a great fire in an anteroom.

This anteroom was built against the curtain wall between the keep and the hall; it was reached from the first floor of the keep by a handsome stone staircase.

'This will be the chamber of parade,' Jehane was saying. 'Those hangings of Theseus and the Minotaur will cover this wall here, two benches can go *there*, no, it will be better to have one against the staircase, or see, why not set a screen at the door and put one bench in front of it? Then a trestle table can stand in the corner, a big one, to be set with wine and comfits, so that the servants needn't come through the hall and solar . . . now here's my lady duchess . . . my lady, this will make a famous chamber of parade. . . .'

Odard was listening politely, but in his gloomy tawny eyes Yolande read a look which might have meant: *Who the devil does she think will use her chamber of parade?*

'I'm sure you'll arrange it beautifully, my lady,' she said, moving forward from the foot of the stair with Douce and Aurania behind her.

'Of course, it's small,' went on Jehane, with an unseeing glance at the white-haired steward standing beside the solar door. "And two, no, three more torch-brackets are needed, and a candelabrum on the table, there's a bronze one in the armoury will do, my mother, God rest her soul, always used to say that the quarrels in hall were fewer by half when the candles were lit as well as the torches, we'll have rushes strewn here, no, pine-needles, at Camors we had pine-needles in all the principal chambers from Christmas until Easter and sometimes even beyond.'

'So please Your Grace, supper is served,' said the steward rapidly.

Yolande led the way into the solar, where the gilded tusks of a boar's head faintly echoed the splendours prepared for Christmas Eve at Bargreant.

'All those costly presents still there,' thought Yolande with dreary amusement. 'They'll have to follow after the guests. What a dim and dingy little castle this is going to be!'

Dom Cyril had fluffy white hair that stood out like a cloud around his tonsure and above the gold-embroidered collar of the white chasuble. When he came to the Gradual, *tecum principium in die virtutis tuae*, 'with Thee is the principality in the day of Thy strength,' Yolande found herself applying the words to Balthasar and the duchy. And when Dom Cyril took the chalice to the right to receive the wine and water, Yolande for the first time in her life was unmoved by the gesture of preparation.

It was made so often, that gesture—with so much love and devotion—and still kind fathers were killed by outlaws, and kittens by jeering boys, vicious noblemen fingered the breasts of helpless girls, and cherished wives died hideously of the black pestilence. . . .

When Dom Cyril elevated for adoration first the Body and then the Blood, Yolande felt no checked heart-beat, no magical or majestical thrill of communion. Instead she was ravaged by loneliness and sadness; in her mind's eye the Sieur Jesus was a Son left to die on the Cross, the Virgin Mary a Mother with seven swords in her heart. Behind their tortured shapes was horrifying fog and silence.

In the fog appeared a vision of what she tried not to remember—a vision of two gigantic staghounds, one white and the other black. A little something twirled in the dimness above their twin heads; they reached aside and caught it and tore it asunder. . . .

Dom Cyril's voice reciting the *Paternoster* seemed to come from very far away. Yolande shivered with pain and rage, setting her teeth to endure the shock and memory of the vision. She supposed it to have been a machination of the devil . . . but at such a moment you might have expected the Sieur God to quench or forbid it.

The maimed and giftless Christmas season brought with it a snowstorm. The snow blew in at narrow windows, the gale whistled and howled in stony corridors and entries, the household went cloaked and hooded all day and huddled around the fires and braziers. By order of the Grand Seneschal, castle and town held a minimum of converse; business between them was conducted in the barbican, where a huge fire of wormwood smoked continually beside the gate. Yolande might not visit the convent; Dom Cyril might not leave the castle; and archers shot from the ramparts at wolves running boldly in the fringes of the woods.

Wind in the worn stone, and shovels in the courtyards, formed an accompaniment for the voice of Dame Jehane. To her strident and sometimes conflicting commands she added scowls and strange gestures, so that the servants who swept and scoured and hauled gear up and down the stairways occasionally stood amazed instead of carrying out an order.

' You'd think she was milking a bloody cow,' said an archer to a kitchen girl, who gasped as Yolande came upon them at the head of the anteroom stair. Yolande pretended not to have heard; the scene below secured her attention. The hangings embroidered with the story of Theseus were going up along one wall. Dame Jehane sat hooded and bellowing beneath the opposite wall; occasionally she fisted the air as if either to help or strike the serving-men who shifted ladders and struggled with the heavy fabric.

' Keeps 'em warm in this weather,' said Griflet, captain of the archers, to the old steward at the stair-foot. Yolande heard him too, but that did not worry the bronzed and handsome captain; Griflet had quickly understood that at Roclatour his duchess was not much more than a prisoner.

Dame Jehane was growing angry; her language became obscure and impacted.

' . . . what I want is what I want—that end further along, don't you see if the, there, you pick it up, pick it up man, don't let it drag on the—give it to him, now move your ladder, come down, move your—come down, don't stand there gaping, you with the green hood, give him a—hand it over, no lift, that's right, no, it's the wrong piece, the next one's the Minotaur in the Labyrinth, *the next one's the Minotaur in the Labyrinth*, I believe they've got that upside down, the Minotaur isn't at that end, Saints why are you so stupid, it's not that piece at all then, hold it so that I can see, so that I can see, put it—see put it on the floor, be quick, you with the blue tunic, hand it up to him, don't tread on the—ship's sails are next but one, if you stand there staring you booby I'll have you whipped—out of my sight. . . .'

'I'm sure you'll arrange everything beautifully, my lady,'
repeated Yolande to herself as she skirted the field of action.
Some of the watchers were staring open-mouthed; the dutiful
Aurania was pink with embarrassment, and Douce, standing
behind Jehane's chair, was still-faced as if at a funeral. Jehane
spared Yolande only one of her wild unseeing glances; it was
Douce who motioned to an archer to set forward another
chair.

'What a fool I was to come out of my bedroom,' thought
Yolande, smiling at him. Then, as she sat down and drew
her hood forward, lightning winked in the leaden sky beyond
the high windows, and a long roll of thunder jarred the antechamber floor.

'Winter's thunder, summer's wonder,' bayed Dame Jehane.
'Get on with your work, it's Thursday, Thursday's thunder
promises plenty of sheep and corn, up with that end, blue-
tunic . . . careless knaves, you've missed a loop, lower it again,
come down, stay where you are, can't you understand a simple
order? You there with your wet boots, stand aside from where
—they have to be told every move, I've seen two lads at Camors
do better than all the pack of you, take up that slack, take up
that slack, help them someone, God have mercy, have you all
nothing to do but stand around staring. . . .'

'Of course they haven't,' thought Yolande, 'with snow
two feet deep on the ramparts. It's as good as as mystery play,
thunder and lightning and all. Jehane is Lady of Misrule . . .
shame on me for finding it funny . . . it's like something out of
my fever . . . *how we rickled the ramkins in the chamber of
parade.*'

In the week after Epiphany the name of Yolande's new
tutor went through the castle like a rustle of dry leaves. 'Dom
Ursus Campestris is here,' they said; and Yolande first saw
the friar as he directed the removal of two chests from the
great horse-sledge that had followed him over the white and
frozen hills from Jarapt.

He was youngish, this Master of Theology—youngish and
florid and bulky in his heavy black cloak and great furred

riding-hood. His beautiful black boots were spurred with silver, and little enamel plaques adorned his fur-lined riding-gloves. His nose was a beak with flared nostrils; he had a sleek blue-black jowl and prominent grey eyes, and a tiny skull of rock-crystal grinned from a great gold ring on the hand he raised to bless Yolande.

'My lady,' he called her, not 'Your Grace,' or 'Sister in God.' She thought he looked both cruel and courtly, and inwardly shrank a little further into her shell of submissiveness.

'I am very happy to greet you, Dom Ursus,' she told him almost in a whisper.

The regard of the bold prominent eyes flicked across her face to the faces of Odard and Jehane. Everybody was very polite; when the floodgates of Jehane's speech were loosed, Dom Ursus waited a moment in the icy blast of the hall doorway, and then at Odard's gesture turned to walk beside her as she talked. Odard and Yolande followed silently behind.

Into the torrent of words Dom Ursus thrust replies that occasioned a swirl or eddy before they were driven under.

'. . . waiting and wondering here how the folk at court are faring, we've had messengers from my lord Grand Seneschal but you never know from day to day what the pestilence will do, my lord how is he, and my lord duke too? My lady duchess has been sorely worried, it was a dreadful shock to us all, the merry-making all undone, you were not at the banquet?'

'No,' said Dom Ursus. 'According to my latest letter, my lords are both well. I came direct from Jarapt, avoiding Bargreant. The plague's not in the castle. That is, not yet. Thirty have died in the city.'

'God have mercy on us. . . .'

'And on them,' said Dom Ursus.

'Yes, yes, of course, as many as that already, so far we've nothing at Roclatour, it's not often the pestilence lasts so far into cold weather, we thought Bargreant had escaped, I said to my husband only a week since, I said we'd do well if so great a crowd didn't bring it somehow, that wretched madman has much to answer for. . . .'

'No doubt he's answering for it,' said Dom Ursus.

' Yes, God forgive him, and Mary have pity on all of us, I
fear he was overtaken in sin, I think the ape died of it, rats
and dogs and swine are stricken like human beings, I remember
at Camors, I'm a daughter of the Duke Philibert, we took
every care we could, it was two years before the old queen died,
God rest her soul, she was always a good friend to me, I
haven't always had to welcome guests to such a place as this,
your chamber is on the second floor of the keep with a fireplace in it, there was a horse, a charger of my elder brother's,
God have him in keeping, they thought it was the staggers,
but in the morning charger and groom were both dead in the
straw, they sent me away to a convent, you'll understand the
first care here is my lady duchess and her safety, we're very
glad to welcome a famous scholar, my brother the present duke
says Grey Friar for mystery, White Friar for history, Black
Friar for company, he-he-he. . . .'

Yolande glanced aside at the castellan, and could have sworn
she saw the tail-end of a sardonic smile on his morose yellow
face.

' He's glad his daughter-of-a-duke has someone else to talk
to,' she reflected. ' But he has to attend in case she says something that needs repair.'

They seated themselves in the solar, and bluish light from
the windows gleamed on the friar's ruddy face. He was served
with steaming spiced wine, and drank it down like a man-
at-arms. Yolande resolved to appear to him to know less than
she actually did. It looked as though life might become
exhausting at Roclatour.

Dame Jehane, she perceived, saw in the handsome Dom
Ursus the first swallow of a stately summer. The lustre of his
learning would adorn this distinguished corner of the duchy,
where famous men and proud women would come to pay
their respects to Yolande, and find themselves paying those
respects also to the dignified, debonair, long-neglected-but-
finally-justified, very-nobly-born, and wholly-meritorious
Jehane.

One of the chests from the sledge was full of books and

scrolls: Dom Ursus and Yolande unpacked them together. Some of the lettered titles were of works known to her, such as the Lives of the Saints, the Miracles of the Virgin Mary, and the *Gesta Romanorum*. Then there were Latin grammars compiled from Priscian and Donatus, and volumes of Plutarch and Livy and Tacitus. Charlemagne and Julius Cæsar jostled Merlin and Robert the Devil; the Geste Historial of Troy and the History of the Kings of Neustria were disinterred from a heap of song-books, bestaries, and metrical homilies. Maps lay rolled and tied with ribands, blue for the heavens, red for Neustria, purple for Baraine. Presently Yolande was absorbed in a magnificent hundred-year-old map of the round world.

In the light of four candles she knelt on a bench beside the standing-table in the winter parlour; Dom Ursus picked up books, blew dust from their edges, and ranged them on a trestled board. Between his movements he sat still and watched Yolande.

Above the map itself was drawn the Sieur Jesus sitting in judgment; at his feet knelt Our Lady, showing to him her breasts in intercession for mankind. Angels blew on the Doom Trumpets; the dead split open their coffins, and terrible little fiends parcelled and drove away the damned at the bidding of a seraph with a sword of flame. On the map were seas coloured black around the land-masses; where the towns thinned out stood all manner of curious figures of infidels and half-men and marvellous beasts. The rivers were red; Danube poured through half a dozen mouths into the Cimmerian Sea, on whose shore cannibals tore human limbs beside the Golden Fleece; Oxus and Jaxartes wound past Samarkand to the mysterious ocean. By Ganges appeared a savage having one leg and a foot so large that he used it as a shelter from the sun; and near the mouth of the Ganges lay the Island of Paradise. Jerusalem sat at the centre of the world, with Babylon and Constantinople, Rome and Memphis, equidistant in their several countries. Nile rolled from the Fire Mountains through desert held by ibis-headed fiend and unicorn and salamander, to the Delta and the granaries of Joseph. . . .

'We had as good a map as this at Bargreant,' Yolande

decided, ' but I shan't say so. It would sound too much like Jehane. And Chevronel was learned, but I'm not going to talk about *her* to any wide-nostrilled Dominican.'

' *Do you know where the Sieur God was when He made heaven and earth?* '

The tutor's question came so suddenly that Yolande was startled; but she had learnt an answer, and gave it politely.

' *In the farther end of the wind.* '

' And what was Adam made of? '

' Earth, air, fire, wind, cloud, dew, flowers, and salt.'

' Which flowers does God most love? '

' The lily and the rose.'

' Which bird or beast? '

' The dove.'

' And you? '

Dom Ursus could smile pleasantly. He was smiling now.

' Kittens,' said Yolande shortly, and delicately touched the map to try to head him off.

' What have you there? ' he asked, to her relief.

' A beautiful leopard, *passant gardant*, but going to the sinister side, towards some mountains. He's in Africa, inland from Carthage.'

' We will go over that map,' promised Dom Ursus. ' It will tell me how much Latin you can read.'

Yolande wished some of the savages were not so desperately naked; but, after all, Dom Ursus was a friar and a Master of Theology. And she could always look at the fascinating crystal skull on his hairy finger.

She looked at it almost every day for nearly two years. At it, and at her ebony hour-glass in which slid the silver sand, and at the strip of lake and pinewood, heather and rock and changing sky, framed in the narrow window opposite her high carven chair.

In the spring, when she first rode abroad with Odard, she speedily found exactly what it was she could see there; and sometimes she would halt grey Tancred—a powerful gelding of the kind ridden by the archers of the garrison—on the brow above that particular pinewood. Then she would look back across the bosom of the lake, and wonder at the two Yolandes into which she was now divided.

One of these two did everything she was bidden to do, whether it were Latin or Italian or Franconian, astronomy or history or the reading of glosses upon Holy Writ, embroidery of an altar-cloth or practice with her harp and lute, or the preparation of salves and tisanes in the chamber beside the armoury. Also she dutifully kept a bald little chronicle of such news from the outside world as Dom Ursus gave her. Barely any indication of her own feelings crept into this record. . . .

'This month the plague abated in Bargreant, but was still spreading abroad in the duchy. At Sanctlamine died the good prior Dom Gilomar, who was a close friend of the late Duke Engelbert. With him died his sub-prior and seventeen of the brethren and many of their servants. In Bargreant died six hundred and forty in the city and four in the castle, from the night of the interrupted banquet until Saint Mark's Day. After that no more, for which praise was given to God. A weaver and three apprentices were hanged for breaking into sealed houses. Six men and eleven women were found to have used unhallowed remedies, and of these one man and eight women were burnt for witchcraft.

'The Duke Balthasar and the Grand Seneschal were summoned to Hautarroy concerning the quarrel between the Dukes of Ahun and Beltany. . . .

'This month, on the day of Saint James Apostle, the queen gave birth to a daughter who was named Jacqueline. In Elquitaine was a great flood. The lord king dismissed from the office of Chancellor the Duke of Saulte, who had held the office for ten years, and appointed in his place the Bishop of Estragon. . . .

'This month the plague disappeared from all parts of the kingdom. At about the time of the Assumption of Our Lady, Saracen pirates sailed up the River Royenne and did great mischief in Trevence. A part of their fleet was caught and destroyed by skill of the Chevalier de Largire, who built a bridge of boats and chains, and cut off the head of an emir, and sent it to the Duke of Trevence. . . .

'This month the Franconian envoys came again to Haut-arroy, bringing the ransom of the lords captured at the Gorge of Arionbel. At Belsaunt in Honoy a church tower was struck by lightning and two people were killed. The Grand Seneschal returned to Bargreant. The Duke Balthasar remained with the lord king, and wore the queen's colours in a tourney on Saint Luke's Day. . . .'

The Duke Balthasar came nowhere near Roclatour. The Grand Seneschal came twice, talked in private and separately with the Sieur Odard and Dom Ursus, and listened impassively to bursts of confused eloquence from Dame Jehane. To Yolande he barely spoke, contenting himself with giving her news of her husband, and praise of her demeanour as reported by governess and tutor. Yolande supposed that he expected her to complain of being kept at Roclatour; she was careful to do nothing of the kind, showing him instead her altar-cloth and chronicle.

'You are happy here,' he told her, kindly but firmly, during his first visit.

'Happy enough, my lord,' she replied. 'But I should be happier if my father's body were taken from the church here and buried with the bodies of the other Dukes of Baraine.'

'Very devoutly said, my lady. But the king will not at present let Balthasar leave the court. When he comes again into the duchy, that shall be our first care.'

When he had gone, Yolande sat for some time alone, looking now at her wedding-ring and now at the doll Amarand, who guarded her secrets the more closely in that she had cut off their key from his sword-belt and hung it by the little gold cross which lived on a neck-chain under her clothes.

'Uncle Azo thinks I'm a simple little body,' she decided, and paused over her accidental choice of words. A simple little body . . . that was what these Montguiscards wanted, and what the other, the secret Yolande, was determined somehow to deny them.

When the shocking news came in from Sanctlamine she pretended to have a headache, accepted a vile-tasting potion given her by Jehane, and lay for a long time alone in her bed, enduring silently this blow at her secret hope for more news of Amarand's fugitive elves. They were becoming little more than that to her now. Poor Dom Gilomar . . . poor sub-prior, of whom Diomede had spoken so kindly. All her past was shredding away; Dame Jehane saw to it that her visits to the convent were few. All the laws of God and man were closing in on Yolande.

She unlocked the doll and took out of him the agate talisman given to her by the apothecary Philastrius.

'A heathen thing to do,' she told herself, as she linked its silver ring to her chain beside the cross and the key. 'But I said I would wear it . . . and I wish I had a hair from the tail of a lion . . . for I very much need protection from thunderbolts. And now I shall never know what happened to *them*.'

A crazy fantasy lurked in her mind, ready to flare up when she was alone. It was a fantasy of escape, with Lioncel and Diomede riding to right and left of her through sun-dappled glades of a forest. It had no beginning and no end; it was safe and lovely and full of music; castles reared up with friends in them, strong friends such as Raoul of Ger. Rivers glittered, sunsets flamed, and the wedding-ring was gone from her finger. It was almost worth the ache of loss when she came back to the real world and the stony gloom of Roclatour.

The only book to feed that fancy, of all her tutor's store, was one which recounted the lives of Byzantine princesses. These young women moved among unimaginable splendours of veined marble and gold and roses; they married kings, wrote poetry, had each other stabbed or strangled or choked with a pearl, fell in love with blond giants of the Varangian Guard, and sometimes ended as devout nuns or grotesque anchoresses. None of them, so far as she could discover, was talked to death by her governess. From this last fate Yolande writhed away in spirit; she liked neither Dom Ursus nor the Sieur Odard, but with them in her eye she began to bear a little on the steering-oar of her own affairs. . . .

In the first winter she had had no hunting; Odard was
devoted to a sport which took him out of range of the tongue
of Jehane. But in the spring Odard saw to it that she had plenty
of riding, and when it became evident that Jehane was not
even a fair-weather horsewoman, Yolande grasped every chance
of showing how well and gladly she rode. Aurania and Douce
were both at home in the saddle; with one of them for company
and up to a dozen archers as escort, duchess and castellan covered
miles of moorland, forest, and smooth lakeside sand.

Odard was dull and grim, and Yolande wished he would not
speak to her after every gallop, as though speech had to be jolted
out of his heavy carcase.

' The verderers say there'll be boar in plenty when hunting
comes again,' he would tell her, or: ' This bridge is kept in
repair by dues from the Friday market.'

But if she did not like Odard, she still was sorry for him, and
very careful not to shame him by showing any awareness of the
oddities of Jehane. And in spite of herself she became aware of
a certain flavour of dumb gratitude in the castellan's demeanour,
very queer considering their ages and relationship. And at the
same time she noticed that Dom Ursus, although no performer,
was attracted by the sound of a well-played lute.

The winter parlour was given up to Dom Ursus; that is to
say, he taught her there, and used it himself when lessons were
ended. In one corner a little staircase rose to a narrow door;
Yolande explored and found herself standing in a turret built
out from the rampart above the southern postern. The cool dry
turret room had three large cross-shaped loopholes for archery,
cut low down, with wooden screens to set against any or all of
them. In the floor was a trapdoor giving a drop for a large
stone or ladleful of boiling oil on anyone battering at the postern.
There was also a door leading out on to a rampart walk above
the little castle garden.

On a fine May morning she asked Dom Ursus if he would
mind her taking her lute there for the daily hour of practice.
His grey eyes bulged glassily as he considered the question.

' In the solar,' explained Yolande meekly, ' it interrupts the
conversation.'

' What says my lady Jehane? ' he enquired, without looking at her.

' I've not asked her yet. If I have your leave, she may not mind. Shall I try, to see whether the sound disturbs you? '

This time Dom Ursus did look at her, and apparently satisfied himself that this docile creature was really concerned for her lute-playing. Like himself, Dame Jehane was no instrumentalist; Yolande, being well-advanced, was left to her own devices in the time allotted to music.

' It would not disturb me,' said Dom Ursus. ' Come, we'll find my lady.'

Yolande preceded him along a passage, and waited for him to open the solar door. Dame Jehane was talking.

' . . . I never do, I said, I can't abide that sort of thing, the woman talks of nothing but herself and her affairs, who cares whether or not the Constable's her cousin, the Constable's only a count and a bad-tempered one at that, it was always a duke in the old days, I said to my sister Muron it's not as though I said —it's not as though . . .'

Aurania and Douce were already standing; Yolande and Dom Ursus waited for the flood to subside.

' My lady,' began the tutor while Jehane's mouth was still open, ' the duchess wishes to use the turret beyond the winter parlour for practice with her lute. It will not disturb me . . . in fact I shall find it agreeable. You have no objection? '

' Turret beyond the winter parlour? ' repeated Dame Jehane in a slightly offended tone. ' Why not here as usual, child? '

She very seldom called Yolande ' child ', but the learned tutor had just called Yolande ' the duchess '.

' Because,' went on Dom Ursus smoothly, ' my lady duchess is courteously concerned lest she interfere with the conversation.'

' But why should—of course not the time's set apart especially for—what do you mean? '

Dame Jehane had begun to glare at Yolande; if no insult were intended she had come near to insulting herself, a very serious predicament for the youngest daughter of Philibert of Camors.

' It's not fitting you should sit alone,' she went on in a milder key. ' Besides, that turret will be very cold, you'll catch a great rheum; there's nothing to be seen there; we like to listen, don't understand ...'

'The turret's on the south wall, my lady,' said Yolande very gravely. 'I feel I should give more care to my practice ... and perhaps I might have a brazier there.'

'Wait till warm weather and then we'll see, I'll have a look at the turret, it's very kind of Dom Ursus, Aurania fetch my lady's lute, Douce another log on the fire, Dom Ursus will you stay to listen, I like to hear my lady play *Dame Carcenet* and the Honoy dances and *Saint Amarand for Baraine*, at Camors we had half a dozen of the best lutanists in the kingdom, one of them, what was his name, made a virelay for me, how did it go? *Dee-di-dee-dee, di-dee-da-dee* ...'

Yolande had a contralto voice, and favoured mournful songs, singing those of other kinds chiefly as a concession to company. She looked through a pile of music, chose a lay called *Autumn in Broceliande*, and took her great lute on her knee, determined that today no prattle should interrupt her. When she was ready she began to sing as though her life depended on it.

> '*In the wild wood the leaves of autumn whirling;*
> *On the dark moor the silver slant of rain;*
> *Across the sunset, smoke of weedfires curling;*
> *Beyond the mere, the wild swan's wings again.*
> *The war-horn of Pendragon groans in vain,*
> *And idly swings Excalibur to sever*
> *The branches of grim thorns that bend and strain*
> *Where in his tomb great Merlin mourns for ever.*'

Yolande paused for a few seconds longer than was usual between verses, and up like a flushed flight of pheasants burst the words of Jehane.

'That's new to me, very gloomy, you can hear the swans' wings and the war-horn in the twilight, I remember when I was young a great hawthorn at the edge of a wood, and my brothers told me it was under there the enchantress imprisoned Merlin, I wouldn't go past in the dark for ...'

Yolande struck a fierce chord and began the second verse.

Jehane was silenced for a moment; but by the middle of the third she was praising the song aloud again. Dom Ursus sat by the table, looking into the fire; Aurania on a bench, Douce on a stool, tried to attend to what she said without disrespect to the singing. During the fourth verse Jehane discovered that she was talking, and checked herself; but during the fifth she began again without noticing it.

'Her thoughts must be very *loud*,' reflected Yolande when the song was done. 'They must deafen her to what's going on outside her head. I'm sorry for her, and I wish she'd give off the quiet wisdom of women more quietly.'

Dom Ursus rose and excused himself, and the firelight was pink on his eyeballs as he glanced round the room.

'This is a sad chamber for echoes,' he said as he went out. 'Ceiling too high . . . a pity . . .'

His voice was cut off by the closing of the door, and Yolande began to sing again. When she laid aside the lute she sat down to the harp, and woke every reverberation the solar could encompass.

'It's very true there's a great echo,' commented Dame Jehane. 'I never noticed it so much as today, perhaps it's that screen before the door, it's nearer this side of the room than usual, I wonder, Yolande, if it mightn't be well to try your turret chamber, there's a brazier never used in the armoury, you'd have to give heed to the fumes in so small a space, the archery slits should bear them away, I'd begin in a warm noon, I don't know about the harp, Dom Ursus won't want it trundled back and forth each day, turrets won't do for harps, too damp, we'll put the brazier in for a day or two at first, you can try, in the summer we'll walk in the garth and hear you at it. . . .'

Yolande began to practise in the turret with a flattened cross of sunlight on the floor at her feet. The south side of the castle faced away from the town; rough woodland came near the moat, but orchards and pasture lay just beyond, with the out-lying hills of the Casque of Baraine thrusting eastwards behind. The *esplanade*, or cleared space with no cover in it for attackers, had been carefully burnt-over in the previous autumn; but the slope on the inner side of the moat bore briars and brambles from the water's edge to the foot of the ramparts.

Yolande hugged her lute and her privacy, gazing out of the calm gloom; then she filled her turret with song or caressed it with cadences of lute-play scarcely disengaged from silence. Pigeons fluttered beyond the slits, and seemed to approve her music. A week or two after she first sat there she made a Latin lay which could not be shown to Dom Ursus or anyone else.

> ' *Musas in turricula*
>   *Servat dux Jolanda;*
> *Columbas canticula*
>   *Fascinat miranda.*

> ' *Clamat in solario*
>   *Domina Johanna*
> *Cum sermone vario*
>   *Et furibunda sanna.*

> ' *Sicut tuba hostica*
>   *Exinanit forum;*
> *Tandem crura postica*
>   *Decidunt asellorum.'*

Not very good Latin, perhaps, but at least she had remembered that *dux* was feminine as well as masculine. ' In the turret Duchess Yolande serves the Muses; her strange little song enchants the pigeons. In the solar Dame Jehane clamours with changing chatter and furious grimace. Like an enemy trumpet she empties the market-place, and finally the hind legs of little donkeys drop off. '

VII

THE WAY OF DOM URSUS CAMPESTRIS

AT odd moments during her days Yolande had begun to sketch
again in charcoal on the backs of her exercise-papers. One
lively scribble showing oxen and a waggon entering the main
gate she left by accident between the pages of the Geste Historial
of Troy. Dom Ursus found it there and gave it back to her at
the end of a Latin reading.

'That is a gift you should not neglect,' he said with stern
approval. 'Have you had instruction in drawing?'

'Yes. My old governess drew and painted.'

'It's a pity there's no one here to go on with it. If I drew a
hawk it would be taken for a heron.'

'I . . . I should like more training. There's an apothecary in
the town, a man called Philastrius, who does both very well.
My lady abbess bought me a kitten at his shop, and I went there
once and saw his pictures.'

'We will see whether he can teach as well as draw.'

So they visited the apothecary together. Philastrius made
Yolande very respectfully welcome.

'How is Topaz, Your Grace?' he enquired almost at once.

'Dead—an accident,' said Yolande shortly, taking no overt
notice of the brother and sisters of Topaz as they stalked among
chests and tables and rubbed themselves against the lean ankles
of Philastrius. Blanche helped her husband display his work,
and Yolande, looking at Dom Ursus to observe its effect on him,
was a little startled by the expression on her tutor's sanguine face.
His eyes seemed bulging in a new mode as their gaze rolled
across the portraits and compared them with the calm beauty
of the original.

Philastrius, doubtful of his possible prowess as a teacher,
agreed to come up to the castle twice a week, bringing with him

all necessary materials. And when the lessons began he made no further enquiry concerning Topaz, for which Yolande was grateful to him. The faint smell of lavender and spices that clung to his gowns became part of the sunny mornings in which the pair of them sat with charcoal and paper, discussing the shapes of flowers and trees, of buildings and horses and people.

Dom Ursus had squared Dame Jehane, taking the hours of new instruction out of his own share of Yolande's time. At first the governess contented herself with sending Aurania or Douce to observe the conventions; but when Philastrius appeared with paint-brushes and pots of colour, Jehane herself began to haunt the winter parlour.

At Camors in the golden age, it appeared, two very skilful limners had decorated the summer-house, one of them it was who painted the Virgin on the door of the old queen's chamber in the great castle of Ingard, the old queen wouldn't have red in the pictures, it made them a little sad in the distance, the summer-house had plenty of red, it seemed to frighten away the birds . . . and so on, and so on, while Philastrius interjected murmurs of guidance with moisture beading his sallow forehead.

Presently he took Yolande to the turret-tops and the stables, and to the chamber over the gate where the great portcullis hung in grease and military gloom. In these places Jehane might not sit at ease, and Yolande on her little stool could work without interruption.

Dom Ursus generally walked abroad when drawing was in progress; sometimes Yolande would see him in a skiff, a far-off figure hooded against the hot sun, with a book or scroll in hand, and his boatman paddling instead of rowing, so that he did not have to stare into the face of the ruminating Dominican.

Philastrius, too, had a rowing-boat, and occasionally he was permitted to give his lesson on the lake. At such times a barge was in attendance, with a group of archers who solemnly kept watch in pairs, while the rest enjoyed a discreet throw of dice on a buckler amidships.

On thin planed boards Yolande drew and painted the little town from a number of angles, and gave one of the pictures to

Jehane and another to Dom Ursus, a third to the abbess, and a fourth, better than any, to Zoster Adela.

'How d'you get on with Dame Jehane, my precious?' asked the nun when they were alone in the convent garden.

'Quite well,' admitted Yolande, 'but only because I pretend to agree with everything she says. At the least objection her voice goes up on a note that rends your ear. And I'm sorry for her, too, for she seems so sad and so . . . driven.'

'Don't worry too much. That lady likes to spin her shroud of everything that comes nigh her.'

After Azo's first visit Yolande often recalled that remark. Jehane began to understand that the household of the duchess was deliberately thrust away into this corner of the hills, and that the end of the pestilence entailed neither the holding of a summer court nor the prospect of return to Bargreant in the autumn. Forthwith she fell into long sulks of which the silence seemed as solid as speech; lowering, haggard, staring into vacancy, she often had to be spoken to several times before she made any answer.

'Yes . . . no . . . do as you like,' she would snap at Aurania or Douce when consulted in household affairs; then, rousing herself, she complained and stormed and reversed their decisions.

As for Odard, it became apparent that she considered him author by default of all her woes; and when he defended himself or deprecated her anger against others, she groaned at him in a most heartbroken and alarming manner. Yolande, aghast at her first midnight awakening to the new noise, roused the damsels and beat on Jehane's bedchamber door. Odard opened it, wearing his bed-gown, carrying a taper which showed his eyes bloodshot and his face ghastly with fatigue.

'My lord, what is it?' gasped Yolande. 'Is my lady ill? What can we do?'

'Gramercy, my lady, you can do nothing,' he muttered. 'And I pray you won't mention it tomorrow. It's a . . . a kind of nightmare. Don't let it disturb you again. I've given her a cordial. She . . . sometimes she believes our children visit her.'

'I wonder if he's lying,' thought Yolande when she was warm in bed again. 'Is she just plaguing herself and him, because she married beneath her and has never had what she thinks is her due? Saints know he's dull and mournful, but that's partly her own fault.'

Next day the kind-hearted Aurania could not forbear to ask how Dame Jehane might find herself.

'Well enough, well enough,' moaned the governess, her tragic whisper belying its words, but also discouraging further enquiry. There were times when Jehane seemed to stand aghast at the spectacle of her own quiet heroism.

Occasionally she was afflicted with a phase of roguish gaiety, in which everyone else stood accused of doleful dumps. At such times she made a great mock of men, calling them half-brutes, half-babies; Odard pretended not to hear, and Yolande and the damsels pretended not to see him. Dom Ursus, vocationally exempted from her strictures, seemed rather to enjoy them. Then, too, she made fun of relatives who had presumed to pity her—pity *her*, gallant Jehane, who had ridden half-across Europe behind her soldier husband, while they sat screened from God's sunlight in castle parlours and convent cells.

Then in some twist of meaningless excitement she would see herself as a spoilt child at Camors might regard her; and again she would plunge into a fog of childless grief and frustration—suffering, watching herself suffering, watching others watching her suffering while she probed for their sympathy with a pitchfork of bad temper.

She was very attentive to fasts and observances, guarding her Candlemas candle-end, her Good Friday crossed cake, and many emblems from shrines she had visited; but it seemed to Yolande that Jehane had found the Sieur God only a dimmer, larger, more forgetful Duke of Camors.

'Mary Mother, have pity on her,' prayed Yolande every night of the year.

At the height of summer Azo sent his young cousin Melania to visit Yolande. Yolande took up her dislike of Melania where she had dropped it; in addition she found herself disposed to regard Melania as in some sense a spy. But to Jehane, Melania was a new pair of ears, and therefore a godsend. Yolande was slightly shocked at her own malicious pleasure in binding Melania as a victim on the altar of Jehane's self-love and self-pity.

' My lady,' she would say as they filed into the solar to break their fast, ' my lady, you must tell Melania how you skated with King Réné by the light of the moon.' Or: ' My lady, Melania would like to hear of the tournament at Camors when your brother unhorsed the Archduke and you were Queen of Love and Beauty.'

' Blessed Saints, does she never stop talking? ' grumbled Melania at the end of her third day with them.

' Ah, my lady Jehane's a rare one for a tale,' said Yolande brightly. ' She keeps us all lively in this dull place. I feel sometimes as if I'd lived at Camors in the old days myself.'

' I'll warrant you do,' muttered Melania. ' Can't you drop your Latin tomorrow and ride out again? '

' Dom Ursus is very strict,' said Yolande regretfully.

That remark, too, she remembered later with amused self-mockery. Melania was the kind of maiden who seemed to pout not only her mouth but also her whole body for the admiration of men. Yolande saw the captain Griflet lick his lips as he eyed the guest's dark ripe beauty. Even the melancholy Odard sometimes watched it with interest; only Dom Ursus appeared immune from response to that kind of provocation.

Nevertheless the morning came when Yolande climbed to her turret, leaving the tutor in the winter parlour, and presently as she played her lute she heard him laugh as he spoke to someone else. Dom Ursus did not often laugh; Yolande was overcome by a mild inquisitiveness, and continued to play, but leaned to the keyhole. She saw below her the standing-table, still littered with books, and then Dom Ursus in his chair, with Melania upon his knee.

Yolande felt shocked rather than surprised, curious rather than ashamed. The confident encrimsoned face of Dom Ursus was pressed against the velvety throat of Melania, who grinned sightlessly up at the ceiling, and presently seemed to squint with pleasure expertly bestowed. The crystal skull on the friar's ring

G

flashed and vanished again, death in the midst of abundant life.

'What kind of a fuss would there be,' wondered Yolande, 'if I were to tell Dame Jehane, or Dom Cyril? *I* know . . . at least I think I know. They would both lie very skilfully, and I should be accounted a desperate sacrilegious liar. And supposing I opened this door on them and stood crossing myself in horror? It would come to the same thing in the end . . . how *dared* I say such a wicked thing about my reverend tutor, who was especially chosen for me by kind, wise Uncle Azo? No, it's no affair of mine . . . except as practice in keeping secrets. And before I get a stiff neck I had better sit up and begin singing. It isn't every friar gets a duchess to sing to his amours.'

In the solar, later that same day, she learnt that the ducal quarrel in the western provinces had exploded in open war. Beltany had defied his king, and drums were beating in Hautarroy. Balthasar had gone with the Constable to chastise the offender.

'I wonder the king lets him go,' Melania told Yolande in the solar.

'It will always be hard to keep my lord duke from serving the king in the field,' said Yolande.

When she had spoken she sat quite still, ignoring Melania's glance of contempt, tasting the sharp realisation that she hoped Balthasar would be killed. *That* would wipe the smugness from the face of the Grand Seneschal.

'We'll pray every day for his safety and glory,' promised Dame Jehane. 'Beltany's a false rogue, of course my aunt the dowager's his aunt by marriage too, she could never abide him, they're a rancorous breed and very headstrong, his younger brother was with mine in Livonia, he threw a man off a bridge for splashing his charger's caparison with mud, he was killed in a brawl not long after, his sons laughed to hear he was dead, it was a judgment on him, they were afraid he'd beat them raw when he found they'd lost one of his falcons.'

'Children are heartless creatures,' commented Dom Ursus.

'Mine weren't!' declared Jehane, her eyes beginning to glow with disputatiousness.

There was a second's awkward pause; Odard cleared his throat and spoke.

'I once saw a chevalier made prisoner because in a gale of wind the caparison blew up over his charger's head. The brute stopped, and when he spurred it, reared and threw him into a holly-bush.'

'And I've heard tell,' went on Dom Ursus, smoothly, 'of a Saracen in a pot helmet, a trophy he was wearing unlaced, which got a thump with a mace that turned it right round on his head, blinding him so that he was bowled over still struggling to right it. The man who captured him kept the helmet, and greatly angered his lady—I was there—by saying that was how half the men he knew might find courage to face their wives after a merry campaign. But there are some women who take everything to themselves.'

'That I *never* do,' said Jehane very proudly.

As summer wore on there were excursions into the woods and along the lake; Dame Jehane was making a collection of herbs and roots for her autumn brewing. She knew all the times and seasons for gathering, and watched the moon narrowly, as though it were not to be trusted. With her pride of exact knowledge went a great impatience in imparting it, so that when Yolande and the damsels tried to learn they were speedily left behind in admiring consternation.

'My mother, God rest her soul, had a wonderful conserve she made of the white root of Saint Hiltrude—ay me, I found it a sad wort later—there were banks of it in the woods to northward of Camors, it grows on dry ground and keeps very well, it's a herb of Saturn, best gathered in the week after Saint Hiltrude's Day, and always with the sun upon it, the leaves have a hot ungrateful flavour, I mind my sister Verville was sick after we dared her to chew one up . . .'

'Even in talking of her childhood,' thought Yolande, 'she uses her sister's title instead of her given name.'

'. . . called it a linctus, it's not a linctus, a linctus is thicker than a syrup but not so thick as an electuary, it's more of a syrup, made by decoction, not by infusion, chop the leaves very

fine, and bruise the root but don't pound it, boil them in spring
water, a handful to a pint, until half the water has gone in
steam, and then let it nearly go cold, and strain through a
woollen cloth, don't press it, let it run out, and add to each pint
a pound of honey and boil into a syrup, and skim it, the skim
keeps a bitterness, it's the Saturnine influence, my mother stirred
the skim in wine and gave it to us for toothache, the syrup lasts
a year, you must remember to keep it in earthen jars, and don't
stopper them, just tie a piece of parchment over the top . . .'

Recipes poured out of Jehane like water going over a weir;
and when Melania had gone and the hay and corn harvests were
in, a kind of bedlam broke loose in the chamber beside the
armoury. The well-chain rattled, the cauldrons steamed, the
air grew full of warring odours; fruit and berries, leaves and
roots and nuts, were stored in a nearby gallery, and there were
frequent collisions in the doorway as Jehane's assistants tried to
keep abreast of her requirements.

Some demon of obliquity sat on Jehane's shoulder; never
could she issue a straightforward command. There was always
an addition, a correction, a modification; and the resulting
hesitancy and muddle Jehane projected fiercely on to the
sufferers themselves.

'Go on, what are you waiting for?' she would shout at the
frightened kitchen lad who carried the heavier supplies.

Scarlet-faced, obviously scared to move lest the current edict
were incomplete, the hapless youth would spin round and
gallop off, only to halt with a clatter of clogs as the next
instalment overtook him. One morning Yolande found him
unnerved and weeping in the corridor; Douce had a kind hand
on his shoulder and was whispering into his big red ear. Even
down the calm face of Douce a sparkle of sweat went sliding;
and as Yolande passed the doorway of despair Aurania came
scuttling out, only to stumble over a bucket and shoot half a
bowlful of walnuts on to the stone flags of the passage.
Yolande exclaimed and knelt to help recover them; wood-smoke
and the mingled smell of blackberries and red-dead-nettles,
came whirling out of the brew-room with the exasperated voice
of Jehane.

'. . . where's Yolande, she said she was coming, I can't do everything at once, who's supposed to be stirring this thing, where's that moonstruck oaf gone, I said those roots were mouldy, it's nearly seven hours now and the pot's not ready, Douce, Douce, hurry up, bring me that wooden basin, Holy Mary, *it's boiling over . . .*'

A loud hissing announced some temporary set-back. Yolande thrust the last of the walnuts into the bowl, gave the hot Aurania an affectionate squeeze, and plunged into the fray. . . .

'These have been left too long,' lamented Jehane, turning a little while later from a trayful of withering blackish-purple berries which might have been grapes.

'What are they?' asked Yolande, who had long since given up trying to remember what was going on.

'The archbishop's apothecary said its name was Herb Paris, but at Camors we called it True Love, it's the same as Leopard's Bane, a herb of Venus, and good against poisons, and the leaves are helpful for green wounds . . .'

That night Yolande could only remember that True Love was Leopard's Bane. But out of all the noise and flurry began to emerge rank upon rank of little casks and jars and vases of ointments and febrifuges, purges and restoratives, balms for the complexion, pickles and preserves and sauces for the table. They were most of them useful or good to taste, or both, and on one bright October morning Yolande, coming out on the hall steps to mount grey Tancred for a stag-hunt, overheard old Julian, the sergeant-of-arms, speaking aside to Griflet.

'By the bones of Saint Amarand, captain, my lady Xantroy knows her physic. I got steward to beg me one of her purges; it rasps the mischief out of your tripes like a birch-broom clearing a gutter.'

Coming out on the hall steps to mount grey Tancred for a stag-hunt. . . .

That was the best way of escape. Yolande disliked killing, and disliked the faces of men and boys as they killed, but she found a wild pleasure in the chase as it streamed across hill and

woodland and along the autumn shores of the lake. Aurania
and Douce came with her alternately; otherwise the hunt was
exclusively male. Each day a couple of archers was detailed to
attend the girls in case of mischance to them or to their horses;
otherwise Odard seldom paid any special attention to her
presence. Neither did anyone else, except perhaps Griflet, who
tended to keep within close hail when Aurania was of the party.

Dom Ursus did not ride out with them; his hunting was of
different kinds, only one of which had been revealed to his
pupil through the keyhole of the turret door.

Then, one day, as Yolande stood with Zoster Adela at the
gateway of the abbey, a mild-faced old woman, gowned and
hooded in green, came past them down the hill, supporting
herself on a staff. At sight of her young duchess she lifted a
hand and bowed her head; Yolande noticed that not only Zoster
Adela but also the convent porter and her own waiting archers
crossed themselves. Aurania, coming out of a shop across the
little square, crossed herself too, and gave the old woman a
wide berth.

' Is she supposed to be a witch, then? ' asked Yolande
curiously, for the old woman looked as if she would scarcely
strike at a wasp until it stung her.

' So they say,' growled Zoster Adela.

Yolande crossed not herself but the air between her and the
receding figure. Then a curious thing happened; as though she
felt the gesture which she could not possibly have seen, the old
woman turned and repeated it, using her staff.

' I don't think she's a witch,' said Yolande.

' After that, nor do I,' muttered the nun. ' There's a kind of
rumour spreading down by the quay . . . someone is stricken
with palsy, someone else's baby has a fit, and the gossips go to
it. So-and-so won't be found at home on Saint John's Eve . . .
her husband said she was sick in bed, but she didn't look ill next
day, and so on. It's said your Dom Ursus is a flail of witch
craft . . . and what would Reverend Mother Abbess say to my
gossiping about gossip? '

Said Yolande: ' I'd rather have gossip about Roclatour today
than about Camors twenty years ago.'

'Have you heard anything of witchcraft down by the harbour?' she asked Philastrius during her next drawing-lesson.

'Something,' he replied after a second's hesitation. 'I think it's only mischief-making. The war and the plague have gone by and folk must have something to talk about. With Dom Ursus here in the castle there'll be no stirring of the old religion.'

Two-thirds of a year passed before Yolande and Philastrius mentioned witchcraft again. By that time they were good friends within the strict limits of their acquaintance, and Yolande was happy in the quiet hours when colour flowed from her little brushes. Otherwise she was not very happy; life in the castle was going awry.

Uncle Azo had come and gone again; Jehane had been ill, and was growing more eccentric, flinging her long body about in attitudes of profound dejection. Odard was duller and gloomier than ever, busying himself silently with his duties as castellan and warden of the forest around Lake Targe. Something had happened to Aurania, spoiling her old tranquillity. Yolande herself was sometimes visited with a sick desperation; no passage of time reconciled her to the wifely prospect ahead.

Regular news of Balthasar reached her only through Odard or Dom Ursus; it was as though a sprightly dummy came back from the war in Beltany and bounced about in Balthasar's clothes at court or upon some embassy. Balthasar's Christmas present to her was a jewelled musical-box; it came with a formal letter signed but not written by himself.

Only Dom Ursus seemed the same—until about ten days before the next midsummer Feast of Saint John. Then, on a hot June morning, Yolande played her harp in the castle garden with only Aurania to listen. She had picked up songs at random and scattered them over the cushions on the stone bench beside her; as she sang and played a glance from Aurania told her that someone had come out and was approaching behind her. She did not choose to break off her song, which had no title and was new to her.

> *'When I was a stone a bolt split me,*
> *When I was a tree a storm threw me,*
> *When I was a snake a hawk tore me,*
> *When I was a hawk a stone hit me,*
> *When I was a stag a wolf slew me,*
> *When I was a wolf an axe shore me,*
> *When I was a man a god rent me:*
> *These be the dooms fate sent me.'*

'*Who gave you that song?*' demanded a harsh voice, so that Yolande turned her head in astonishment. Dom Ursus stood there, with a black frown on his red face; never since his first appearance had he spoken to her like that. He extended the hand with the skull-ring on it to take her song from her.

'It came with the others from Bargreant,' she answered, too annoyed to be properly scared. 'I never saw it until today. What's the matter with it?'

'What's the matter with it? My lady, you're well able to learn what is set before you, but it seems that in some sort you're still very much of a child. That song is altogether heathen, figuring the passage of the soul from rocks and trees into birds and beasts . . . the damnable error of Pythagoras . . . who do you think is supposed to speak of *a* god like that? There is one God, and you know it.'

'Some wandering poet, I suppose. Poets are mostly mad, are they not? Have I done wrong to sing it?'

'Yes, and you don't appear to be ashamed. What wonder the base herd goes astray, if the rulers of the land are lax? It's time you were told what wickedness lurks in the very shadow of your ramparts. You know it's written *non potestis calicem Domini bibere, et calicem daemoniorum.*'

'"You cannot drink of the Lord's cup and of the cup of devils." Who wants to?'

'Wretched women of Roclatour, deluded to their own damnation. There's a Sabbat planned for Saint John's Eve somewhere to the west . . . a man came to me sweating with horror . . . his wife talked in her sleep . . . we've got her in the town prison. She had a toad in a pot . . . one of her neighbours was paralysed only last week, and another found all his hens dead at one time. She won't give the names of her companions, but once or twice she has called out upon Zannico, so that's what their devil is called here.'

'Holy Mary defend us!' whispered Yolande, chilled along the spine at this sudden revelation. 'Why does witchcraft stir after a pestilence?'

'The fiend is skilful in his use of human extremity. He tells the bereaved that God has abandoned the world and given it over to himself. And if enough of the base sort wear his amulets, those who escape the plague will let it be known, and point to Christians smitten down, and say: *Zannico has the power.*'

'But are there . . . are there many?'

'That is what I shall find out.'

The nostrils of Dom Ursus seemed wider than usual; his hand, that had gone to his pectoral cross, came out again.

'Meanwhile, give me that song,' he commanded. 'Yes, and the others with it. They must be examined. This does your former governance no credit.'

Yolande stood up and tossed the song on to the bench.

'Take them,' she said. 'I will make my confession to Dom Cyril.'

She glanced aside at the flushed face of Aurania, who seemed distressed even beyond the demands of the occasion.

'Perhaps you would like to help Dom Ursus gather up the songs,' she said, and had time to see Aurania go white before she moved away. It was a chance form of words, and its effect twisted in her thoughts as she went up to the turret chamber.

'Are we all going daft?' she asked herself angrily, taking up the lute which lay there. But her fingers plucked no sound from the strings; she noticed through one of the flanking archery-slits a movement among the bushes between the rampart and the moat. A young man and a girl sat there, hidden from anyone on the battlements above them, holding hands as they gazed out across the *esplanade*.

'How the devil do townsfolk get inside the moat?' she wondered, when she had stared to make sure they were not of the household. ' I suppose I should see them turned out, and then Odard would have the bushes cut down. But . . .'

She watched the pair gradually abandon themselves to each other. Their shy tenderness was fascinating; it brought an alien charm into the sunlight. Yolande forgot her anger with Dom Ursus, her suspicion of Aurania's sudden pallor; she wanted the young man to go on kissing the girl.

' Here's a love-lay for you,' she whispered after a while, and began to play softly. The lovers' heads came round, but to them she was quite invisible.

' This is likely as near as your duchess will come to true love,' she reflected. ' What, have I driven you away? No, stay and listen. I wish you very well.'

The shadow of the corner tower beyond the pair enveloped them, and they rose to go, by means which Yolande found beautifully simple. The young man rooted about in the briars and dragged out a long plank, which he laid across the water for the girl. When she had crossed he pulled it back, and hid it again, producing in turn a long staff with which he pole-jumped neatly to the opposite bank.

Yolande chuckled at their impudence, wondering how long it would be until some sentinel noticed them and warned them off. When they had vanished into the orchards she felt suddenly lonely.

' True Love is Leopard's Bane,' she told herself sombrely.

On the following day there was no Latin reading, no lesson of any kind. A townsman had found a waxen image hidden in a chamber-pot. There was a nail through its middle, and a forked beard of strips of cloth adorned its waxen chin. A fork-bearded neighbour was lying at death's door. Dom Ursus and the provost had the wives of both men hauled before them. . . .

Dom Ursus was in his element; at supper that night he discoursed of old crusades, and Yolande noticed Odard watching him with a withdrawn expression. Jehane was caught in a cleft stick; she wished to boast of past cases of witchcraft at Camors, but was restrained by the fear of bringing ill-fame on the home of her girlhood. Yolande sat quite silent, but as she not infrequently did so, this occasioned no surprise.

Witchcraft was loathsome, but so to her was the scavenging pleasure of the sleek relentless Dominican. Griflet, she saw, was more friendly to the friar than he had ever been; Griflet would no doubt enjoy posting his men around a scaffold.

On the following day again, Yolande went riding. It was Aurania's turn to be with her, and it was Aurania who screamed in her saddle by the edge of a wood overlooking the lake. First Yolande, then Griflet, then Odard himself, galloped up and reined in to stare where she pointed; a mandrake-root some eight inches tall, roughly habited in the white and black of a Dominican friar, hung from a beech-bough, with a sliver of wood driven through what corresponded to its stomach.

Yolande watched Griflet pull thoughtfully at his long straight nose. It was Griflet who cut the manikin down and stowed it in his saddle-bag to take back to the castle. Aurania seemed sick with fright; Yolande rode close beside her, trying to comfort her without appearing to know that she was too fond of Dom Ursus.

The friar himself was hugely pleased with this tribute to his enmity. Saint John's Eve was very near, and innocent townsfolk had begun to dodge round corners when they saw him coming. That same evening Yolande passed through the winter parlour, as much to see if the lovers were under the rampart wall as to fill in her hour of lute-practice. . . .

Dom Ursus was not there; seeing among his papers a book open at a brightly-coloured page, she moved behind the table to look at it. The book was about the prophets of Israel, and the picture showed some of the troubles of the patriarch Job. And under the book, sticking out beyond it, was a paper bearing a list of names and remarks. The list had no heading; Yolande read it with staring eyes.

' *Euphemia Tarcot, the laundress, has a little black dog that performs tricks.*
Vivienne, wife of Jurgelin the coppersmith, seen feeding a squirrel in the woods.

Madeleine Macaras, a manifest whore, seen stroking the
lake with a wand.
Blanche, wife of Philastrius the apothecary, breeds cats
and is said to make philtres.
Lymis, daughter of . . .'

Distantly a door banged, and Yolande scurried away up into
the turret. There was no sign of the lovers, and she found the
evening cold and strange.

In the morning Philastrius came again, no graver than usual.
Yolande looked about on the table and turned to Douce, who sat
tranquilly sewing in the sunshine.

' Douce, will you please fetch the box of charcoal from the
hutch beside my bed? '

' Yes, my lady,' said Douce quietly, and was gone like a
shadow. Yolande and Philastrius were alone; Yolande gripped
the nearer of the long stained hands and whispered urgently.

' Hide your wife or send her away . . . she's in mortal danger
. . . Euphemia, Vivienne, Madeleine Macaras, Lymis, are all
suspected with her.'

The long sallow face of Philastrius went green with terror.
He bent his head and kissed Yolande's knuckles savagely with
dry lips. Then he rose trembling, to walk to a window.

' Our Lady requite Your lovely Grace,' he said hoarsely, and
stood looking out, so that Douce should not see anything strange
in him. When she had come back he turned, and for an hour
controlled himself and his clever hands. Yolande admired the
deliberate pace with which he finally left her presence.

' Suppose Blanche *is* a witch,' she reflected. ' I must be in
great peril of hell. Nobody ever called me lovely before. He
must have meant lovable. Dear Mother of Jesus, let him get
her safely away. I don't believe she's a witch at all. *I don't care*
if she is, I like her! '

The next time Philastrius came he tested a piece of charcoal
on a scrap of paper, and Yolande saw that he had drawn a boat
with four people in it. One of the figures he labelled B and
another V, and scribbled *safe* under the boat, and blacked the

whole drawing out when Yolande had nodded and smiled. Evidently Philastrius and his neighbour the coppersmith had rowed their wives away out of immediate danger. The women were sisters, and had relatives in villages along the lake.

Dom Ursus gave no sign of vexation at the scattering of some of the suspects. He had his prey, and on the whole was in good humour for the rest of the summer. On a calm July morning the two women who had made the waxen image, and the other who had given the name of her devil under torment, were burned alive near the barbican.

'I hope you will watch this act of cleansing,' Dom Ursus told Yolande.

'It's an act of the secular arm,' she replied, not without malice. 'I shall take counsel with the Sieur Odard as to whether my presence is advisable or necessary.'

The Sieur Odard let her off. At the hour of the burning she sneaked into her turret, intending to play the lute as loudly as she could; but the lovers were there, advancing hand in hand among the bushes. They halted immediately beneath the turret, and Yolande pulled a face at herself and moved the trapdoor a very little. There they were, thirty-five feet below her, lying close to the postern door, smiling into each other's face, sure of an uninterrupted hour while all the town gathered on the other side of the castle.

When the first terrible screeching drifted over the bulk of stone, Yolande put her fingers in her ears. So did the girl at the foot of the wall, yielding herself completely to her lover. Yolande watched for a while with shortened breath and quickened pulses; then she replaced the trapdoor, and said a prayer for them, and cried a little. She wondered if the spirit of any of the witches could leap from the flames and take the chance of life just offered among the briars and brambles above the moat. That no doubt was heretical or heathen; Yolande felt a ghostly wringing of her flesh by the tensions of those opposed solemnities.

After that she began to be aware of something new in the

eyes of men who looked at their duchess. Was she really growing beautiful, or was it just crude male interest in the coming
end of her virginity? Odard seemed to grudge his own attention
to her; Griflet turned on her the greedy mocking glance he kept
for all women. Philastrius regarded her with a devotion she
found a little embarrassing, but at least his greenish eyes were
innocent of that other expression; Blanche and her sister had
come home again, for Philastrius had procured letters from the
abbess and the Prior of Saint Michael's, countersigned by the
provost, declaring that no suspicion of witchcraft attached to
either of them.

At Dom Ursus Yolande now hardly ever looked directly, and
when she did she thought of Aurania rather than herself. But
even archers and townsmen seemed sometimes to be thinking,
as their glances dodged away from her own, of the duty she
owed the duchy; and her repugnance grew and frightened her,
and only Zoster Adela had the least inkling of it.

Dame Jehane was laid low again, this time with a swinging
fever. After vociferous indecison she had elected to watch the
burnings from the battlements of the barbican. Arriving late
at her point of vantage, she looked and listened for a moment
and then collapsed in a faint; and now it was evident that
something which had waited for years had pounced upon her
from within.

For the first time Yolande was aware of Jehane as frightened;
and, also for the first time, she observed pathetic shreds of the
love and tenderness which once must have bound Jehane and
Odard together. Odard's fear of his wife's working some folly
ruinous to their joint fortunes was eased by the sight of her
tucked up in bed. Everyone who dealt with Jehane was seasoned
against her oddities, and now, when she began to talk to her
children, no one betrayed undue surprise.

Now, too, Jehane seemed disposed in her chatter to blame her
family for telling her that she had married beneath her, rather
than Odard for overcoming her own family pride. Also there
was now no shadow of doubt that the household revolved
around Jehane rather than around its duchess; Yolande took
her turn with the damsels in no grudging spirit, preferring to

read or listen to the sick woman rather than to extend her lessons with Dom Ursus.

Sometimes Jehane revealed deep rancours, as on the day she cursed the king who had taken her rebel brother's head off. Yolande herself was in the room when that happened, and turned out the women who had just bathed Jehane.

'Damned little red-headed lecherous fox,' she called her sovereign lord and Yolande's. 'His cousin whom he slew at Pont-de-Foy would have made twice as good a king.'

'My lord Grand Seneschal wouldn't like to hear you say that,' Yolande told her.

Up went Jehane's voice into a scream of assertion.

'My lord Grand Seneschal! Much he cares about anyone but my lord Grand Seneschal and my lord Grand Seneschal's lord duke of a precious son! There's a nobleman for you after the king's own heart! Fair and brave as Achilles and Alexander! Gallant soldier, born courtier, the makings of a general and a statesman! The king's son holds his hand when they go to Mass at Hautarroy! He wears the queen's colours in the tourneys there. . . .'

'I beg you will not excite yourself like this,' said Yolande.

'You beg, you!' yelled Jehane. 'You, the duchess, going slyly about with your hands crossed on your maiden stomach . . . it's little you know what life has in store for you! King Solomon shut up demons in urns and buried them for others to discover . . . you've got a demon in an urn, but you're the only one who hasn't discovered him!'

'Go on,' said Yolande, quietly.

'Everyone tells you he's a paladin, your lord duke . . . no one tells you he's stuffed as full of evil pride and cruelty as an egg is full of meat. His men hold peasants for him to burn their beards off . . . he plunders and rapes for sport . . . he makes men fight animals for gold, and robs them afterwards of the purses he has thrown to them. In Beltany he burned a barn full of wounded. Balthasar, Peer of Neustria . . . no one calls him that now. His new name's Belphegor, Peer of Hell!'

Yolande said nothing for a moment. She was sitting by

Jehane's bed, staring fascinated at the wild eyes and tormented
face of her governess.

'I must thank you for telling me this, my lady,' she got out
finally. 'I'm glad to have someone about me who's not afraid
to let me hear the truth. But indeed, I'm not so surprised as you
might expect. Drink your draught now, and try to be quiet.
Belphegor, I'm sure, is a very good name for him.'

With Dom Ursus Yolande was reading the *History* of Tacitus,
and on the following day she translated a passage and paused,
so that the tutor glanced at her across the corner of the big table.

'"For Otho's had been a neglected boyhood and a riotous
youth, and he had made himself agreeable to Nero by emulating
his profligacy. For this reason the Emperor had entrusted to
him, as being the confidant of his amours, Poppæa Sabina, the
imperial favourite, until he could rid himself of his wife
Octavia."'

Yolande gazed out of the window.

'If my lord duke has mistresses,' she enquired, 'how do you
advise me to treat them?'

Dom Ursus sat back in his chair and set his finger-tips
together.

'*Sicut Ecclesia subjecta est Christo,*' he quoted, '*ita et
mulieres viris suis in omnibus.*'

'"As the Church is subject to Christ, so let wives be subject
to their husbands in all things." Yes, but suppose I am commanded to sit at table with them?'

'My lady, do not anticipate so unhappy an eventuality.
There's no cause to expect that such a situation will arise. I . . .
we . . . all hope that you have many happy years of married
life before you.'

Yolande made strokes with a dry quill upon a piece of parchment. The tiny squeaking sound shared the silence of the winter
parlour with the snap and chuckle of flames in the great fireplace.

'I will courteously ignore them,' she decided aloud. 'But if
one of them should seem to be a witch, I will tell you about it.'

Dom Ursus was silent for a moment, as if considering
whether this speech was prompted by innocence or impudence.

But Yolande realised that he could never admit to himself that she was making bitter fun of him.

'These matters can be considered when they arise,' he said coldly. 'Meanwhile, let us return to the affairs of Imperial Rome.'

'Yes. I like reading of the deaths of tyrants. It's good to know that rulers nowadays are better than those of old time.'

She waited another few seconds, smoothing the pages of Tacitus with a hand that bore the black pearl and thunderbolt of Montguiscard. But to allow more than one digression during a Latin reading was not the way of Dom Ursus Campestris.

VIII

BELPHEGOR'S WAY

'THERE they are,' said Lioncel, drawing rein in a high forest clearing three leagues south of Hautarroy.

'What is it?' asked Diomede, riding out of the thickets behind him.

'There in a row—the mountains of Baraine.'

The pair of them sat gazing eastwards over the last colours of the autumn woods.

'That's not Siege Orgulous and the rest,' objected Diomede.

'No, it's the range they call the Talon. The Casque's a long way beyond.'

The blue skyline, far and fretty, suffered an absurd diminution of magic in Diomede's eyes. Lioncel and he were squires now, well-grown and bronzed with a year of service overseas. They had fought Saracens and Levantine pirates, and had walked in the streets of Rome and Constantinople; but they had never ceased to treasure their old loyalty, and this, the first sight of the duchy since they had fled from it, held them silent for a long moment above their northward road.

'The two years are nearly gone,' said Lioncel glumly. The terms of Yolande's marriage-contract were known throughout the kingdom.

'I suppose she's still shut up at Roclatour,' said Diomede. 'I believe no one there would know you now. Me they never knew. In the spring, if Janus would allow it. . . .'

'We might turn troubadour, you mean? Yes, he's the one man in these parts who wouldn't think us daft to ask.'

'Hautboy and harp in Maytime, like something in a romaunt. We know enough songs of different kinds. It might be very sad and ghostly.'

'Yes . . . yes, it might. But let's do it if we can, on the

chance of getting a glimpse of her. She may have thought of us sometimes . . . after all, your uncle's last letter to Janus said he had sent Amarand back to her.'

'If only that damned last lick of the plague hadn't reached Sanctlamine . . . or if my uncle Dagobert hadn't left everything to Janus . . . but it's no good *iffing*, the water's gone under the bridge now. We'd have to stop short of Bargreant; your young cousin would know you if no one else did.'

'Berel? Yes, he would. I don't suppose Azo troubled to appoint new pages there. Now if Janus took it into his head to ride out that way . . . but there aren't enough castles, or friends of his. Besides, in his train we should be seen by everybody. I don't want to sing in front of my lord the Duke Balthasar.'

'Nor I. *He* might remember. He isn't there yet, but by the spring he may be.'

'Yes, damn him. I suppose it's only knowing what we know about Azo that makes her marriage seem a desecration.'

'Many a man in Azo's place would have tried to marry her himself.'

'Yes, that's true enough . . . come on, we must be going now.'

Lioncel gathered up his bridle and saluted the horizon. Diomede only scowled at it.

'No need to go straight downhill,' he pointed out as they wheeled. 'We can keep to the hillside for a while.'

'Look, across the valley there. A mounted troop just going out of sight up that branching westward road.'

They watched the distant sparkle of steel vanish behind a wooded slope, and set their own horses to trot through a great beechwood. They were commissioned to ride ahead of Janus on the task usually allotted to Scipio, who had leave of absence to visit his family in the province of Camors; that is, they had to find quarters and summon a famous armourer to be in attendance when the chevalier should arrive there.

Janus was a day's journey behind, and his younger squires were enjoying their new responsibility. Their half-armour was brightly polished, their swords were now as long as most, and each carried a loaded crossbow cased behind his right stirrup. Wayside robbers would recognise them as travellers likely to shoot first and hold parley afterwards.

Lioncel whistled a lilting air, and Diomede joined a harmony to it. It was the song of Dagonet, King Arthur's jester-chevalier, dying alone at the edge of a wood with only his memories to console him.

A strange deep bellow interrupted their duet; Lioncel's gelding shied, and Diomede had his crossbow out before his comrade regained control of the frightened animal. Then both squires sat still again, staring at an apparition arisen among the twisted roots of a great beech beside their way.

It was a queer misshapen figure, bruised and bleeding and naked to the waist, supporting itself on magnificent bronzed arms, peering mournfully at the riders out of intelligent greenish eyes. As it moved they saw it to be a dwarf; his thick short legs were clad in good blue woollen hose, and on his big feet were iron-studded clogs. His nose had apparently just been broken, for his lips and chin were masked with blood that had run down on to his broad copper-haired chest. His rather finely-shaped head sat strangely against powerful shoulders, for he was slightly hump-backed; and his auburn curls were crowned by a blue cap of Phrygian shape, which set a last seal of oddity upon him.

' Who are you, and what's happened to you? ' Lioncel demanded.

' I am named Quargis,' answered the dwarf calmly. His deep melodious voice had a lisp in it because of his bruised mouth. ' An acrobat of sorts. I had a kind master until this morning, but I've carried so many of his secrets he must have decided to bury me with them. The two knaves appointed to slay me seeem to have botched it. They knocked me off my horse and stunned me, but this cap's lined with mail. They've broken my nose, a needless addition to my beauty. And they half-stripped me and left me for dead. I can't walk . . . my knee's sprained, and it hurts like hell if I try.'

' Could you sit in a saddle? ' asked Lioncel. ' If so, we can give you a lift to that village in the valley ahead.'

'That would be a Christian deed, young masters. I expected to crawl there on all fours when my head should have stopped pealing a carillon.'

'You'd best sit still awhile,' said Lioncel, tossing his bridle to Diomede. 'We've a wineskin here, and water, and I'll find some linen.'

A few minutes later they had wiped away most of the blood, and bandaged an arm where the skin was torn. Diomede put his cloak round the cold broad shoulders, and Quargis clutched the wineskin and cocked a curious sideways eye at him.

'I see you're neither priests nor Levites,' he remarked. 'I should like to know whom you serve.'

'The Chevalier de Largire,' replied Lioncel, who was shortening his stirrups.

'Him they call Janus of the Silver Shield . . . he's coming to the king's birthday tourney?'

'Yes.'

'A famous chevalier. I trust he won't grudge your delay.'

'We're alone this journey, but he would probably have done the same.'

'I've heard strange tales of his courtesy to simple stricken folk. Now I shall believe them.'

'And who is . . . was . . . your own master?'

'One I am loth to name.'

'Well, that's your business.'

'Yours too, maybe, if you were known to have helped me.'

'We'll take our chance of that. Come now, try to stand up.'

They prised his bulky body from the ground; his head was below their chins, but his great hands easily gripped their outer shoulders. With some trouble they hoisted him into Lioncel's saddle, and got his feet into the stirrup-irons. Lioncel took the bridle, and Diomede rode close behind. Quargis clasped the saddle-horn with one hand, and with the other signed the Cross over Lioncel's head.

'Keep straight on for a while,' he advised. 'After a quarter of a mile a path slopes down to the village—I know, because that's the way I came. I believed I carried a letter to a crony of my lord's, whose castle lies a league to the east. You think i odd that I should be trusted with such errands, but I can climl —I *could* climb—where others find it difficult, and hide wher others would be seen.'

'Something's going on in that village,' said Diomede suddenly. 'They're searching in the thickets round about.'

'And something queer's dodging between the trees up there,' added Lioncel, pointing to their right front. 'Holy Saints, what *is* it?'

An extraordinary brown-and-white bundle was blundering among the beech-boles fifty yards away. It seemed to move on bare legs, and as they watched it fell flat and struggled to get up again. Quargis leaned forward, peering, and spat before he spoke.

'It's a peasant woman with her gown tied up over her head,' he growled. 'The sign manual of my golden lad, my Angel of the Peacock. We'll likely find someone else dead or maimed down yonder. He spreads such jests wherever he goes, outside the cities. Look, she's heard us . . . she's trying to hide.'

Diomede thrust his mount past the other and approached the unfortunate creature at a trot. She was now kneeling in the beech-mast, whimpering miserably in her prison of corded cloth. Her clumsy bare legs and feet had been slashed with a whip; a linen smock, torn and grubby, only half-protected her nakedness.

'You're safe now,' called Diomede, angry and ashamed. 'Keep still, and I'll cut you loose.'

The only answer was a muffled howl. The woman clapped like an enormous partridge, and autumn sunlight slid and quivered over her helpless flesh. Diomede swore distressfully, and tethered his horse before dismounting to advance, dagger in hand.

'We're friends,' he said quietly. 'Kneel up, we're going to take you home.'

He cut the cord and parted the cloth, which opened and fell apart like the bud of a huge flower. A yellow kerchief, a tangle of hair, a round face mottled with terror, burst into view; bright blue eyes glittered, focusing first on Diomede's dagger and then on the cloaked shape of the dwarf riding up behind him.

'You were with them!' the woman screamed, pointing a red finger at Quargis. Then she scrambled to her feet and dashed away downhill at surprising speed, leaving the three staring after her.

'Now she'll raise the village on us,' said the dwarf sombrely. 'I wasn't there when they trussed her up. They were drinking at the inn when I left. The fun hadn't started. We'd best make off and skirt the place . . . unless you'd like to leave me here to settle my brave master's debt.'

'Come on,' said Lioncel. 'They'll have dogs. We don't want to have to use our bows. Hold tight, I'm going to run.'

He tossed his own cloak up to Quargis, caught the near stirrup-leather in his hand, and started off at a swinging pace. Soon there was undergrowth to screen them, and the hillside flattened out in a grassy plateau. A faint tumult drifted up as the woman was greeted by her neighbours. The slope steepened beneath them, and Diomede scouted between the coppices. When they had gone a mile or more Lioncel began to puff and tire, and at last sank down on a fallen tree-trunk to get his wind again.

'That's what comes of doing a kindness,' said the dwarf, looking down at him.

'Was it your master who rode away up that other road?' asked Diomede.

'Ay.'

'Tell us his name now. What was it you said about a peacock?'

'Just one of my names for him. He's the Duke of Baraine, the king's favourite, the young limb they call Belphegor, who goes abroad with the curses of all decent folk rising like dust behind him. And in his company a dozen of his kind, Camus de Caherne the chief of them, with a score of cut-throat archers, and just now a team of monstrosities such as your humble servant, to make the Duke of Ahun laugh when he visits him two days hence.'

'*Belphegor*,' said Lioncel reflectively.

His glance encountered Diomede's and both of them looked away.

A few miles nearer the city they hired a palfrey for Quargis, leaving money in pledge for its return. Also they bought him a shirt and tunic, and a long cloak, with a hood to hide the too-remarkable Phrygian cap. They were taking him to the house of a kinsman, and their ungrudging confidence in him broke down the dwarf's last reserve. In the final league of their journey he regaled them with stories of the exploits of Balthasar-Belphegor.

'The king dotes on him,' said Quargis, when he understood that his rescuers were newly returned from abroad. 'You know that Fulk, Count of Olencourt, who's been Constable since Pont-de-Foy, was also Castellan of Montenair, the key to Nordanay?'

'*Was* . . . why, isn't he now?' asked Lioncel, to whom this was military intelligence.

'No, not he. Belphegor's made Castellan instead. Part of the king's new game of slighting his old supporters. He's made Count Fulk a marquis, with a manor or two in Queranay.'

'But Belphegor . . . the Duke of Baraine . . . is only nineteen.'

'No matter, he's got his papa to prompt and advise him. And the mob in Hautarroy to cheer him. He keeps his antics private there, and only shows his filthy cruelty in the country-side. In the city he scatters largesse and goes to Mass with trumpets. Listen at the jousting and you'll know how much he's loved there. He's tall and very strong, and like a tiger in battle. In the war against Beltany he was chased across open moor on horseback, and leaped his charger over a crag into deep lake water, and swam it ashore. That's the kind of adventure that makes good talk in the taverns. The others they hear less about; even his bullies don't boast of them.'

'Others? Such as . . . ?'

'Burning rebel wounded piled up in a barn. Disembowelling a prisoner by walking him round and round a tree. Impaling a whole family, down to the cradled infant. I wasn't too surprised . . . I first knew him at Hastain after the battle of Arionbel. I saw him and his friends snowballing a blind man and making

dogs drunk. The king gave him the castle of Sabloyn up there
in the hills. I thanked God the plague interfered with my going
there at his bidding. He has wild beasts in pits and makes
prisoners fight them. The prisoners can choose their weapons
from his armoury, but they don't often win. And he's fond of
torturing men and women together. . . .'

' What's he *after*? ' broke in Diomede after a while, finding
his forehead damp to the wind. ' Why with all his fame and
success, his riches and rank and beauty, does he have to work so
hard to earn the name of a fiend? Whom or what's he paying
out? '

' God in his inscrutable wisdom may know but doesn't tell.
Maybe he, Belphegor I mean, is just a mad animal in semblance
of a man. But he has dainty finger-nails and a skin like a girl's.
I don't know . . . they say he was nearly starved to death as a
boy in the siege of Ferisgar, and his mother died soon after.
For years the Grand Seneschal was a luckless mercenary
captain, dragging his son around the frontiers of the Empire.
And now the world's at his feet, and the devil's at his elbow,
and to all whom it may concern I say: *keep out of Belphegor's
way.*'

' How did you first come in it? ' asked Lioncel grimly.

' He saw me and my troupe at Hastain, and took us into his
service. That was when the king made him Count of Jarapt. It
was livelihood for six of us . . . you expect a young lord to be
wild . . . and he found out how I could climb. I've stood with
Camus on my shoulders, and him on the shoulders of Camus,
when he wanted to reach a lady's window. What gave me a last
grue was a rape at a village bridal. What offended him in me
was my strangling one of his bully-boys who had set my hair
on fire. At least, I think that was it. I know I'll have to lie low,
and dodge my old acquaintance, and get away when I'm able.
My cousin is the physician Sylvanus . . . you may see him when
blood is shed in the lists . . . and although he's ashamed of our
kinship he's kind to me by stealth.'

Quargis broke off for a moment, brooding with his chin on
his chest, a habit made easy for him by nature. Then he turned
a speculative eye on the youths whom he had reduced to silence.

'.It's worth a crown or two to Belphegor to know I'm still alive,' he told them.

'Don't talk like that,' said Diomede savagely. 'I'd give all the crowns I possess to know him in hell where he belongs.'

'Why, what's he done to *you*?' asked the dwarf with a sort of kindly malice. Not waiting for a reply to so cynical a question, he looked ahead and summoned another reminiscence.

'At the back of the Hotel de Hastain,' he said, 'there's an alley with a postern opening on it. I used sometimes to haunt that alley by night, to give a lantern-sign to my lord when the coast was clear for his entry or departure. And one night he and Camus de Caherne were just going up to the postern when a man came hurtling along as if he'd done murder . . . no time for any of us to move. He ran full tilt into the pair of them, and they grabbed him before he could make a sound. Camus pinned his arms, and Belphegor got him by the head with one hand over his mouth, and they screwed him different ways until his neck broke. I'm not what you call finicky, but I've dreamed of that sound sometimes since.'

'But why should Belphegor seek the king in secret?' demanded Lioncel.

'It wasn't the king he sought at such times.'

'Who was it, then?'

'The queen.'

Diomede remembered that story later in the afternoon, when Quargis led on beneath the towering Hotel de Hastain and past the cathedral apse to reach the house of Doctor Sylvanus in quiet Street of Scales. It was a tall stone house, with its own court-yard beside it; the gilded pestle and mortar gleamed over the street door. In the courtyard Lioncel and Diomede lifted down their fellow-traveller; he stood for a second with one great hand on an arm of each of them.

'You go to the Burning Bush?' he said.

'Yes, if there's room.'

'They'll make room for the Silver Shield. It's not the place for me, even if I wanted to show myself. I'm going to grow a beard to go with this new nose they've given me. My tavern's the Cup and Ball, in the first alley to the left as you go on your way from here. Any day at noon will find me there. Come tomorrow . . . not tomorrow? Come when you can . . . you promise? Your money will be ready. Eh? No, I shan't beggar myself by repayment. I was the master of the acrobats. I have a little hoard with a goldsmith. God be with you . . . here come my cousin's servants.'

Two very subdued young squires lay side by side in one bed that night above the Sign of the Burning Bush. They could hear other people talking beyond the wooden walls of their chamber, and took no chances of being overheard themselves. Their master's name had commanded the usual respect; it was easier for two than for one to keep fellow-guests at a distance, but they had withdrawn from the public rooms as soon as their meal was ended.

For an hour or more they spoke softly together about Quargis and Yolande and Yolande's husband.

'There's always the hope he'll be killed in the lists,' murmured Diomede.

'I pray he comes up against our Janus,' breathed Lioncel between clenched teeth.

'Here's your prayer answered,' said Diomede a week later. Lioncel glanced at him and grinned.

It was late in the year for jousting, and the green turf beside the red-draped tilting-barrier was soon trampled to a grey slime. Mares'-tails patterned the blue sky, October wind tossed the last leaves among the many-coloured pavilions at either end of the lists, and sunlight was still warm in the lee of the packed stands. Red-haired King Thorismund, black-haired Queen Fredegonde, and the little pink-cheeked Duke of Honoy who so admired his friend Balthasar, sat amid great lords and ladies in the blue-and-white balcony under the White Lion of Neustria. Lioncel and Diomede stood by the famous silver shield at the door of the black-and-white pavilion of the Chevalier Janus.

In front of them the tail of black Pollux was braided with cloth of silver. The tall bulk, charger and chevalier, was a splendour of black and silvered steel, again with no other colour

showing save that of the long gilded spurs. At the far end of
the lists was an even more wonderful panoply; the armour of
Balthasar Duke of Baraine was gilded all over, and his charger
—caparisoned with cloth of gold—was of a fawn tint that carried
the note of colour down to gilded hoofs. Only the bright
purple shield broke the harmony; for the rest, it was *Or* against
Argent, and the crowd yelled for its golden lad.

Diomede crossed his fingers and wished he could cross
himself. He thought of the glade by the wishing-well; since
that day he had many times watched Janus ride in such
encounters, always to win or draw, never yet to lose. And now
he, Diomede, had to wish misfortune to the blazon of
Yolande.

The Constable was Master of the Tourney; he sat immediately
before and below the king. Diomede spared him a glance,
wondering if he, too, wanted Janus to kill Belphegor. The
Constable let the crowd expend its bellyful of cheers before
raising his white baton and nodding to the trumpeters. A
marvellous cadence in sustained thirds pierced and frayed the
shouting and outlasted the babble that followed it.

The baton thumped on the rail of the Constable's balcony.
The silver bells on the bridle of Pollux rang sweetly all
together as his great hoofs pounded forward towards the red
barrier.

One golden Leopard of Baraine glittered on the purple shield,
another flashed on the closed helm that hid the beauty of
Belphegor. Over the charger's gilded chamfron they grew out
of the sunlit distance; the silver imperial eagle rushed sparkling
to meet them. . . .

The crack of splintered hornbeam was swallowed by the bang
and crash of metal. Pollux slipped, slid, and staggered sideways,
one rear hoof dealing the barrier a dull tremendous thump.
Janus fell like a thrown tree, clanging to the ground with
Belphegor's lance-tip broken off in his visor-slit. Belphegor,
battered backwards along his charger's crupper, was carried
a score of yards before he swung himself upright and tugged
the fawn monster to a halt.

The city of Hautarroy seemed afloat on a tide of roaring

sound, but Lioncel and Diomede, Rosso and Verde, were blind
to the victor and deaf to his triumph as they raced forward over
the grass.

Afterwards Diomede only remembered wondering if they
had emptied the silver coffin. Rosso captured the stallion's bridle
and got him out of their way as they bent over the motionless
chevalier. Lioncel tore the lance-head away; its pronged plate
had jammed in the slit without doing damage beyond.

' Leave my helm on,' commanded Janus in his ordinary voice.
' Drag me back on a cloak. My right leg's broken.'

Round one end of the tilting-barrier trampled the fawn-
coloured charger; the golden splendour of Belphegor towered
above them as they crouched and laboured to get the cloak under
its glittering burden. Round the other end rode one of the
tilting-marshals; Lioncel rose and called to him through the
din. The marshal nodded and reined round to face the royal
balcony, making a sweeping gesture towards Belphegor. The
cheering which had begun to slacken, broke out in renewed
thunder. Diomede found his eyes filling with tears of rage.

Hauling the fallen paladin away was a tedious business.
Some of the crowd were joyfully booing before the pavilion
door gave shelter. The Constable's own barber-surgeon was
waiting to attend Janus; on the floor of the tent they unhelmed
and unarmed him, and skilful fingers discovered the fracture
before a swelling had time to mask it. Janus stared crossly at
the silken ceiling, but made no complaint and did not raise his
voice.

' This had to happen some time,' he said to Rosso, ' but by
God's Monday I wish it had been someone else to do it.'

Nobles and clergy began to appear to find out what had
happened to him. Among the first was a fat abbot in a crimson
cloak and furred hood; he sank down on a camp-stool and shook
a ringed finger at Janus.

' Remember your ancient promise,' he said. ' If I can't have
you hale I must have you damaged. I've sent for a horse-litter,
and my chaplain's ridden off to make arrangements.'

' Boys,' said Janus, ' salute my friend the Lord Abbot of
Saint-Maur. Old comrade, I present my squires and servants.

We'll gladly exchange the Burning Bush for the precincts of
your hospitable abbey.'

'You must command my servants,' said the churchman
courteously to Lioncel and Diomede. 'And you, Janus,' he
added, turning back to the supine chevalier, 'you will now have
time to dictate to my clerks the story of your wanderings.'

'God send them kind hearts and easy quills,' said Janus.

The Duke of Saulte came then, and the Archbishop's
chaplain, and the Constable's brother, and the king's own
chamberlain; Diomede bowed and made answer and bowed
again, while Janus calmly superintended his own removal in the
litter. The abbey servants took him away, with Rosso in attendance. Lioncel remained with Verde in charge of the coffin, the
armour and gear, and the black-and-white pavilion, which must
in courtesy stand with furled banner until the end of the tournament. Diomede rode to the Burning Bush, where Nero had
remained to keep an eye on the rest of the horses and baggage.

'Belphegor wins all the time,' Diomede told himself dolefully
as he rode in at the South Gate and began to thread the silent
and almost empty streets.

Westering sunlight flashed on the paint and gilding of the
shop signs; the shadow of Diomede and his horse was blue-grey
on the cobbles between the forward-leaning house-fronts. Cold
wind blustered round corners, and brown leaves lay thick in
the gutters of courts and squares and alleys.

Winter had promised to be cheerful here, but now it would
be . . .

Diomede stared between his horse's ears with a sudden blankness of realisation. In the great abbey by the North Gate Janus
would have little need of his squires. It was late in the year for
dawdling among villages, but not too late for a harp and a
hautboy to visit Roclatour.

'First of all,' said Janus, 'I must have Scipio here. Rosso shall
ride to fetch him. That will occupy a week or more. Then,
when Scipio arrives, you may make this journey into Baraine.
I shall give each of you a letter to show that you travel with
leave from me. There is now, I understand, a chapel in the

Gorge of Arionbel. You shall make there for me the offering
I should have made long ago; and there is no need to hurry.'

This was more than Lioncel or Diomede had expected, and
they said so.

'It may be I lie here on my back because of that same
omission,' said Janus, and then was silent for a while, as if
pondering the terms of some gentleman's agreement between
the Sieur God and himself.

'Meanwhile,' he went on at length, 'you boys must go about
unbadged in the city, and keep your tempers concerning what
may be said about my overthrow. I have hitherto broken an
arm, a collar-bone, and three ribs, and have been wounded
eleven times, beyond snicks and scratches; so don't repine too
much at this calamity. In the spring I shall be jousting again.'

They noticed that he never mentioned his charger's slide in
the mud. Such an excuse was far beneath the dignity of Janus.

So it came about that they moved discreetly among the shops
and taverns, finding here a song or a basket of candied fruit for
their bed-fast chevalier, and there the gossip of unbuttoned
burghers. Mindful of the warning to keep their tempers, they
listened to a new couplet bawled to an old tune in honour of
the golden lad, the Angel of the Peacock:

> ' Fee, fi, fo, fum,
> Bang in the occu-lar-i-um! '

Janus was variously reported to have lost an eye, to have
been emasculated by the horn of his saddle, to be dying of
chagrin, and to have taken the cowl. The Duke of Baraine had
gone on to distinguish himself on the second day of the jousting,
and the queen had hung a wreath of laurel on his lance-tip.
Lioncel and Diomede rolled pellets of bread, looked thoughtfully into their wine, caressed their dagger-hilts, and sometimes
took themselves out of earshot in something of a hurry.

The Sign of the Burning Bush they avoided, but several times
they paused at noon beneath the undistinguished Sign of the
Cup and Ball. There, sure enough, was Quargis, villainous with
the beginnings of a beard.

' I knew you'd plenty on hand,' he said on the first occasion, when the tavern-keeper had shown them into a little private room. ' Oh, yes, I was at the jousting; I climbed a tree and saw very well . . . yes, yes, my leg's in order, acrobats know how to deal with a sprain.'

Quargis was a mine of gossip; the two squires learned from him how one lord and another lord had quarrelled over a third lord's wife, how coiners had been caught three doors away from the tavern where they sat, how a boat had rammed the bridge in a fog and gone down with all on board.

' I move no further than this by daylight,' he confessed. ' Until Belphegor's out of the city I mean to hug my lair. They say he's going to keep Christmas at Hastain again with the king.'

' He is, is he? ' said Lioncel flatly. Diomede read Lioncel's thought: if Belphegor were at Hastain, he could not be at Roclatour.

' Yes, yes,' went on the dwarf, parodying the voice of some fat burgher. ' You know how fond the . . . little Duke of Honoy is of him.'

Quargis was silent for a minute or two, sipping his hot spiced wine, or grinding his palm softly over the pewter goblet. His glance frisked several times from one squire's face to the other's, and he seemed to come to some decision.

' You know the queen dowager died a few weeks back? ' he murmured.

' No,' confessed Lioncel. ' I thought her dead long ago, if I ever thought of her at all.'

' That's doubtless what my lord the king would have had you believe,' said Quargis. ' After the battle of Pont-de-Foy, when her son was killed and his party destroyed, she was sent to the Convent of Saint Rose, a league to the south of the city. We passed within a mile or two before you bought me my new shirt. There she lived and there she died, and now there's a muttering about some treasure she hid before they shut her away. She had none of it with her, and the rumour goes that all she said before dying was that only Gaston de Volsberghe knew where the hoard lies.'

'Gaston de Volsberghe? The only rebel commander who escaped from Pont-de-Foy?'

'That's the man. A great tall blackguard, who once swore to impale Raoul of Ger. No one knows where he is, or indeed if he's alive at all. Attainted and exiled these twelve years. A very good soldier, so he'd not lack for a living. The king broke the duchy of Volsberghe in pieces, and Gaston's brother is only a count these days. Once or twice I've heard a whisper that Gaston had been seen in Nordanay; there's still a tidy price on his head, our lord the king having a good memory when it suits him.'

'What about this treasure, then?'

'The dowager's young nephew-by-marriage, Guy Count of Burias, is said to be after it by fair means or foul.'

'Foul?'

'Ay, he's for having her out of her grave.'

'But how can he do that when she's buried at——?'

'Black arts, Master Lioncel. Necromancy, they call it. Would you two like to come and see?'

'Er. . . .'

'I shan't attend in the front row. In fact I shall be well behind.'

'The front row! Why, will there be a crowd?'

'A dozen or so, court rips and their trollops. Nothing like it's been tried for years; these pleasure-wearied young men will go far in search of entertainment. Burias is not too bad, but he mixes with some that are worse.'

'How d'you know all this?'

'From my kind but curious-minded cousin . . . one of his patients, scared half to death, wanted a philtre to stop her lover having any part in this expedition. Sylvanus knows that I am not readily impressed; he's asked me to observe the occasion and report what goes on. The necromancer is a rival of his—not in magic or medicine, but as an alchemist.'

'Where and when is this going to be done?'

'Say rather, attempted. In the graveyard of a deserted village half a mile from the convent. Maradette, it was called; it was in the royal forest, and the king moved his serfs away

H

years ago. I knew it when I was a lad; there's nothing much
left now but the ruins of the church and the priest's house. The
rite's planned for three nights hence, All Saints' Day and All
Souls' Eve.'

'D'you think anything will happen?' asked Diomede
curiously.

Quargis shrugged his great shoulders and spread thick
fingers in the air.

'I'd say half-a-mile's nothing to a good ghost,' he replied
'Especially on that night, when graveyards are reputed to stir
I don't know . . . I'm not a good Christian . . . I've seen too
much contented evil, and it seems to me that prayers and psalms
drain the good away from earth without adequate return. I
don't think the Sieur God much minded what happened to the
Sieur Jesu . . . but this is no way to talk a bowshot from the
chief church in the land. The magic that goes on in there needs
faith like any other, and faith needs the kind of vision and
blindness that I haven't got.'

It was not easy to shock young men who had been to Rome
and Constantinople, and Quargis noted with approval that
neither of his listeners quailed at his words.

'Well, are you coming?' he went on. '*Something* may
happen.'

Lioncel and Diomede exchanged glances.

'Say a kinsman of Doctor Sylvanus has asked you to supper
and morning Mass. We'll attend at Saint Andreas on our way
back. I haven't offered my candles yet in gratitude for your
rescue of me.'

Quargis grinned a little sadly.

'Our horses . . .' began Diomede.

'I'll find three horses,' promised the resourceful dwarf.
'Tell me tomorrow how the chevalier takes it.'

Janus took it very well, complimenting them on their treatment of a luckless wayfarer. If their story sounded as though
Quargis was a burgher rather than an acrobatic dwarf, that
was because they emphasized his scrupulous repayment of the
money spent on him. And so, in the afternoon of All Saints'

Day, Lioncel and Diomede sallied forth with swords under their cloaks.

The horses were waiting in the yard of the Cup and Ball; Quargis had bespoken an early supper. The vesper-chimes of Hautarroy followed on a light north wind as the adventurers galloped into the twilit woods.

Before it was quite dark they reached a dreary deserted hamlet, and tethered their mounts in a dell on the eastward side of it. Then they stumbled among mounded graves and stole through long grass and nettles to the porch of the little church. The door had disappeared with all other movable woodwork, and the wind mourned eerily in the gapped roof. Inside, they lit their lantern at the foot of a stone stairway.

Diomede confessed to himself that he would have been terrified to come to this place alone; but Quargis was so matter-of-fact and Lioncel so interested that it was impossible not to feel a grim excitement.

Quargis had a rope ladder and a wineskin under his cloak. For weapon he carried a battle-axe; his squat figure, Diomede decided, was enough to daunt the devil himself. Up on the cold tower-top they found the lead had been stripped from the timber, but enough flooring remained to let them lie sheltered behind the battlemented parapet. Diomede, climbing last, had missed most of the cobwebs, but the wind of a bat's wing had brought sweat to his forehead, and when the lantern-candle was snuffed he was the first to suggest recourse to the wineskin. Lioncel's hand, as he passed it, was comfortingly warm and steady.

'The moon will be up in an hour or two,' Quargis reminded them. 'Let's keep silent for a time, to sort out the noises.'

Diomede pushed back his hood, and set himself to listen. A screech-owl's cry split the moan and hiss of wind with ghastly recurring clamour; somewhere far away a stag belled repeatedly in the darkness. Down below, a window-slat clacked and rasped and rattled; Diomede loosened his sword and tried to measure distance for a swipe at the stair-head if need should arise.

The constellation of Orion signalled through travelling

cloud-wrack. Sometimes Betelgeuse and Rigel shone dimly
when the rest were hidden. To the west of them Aldebaran
and Capella came and went as though playing a game. After
a while two yellow lights began to flicker from a fixed point
beyond a web of shifting tree-tops to the north-east.

' Is that the Convent of Saint Rose? ' asked Lioncel.

Quargis grunted assent, and Diomede was suddenly glad
that he was on a tower-top. It seemed safer than the naked
woodland, where suddenly the ghost of a queen might glide
between the oaks. He hoped that if she came the horses would
not see her.

After a while Lioncel spoke as if staring across Diomede's
back.

' Someone's bringing lanterns from the river side of us.'

The hooded bulk of Quargis reared up and hid the glittering
Square of Pegasus.

' That's not the way Burias should come,' he muttered. ' Of
course, a boat up the river . . . but there don't seem to be many
of them. Three lanterns . . . and now we must be very quiet.
This is a freakish wind for sound.'

Watching at the crenels, the three of them saw five men
striding in file under the trees, amid the bushes, and between
the last tumbled remains of mud-and-wattle huts. They were
cloaked and hooded, and carried what seemed to be bundles
and weapons. A beam of lantern-light gleamed on what
looked like a fishing-trident, and one tall silhouette was
revealed with a pickaxe over its shoulder.

' Our footprints! ' breathed Lioncel, and Diomede felt a
chill in his spine, but the newcomers passed purposefully
beneath the south wall of the church. With lanterns swinging,
they went round the four sides of the churchyard, plainly not
concerned with looking for signs of previous visitors. At gaps
in the low ruined walls they paused and spoke together, halting
at length in a group by the doorway of the tumbledown
vicarage. Height and distance and drawn hoods prevented
any sight of their faces; their voices were no more than a
mumble against the cold wind.

For a minute or two they stood talking, their figures shaping the core of an intricate pattern of cross-lights and shadows. Then they moved into what had once been the vicarage garden, and hung two of the lanterns on boughs of a great hawthorn. Presently two of them were uncloaked and digging with pick and shovel. One was bearded, the other was not; they might have been soldiers, watermen, woodcutters, or foresters. A third, still cloaked, stood watching them; a fourth took a lantern with him into the little ruined house, and its movements flung wedges of wheeling light out of the narrow windows. The remaining man walked back to the point where the party had crossed the overgrown track from Haut-arroy; there he stood as if on guard, hardly to be seen at all.

Diomede stared and stared at the glow beside the hawthorn. 'No graves there,' he reflected. 'Are they digging for the treasure? Or are they in league with the necromancer and getting ready a sham apparition?'

These suspicions so engaged him that he whispered them to Lioncel.

'M'm, maybe a plot of some kind,' Lioncel murmured in his ear. 'I wish we'd brought crossbows. I'd like to go down and see what they're doing, but there's too many of them to risk it.'

'I'd rather watch from here, thank you.'

After that they lay quiet again for what seemed a long time. Diomede moved, and one of his spurs screeched very faintly on the stone behind him. Neither of the others spoke, but he felt their cautionary tension like a touch in the darkness. Beyond the corner of the priest's house the digging was still going on. The light inside the building was stationary; Diomede was watching it when suddenly it went out. The man inside rejoined his companions, using some back exit. They looked up and laughed, and he held out a wineskin. One of the group whistled, and the sentinel stalked back to them. He, too, laughed, and his head was tilted against the lights with the wineskin held beyond it.

'Damnation, I wish something would happen,' Diomede told himself.

The clouds above the eastern horizon were suddenly veined

with silver. The moon was coming up behind the Talon of Baraine. Diomede thought of his night in the pass above Lake Falchion; then he was softly thumped in the rear by Lioncel.

Turning, he saw a red smear growing out of the distance. He ducked as the moon came out and brushed the battlements with level light. The glims were doused by the hawthorn; the churchyard of Maradette lay utterly desolate. . . .

There must have been twenty riders in the procession that presently filled with torchlight and chatter the rough track beside the churchyard wall. Moonlight and cloud-shadow chased each other across the scene; there was a snorting, a jingling of bits, and a good deal of dismounting. Three figures advanced with something which looked like a woven mat; this they unrolled and laid among the grave-mounds at the bidding of a tall white-bearded man who carried a metal tripod under one arm. . . .

Soon, by the light of the torches, the white beard was bowed low as its owner bent and chalked a circle on the matting. This circle he filled with other markings; over one of them he placed the tripod. Then he put on a wide-brimmed hat with a crown shaped like a steeple, and suppled his hands as if washing them in the moonbeams. Two assistants busied themselves preparing something in the bowl.

The gibbous moon was peering down from a black expanse of sky when at length the necromancer lit a taper and waved his helpers back from the circle. He turned to the company that now lined the western wall of the enclosure, and silenced them with a gesture.

The Count of Burias stepped forward and stood beside him. Moonlight showed him to be a personable young man, dark and haughty and clad in half-armour, with a hunting-hat on his head. The old man touched his taper to the bowl, and thick white smoke began to rise, with yellow flames curling beneath it. . . .

The crowd stood silent and rigid; the necromancer's voice went up in a reedy declamation. The smoke whirled and billowed away across the southward wall, sometimes hiding the roof of the vicarage from the watchers on the tower.

Diomede found himself clutching Lioncel's arm; they hung back, afraid of the wavering glow, yet anxious to miss nothing.

A brazen rod flashed in the necromancer's hand; brazen serpents were twined in opposition beneath its winged tip. The moon was suddenly clouded again; the wind, which still crashed softly in the trees around the derelict village, seemed to abate in the churchyard, so that the smoke steadied and rose more straightly into the air.

'A-ah!' said Quargis softly, as a blue-white radiance struck up from under the great hawthorn. Brighter and larger it grew, illuminating the twisted branches. The necromancer paused in his incantation, the Count of Burias set hand to his sword, and a gasp went up from the ranked company behind them.

A shape leaped in front of the blue-white glare; a ghastly exultant bellow broke out, like that of a group of cattle all gone crazy together. The moon came out once more, and the wind scattered the tripod-smoke, and a black thing like a Minotaur charged through a gap in the eastern wall, with a trident poised in its black man's-hand, and a black foot-long phallus spiking up from its shaggy loins.

A yell of terror pealed from the panicking courtiers and their servants. Torchlight broke in a whirl of sparks and plunged away into the woods as men and women and horses fled in shrieking confusion. The apparition danced and whinnied and kicked the tripod over; flaming sticks and powder flew wide in the long grass, and through the eddying smother the trident went lunging into the necromancer's stomach. The old man doubled up with a groan, and collapsed against the low wall; a second thrust, darted at Guy of Burias, was parried by his flashing sword. An arrow leaped out of the dark behind the demon, and struck the count in the throat, so that he dropped his weapon and fell choking in the nettles.

No one of his friends was left; the stampede was complete, crashing away with a lessening din along the moonlit oak-glades. The bull-headed monster caught up a torch that flared at his feet, and by its light dealt another blow at the necromancer, who kicked and lay still with his staff fallen across his neck. Then the trident was poised over the young nobleman; but he, too, grew still before it could descend. The bull-man laughed, and stuck the weapon upright in the ground, and pulled off his animal headpiece, disclosing a shapely golden head which could not be mistaken.

Still laughing, Belphegor turned to his companions as they came out of the priest's garden.

'The old trot can lie quiet,' he cried. 'Her secret's safe yet awhile.'

On the tower-top the watchers huddled fascinated, afraid to stir, while he ground the lit end of the torch first into one dead face and then into the other.

'This'll discourage the black arts, if anyone comes to look for them,' he went on in the same clear voice. 'And treasure-seeking too. . . .'

His words became indistinct as the others came around him. One of them carried a great conch with a mouthpiece of silver. Another knelt and pulled out the arrow, thereafter rifling the dead count's body. A third held a lantern for the operation, while Belphegor himself twitched up the brazen staff and tucked it under his arm. Then he took his torch and trident and headpiece with him into the priest's house, emerging a few minutes later in the hunting-clothes he had worn before.

The wineskin went round again before the group broke up. They gathered their sacks and tools and cloaks, and made off towards the river, laughing and talking in great contentment; the next flood of moonlight showed the graveyard still again, except for the curl and drift of smoke from the spilled fuel among the mounds.

The wind lamented, and the owl took up its tale, and the wink of the distant convent's lights was answered from the sky by more deliberate winks from Rigel and Capella.

'Well, you've seen what the golden lad can do,' said Quargis, almost with satisfaction.

'And *that's* what's married to my lady,' though Diomede.

'Can't we somehow . . . *use* this?' demanded Lioncel grimly.

'Yes, if we want our throats cut,' Quargis assured him.

'It seems so damned pointless,' Diomede grumbled. High-spirited cruelty always baffled and enraged him; his own savagery was of a kind that awoke only in reaction.

'Pointless to you and me, maybe,' said Quargis bitterly. 'And to my kinsman when I tell him of it. Except that he's lost a rival here. Come on down now, and I'll see if there's anything left I can take as a token to back my tale.'

They relit the lantern and filed down the tower stair. If any inhabitant of the graveyard meant to use his night's privilege, he had determined to wait, thought Diomede. Too much crowd and noise for quiet courteous haunting . . . Quargis was unbuckling the old man's belt, a beautiful piece of coppersmith's work with the Signs of the Zodiac on its plaques. Diomede crossed himself at sight of the disfigured face and scorched white beard.

'We must make a cast aside and go in at the East Gate,' said Quargis, when they had stood by the hawthorn and seen the last guttering flare die out at the bottom of the grave-like trench. 'It's lucky there's this moonlight. We don't want to get mixed up with that frightened rout yonder.'

As they made off to find the hidden horses, Diomede turned for a last look at that ill-omened place. The moon picked out a limp dead hand, a glittering leg of the overturned tripod, a stone beast on the porch roof, a wisp of smoke like a spectral serpent. . . . He turned to follow his companions, and trod on something metallic that clinked under his spur. It was a dagger, jewel-hilted, which must have been tipped from the plundered sword-belt, for its pommel was a boar *passant*, the crest and device of Burias, cunningly carven in some darkly-crystalline stone.

'*In memoriam*,' said Diomede, and slid the blade into his thigh-boot top as he followed the lantern light ahead.

Before dawn the three of them drank at an inn in the suburb beside the East Gate. A groom and a drawer were awake to serve them; on moonlit nights, said Quargis, this house of call was never closed. Eat before Mass they would not; and so when the gate opened they rode straight to the cathedral. By then Diomede had pouched the dagger with

the boar on it; he regarded the morning scene with the aloofness of one who had been up all night. When trumpets and
torchlight bore down from the Hotel de Hastain, and an
excited burgher turned to tell him that now they would be
able to see the Duke of Baraine, Diomede accepted the rôle
of stranger thus thrust upon him, and put what he imagined
to be a southern accent into his voice.

' This is the son of the duke who was murdered? ' he asked
very politely.

' Nay, nay, nay,' said the burgher scornfully. ' He's the
husband of the late duke's daughter, and the son of the Grand
Seneschal—him that beat the Franconians to shreds two years
back. He's a great friend of the king, and as doughty a spear
as ever downed champion in the lists.'

' Blows a good trumpet, too,' said Diomede, and yawned as
he went away up the steps.

When, later in the morning, Lioncel and he paid their
respects to the Chevalier Janus, the latter laid down his comb
and mirror and eyed them very gravely.

' Boys,' he said, ' for six months I shall stay here to meditate
and dictate my memoirs. When you have visited Arionbel, do
as you please; come back to me, return to Gax, or go on to
Largire and wait for my word. Scipio will be in charge there.
Rosso will stay here with me. Lay your plans and tell me what
you intend to do.'

' What's come over him? ' asked Diomede, when he and
Lioncel were next alone together.

' It's in the family, of course,' said Lioncel ruefully.

The sister of Janus was an anchoress of formidable sanctity,
who had terrified both Diomede and himself. Beneath her
attacks on his way of life Janus had shown surprising meek-
ness; in fact, he had looked sheepish, and neither youth had
ever forgiven the celebrated recluse.

' Pray God he doesn't take to religion,' went on Lioncel
devoutly.

' We must try to bring back a holy sign from Arionbel,' said
Diomede. ' Something to discourage him from . . . er . . .
well, from too much holiness.'

'Like setting a little fire to burn across the path of a great one.'

'Yes, that's it. I'm going to light for Saint Andreas a candle the height of the Silver Shield.'

'And I another, the length of his longest sword,' said Lioncel.

'Meanwhile, are we going to ask Quargis to come away with us?'

'I've been wondering about that. I feel as if we should keep him with us in case. . . .'

'In case we can somehow . . . it's daft to think of it.'

'I've thought of it a lot, if you mean we might add his hatred to ours, and work some mischief to the Angel of the Peacock.'

'Yes, that's what I meant,' said Diomede desolately.

'Of course, she may not know what he's like . . . and he *might* treat her properly.'

'Huh!'

'Yes, I know. The odds are all against it.'

Quargis was glad to be invited to follow their fortunes with them. According to his information, the death of the Count of Burias had occasioned a grave scandal at court; the king was enraged at the death of his friend, but unable, in the circumstances, to bring anyone to justice. The archbishop flatly refused to bury the count in the cathedral; but, considering that he died fighting the devil, the Bishop of Belsaunt conducted the service when he was quietly laid among his ancestors at Burias in Beltany.

So Quargis was with Lioncel and Diomede when at length they took the muddy eastward road towards the mountains of Baraine.

'No young women to bid farewell to?' he asked with sly good-natured concern.

'No young women,' said Lioncel, cheerfully.

Diomede said nothing at all.

On the third day out they paused at an inn which commanded a narrow wooden bridge that crossed a willow-bordered stream. This stream wandered out of the foothills of the Talon; the travellers were rounding the northern end of the range, preferring to lengthen their journey rather than plunge into wooded ravines. Pale sunlight glittered on slow-moving water as they drank a cup of wine in their saddles.

Few wayfarers were abroad on the bleak November roads; it was natural to look with attention at the two cowled and sandalled palmers who strode manfully towards them over the two-plank packhorse bridge. Each carried in his wide-brimmed hat a cockle-shell and one or two leaden signs from Neustrian or Franconian shrines. One was tall and lean, with a pointed sandy beard and a beaked nose scarred near the eyebrows; the other was immense, grey-eyed, thick-lipped, with a black square-cut beard that reached half-way to his girdle. The giant gave the mounted trio a resounding *Pax vobiscum*; his companion signed the Cross at them, but barely raised his eyes, being no doubt engaged in profitable meditation.

When the muddy black frocks were gone beyond earshot Lioncel let out a hissing breath.

'Diomede,' he began softly. 'Did you see?'

'Yes, I saw, but I wasn't sure. You've been closer to him than I have. It's that damned soldier again, the helmsman in the long boat.'

Quargis, sitting a little apart, nodded and winked at them, but said nothing for a moment, as an inn servant came to collect the wine-cups. When the three of them were away from the wall of the building, Quargis drew rein.

'Now what?' he demanded quietly.

'What d'you mean?' asked Diomede, as Lioncel and he halted.

'I didn't think *you'd* know him. He must forget that his great beard makes him look like his father.'

'His father?' repeated the mystified Lioncel.

'Of course. The old Constable, who was killed at Pont-de-Foy. I lived at Belsaunt then; his head was stuck for six months over the south gate there.'

'*What* are you talking about?' muttered Diomede.

'Him that's just gone by, of course. Gaston de Volsberghe.'

'Is *that* Gaston de. . . .'

'Ay. I'd swear to it anywhere.'

'We were talking about the other—a man of the Grand Seneschal's. The Grand Seneschal seems to use him on . . . er . . . on secret business.'

'I've never seen *him* before that I know of, but I'll warrant this business is secret enough. Young masters, you'll remember the price on Gaston's head. What's to prevent our dogging that pair and giving word to the Provost when they reach Hautarroy?'

The three of them sat silent for a moment beside the empty bridgehead. The long shoots of willow and poplar shook and waved in the gusty wind, and the innkeeper's ducks explored the brown sedges. Behind them, the innkeeper came to his door and spat after surly palmers who needed no refreshment.

'What's to prevent us?' repeated Lioncel. 'It seems to me Belphegor's to prevent us. God knows I'd like to put a spoke in his winged wheel of Fortune. But if Gaston de Volsberghe's abroad with that knave there, he's in league with Belphegor and Belphegor's daddy. They must . . . by Our Lady, that's it, they must be after the old queen's treasure. They're smuggling Gaston into the realm . . . it means the king doesn't know!'

'I told you,' said Quargis patiently. 'I believe there's a thousand crowns on his head.'

'Some kind of a bargain between three very crafty knaves,' went on Lioncel. 'If we stick our noses in, we'll get them scalded off us.'

'We could ride after them and shoot them down,' said Quargis. 'Gaston's head in a sack would be as good as Gaston in chains.'

'It's a coil,' growled Diomede. 'Whatever we do is wrong now. Murder them, and it's murder, and chalked up as sacrilege; I reckon there'll be nothing to show they're not real pilgrims. Yet there they are, two great villains, and it feels a crime to let them go. If we try to capture Gaston and fail— and it means taking the other as well—we're killed or exiled for nothing. Succeed, and we're caught in the net with them, and not likely to live long that way either. D'you think the king would believe *us* against his boon companion? There'd be some tale to explain away Gaston's coming in this guise. Besides, can't you hear us accusing Azo of murdering the Duke Engelbert?'

'What's that?' exclaimed Quargis, astonished.

'Time we told you our own little story,' said Lioncel drily. 'Come, we'll go slowly on. It'll be easy to turn and catch them up if that's what we decide to do. That innkeeper'll think we've taken root beside the flowing stream.'

The horsehoofs clumped leisurely over the wooden bridge. When they reached the far bank the squires closed in on either side of Quargis. The dwarf listened almost silently, his chin sunk on his breast, his eyes focused far ahead. When they had both done he drew rein again.

'It's a very thin noose for very thick necks,' he said in his matter-of-fact way. 'But I still think we should track them and at least see what they do.'

'No need, I fancy,' Lioncel told him, nodding at the distance.

Six horsemen, with two led horses, were galloping westwards round a bend of the pine-shadowed track. Their black coats were badged with the Thunderbolt; the leader wore full armour, and beneath his lifted visor he scanned the little silver wolves of Largire in the hats of Lioncel and Diomede.

'Have two palmers passed you?' he demanded, civilly, but without preamble.

'Two miles back,' replied Lioncel. 'Just beyond the next bridge.'

The man-at-arms saluted him, and spurred away at the head of his party.

'That's how battles are lost and won,' said Quargis, a little obscurely. 'Master Lioncel, Master Diomede, your humble servant will continue to keep out of Belphegor's way.'

IX

THE SECRET SERVANTS OF YOLANDE

ON a misty November afternoon Yolande and Douce, with old Julian and three archers in attendance, rode up the stony streets from the east gate to the castle. As they passed the yard entry of an inn called the Spurs, a greasy-looking woman came stumbling out and caught at Yolande's stirrup.

'My lady duchess!' she pleaded, and Yolande waved back the archer who crowded forward with lifted whip.

'What is it?' asked Yolande, reining in, and pushing at her hood to get a clearer view of the crowd that gabbled beside the inn stable.

'One of your men, my lady duchess—a harper has knifed him, and they've sent for the provost.'

Yolande hesitated. This was the kind of affair from which she instinctively shrank; but Odard de Xantroy had ridden away to Pardelin, and no one had ever before made such a direct appeal to her authority. She turned the grey gelding Tancred into the yard, and the others came clattering and crowding after her. A glowering soldier, with the Leopard on his coat, stood holding a gashed and bleeding wrist. The fat innkeeper was storming at a tall shifty-eyed man who carried a flute sheathed at his belt. Inside the stable someone was lying on the straw; the group fell silent, hats came off, and again Yolande halted her mount.

'Where is this harper?' she demanded.

The innkeeper gestured unhappily towards the dark interior.

'What's he doing there? Is he wounded?'

'It's . . . it's a young woman, my lady,' stammered the innkeeper. 'She's hurt her leg and can't walk, and I gave this knave leave to shelter her and the rest of his company here, never expecting any trouble of this sort. . . .'

215

'A young woman? Let me see her. Take my bridle.'

Yolande slid to the ground, and the innkeeper reached for the gelding's rein. The travelling flute-player shrank back, and the soldier made a clumsy effort to salute, still holding his wrist. There in the heaped straw was a mop of frizzy dark hair, a pointed sallow face lit by defiant blue eyes, a dirty blanket, and two thin fists, one of them clenched on the hilt of a dagger.

'What's your name?' asked Yolande. 'Tell me what happened. Why did you . . . what did he do to you? '

The blue eyes stared fearlessly up from beneath fine black eyebrows. A sullen voice rose quietly and quickly from pale, bitten lips.

'I am called Heuradys, my lady. I play the harp. The soldier says he paid to have some fun with me. I don't sell that sort of fun, and he never even tried to pay *me*. That long knave with the flute is the chief of our troupe. He must have taken the money, thinking I couldn't defend myself and wouldn't dare to make a fuss. The innkeeper wants to turn us all out for brawling. If you're a great lady here, I pray you don't let him, for we've nowhere else to go this winter. And don't come too near . . . I smell, and it makes me ashamed. I was thrown by a mule and cut my leg, and the mule kicked out and hurt my ankle. The cut's going rotten, and I don't want to die at the roadside.'

Yolande exclaimed and knelt down, ignoring the mixed and miserable odours. She reached for the grimy hand that did not hold the dagger, and felt anger mount to her own throat and eyes. For a few seconds she and the waif looked steadily at each other. Then Yolande turned to the faces fringing the doorway.

'Douce,' she commanded, ' send a man to bring Master Philastrius at once. Tell him to come with bandages and salves for a dirty wound. You, innkeeper, bring a cup of Malvoisie . . . and let it be good, for I shall taste it. Julian . . . Julian, I want you. Take this garrison man in charge. Tie up his wound, and tether *him* to your saddlebow.'

An incredulous glow in the blue eyes, a tightening of grubby fingers on her own, rewarded Yolande for her interference. The soldier looked viciously unashamed, the man with the flute stood scared and silent; Douce calmly transmitted the order given to her, and Julian obeyed without moving a muscle of his wrinkled face.

More and more people came into the yard; when the provost arrived, his tipstaves had to prod a path for him.

' My lady duchess! ' boomed the provost, who was appointed from among the burghers. ' I beg you, do not kneel there! You mannerless churls, bring a chair for Her Grace! Keep back from this doorway! Let the innkeeper pass there, and bridle your clattering tongues! '

Briefly Yolande explained what had been told to her.

' Do either of you deny these charges? ' demanded the provost sternly.

' I paid my due,' muttered the soldier. The musician said nothing. The innkeeper proffered a goblet in a cloth, and Yolande took a sip of the wine before turning to prop and serve the wounded girl.

' Our Lady bless you,' came in a whisper over the rim of the goblet. Yolande saw the little harp in its canvas case, and a bundle of clothing tied up in a grimy kerchief.

The provost ordered the other members of the troupe to stand forward. A surly man, a pinched-looking boy, and a frowsy older woman obeyed; they bore witness to attempted rape, but denied all knowledge of money offered or received.

Next a chair was brought for Yolande, but she stayed on her knees in the straw until Philastrius thrust his way through the crowd. Then she set the chair in the doorway, screening the sallow flesh laid bare by the apothecary.

' Can I move her to the castle? ' she asked.

' Yes, my. lady, quite safely. The wound and the ankle only need care. I'll come with her and see she's properly cleansed and bandaged.'

Yolande stood up and pointed with her riding-switch at the stout stable-door.

' Take that off its hinges,' she said to the innkeeper. ' It shall come back to you at once. Here's a coin for your wine

and your trouble. Master Provost, arrest this procurer and
deal with him according to law. Let the rest of the troupe
remain; I will settle the dues for them. And I will deal with
this archer; I will have no such offences in a loyal and peaceable town.'

'God bless and save Your Grace,' said the provost, and a
kind of pleased growl went up from the crowd. Then the
provost's silver-headed staff was sweeping a space for the
unhinging of the stable door.

Yolande got to her saddle again and looked round for the
greasy woman, who stood humbly enough by the wall and
stared in alarm when she found herself beckoned.

'You did good service,' said Yolande clearly, and bent to
give her a silver crown piece.

'God save Your Grace!' bawled somebody who cared
nothing for what happened to garrison men or strolling
musicians, but had an eye for friendship between the duchess
and the townsfolk. The cheer was taken up, and it rolled out
of the courtyard, startling the pigeons from the roofs, staying
the hands of men and women over their looms and hammers
and vats and cooking-pots, setting doors and shutters wide,
filling the narrow streets with questions and the clatter of
clogs and wooden shoes.

Yolande lifted a hand in salute, half-angry, half-delighted.

'This is the first time I've been cheered as *me*, and not as
a dummy,' she thought. 'Saints, how they crowd round . . .
no, they want me to lead on.'

So she led on uphill, amused to see the astonished guard come
tumbling out at the barbican.

'You'd think I was going to capture my castle,' she told
herself, and turned in her saddle to wave as she passed under
the arch.

'A good thing Jehane's in bed,' she reflected. 'I'll tell Douce
and Aurania to keep as quiet as may be about this. I'll have
to put the poor wench in my own antechamber. A queer name,
Heuradys. I wonder if Dom Ursus will feel it touches *his*
dignity.'

Dom Ursus had ridden abroad in some other direction, and

heard nothing about the waif until supper-time. Before that,
Yolande had an encounter with Griflet. The young captain
confronted her with a half-smile on his handsome, brutal face.

'This archer, Your Grace,' he began off-handedly. 'Shall I
let him go?'

Yolande looked up from the chess-board and saw that
Griflet would rather like to embarrass her; she had never yet
given him a direct order. Aurania glanced from one to the
other of them. Aurania was looking her best that evening—
clear-eyed, calm, unwontedly contented—and Griflet shot one
heavy-lidded glance in her direction.

'Where is he?' asked Yolande.

'In the guardroom, Your Grace.'

'His wound is bandaged?'

'Yes, Your Grace.'

'Put him in a dungeon until the Sieur Odard can deal with
him.'

'But Your Grace!'

'Yes, captain?'

'He did nothing . . . in fact, he was defrauded.'

From some thicket of anger darted a snake-like certainty.
In the presence of Aurania it would be best to use mockery
against this insolent young man.

'Captain, I'm afraid you don't understand what he tried to
do. Ask old Julian to tell you. Your modesty does you credit,
but I will not have my device disgraced by foul misbehaviour
in the shadow of my castle. You may go now.'

A dark flush overspread the brown face of Griflet. He
bowed, lowering his gaze to the floor.

'Your move, Aurania,' said Yolande gently, as though he
had already disappeared.

When they were alone again Aurania shot an admiring
glance across the embattled board. Yolande was deliberately
staying away from the truckle-bed in her antechamber; she
was alarmed at her own pleasure in saving and sheltering a
fellow-creature in distress.

At the supper-table she told Dom Ursus about Heuradys. A
frown darkened his face as he listened.

' But is this wench of a good life? ' he asked, when the story was ended.

' I think so, as long as she has a dagger,' said Yolande innocently.

' These strolling players are not often of a sort to merit such condescension.'

Yolande pondered this remark.

' Perhaps a little condescension is needed to sort the wheat from the chaff,' she said, with the respect she always accorded to her tutor.

She glanced down the hall, noting which serving-woman was absent on duty in Jehane's bedroom. Douce seemed exhausted; she had just come from the presence. But now Douce, and Aurania, and the sulky Griflet, were all watching Yolande.

' I'll take counsel with my lady abbess concerning this harpist,' said Yolande. ' Dom Ursus, do you think we might ask her to let Sister Marcelle come to read to Dame Jehane? Sister Marcelle reads beautifully; it is her recreation.'

Yolande could feel the silent blessings called down upon her in the minds of Douce and Aurania.

' Yes,' returned the Dominican, but he was not to be headed off. ' This wench must be removed as soon as possible. It's not fitting that she should lie in the chamber next to your own.'

' She'll be well enough to move in a day or two,' said Yolande. ' I would rather she didn't reward our charity by dying in a ditch.'

Inwardly Yolande was determined that Heuradys should stay as long as she had need of help. To be sure, this tartness was not the way to secure support from Dom Ursus; he was considering her last remark with one eyebrow slightly raised.

' He'll tell Jehane,' she thought. ' Then there'll be turmoil. Very well: I must talk to Philastrius.'

And after supper she betook herself to the antechamber. There, alone by the light of a candle, the strolling player who could not stroll turned her uncovered head, with its crisp dark hair cut short at the neck, and looked curiously up. One slim hand, now clean and trim, lay outside the furred coverlet; it twitched and then was still again.

Yolande sat down on a stool and was suddenly shy.

' You're easier? ' she whispered. ' They did all they could for you? Philastrius is a good man, and skilful.'

' Yes, my lady duchess. May I kiss your hand? I smell only of salves and violets now.'

Her lips were hot on Yolande's fingers. Then she laid the back of Yolande's hand against her forehead and cheek.

' This completes the dream,' she said, as though to herself.

' The dream? '

' A dream I have often had, of comfort and safety and cleanliness. I never expected it to be more than a dream.'

' Where's your harp? '

' It wasn't mine. That rogue you saw lent it to me, paying himself out of my share in our takings.'

' How long have you travelled in his company? '

' Two years, my lady duchess. My home was near Jarapt. My mother and sisters died of the plague. My father vanished just before . . . he seemed pleased, said he had some secret profitable undertaking, left us a bag of silver crowns and promised to come back with more . . . and then he never came. The plague must have overtaken him too.'

' What was his work? '

' He built boats on the river there.'

Yolande slowly tightened her clasp of the strong hand smaller than her own, and sat like one who has suddenly heard a horn wound far away in the night.

' Have I said something I should not? ' asked Heuradys, sadly.

' No . . . indeed, no. I am sorry you . . . you were orphaned so cruelly and left alone like that . . . and ashamed that it was one of my men who made a beast of himself today.'

' Oh, dear my lady, half the soldiers you meet are like that, except that some of them don't even offer to pay anything or anyone.'

' That man will be punished.'

Heuradys closed her eyes, and at once appeared childish.
Yolande bent nearer and put her other hand to the thick frizzy
hair.

'That sounds as if I were powerful,' she whispered. 'But
really I am not. If you want to stay here for a while, we must
pretend you're quite ill. The apothecary will see to it. But I
think I can promise that you never need to go back to that
grim life.'

'It's not always quite grim . . . but . . . this goes beyond my
dream. Dear my lady, why do you do it? '

Yolande was silent, wondering why.

'I think we were meant to be friends,' she said, after a
pause. 'Since *my* father was killed I have had very few friends.
A nun in the convent here . . . Philastrius, whom you know . . .
a kinsman whom I have met once . . . and two others, who
disappeared before I was married.'

Heuradys opened her eyes, and again was older than
Yolande.

'I forgot that you were married,' she murmured. 'It seems
wrong that you should be married.'

Yolande stooped and kissed the pale forehead before she
took her hands away.

'It seems wrong to me too,' she said, 'and you are the only
person who has ever agreed with me aloud.'

Next day the Sieur Odard returned, and found himself in a
hornet's nest. Dom Ursus had talked to Jehane; Yolande had
talked to Philastrius. Jehane sat up in bed and screeched at
her husband. Odard, still in his riding-boots, sought Yolande
in the solar.

'Can't you move this wench to the convent, my lady? ' he
asked wearily.

'Philastrius says she may die if I do. Besides, what harm is
there in *my* taking care of her? '

'God knows there's none whatever,' snapped Odard, and
suddenly looked Yolande in the face.

'What's Dame Jehane been telling you about my lord
duke? ' he asked. 'She's worried because you haven't been

near her since. She swears she was so ill she didn't know what she was saying. That means it was something she wishes she hadn't said.'

The wretched man's defences were down, but he seemed to have some reserve of fortitude behind them. His gloomy face was seared with fatigue, but his eyes were wary rather than ashamed.

'She only told me he's called Belphegor, and that he ill-treats women and serfs and prisoners and anyone else who can't stop him. Nothing very surprising. I shan't write to tell him about it. I thanked Dame Jehane for telling *me*, and stayed away because my being there seemed to offend her. Shall I go and talk to her now?'

'It might ease her, my lady ... it would be kind ... but she's very angry now about this little wench.'

'What's been done with the soldier?'

'The soldier, my lady?'

'The soldier who tried to ravish this girl, knowing her to be injured ... so handy for him, she couldn't run away.'

Odard looked a little embarrassed at such plain speaking.

'He's in irons for a week, on bread and water,' he told her glumly.

'I want him dismissed at the end of the week.'

'My lady, I beg you'll wait until then, and tell me if you still want that.'

'Very well, my lord. The captain Griflet wanted to release him, which told me all I want to know about the captain Griflet.'

Odard was silent. Yolande stood up, and paused by the solar door to plumb another mystery.

'Dom Ursus said nothing to *me* today about her, about this musician I mean. If I refuse to turn her out, will Dom Ursus write to the Grand Seneschal and tell him Dame Jehane is ill and I'm out of her control?'

Odard turned upon his duchess an eye suddenly crafty with soldierly speculation.

'I don't think he'll do that, my lady,' was all that Odard said.

Jehane had reached one of her heartbroken moods when Yolande entered the principal bedchamber.

' Child, why must you do these things? ' she wailed from her heaped pillows. ' God knows I've tried to be a mother to you. I know I'm hasty sometimes, perhaps I don't talk to you enough about what's fitting, what would my lord your father have said, dragging this creature from the streets into your very bedchamber, I warrant she's scabbed and lousy and filthy, you may catch some vile distemper from her, she's a stabber and most likely a whore, none of that sort's fit to be trusted. . . .'

' Listen! ' said Yolande firmly. ' She isn't a whore, she isn't in my bedchamber, they stripped her on a sheet, they bathed her in my tub, they washed and combed her head, Master Philastrius shaved the hair from her body and gave her a vial of strong spirits to rub into the roots and kill the eggs. They burned all her clothing, and now she's as dainty as a princess. If anyone tries to frighten her she shall sleep with me until she's able to walk, she with one dagger under her pillow and I with another under mine.'

' And you the Duchess of Baraine! ' moaned Jehane.

' Even a duchess may be allowed her own way for once! ' said Yolande, and then was filled with compunction, because she had meant to soothe this tormented creature.

' Surely, my lady,' she went on gently, ' you wouldn't want me to have had her turned out of the stable? '

' No, no, you're cruel, you twist my meaning, there's a hospital in the town.'

' It's full.'

' The lady abbess would have taken her in. . . .'

' Why should I thrust *my* duty upon the lady abbess? '

' What are convents for? You could have borne the cost of it! '

' Yes, I could, but I like this girl, I'm going to look after her, and I won't be talked to as though I've sinned by doing what Holy Writ enjoins. Sometimes I think I had rather be tutored by a Franciscan. . . .'

' Oh, God, after all I've suffered, to be told I'm blaming you for charity! Leave me, leave me, go your own way, take in the whole town, fill the wards of the castle with lepers, tell the Grand Seneschal I'm ill, there's a raven in the north tower, I've heard it croaking these three nights past, lying here sick and lonely, my husband nowhere near me. . . .'

'There's your handbell on the table,' said Yolande quietly. 'Aurania and Douce are in the next room. Your tirewoman can sleep here if you want her to. The Sieur Odard was only three nights away . . . *and* he was on duty of the duchy. I'll see about the raven. Let me give you a drink.'

'No! How can I tell what . . . why do you all hate me? You all wish me dead . . . I'm in the way . . . everything goes awry when I'm not there to see to it . . . no one pays attention to what I say, lying here. I haven't the strength, I've done all I could, I've wasted my life, I've been a fool, a fool, a fool!'

Yolande cast about for something to say that would not sound brutal to Jehane or insincere to herself. There seemed to be nothing, for she would not take upon her the blame for Jehane's unhappy past.

Only when she had left the room did she remember that nothing had been said about Belphegor. Heuradys had replaced him in the vortex of the whirlpool. Tomorrow, perhaps, it would be something else.

Wiping her forehead on her sleeve, Yolande turned in at the solar door. Aurania was flushed, Douce very pale; they seemed to be having the first quarrel Yolande remembered between them. She went away again towards her own room. As she passed the door of the winter parlour angry voices resounded within; when she had gone by, it was flung open, and Griflet strode out.

'Remember the bridge at Klingenstein!' Dom Ursus shouted after him, and Yolande saw the younger man turn in the passage and look back with the face of a wild beast. One hand gripped his dagger-hilt, the other clasped and unclasped in empty air; Yolande, rooted in the shadow beyond, reflected that Griflet was not often crossed twice in two days.

'It's a good name to remember, the bridge at Klingenstein,'

she thought. 'The valiant captain did something there he would not have recalled to him.'

The castle of Roclatour tonight was not a very happy place; but there was still Odard, doubtless in the barrel-vaulted chamber where he kept his rolls and strong-boxes, and where a mournful lay clerk wrestled with the accounts of castle and forest. Odard was alone there, warming his hands at the brazier.

'My lady's very depressed,' said Yolande, 'but she seems to have forgotten her anxiety about the recreations of my lord duke. She told me . . . my lord, can you have the raven shot or driven away, the raven that plagues her from the north tower?'

Odard's humped shadow on wall and vault endorsed Odard's own depression.

'There's no raven there,' he said.

'Oh . . . oh, I'm sorry, my lord. Tell me, what happened at Pardelin?'

'A quarrel between two archers; one of them was stabbed, too. I'm changing the garrison there, and sending Julian to take charge.'

'Is that a mark of disgrace for him?'

'No, my lady, it's a promotion.'

'Is the village filling up again? My lord Grand Seneschal told me he was putting in a miller and two or three farmers from the north border of the duchy, with leave to take serfs from demesne land there. Is there a new priest yet?'

'Yes.'

'Do you know if any more was ever found out as to how Turlequin got his boat on to the lake there?'

'No, my lady. I'd like to know. A rogue like that some-times pulls long strings among the peasantry. And peasants will take great trouble to spite or injure their lawful lords.'

'Tell me if ever you hear, will you?'

'Yes, my lady. I've had that *esplanade* trimmed back so that nothing bigger than a weasel can get unseen to the moat-side.'

'Yes, of course, it was partly that which . . . so there's no one in the castle now but a handful of soldiers?'

'Six there, and four more by turns at Quatrelances.'

'Poor souls, they must find it a penance.'

'Maybe. They're paid regularly, and they don't have to stand on parade, and nobody sees what game they poach, and there's wonderful fishing in the lake.'

'Yes, I used to fish there.'

Yolande felt Odard glance at her sideways as she sat staring into the brazier.

'Tell me if you hear,' she repeated. 'I'm always interested to learn what goes on at Pardelin.'

The moment's silence that followed was pierced by a thin distant yell. Odard made an abrupt movement. If the voice were not Jehane's own, it was probably that of her tirewoman; Jehane sometimes threw her handbell, or even a book or a goblet at those whom she saw in her bedchamber. At other times she welcomed them; but the welcome was oftenest for those whom only she could see.

Next morning, before her drawing-lesson, Yolande took Philastrius to examine Heuradys. A November gale was roaring down the mountains; hail battered the stout oiled paper framed in the narrow windows.

'Better here than out on the roads,' muttered Philastrius, skilfully kneading a golden-brown ankle, and pressing the foot to flex and extend it.

Heuradys made a sound that was not quite a chuckle.

'Three travellers visited me last night,' he told Yolande as she watched him. 'Two young squires and a dwarf, bound on a journey of devotion to the battlefield of Arionbel. The dwarf is a kinsman of my old teacher of medicine at Hautarroy. The young men were very civil; they carry a harp and a hautboy, as if they were troubadours of the old days. But they have letters from a famous captain, the Chevalier de Largire.'

'Whom my lord duke overthrew the other day in the lists.'

'Yes, that is he. Would you like to hear these young gentlemen sing and play, my lady?'

'I'll see what the Sieur Odard says,' Yolande decided. 'They

sleep at an inn, these squires? We mustn't put a further strain
on our celebrated hospitality.'

Philastrius smiled discreetly, drew up the blankets, and
patted the hand of Heuradys with his long stained fingers.

'You must lie quite still,' he told her. 'Any attempt to move
you would be dangerous. Eat and drink and sleep, and I'll
bring you tomorrow a medicine with a very powerful odour.
No need to drink it; my lady will see that everyone smells it
. . . except the Dame de Xantroy.'

'Yes, we must keep it from her,' said Yolande. 'She'd want
to dilute it with an infusion of vervain, betony, elecampane,
and the white wort of Saint Hiltrude. But Philastrius, she's
really ill . . . or she'd have been out and about yesterday.'

Philastrius nodded gravely.

'That lady should now be told anything she likes to hear,'
he said.

'Troubadours out of time and season,' said Odard when
Yolande spoke of the strangers. 'But let them come and sing;
I wish Dame Jehane were well enough to listen. The worst of
gentlemen in that trade is that it's hard to stop them as you can
the common sort. And they have to be paid more than gleemen,
and fed like chevaliers.'

'The hall's draughty,' declared Yolande. 'My lord, let's have
the household in the chamber of parade.'

Having ordered the fire to be lit there, Yolande like a careful
mistress of household went later to see if it burned well in the
seldom-used fireplace. The gale boomed in the corridors;
draughts whooped and whined as doors were opened and shut.

'A shame when we *do* use this place that Jehane's not with
us,' she thought, as she came out on the stair-head. Then she
saw the two young men, still cloaked but without their hats
and gloves, warming their hands at the great glow before
uncasing harp and hautboy.

Nobody else was there; for a few seconds they did not see her.
She had just that fraction of time in which to rally after the
stifling blow in her breast. . . .

'*Lioncel!*' she cried. '*Diomede!*'

Afterwards she wondered if her voice had been harsh, and if her face had seemed silly with surprise. But the wind was hammering and whistling outside, and the logs crackled loudly on the hearth. Dark head and fair head came round; brown eyes and blue shone in the cross-lights of fire and tawny, gloomy sky. Lioncel and Diomede each sank upon one knee, waiting silently with face upturned, a face strained and glad and afraid.

Yolande's feet felt for each stair as if it topped a precipice. Twenty-four stairs in sets of eight. She was on the first landing when they saw her. Sixteen stairs to go, into the narrow stony pine-scented firelit tapestried chamber of parade.

'*Are you the same,*' she thought wildly, '*or have you grown into hard, cunning creatures who'll wonder why you liked being at Pardelin with me? No, or you wouldn't have come back.*'

Dignity, Yolande: keep your hands from fluttering out, your breath from deepening and catching in your throat. It's two long years . . . Lioncel's as beautiful as ever, he's got a scar by his left eye. Diomede's grown more beautiful. Can they be as glad as you are? Which would you rather have more glad? Neither: you love them both . . . they're your brothers . . . your Sign of the Zodiac is Gemini . . . silly to think of it like that . . . Jesu, Mary, Diomede's crying, two great tears sliding down, but his face is stiff as though he were hurt . . . Lioncel looks as if you were a ghost . . . what *do* you look like?

When her foot touched the carpet of pine-needles she darted forward, careless of self-betrayal. Halting between the kneeling pair, she stretched out eager fingers.

'*O my dears,*' she said quietly, gathering kisses with both hands. Dry-eyed, hot-cheeked, laughing a little, she pulled them away, caught Lioncel's head between her palms, tilted it, kissed his forehead and lips. Lioncel gave a gasp; she turned, took Diomede by the hair, and kissed him on the mouth and eyelids. Diomede only sighed, and she stepped back with his tears salt on her own lips.

'Stand up,' she bade them quickly. 'This place is full of eyes and ears. Pretend this is our first meeting.'

'My lady,' muttered Lioncel, 'how may we talk to you alone?'

' Wait, I must think . . . someone's coming.'

The door behind the squires opened; it was the old steward with two serving-men.

' You've travelled far? ' Yolande asked, in her haughtiest company voice.

' From Hautarroy, Your Grace,' drawled Lioncel, playing up at once.

' You saw my lord duke overthrow the Chevalier de Largire? '

' Indeed we did, Your Grace. We have the honour to serve that same chevalier. We picked him up in the lists that day.'

' Then you must drink a cup with me now, to show no grudge remains between the Leopard and the Silver Shield.'

At Yolande's bidding the steward went to order the wine; the serving-men she despatched to bring the great harp from the solar. For a moment she was alone with Lioncel and Diomede.

' You've seen the Sieur de Xantroy? ' she asked, and Lioncel replied.

' Yes, my lady. He sent us in here. May we set you a chair? '

' Yes . . . yes. Listen to me. Philastrius is to be trusted . . . he's my drawing-master. How long do you stay in Roclatour? '

' When the gale abates we shall go on to the Gorge of Arionbel, but we shall come back this way.'

' When? '

' In a week's time, perhaps. Then we can . . . er . . . I mean, there's no need for us to go back to Hautarroy.'

' Then I'll somehow find a way to meet you alone. In the castle it's hopeless . . . I've no one to trust, and nowhere to go where you could come too. When you return from Arionbel I'll have made some plan.'

' *O my lady,*' whispered Diomede, as though talking to himself.

Yolande looked at him, and was shocked and happy to recognise a bitter depth in his devotion. She looked again at Lioncel, and thrilled at the old tenderness rescued from Pardelin. For the first time in her life she began to feel something like a Byzantine princess, and it was silly and sad and exciting all at once. But, of course, it was always *one* soldier or courtier or

priest, not two, who broke the palace rules and landed eyeless
in a dungeon.

'I want to hear you sing again,' she said, suddenly nervous.
'But take care what you sing—my tutor, Dom Ursus, is a
Dominican, very strict about other people's behaviour. Which
of you wrote the verses about Amarand and the elves?'

'He did,' said Diomede, nodding at his comrade.

'They . . . they were like a cool drink in a desert,' said
Yolande unsteadily.

Then the steward came in, with a server carrying a flagon and
silver cups on a tray. Three faces stiffened into masks of politeness. The steward poured the wine and stood solemnly in
attendance. A duchess and two squires drank to their lord
King Torismund, to Duke Balthasar and to the Chevalier
Janus de Largire; and they drained the cups in honour of Saint
Amarand of Baraine.

'I shall see you at supper,' Yolande told her guests.

They bowed magnificently, and she inclined her head a little
and moved away to climb the stair.

'My lady, what is it?' asked Heuradys, three minutes later.

'Nothing that matters,' said Yolande, not even resenting the
question.

She lit a taper at the bedside candle, and moved on into her
own bedchamber. There she lit another candle, sat down on
her bed, took Amarand from the bedside chest and stood him
up and stared at him, and finally shut her eyes and held herself
motionless.

Somewhere a thin high note of storm-wind screamed and
whistled in creviced stone. It seemed a warning, a desperate
attempt to tell her something she must do . . . or not do. After
a moment she knew what it was; she wanted to escape with
Lioncel and Diomede, and never come back.

'And then,' she told herself coldly, 'you'd be chased and
caught, and Lioncel and Diomede would be hung and drawn
and quartered for treason, and you'd be accused of God-knows-
what . . . and there'd be a committee of matrons . . . and Odard
and Jehane would be disgraced, and Heuradys flung out . . .

and only Belphegor and Satan themselves know what your noble lord would do.'

But no matter what happened, she was determined to meet the squires in private, to hear their story, and to tell them her own. Presently she got up and went into the antechamber and sat down on the stool beside the truckle-bed. She took the hands of Heuradys, and held them together.

' It might help me very much,' she whispered, ' if Philastrius were to take you to his house in the town. His wife is gentle like himself; they would tend you carefully, and I could come to see you every day. Understand . . . I should be using you to get out of the castle . . . it would be such a service as I could scarcely repay. You would be quite safe there, safer maybe than you are here, and when your wound and ankle are healed I mean to have you with me again.'

' You mean . . . take me into your household, my lady? '

' Yes, if I can contrive it. If I can't, I shall still look after you, perhaps more easily if you're not with me. But I want you with me for as long as you wish to stay.'

' It might be for always,' muttered Heuradys, with a sudden twinkle of her shrewd blue eyes.

' I should be glad if it were for always,' said Yolande, holding on to the warm strong fingers beneath her own.

' So should I,' said Heuradys, ' but not if it were just in payment. Let me go to the apothecary's house . . . let me be useful like that . . . but only let me live with you if I may love you and . . . and guard your back with my dagger.'

Yolande knelt down and put her arms around the thin body.

' I should feel much safer,' she said, ' if you would do that. There may be no need to move you at all; but whether you stay here now or not, you have helped me already to find courage.'

At supper Yolande sat all but silent, listening as Odard and Dom Ursus probed the more recent adventures of Janus of the Silver Shield. Lioncel answered most of the questions, but sometimes Diomede took up the tale. Griflet maintained an air of detachment until he learned that Janus had sent one of his Saracen prisoners home without ransom.

'I have heard it said that prisoners at Largire are kept in silver fetters,' he announced, looking along the board to where Lioncel sat opposite Dom Ursus.

Lioncel smiled courteously; Yolande allowed herself a glance at him, and admired the way his fair skin had sunburned without going red.

'None whom I saw were fettered at all,' he said. 'I think that story may have got abroad because in the solar there hangs a pair of silver fetters, with a very fine silver chain, which one of the chevalier's ancestors wore to symbolise his enslavement by some beautiful lady.'

'I see,' said Griflet politely. 'An old custom of Elquitaine.'

'An old custom of the troubadours,' amended Dom Ursus. 'They had many such fantasies, and those who held to the true faith fought no less bravely because of them.'

'Did the others?' enquired Griflet. 'Perhaps these gentlemen can tell us whether the paynims are notably weaker in the arm than our own Christian warriors.'

Griflet wanted to make mischief; Yolande saw a gleam of mockery in his bold square-jawed face. She addressed herself to Diomede before Lioncel could reply.

'Did you see the Empress and her ladies when you were in Constantinople?'

'Several times, Your Grace,' said Diomede calmly. 'Generally at a distance, in Santa Sophia, but once close at hand on the Golden Horn. They were on a state barge under the walls of the Palace of Blachernae, and we were in a Genoese galley.'

'And they are very beautiful?'

'Yes, Your Grace, but not more beautiful than the great ladies of Neustria.'

'And is there really danger that the Turks will one day conquer the city?'

'The Chevalier de Largire believes so, Your Grace.'

'Why?'

'Well . . . the gate guards go home to dinner, leaving only one or two men to watch. And the fortress built by Bajazet on

I

the Asiatic side of the straits is only five miles from the city.
And the Greeks hate us Westerners as much as they hate the
Turks. And the Turks are learning more and more to use
cannon; the Chevalier Janus says that the next time they are
united among themselves, it will be the end. Unless of course
a great crusade were undertaken to support them.'

'The Greeks should come out of their damnable schism,'
began Dom Ursus harshly.

Damn the schism and you too, thought Yolande impatiently.
She would have liked to go on listening to Diomede.

In the chamber of parade the great harp stood at one end of
the half-circle of chairs and stools and benches. Yolande's chair
was in the centre; it had a little coronet at the top of its high
back, and a leopard's head on each arm-rest. Yolande fitted a
finger-tip into each of the four carven eye-sockets, and held on;
the two loved faces, the remembered voices, tore down the veils
of time and circumstance, enchanting her into terrified pleasure
which had to be hidden as if it were a crime.

Lioncel sang first, Diomede accompanying him. The song
was *Alianor and Meriodon*: Yolande had not heard it before.

> *'The Princess Alianor was tall*
> *And sweet to look upon.*
> *She held her father's court in thrall,*
> *And her closest friend among them all*
> *Was the Sieur de Meriodon.*

> *'She spoke aside with rigid face:*
> *"My lord, I call it shame*
> *That I may never cut my trace*
> *Or find, in this enormous place,*
> *Peace for our gentle game."*

> *'Dark Eudo heard beyond the screen,*
> *Pricking his ears for spite,*
> *Cracking his finger-joints with spleen.*
> *Rare tidings for the king and queen!*
> *Mud for a name so white!*

' " *I'll shame you, pretty,*" *Eudo vow'd.*
  " *I'll set the gleemen winking!*
  I'll see you shaken, glum and cow'd!
  When his blood spurts before the crowd
  They'll snigger in their drinking! "

' *He spied when from a postern gate*
  They strode into the waste,
  And, flown with pride and power and hate,
  Ran spluttering to the chair of state,
  And led the hunt in haste.

' *The king came after, breathing hard,*
  To find that reckless lover,
  With the Princes Guelf and Lionard,
  And seven archers of the guard
  In case their man broke cover

' *So, grovelling in the undergrowth,*
  " *My queen!* " *they heard him cry.*
  " *My chevalier!* " *she groaned, and both*
  Laught, and Lionard check'd an oath,
  And set the bushes by.

' *Behold them sprawling on the sward:*
  Between them, joy and stress,
  And, red-and-white, a carven board;
  For proud princess and valiant lord
  Were desperate-deep in . . . chess! '

The anti-climax was mild enough, but there was not much to laugh at in the castle of Roclatour; Dom Ursus actually uttered a loud snort of amusement. Yolande happened to be looking at Aurania; the fair girl's face twitched, and then was twisted to a smile.

Next, without a glance at Yolande, Diomede began to play and sing the song about Eglantine, linking the chamber of parade with a sunlit afternoon two-and-a-half years gone by. Then Lioncel joined him in a harp-and-hautboy duet which they had composed together and called *The Silver Shield*.

' Does that famous shield often startle those who first see it? '
asked Odard when the duet was done.

' Not often, to our knowledge,' replied Lioncel. ' But in
Greece this spring there was an oddity which you may like to
hear.'

At Athens, it seemed, an Irish captain had sworn that *Argent*
uncharged was the blazon of the Blessed Virgin, and that Janus
de Largire blasphemed by claiming it as his own. Janus
challenged him to fight as became a chevalier; but as a joust
would entail the breaking of lances or strokes with sword or
axe upon the plain shield, the Irishman refused to meet him
unless for the occasion they were to use archers' bucklers of
brass and leather. This irregularity Janus in his turn condemned, offering instead to shed all body-armour and fight it
out with sword and buckler only. If the Irishman pleased, they
could go on to quarterstaff and wrestling. The Irishman would
have none of these, denouncing them as the military accomplish-
ments of churls; but that night he dreamed that the Blessed
Virgin appeared to him and showed him her shield, which
seemed to be *Azure, a fleur-de-lys or.*

Thereupon the Irishman announced that he would apologise
to Janus; but Janus refused to accept the apology. The Irishman
grew very angry, and promised to make Janus accept that
apology if he had to kill him first. Janus swore by the ghost of
Duke Theseus that the Irishman would do neither—he, Janus,
scorning to use a Christian oath to one who had called him a
blasphemer, and was moreover an ignoramus in matters of
blazonry.

The Irishman foamed at the mouth and began to haunt the
harbour of the Piraeus, hearing that Janus meant to take ship
without giving him satisfaction. Lioncel and Diomede, with
Scipio and the Apulian brethren and the delighted crew of a
Venetian galley, were privileged to see the upshot of that
quarrel; the Irishman wheeled his charger between bales of
merchandise, and bore down the length of a quay upon the
unmounted Janus.

Janus picked up a great block of wood and hurled it at his
attacker, knocking him clean out of his saddle. While he lay

half-stunned, Janus picked him up and carried him to an ancient olive-tree standing beside a ruined chapel, and there hung him up in his armour, using a length of ship's rope wound under the arm-pits, and laying his lance and shield neatly on the ground beneath him. The last sounds the squires heard from the sunlit Grecian mainland were curses boomed and squealed out of the Irishman's helmet, and the gabbling of dock-labourers afraid to go near him.

'And somewhere in the Levant the Irish captain is doubtless still looking for the chevalier,' finished Lioncel, turning to reach for the wine-cup set on the bench beside him. He was wearing a violet-coloured tunic and bronze-brown hose, and the flash of his white-gold hair filled Yolande with delight.

'If they weren't coming back again,' she thought, 'tomorrow would be the deadliest day that ever I remember.'

The best song of the evening was called *Tripping-Go*. Diomede harped and sang it, while Lioncel's hautboy wove a flute part round the singing.

> '*Man and brute admire my flute*
> *Whether they will or no;*
> *I am an elf all by myself,*
> *And my name is Tripping-Go.*

> '*Hunting-horn of an autumn morn,*
> *Stuttering " tro-ro-ro",*
> *Feathers a flight of less delight*
> *Than the flute of Tripping-Go.*

> '*It troubles the lords who serve their swords*
> *With fee and fie and foe;*
> *It tickles the bones of a monk at nones,*
> *The flute of Tripping-Go.*

> '*Lovers forget to laugh or fret*
> *Or conjugate " amo"*
> *As they lie in the grass and hear it pass,*
> *The flute of Tripping-Go.*

'Shepherd and sheep a vigil keep
To figure a Morisco;
The red-deer dance, and foxes prance
To the flute of Tripping-Go.

'Rainbow-gleams and sovereign dreams,
Misery-me, heigh-ho,
Twist and turn and quiver and burn
To the flute of Tripping-Go.

'You may curse and cry, but what care I,
Who tormentise you so?
Over the hill you'll hear it still,
The flute of Tripping-Go.'

'Perhaps I shall never again know so happy an evening as this,' thought Yolande. 'But by Saint Amarand's bridle-chain I mean to have some more like it.'

When she went to bed that night she found Heuradys was asleep; after her tirewoman had left her, she heard Heuradys cry out. Springing up, she pulled on her furred bedgown and slid her feet into furred shoes; the door to the antechamber stood ajar, and when she pushed it open she saw that Heuradys was dreaming. She went and stood by the truckle-bed; as she watched, the fine worn face of the harp-player composed itself. Heuradys sank into deeper slumber; and as Yolande turned away she heard through the moan and whistle of the gale another voice, this time in the corridor.

Her instant thought was of Jehane; she moved to the outer door and softly unlatched it. A lantern burned in a niche to her right; past her feet swept the shadow of someone just gone by. Peering round the edge of the door, she was in time to see Aurania disappear into the bedchamber of Dom Ursus.

Yolande glanced to her left; Douce stood there, watching her. Douce could have stepped back round a corner, but made no move to hide. Yolande found Douce a little stupid, but liked her because of her patient kindness to the exasperating Jehane.

'Douce!' she whispered. 'Come in here!'

'Yes, my lady,' said Douce mechanically. She was half-dressed, with a cloak thrown over her bare shoulders, and a taper in one hand. When she stood inside the antechamber she glanced incuriously at the sleeping Heuradys, and turned stolidly to look at Yolande.

'Does she often do that?' asked Yolande, with a sideways motion of the head.

'Since my lady Jehane has been sick, yes.'

'Did you try to stop her just now?'

'Yes, my lady.'

'Why?'

'My lady! It's a dreadful sin ... a friar ... it's counted as incest....'

'Dom Ursus can absolve her, no doubt, and arrange his own absolution. It makes Aurania happier ... I've wondered at her ups and downs lately. And it puts Dom Ursus in a better temper ... perhaps it'll save some other girl from being burned as a witch to please him.'

'My lady! How can you say such things?'

'Other folk do them, I can talk about them. Those two hurt no one but themselves ... oh, it's a very bad example, but you and I are not likely to follow it. Douce, pretend it hasn't happened. There's enough misery loose in this hold without our stirring up any more. You promise?'

'Yes, my lady.'

'You're shivering. Come and get warm by my fire, and drink a cup of wine with me.'

There had only been wine in Yolande's cupboard since Jehane had been bedridden. Presently Douce was sitting with the cloak thrown back and firelight dancing on her plump bare arms. She stared into the fire and listened with Yolande to the fury of the storm.

'When I die I want it to be a still, sunny morning,' said Douce.

This was almost the only unprompted remark Yolande had ever heard from her.

'Why?' asked Yolande gently.

'I don't know ... it needn't be summer, and I should like

it to have rained in the night, so that there are drops sparkling on the trees and in the grass. I hate these storms, and the wild noises, and things stalking round corners that aren't there when you look again.'

'Douce! Has something frightened you here?'

'No, my lady . . . at least Griflet going his rounds sometimes startles me. It's silly of me, because of course he's here to guard us.'

'Was Griflet long in Franconia with my lord Grand Seneschal?'

'Some years, I believe. I think he finds it very dull here. I asked him once why he didn't have himself sent to Bargreant or Jarapt, and he said the hunting here was better. But of course I know it isn't.'

Griflet's pursuit of Aurania hovered unmentioned between the girls. It occurred to Yolande that Douce and she were probably the two most unsatisfactory gossips in all Baraine.

'Would *you* like to go to Bargreant?' she asked.

'No, my lady,' replied Douce firmly.

'There's one person likes being here, then,' said Yolande largely to herself.

An old wonder awoke in her—did Douce realise that Aurania and she had been included in the household because of their insignificance? No one with influence must be allowed near the Duchess of Baraine, in case she were to begin to build up a faction of her own. . . .

And now, in spite of the Grand Seneschal, a faction was beginning to assemble. Lioncel, Diomede, Philastrius . . . and now Heuradys. A formidable faction!

Yolande smiled, and poured out another cup of wine for Douce. She watered it sparingly, and raised her own cup in the firelight.

'Let us drink to the lonely maidens of Roclatour,' she said.

A most becoming blush mounted slowly beneath the creamy skin of Douce. Yolande was too tired to try to discover the reason for it.

The storm lessened during the night; by noon of the next day there were gleams of intermittent sunshine on the lake. Yolande climbed a turret and watched for a while the road that led eastward into the forest. There was no sign of three horsemen headed for Jarapt and beyond; probably they had started soon after dawn. Yolande sped a prayer after them, and hugged her cloak about her; where Lioncel and Diomede were concerned she felt she had it in her to be crazy.

By evening the wind had dropped, and mist was thickening along the hills. The next morning was yellow with fog, and no one rode abroad for pleasure. Yolande heard Odard talking to Griflet about the garrison store of hides. Griflet got to horse and disappeared into the dun gloom of the streets. Dom Ursus set Yolande a piece of Tacitus to translate, and left her writing by candlelight. She watched him leave the winter parlour, having in her mind reflections which might have astonished him; as usual, his departure raised her spirits a little. His prominent eyes and flared nostrils bored the gloom and snuffed up the fog with a sort of avid complacency; the crystal skull grinned at Yolande before it disappeared into a glove of embroidered Cordovan leather.

'Do you suppose,' wrote Yolande, 'that Nero will be the last of the tyrants? Those who survived Tiberius, those who survived Caligula, thought the same; and yet after each there arose another ruler yet more detestable and more cruel.'

Yolande paused and turned back to the passage describing the end of Vitellius.

'When the city had been taken, Vitellius caused himself to be carried in a litter through the back of the palace to the Aventine, to his wife's dwelling, intending, if by any expedient he could escape for that day, to make his way to his brother's cohorts at Tarracina. Then, with characteristic weakness, and following the instinct of fear, which, dreading everything, shrinks most from what is immediately before it, he retraced his steps to the desolate and forsaken palace, whence even the meanest slaves had fled, or where they avoided his presence. The solitude and silence of the place scared him; he tried the closed doors, he shuddered in the empty chambers, till, wearied out with his miserable wanderings, he concealed himself in an unseemly hiding-place, from which he was dragged out by the tribune Julius Placidus. . . .'

Yolande remembered the heedlessness of the great castle of Bargreant, where well-remembered hearths and corners had mocked her with indifference on her return from Roclatour at the time of her wedding. She found fascinating the picture of the lonely frightened emperor stealing through vast and echoing emptiness in search of he knew not what habitude and reassurance.

' I must ask Dom Ursus if the palace of Vitellius is still there,' she decided, ' and why, when a villain is betrayed and ruined and beaten to death, one should begin to be sorry for him.'

All day the fog swathed Roclatour, and at early nightfall the still air of the castle was further thickened by hanging smoke of torch and brazier. Douce and Aurania in turn read to Jehane. Yolande had the bed of Heuradys carried into her own room, leaving the formidable smell of the new medicine to occupy the antechamber. With Heuradys cushioned near the hearth, Yolande played the lute and sang; one song of those she remembered without music had disappeared from her collection when Dom Ursus purged it of Pythagorean and other mischief.

> ' Her will I not admire,
>   Nor her defence assume,
> Who bids desire mount up as fire
>   To fly away in fume.
>
> ' Count not the raptor's blame
>   Ere all defence is known;
> Who jests with flame deserves the same
>   For torment of her own.
>
> ' Her only will I sing
>   Who, challeng'd by the Boy,
> Or bids him wing or crowns him king
>   In courtesy and joy.'

' That's fair enough,' said Heuradys, baring regular white teeth to deal with a chicken-bone.

' It was made by the Count of Ger,' Yolande told her.

'Him I should like some time to see,' said Heuradys thoughtfully.

'You shall if I can manage it,' promised Yolande. 'He is my friend, if he hasn't forgotten me, and my next kinsman on my father's side. In fact, if anything happened to my lord duke and me before we have a child, my lord Count of Ger would be the next Duke of Baraine.'

'The Holy Trinity forbid that anything should happen to *you*, my lady,' whispered Heuradys, crossing herself with the chicken-bone.

Yolande noticed that the petition did not include Balthasar-Belphegor. She was uncertain how much of his fame was know to such people as Heuradys.

At supper that night Dom Ursus did not appear; no one knew where he had gone, and Yolande told herself that at any rate it was not likely he was wenching. The castle porter had seen him, soon after midday, walking out of the barbican as if towards the Priory of Saint Michael. The Sieur Odard sent an archer to the priory, but no one there had word of the Dominican. Odard then called Griflet into consultation, and pairs of archers with torches were sent to the convent, to the provost's house, to the harbour, and to each gate of the town. A scrivener who did copying for Dom Ursus told of his passing in the fog near the quay some time before dusk; and that was the sum of information gathered by the searchers.

Yolande and the damsels sat up later than usual; Aurania betrayed no anxiety, and Yolande wondered if she knew more than the rest of them. Odard appeared in the solar and talked desultorily. Finally, near midnight, Griflet came in to report that the castle gates were shut.

'It begins to look like a villainy,' said Odard gloomily.

Griflet stood pondering, his corselet dimmed with moisture, his leather bonnet and gloves steaming a little as he gazed into the fire.

'He made enemies during the summer,' said Griflet, and added after a pause: ' the fog's damnably thick.'

In the morning the fog was still there, and frost had crept

under it. The town hummed with a new search; Philastrius, kneeling beside Heuradys to change her bandage, told Yolande that men were dragging the harbour with nets.

Suddenly the door opened, and Douce stood whitefaced on the threshold. Yolande rose to her feet, unpleasantly thrilled.

' What is it? ' she asked.

' My lady . . . they've found him . . . Dom Ursus . . . dead. In an empty house by the East Gate.'

' Jesu have mercy,' said Yolande, as she and the others crossed themselves. ' What had happened to him? '

' His throat was cut, my lady. Someone had locked the door and left him there.'

Yolande stared at her, appalled.

' Have you any idea who . . . ? ' she began, but Douce interrupted her.

' No, my lady. They say the house was his own. The Sieur Odard has gone down there. He asks us to keep it from Dame Jehane.'

Douce glanced at the apothecary, and beckoned Yolande with one finger. Yolande followed her from the room and closed the door behind them.

' Aurania? ' she asked.

' I've put her to bed. She's half-dazed. I'll tell my lady she's sick after the pynnonade last night. Pineapple never agrees with her. My lady, is it a judgment? '

' I expect so,' said Yolande shortly. ' We must be as kind to her as we can. Go back and stay with her. I'll come to the dame presently.'

Douce went silently away, and Yolande, a little dizzy, re-entered her own chamber.

' What a horrible way to die,' she muttered. ' Philastrius, if they find the murderer, what will they do to him? '

' Break him on the wheel, my lady.'

' What do *you* think Dom Ursus was doing there in an empty house? "

' He kept himself closely informed of events in the town,' said Philastrius. ' Maybe he quarreled with one of his . . . er . . . informants.'

' Philastrius! '

' Yes, my lady? '

' If need arise, will you and Blanche take Heuradys in for me until she can walk and come back to me here? '

' That we should gladly have done, my lady, but there is something I must tell you . . . nothing to do with Dom Ursus, God rest his soul.'

' What is it? '

' Before the fog came down a merchant of furs rode in from Jarapt. He put up at the Sign of the Keys, and he's fallen very sick there. His two servants are sick too, and today the inn-keeper's wife and a groom have both gone down. It might be . . .'

' Holy Mary! Has the plague come back? '

' No, my lady, but it may be a winter pestilence. It sounds like the sweating sickness I remember five years ago in Beltany. If so, it can be deadly . . . I shall be busy, and could not come here again until I can visit you safely . . . or unless I were needed for sickness in the castle, which God in his mercy forbid.'

Yolande stared down at him, and put out a hand to touch his shoulder. Philastrius smiled up at her and down at the watchful Heuradys.

' Fortunate Roclatour, that missed the plague! ' said Yolande. ' Guard yourself and Blanche, dear friend. And when . . . if those two young men come back from Arionbel, tell them from me to ride away again very quickly. Say I shall hope to hear them sing again in happier times.'

' I will, my lady. Now, listen. Burn wormwood in the ante-chamber. Hang up a string of onions by the door, and keep an even warmth. If anyone near you sneezes, send her to bed; give no food or purges, avoid both heat and cold. If anyone begins to sweat, send for a physician or for me. I must go now . . . this wound is healing as it should. In three days' time this damsel may walk, using a staff at first. The Holy Trinity have you both in keeping.'

' And you, Philastrius,' said Yolande as he bowed himself out. Then she looked down at the harp-player, and was almost

ashamed at the glow of love and trust in the bright blue eyes
between their black lashes.

' You'll think it an evil hour in which you came to Roclatour,'
she said.

' No matter what happens now,' said Heuradys, ' I shall never
think that.'

' Grim tidings for my lord Grand Seneschal,' Yolande
remarked to Odard when she met him towards evening.

The castellan blinked at her; his nights were disturbed by
Jehane's demands for this decoction and that infusion.

' My lord Grand Seneschal's gone to Zurland,' he told
Yolande glumly. ' He's sent to arrange the marriage of my lord
Duke of Honoy.'

Yolande waylaid him beside the door of the little chapel,
where she had intended to pray for the soul of Dom Ursus.
The body of that sleek Hound of God already lay at Saint
Michael's Priory; and still the yellow fog hung close and blurred
the passages and entries of the castle. It seemed to Yolande to
typify the muffled quality of her life; after the fantastic reunion
everything was dimmed again.

Sitting beside Jehane earlier in the day, she had courted the
retelling of stories of Camors, and played the lute and read
from the *Gesta Romanorum*. The sick woman seemed easier,
content to believe that fog had put an end to active life beyond
her observation.

' Dom Ursus has not been to see me,' she complained once,
and Yolande said she believed the tutor now to be at the priory.

' He'll soon be quit of his tutoring,' went on Jehane quietly.
' And I of my task as governess You'll not have much to
unlearn, child. Show me your embroidery.'

Yolande showed her the gorgeous banner she was preparing
for Balthasar to hang above his stall as a chevalier of the Order
of the Bridge of Faith. This order, originally consisting of the
king himself and sixteen of those who distinguished themselves
on the field of Pont-de-Foy, had been kept up to strength by
addition of friends and favourites of Thorismund. First of
those to be thus included had been Yolande's own father and her

first betrothed, Drogo Duke of Boqueron; the Grand Seneschal, and now his son, were the most recent to be so honoured.

' I should have set the Thunderbolt an inch to the right,' said Jehane, pulling the bright silk about with dry, restless fingers. ' I remember helping my aunt of Beltany with her son's banner of the Order of Saint Andreas. She said that for my age I was the best broiderer in the province. I was making it when I first met my husband. I liked dark sulky-looking men; I thought there was maybe something behind, but it's turned out to be sulks all through. Kings and commanders don't like that. Then when my family fell out of favour ... '

' Rebelled against the king, you mean,' thought Yolande mechanically.

' ... he started us off on our travels with more valour than sense. A word to the old Archbishop, I told him, and he could have had a place at once. But no, Odard must go his own way into exile. Four years it took us to find a roof that didn't leak. These Franconian noblemen often live like peasants, except that they have castles instead of farmhouses. Saint Catherine witness I've shelled peas with arrows thudding into the shutters, and milked a goat with the stones from a trebuchet smashing into the houses near by. You, now, you've never known what it is to lack a meal ...'

' No, my lady,' said Yolande patiently.

' *Ecco,* as the Italians say, I've got my hiccough coming on, will you dip into the second napkin, it's fennel-seed boiled with mint, and add a finger of white wine, I mind standing at a window when I was six years old, hiccoughing like fury, it was evening, and a white owl rose and floated away in the blue twilight, I thought it must be the shape of a hiccough, it eases the pain in my right side, I wonder if Douce dosed Aurania, my lord tells me there's sickness in the town, I reckon the strolling minstrels brought it in with them, you must give all the kitchen wenches a dose of my brew of angelica, there's a jar of the powdered root in the brew-room, half a drachm to a dose in treacle, and there are stalks and roots candied, they should be eaten fasting, don't stint them, it's what they're for, I shall be up again soon, this fog lies on my chest, you'll have to be getting back to your lessons, tell Dom Ursus to come and see me, he's rare good company with a cup of Chian in his fist . . .'

'Yes, I'll be going,' said Yolande, collecting the crumpled banner. 'You try to sleep, my lady. The fog can't last much longer.'

She went out by the door which led into the damsel's room. Aurania, too, had the hiccoughs, but that was because she was drunk. Douche had taken the shortest way to ease her misery. Yolande watched for a moment, and then went back to Heuradys.

Kneeling down by the truckle-bed, she pulled back the coverlet and blanket, looked at the firm breasts pouting beneath a fine green smock of her own, cupped a hand around each of them, and buried her face in the fragrant silken valley between.

Heuradys put protecting arms around her shaking shoulders.

'My lady,' she breathed. 'My dear brave lady.'

'Yolande,' whispered Yolande.

Heuradys was silent for a moment.

'It's too soon,' she murmured. 'Tomorrow you may wish you had not said that.'

Yolande gently shook her half-imprisoned head.

'Yolande,' said Heuradys, and hugged her with sudden surprising strength.

'That was what I needed,' Yolande told her, raising a flushed wet face and staring up at the twilit windows. 'There was a giant who grew stronger every time he touched the earth. Your heart thumps like a charger's hoofs coming slowly over the grass, coming to help me behave like a leopardess instead of a rabbit.'

Heuradys made a quiet but complicated movement, and a little slitting pain came in Yolande's left hand near the base of the index finger. Startled, she looked down; the glittering dagger rolled to the floor, and Heuradys caught the hand close and set her lips fiercely to the tiny bleeding cut.

'There,' she said happily after a moment. 'Now I am not ashamed to call you Yolande.'

The delicate extravagant gesture set a glow in the dreary day. Yolande let Heuradys dab and bandage the cut, and got up to

go to the chapel. Then she met Odard, and heard that the
Grand Seneschal had left the country, and that the sickness
which Philastrius had spoken was running riot in the lower
town.

'If my lady could be moved I'd say the household should
make a bolt for Pardelin,' said Odard.

'Will you now dismiss the soldier who offered violence to
Heuradys?'

Odard blinked. Yolande thought: *so this is what it's like to
nag a man.*'

'Very well, my lady.'

'And have you any idea who could have murdered Dom
Ursus?'

Odard shook his tired head and said that his men and the
provost's were turning the town inside out.

'What was it Griflet did at the Bridge of Klingenstein?'

Odard shot an astonished glance at her.

'I don't know, my lady,' he answered slowly.

'Dom Ursus knew,' said Yolande.

Odard shrugged his shoulders and harked back to the sweating sickness.

'It would be best if you stayed away from his funeral,' he
told her. 'And if you kept to your own rooms here . . . and
received no one from the town.'

'I suppose so, my lord.'

Presently she was kneeling alone in the gloomy little chapel.
The dull stained glass of the single window showed Saint
Amarand in a heathen temple with a stone idol shattered before
him. It reminded her of Vitellius, who saw the statues of
himself hurled down before he was killed. Something about
Vitellius she had to ask Dom Ursus. . . .

And now she could not, for Dom Ursus was dead, and she
must say prayers for his soul, and wonder in what stead his
works on earth would stand him. Plenty of people were shocked
at his death, but no one except Aurania seemed sorry. Somewhere in Roclatour a murderer was probably glad. The pattern
of two years' life was broken; around its edges prowled the
shadows of the secret servants of Yolande.

X

PASSING-BELLS AT ROCLATOUR

ON the fourth day of the fog they buried Dom Ursus in the crypt of the priory of Saint Michael. Jehane was told that his passing-bell was for a victim of the sweating sickness. During the ceremony one of the canons collapsed in the choir, his candle guttering out on the pavement as if at an excommunication. In the castle that morning two of the archers could not rise from their pallets; by noon another archer was lying beside them, and by vespers two more had gone down, with a groom and one of the porter's children.

A physician appeared at Odard's summons; the castle was filled with strong odours of vinegar and burning herbs. The higher household was almost cut off, taking its meals in the solar. Zoster Adela and three other nuns came in at the barbican, their great headdresses set like the sails of a relieving fleet. Yolande spoke to Zoster Adela out of a window; the nun told her to stay in the keep and look after Jehane and Aurania.

So it was that Yolande never noticed the lifting of the fog. For several days she was in effect Jehane's tirewoman; she served medicines, carried water, emptied commodes in the garde-robe, swept and dusted, took Heuradys her meals, and fell asleep as she lay down. Heuradys limped about in the bedchamber, taking more and more of the work there, keeping a cauldron near the boil so that Yolande and Douce were never without hot water to wash in.

Jehane they guarded from everyone except Odard himself, and he took to a truckle-bed in the corner of her room. The passing-bells began to toll all day long; Jehane gave a great deal of husky advice, but no longer constantly announced that she was going to get up. Odard let her understand that Dom Ursus was dead of the sickness; after that she was quiet for a day, and sent for old Dom Cyril, who was now living in the keep.

Also Jehane began increasingly to take the wine offered to her; its effect seemed to be to reveal her to herself as possessed of a calm massive Sphinx-like character, whose iron sense splintered saws and riddles from the rocky core of circumstance.

' Blossoms are not fruits,' she would mutter. ' It's ill luck to dream of fruit out of season. But with flowers it's different. I dreamed last night of roses growing over the grass towards me . . . I saw them move, red and white and the shell-pink my mother grew at Camors. The rose is the emblem of silence. I knew when roses and violets bloomed late in the autumn that some pestilence threatened. It's always like that. After the plague, the sweating sickness; after the scythe, the fire in stubble.'

Or it might be: ' Last night I dreamed of unshod horses. It's moonwort that unshoes them when they tread on it in passing. It's moonwort that opens locks, too, if you put a leaf in the keyhole. This dream is a key, maybe. It signifies danger from too much knowledge. Horses with shoes will be passions doomed to misfortune, as anger, greed, envy, and lust. God and Our Lady be praised they never molested *me*, but there are some in high places who've yielded time and again. For them a sword is made sharp and a pit smokes with brimstone.'

No one knew what old enmities whirled in her muddled head; Odard sat with her for hours, speaking gently, prompting with a name when her voice rose in anger because she had forgotten it, but even he was puzzled for much of the time. Often she talked to herself, but then again she would address someone in the room.

' Douce,' she said once, ' you know my pot of myrtle down in the brew-room. Are you watering it every day, and remembering to *look proud* when you do so? It will never thrive unless you look proud. When I married they bound a wreath of myrtle round the scabbard of Odard's sword when he laid it aside for the wedding. In the morning the wreath had dropped off, and that's how our cruel mischances began. . . .'

One night, for the first time since she had known Jehane,

Yolande deliberately touched her in pity; when giving her a drink she slid an arm behind the bony naked shoulders. Jehane shrugged impatiently, and Yolande took her arm away. Jehane let out a long shuddering sigh, as if to say: *such sympathy is in bad taste, and comes much too late.* Then she leaned back on her pillows, eyeing the towers of Jerusalem in the faded hangings across the room.

'The castles crowd close,' she muttered, and suddenly embarked on a list of names that zigzagged across Christendom.

'Camors, Ahun, Beltancourt, Drufontaine, Malcantarre, Saint-Emeraud, Haut-Ypod, Lestembourg, Adlersbrück, Irmingen, Trenzburg, Klingenstein, Bartsch, Hios, Karnovic . . . but nowhere a home for poor Jehane.'

Yolande, listening as dim turreted shapes sprang from the soil of ever more distant duchies and kingdoms, turned from the sideboard where crowded jars and flasks and flagons reflected the dull light of afternoon.

'Klingenstein,' she repeated firmly. 'Is there a bridge there, my lady?'

'Eh?' grunted the sick woman, turning memory-glazed eyes upon her. 'Klingenstein? Yes, a high-arched bridge with a chapel on it, and barges sailing underneath into flat freezing country. We met the Count of Montguiscard there . . . him that's Grand Seneschal now, and pokes old friends into corners where nobody can see them. He was mustering a company against his return to Baraine. He was glad of a lady then, to keep his captains' harlots in their places.'

'Was there a fight on the bridge?' pursued Yolande.

'No, not that I ever heard tell of. While we were there a man-at-arms broke into the chapel and robbed the altar and slew the old priest.'

'Did they ever catch him?'

'I never heard that either. It was a cursed place to me. *My* Yolande was born there, and died three days after her christening.'

An accusing note crept into Jehane's voice; she was blaming Yolande for having the same name as her own child, or for being alive when the little Xantroy was dead. Yolande's attention strayed along the eastward roads of Baraine.

'Lioncel and Diomede should be back any day now,' she reflected. 'Jesu, Mary, protect them from the sickness, let me see them again soon.'

She pressed a hand against the cross that shared with the key and the agate charm the deepening valley between her own breasts. A great horror reared up behind her physical weariness; soon she would have to submit herself to Balthasar-Belphegor. It was like being doomed to couple with a beast . . . some strange monster might grow in her body and break out breathing fire, shrivelling her to death in a coroneted bed, making her name a ghastly wonder for all generations to come.

'I won't,' she told herself desperately. 'I'll kill myself first . . . if I can somehow find the means and the courage.'

On the way to her bedchamber that night she paused by a window, and saw Orion stalking Aldebaran up the south-eastern sky. Behind him Sirius, blue-white and desolate, topped the black hills above the lake. Her own Sign of Gemini was just too high to be seen . . . her friends were too far and too powerless to save her from stalking Fate.

The means and the courage. The one might depend on the other. If she wanted to make an end of herself it must be with an accustomed gesture. To push home steel, or jump off a height with or without her neck in a noose, meant coming up to a moment when fear of life might be miserably vanquished by fear of death and damnation. To leap into water would mean that she would swim. But to empty a wine-cup she might cheat her nerves; it could just be a drink like any other. Only she did not want to dissolve in a hideous heap of squealing agony. . . .

Philastrius did not deal in poisons, but he knew how to make them. In him was her only hope, and the sweating sickness threatened it. The sweating sickness! Death crept through Roclatour, and she was wondering how to die!

'But there's Heuradys to consider,' she reminded herself.

' Or am I hiding cowardice behind my care of her? Certainly
if I die she'll be thrown out before my body grows cold. No,
I must live until she's somehow safe. But I must see my dear
apothecary . . . without anyone else's knowing.'

A steady north wind was blowing by midnight, and in the
morning a first thin snowfall had whitened the roofs and
ramparts. Yolande dressed and went along to see how
Jehane was faring; when she rapped on the door it was opened
surprisingly by the abbess.

' Child, keep away,' the abbess said, motioning her back.
' The Sieur Odard sent for me before dawn; my lady is down
with the sweating sickness, and Sister Marcelle and I have
come to take care of her. You must stay in your own rooms.
The servants lay the meals in the solar, and you wait to eat
until they have gone? '

' Yes, Reverend Mother in God.'

' Good. You had better not use this passage, or try to talk
to us. Go now, and Saint Marthe guard you.'

' Reverend Mother . . . Philastrius . . . have you news of
him? '

' Yes, God have him in keeping. He's attending two of my
sisters who are stricken. He works all day and half the night.
His wife is down too.'

' Oh . . . Blanche . . . oh! '

' Remember, your duty is to keep yourself safe.'

' Safe for Belphegor and Uncle Azo,' thought Yolande,
crossing herself and turning away. And as she sat down to
break her fast the sky darkened and the snow raged in a grey-
white whirl across the town.

Later, with an arm around the waist of Heuradys, she
watched the comings and goings in the blurred courtyard.
Hooded figures stumbled in and out of the main gate; firewood
came in, and a waggon-load of flour. Serving-women scurried
across the bridge on obscure errands, their heads bent against
the blizzard. Yolande tightened her grasp on her friend's
slim body.

' Riding-boots would be best,' she muttered, ' but it will
have to be wooden shoes, and the oldest cloak I can find.'

'Where are you going?' asked Heuradys simply.

'To speak with Philastrius. No, I'm not in need of his physic. It's the future I'm worried about. Douce is busy with Aurania. If she or anyone else should come, you don't know where I am.'

'Very good,' said Heuradys. 'I wish I could come too. I'll keep my fingers crossed for you the whole time you're away. Philastrius will likely be on his rounds.'

'I know. I must risk that. And thank you for not trying to stop me. It'll be easier for one than for two.'

'I shall never try to stop you from doing anything you want to do,' said Heauradys, as she limped to the great clothes-press.

A quarter-of-an-hour later Yolande made her first un-attended dive into the world beyond a castle. She wore no headdress but a kerchief under her thick hood. A solitary soldier stood guard under the gateway arch; scuttling past him with her head well down, she met the full blast on the bridge and gasped at its weight. The snow-whirl bundled her into the tunnel of the barbican; the teeth of the third and outermost portcullis seemed waiting to champ her, but there-under, too, the single sentry was niched and blowing on his hands.

'There's a tough wench for you!' he bawled, no doubt mistaking her for someone else. She replied with a kind of laughing grunt, and was out again in the storm, heading for the main street with her hood clasped before her nose. Under the hood and over her mouth was a linen cloth wrung out after being soaked in a scalding mess of herbs of the kind kept seething in the brew-chamber.

Few people were in the open. One alley held the noise and flurry of boys snowballing each other; another was half-blocked by a death-cart. The driver was struggling to fasten a blanket round the body of his waiting horse. A bell was tolling down by the harbour, its strokes coming gustily round the steep corners.

Bare-fisted, as became a servant, Yolande beat on the shop-door under the pestle and mortar. Turning, she glanced at the snow-caked boats and the grey water that vanished in spinning murk beyond them. A man came blundering past, tainting the storm for a second with the odour of cheap wine; he laughed nastily at her, and said something she barely caught.

'A lot of good you'll do yourself. His wife's ill, and damn all else.'

'I should think so too,' said Yolande to herself, and could have laughed at her own errand. Then Philastrius opened the door, and peered down at her.

'From the castle,' she said, and uncovered her face. He blinked at her with red-rimmed eyes, stood aside for her to enter, and shut the door quickly.

'My lady,' he whispered. 'Why are you alone?'

'To see you. How is Blanche?'

'I've sponged her with a strong water . . . she's sleeping easily at last. A neighbour's watching by her just now. You mustn't go near.'

'Our Lady knows I'm glad to hear it . . . she married the right husband, did Blanche. Take me where we can be secret. No one knows I'm here, except Heuradys. Have you a moment to spare?'

'Yes. I'm cooking myself a meal.'

With hood thrown back, and the smell of a stew in her nostrils, Yolande sat in a dark kitchen and looked at her drawing-master. He, too, wore loosely round his mouth a linen cloth, and his clothing reeked of medicaments.

'No word yet of those two young squires?' she asked him steadily.

'No, my lady.'

'I hope they mayn't be delayed in places where the sickness is heavy. But that isn't what I came to see you about. Philastrius, will you help me? I've no right to ask at such a time or in such a matter, but the storm gave me a chance, and I've no one else to turn to.'

'I'll help with anything in my power, my lady, so long as it doesn't take me from home for too long at a time just now.'

'It won't do that. Have you a very strong poison, which will kill in an instant . . . or two?'

Queer to make with a couple of words the possible difference between painless night and a last unbearable torment.

'My lady! Dear my lady!'

'With anything in your power, you said,' she reminded him, smiling a little. 'Only *you* know if it is in your power. Until now your help has been one of my happy things; now it may be grim, but it's still help, and I need it. I need it very sorely, if you can give it without danger. I'm coming very close to the other side of being a duchess.'

Philastrius sat down on a stool, cupped his hands over his knees, and looked wearily at her. A knocking began on the shop door, and he excused himself and rose to go into the next room. He opened a window and spoke to someone in the street, telling him not to wait, promising to come as soon as he could. Yolande felt life as a tangle of selfishness; and this time her own selfishness was pulled taut and not to be hooked and drawn aside.

Philastrius came back and sat down again.

'My lady,' he said quietly. 'I must first tell you this, in case it helps or hinders you. I believe that death is utter extinction. You are the only creature to whom I have ever admitted it. Blanche thinks I believe with her that we may find Paradise together. My confessor thinks I believe anything he chooses to tell me. Perhaps if I were not so tired I should disguise my belief from you, but I want you to know that to me the tales of God and the devil are only man's attempt to evade a true perception of his fate, which is that of the animals and plants, a perishing without spiritual trace or redemption. For this opinion I could be burnt . . . except that I have carefully studied the means of avoiding just such a fiery consummation.

'But you are my lady duchess, who warned me of danger to Blanche . . . and although you are so young in years you have known sorrow and shown mercy. Gods and devils are men's excuses for greed of power and for meanness and cruelty . . . but goodness and love and friendship and loyalty and beauty are real too, and when power is needed to guard them I wish that power to be in the hands of such great people as yourself. There are plenty of the other kind. My lady, I am at your service, knowing and wishing to know nothing of what you intend.'

Philastrius stood up and jingled his keys, reaching to thrust one of them into the lock of a high wall-cupboard.

' As I told you when first we met, my lady, I don't deal in poisons,' he said. ' But I'm known as a perfumer, and I have several sets of perfumes which I sell together . . . as this.'

He took down a little flat box and stood it on one edge. The front fell open on a hinge, disclosing four tubular bottles of thick white glass, each with a gilded stopper of slightly different shape. Dimly through the glass could be seen the colours of liquids—violet, crimson, green, and yellow, in columns a little more than the length and thickness of the apothecary's forefinger. Philastrius contemplated this array, and sat down again. He listened to a movement upstairs, and then took out the violet bottle and unstoppered it for Yolande.

' This is really a perfume,' he said. ' I call it Memory of Doves, a silly name to please ladies. It's a blind; the other three are drugs, and deadly. See, the label I have stuck in the lid. It says: *If these liquors have lost the perfumes of flowers they have suffered a change of nature and must be thrown away.* As they never had the perfumes of flowers, they may thus be destroyed before doing harm.'

' This is a lovely scent,' said Yolande, sniffing at the bottle she held. ' And that is a clever precaution against . . . trouble.'

' I hope so. Now, listen, my lady. These three are liquors prepared according to Saracen recipes of power. They are called *capagot, beym* and *adzin.* You see this shell? It's the measure to be used . . . and scalded after use.'

Yolande leaned forward, staring. She had expected nothing like this. Philastrius went on, tapping each bottle in turn.

' The crimson is the *capagot.* A shellful in a cup of wine kills in the space of a dozen heartbeats '

' Very painfully? '

' Apparently not. More as if with a rushing faint. No grimaces or clutchings at the belly.'

'You've seen someone die of it?'

'Yes, in the prison at Hautarroy. Men condemned to be hanged.'

'Ugh! And does anyone else know you possess it?'

'No one at all. I have hitherto never been asked for such ... er, advice. And I have prospered enough to be able to do without such dangerous traffic.'

'Then I could use it without danger to *you*?'

'Indeed, yes, my lady. But I beg you would consider where blame could fall. Innocent servants might be flayed alive. It carries a dreadful weight of accountableness.'

'On earth if not in heaven,' whispered Yolande gravely. Of course, if she poisoned herself, someone . . . probably Douce . . . might be accused of doing it. If she left a letter of explanation, Uncle Azo would burn it and blame Douce just the same. He could hardly admit that a duchess would die rather than let his son deflower her in lawful wedlock. Or Heuradys might be accused, or both of them. . . .

Yolande looked down and up again, meeting the sombre gaze of Philastrius. Then she laughed, not very mirthfully, and saw a flicker as of pain in his brooding greenish eyes.

'I'll remember that,' she promised. 'I see you think I meant somebody else to drink it.'

Philastrius sat very still. The stew bubbled in its pot, the blizzard raged and whistled beyond the window.

'Dear my lady, it was so,' the apothecary muttered. 'I drew on the knowledge of twenty years, and it seems I was wrong.'

'Never mind. You've suggested a possible alternative.'

'One that would load *my* conscience more lightly, whatsoever it might be. And that being so, let me tell you about the other two potions. The yellow is the *beym*; half-a-shellful in a cup of wine stuns anyone to sleep in a moment or two. The sleep lasts twelve hours or more, and leaves nothing worse than a headache.'

'It might be as useful as the other. And what is the third?'

'The green is the *ezd* or *adzin*. It nips life off at the very source. It is drunk in Constantinople, and Cairo, and Baghdad, by ladies who from vanity or dread or indolence wish to avoid the fruits of love.'

' Oh . . . and does it make them ill? '

' Not unless they follow the lead of the Empress Messalina.'

' And how many shellsful. . . .'

Philastrius instructed his young duchess, keeping his eyes from her in case she were embarrassed, tucking the flat box into a leathern wallet as he talked. Yolande took off her cloak, slung the wallet over one shoulder, and cloaked herself again. On the kitchen table she laid a purse; Philastrius picked it up, spilled out the score of gold nobles it contained, and handed the purse back with a little bow.

' My lady,' he said, ' there must be nothing to show that you have been here today.'

' Of course . . . Philastrius, I swear that you will never regret my coming. My love to your beautiful Blanche, and tell her I shall pray to Our Lady for her health and your protection. And as that prayer means nothing to you, I wish you all you wish for yourself. And if I were to send to you for more of the red or the green or the yellow perfume, my full payment would have to wait, for a messenger might wonder at it.'

' My lady, I know I shall never regret what has been said or done here. Come now, and I'll see that no one is near my doorstep to know you.'

Presently he let her out into the raging storm. She took a deep breath of the stinging air, and blew it out again hurriedly, dipping her nose into the medicated linen. The footprints of her coming had already disappeared; and now, as she leaned against the gale, she felt very much more like a Byzantine princess. Perhaps both she and Philastrius were a little mad, she reflected; never mind, it was good to know that such potency swung beneath her cloak.

She had been away less than an hour, she supposed; and her solitary trudging figure passed unnoticed up to the castle. Once she hung back to avoid overtaking someone who looked like a forester lugging something in a heavy sack. Then she looked up at the dim bulk of snow-beleaguered stone, trying to imagine how it must seem to a burgher's daughter, or to one of the servants whom she now pretended to be. Then the sense of her warm firelit chamber, of bright-eyed Heuradys waiting to welcome her, sharpened the edge of this adventure and set her plunging forward again.

'A leopardess with claws at last,' she called herself with a grimace that held more mockery than amusement. Courage and skill to use those claws were two different and separate matters.

'Saint Amarand preserve Philastrius!' she muttered with sudden fervour. Saint Amarand seemed the person to address in a matter which might bear shrewdly on the history of Baraine.

She won into the castle again with bowed head and shuffling feet. Both sentries let her go by without comment; only from men were passwords expected. Yolande reflected that this might be a military mistake.

Two or three people were moving about in the courtyard, but she did not need to approach them. She dodged up a stairway into the armoury passage, and caught a glimpse of Zoster Adela sailing out of the brew-chamber door in the opposite direction. Yolande's heart smote her that she should have to flee away up a turret stair without speaking to so true a friend. In two years that trustful relationship had become a casualty of circumstance.

She found Heuradys roasting chestnuts with the fingers of one hand still carefully crossed; the friendly chestnut smell bore down the medical stink of the antechamber.

'Did Douce or anyone else ask for me?' she enquired, flinging down the snow-covered cloak and kicking off the wooden shoes.

'No one,' Heuradys assured her. 'I might have been alone in the castle. It's a frightening place when you aren't here.'

Yolande kissed her, and let her smell the perfume called Memory of Doves.

'Any news of your squires?' asked Heuradys, rubbing her cheek on Yolande's sleeve.

'Not yet. I'm worried about them. If they get thus far in the snow it may keep them in the town. All my eggs in one basket.'

'Except the great Count of Ger.'

'Oh, he! I expect he's forgotten me.'

'And he your heir-presumptive!'

'The presumption is recent and remote. And now I must put on my head-dress and find the Sieur Odard to ask how things go with Dame Jehane. Then I'll come back and give you a lesson at chess.'

Things went badly with Dame Jehane. At noon of that day she dismissed the ghosts of her children in order to make confession. Dom Cyril administered the Last Sacraments, and shortly before the time of vespers she died almost as she had lived, in the middle of a sentence.

'If my brother had any sense,' she began, and instead of going on, paused, and went in search of the little ghosts, leaving her husband holding a hand that grew cold. The blizzard had blown itself out, the sky cleared, and snow lay thick under glittering stars when the convent bell began to toll for her.

After a whispered word with Odard, who backed away from her as she spoke, Yolande spent another strange time of prayer in the cold chapel. She was not so much sorry for Jehane's death as for her whole unhappy life; and that seemed an impertinence to Jehane's Creator. How simple and how dreadful to believe as Philastrius believed!

Then she sat with Aurania, who had come through a fever without sign of the general infection. Douce was there with them, white and crushed-looking without Jehane to worry her. Yolande stitched at a pair of gloves she was making for Heuradys.

Aurania laid down her breviary and turned a shapely tousled head wretchedly towards Yolande.

'My lady,' she whispered, 'what will happen now?'

'I don't know,' replied Yolande. 'Is the sickness at Bargreant?'

'Yes, my lady,' said Douce from the shadows.

'Then we shall be as well here as anywhere, I suppose. After Christmas I think it likely my lord duke will take us away, perhaps to Hautarroy.'

This was invention on Yolande's part; she had no idea what stony shape would frame the grim immediate future. For all she knew, Balthasar would whisk her away to Jarapt, or to one of the northern castles of Baraine, or to ill-famed Sabloyn in the Uplands of Honoy; but she suspected that he would follow Azo's example and keep her in the background. Hautarroy and Bargreant were neither of them likely; but there was no need to add to the dolours of Douce and Aurania. They were her damsels now, in fact as well as in name, and Yolande would not admit to them in words how cheaply she was held by her husband.

Aurania, she could see, was growing daily more frightened; Dom Ursus might have absolved her, but it seemed that nature had refused to second him. She complained only of loss of appetite. Perhaps it was time for some of the quiet wisdom of Philastrius.

Jehane lay dead in the next room, beyond the door that had not been opened for nearly a week. No one but Jehane had kept tally of the material brewed and distilled and compounded during the autumn. Here was a chance at once to rescue a damsel in distress and to test the strange green liquid called *ezd* or *adzin*.

Yolande carried a candle down to the brew-room, and confronted the array of remedies and condiments, of pans and spoons and dishes, standing as if under the command of the pot of myrtle. Tonight their shapes looked pathetic, as though they knew themselves orphaned. Yolande lifted her chin and gave the myrtle a ducal curtsey. Then she stood thinking for a moment, and finally picked up an empty jar, with two flasks whose uses she remembered. Cobwebs and silence and gloom, and a score of faint warring odours, reproached her with the memory of her mirth at Jehane in action.

Then she climbed back to her bedchamber, and poured out a cup of wine of Estragon. Heuradys, who could read a little, was spelling out a story in the Byzantine sequence.

'A cheering draught for Aurania,' said Yolande, as if to herself, and doctored the wine behind the open door of the great press. Then she took candle and wine-cup along the passage and round the corner to the room shared by the damsels.

'I've been to the brew-room,' she told Aurania. 'Here's a dose should settle your stomach and let you eat again.'

Aurania accepted the cup with a mechanical politeness. Yolande regained her own bedside sweating a little, but not with the sickness. That night she took Heuradys into her bed, and slept in the comforting clasp of a thin strong arm.

In the morning she confronted Aurania's glare of slightly bewildered gratitude.

'My . . . my lady, gramercy . . . gramercy for the draught you gave me,' stammered the plump flushed beauty, clasping her hands as if to pray. 'It . . . I'm wonderfully eased . . . I didn't know you were so skilled with physic.'

'I'm not,' said Yolande, wanting to both laugh and cry a little. 'It was a chance remembering. I used the last of a syrup, and I can't recall its name or prescription.'

'That was wise of you,' she told herself. Aurania, sitting half-naked in bed, looked just the kind of young woman who might be glad of that treatment again.

Going out into the passage, Yolande encountered a different glare in the eyes of the Sieur Odard. Odard had slept, or at any rate had lain, in the chamber once occupied by Dom Ursus. He looked so haggard that Yolande wondered whether he would be the next to go down. Then she realised that he, too, was near some extremity of emotion.

'My lady,' he said hoarsely, still keeping his distance, 'the abbess is taken sick. She sends word, and I agree, that I should take you out of this pest-house. You and the damsel Douce . . . as quickly as may be.'

Yolande stiffened where she stood, and crossed herself twice.

'Where to?' she demanded. 'Bargreant? I heard say the sickness is there too.'

'It is.'

'Where then?'

'To Pardelin.'

A cold thrill climbed through Yolande's crowding per-
plexities.

'But Aurania . . .' she began.

'Sister Marcelle will nurse her. Or one of the other nuns.
When she is well she can come after you, or go to the convent.
The abbess left by litter last night; I had this news, and her
message, just now.'

'I must have the girl Heuradys with me.'

'Heuradys? Yes, yes, you'll want a woman, and she has
kept clear of infection. Dom Cyril will come with us.'

'But the snow . . . and all the household gear. . . .'

'It's freezing hard. There are plenty of horse-sledges.
Several of them are covered. I can find a dozen men to go;
none of those in the North Tower have sickened or look like
sickening. My . . . my lady will be buried today. We must
start at dawn tomorrow. This, I believe, is how my lord
the Grand Seneschal would order it.'

Yolande stood still for another moment, and crossed herself
yet again.

'You are in command here,' she said. 'I must be guided
by you, my lord. But what if we take the pestilence with
us?'

'Then we shall be in God's hands.'

'That will be a sore mischance,' escaped from Yolande
before she could stop it. But Odard was too worried to notice
what she had really said.

'We shall have done all we can,' he went on, gloomily.

'It doesn't affect the horses, does it?' she asked him
suddenly.

'No. I'll send riders at once to warn Julian we're coming,
and to prepare the people at that village inn half-way.'

'Very good, my lord. I hope you are caring for yourself?'

Odard looked at her oddly.

'I am, my lady,' he said, as though taken off his guard,
for a dull flush suddenly crept up under his yellow skin.

'I'll send the steward and two men to roll up your bedding,'

K

he went on. ' I fear you must use a truckle-bed tonight . .
the bed I slept in must be taken for Dom Cyril.'

' No matter,' said Yolande, suddenly flat-voiced. For the
second time a household had suddenly dissolved around her
Beneath the excitement of change and return was a chill ache
of desolation.

' There'll be sledges for three or four chests,' went on Odard
' We can send for more gear as need arises. At least Pardelir
is warm and dry . . . I'm sorry, my lady, to have to ask you to
waken unhappy memories there.'

' That is no matter either,' said Yolande.

She took Heuradys in her own sledge. Douce and Dom
Cyril shared a second. A third and fourth were loaded with
canvas-wrapped bedding. Each of these great sledges had
two shaft-horses and a leader out in front. Lesser sledges
followed, heaped with chests and wineskins and firewood and
braziers and Yolande's bath-tub. First of all went a kind of
snow-plough, for which spare horses were led in rear. A
dozen fully-armed soldiers, besides three grooms and two
cooks and a couple of serving-men, rode in the convoy.

Yolande and the others had slept in most of their clothes,
and risen by candlelight. In the rosy glow of a wide clear
dawn they hurtled out of the side gate and over a little-used
drawbridge that had no barbican to protect it. The runners
of the sledges rasped and roared on the dry planks between
snow and snow; the horse-hoofs drummed and were muffled
again. Odard wore full armour except for a leathern hood and
hat and great leathern gauntlets. His charger, with thirty-
five miles to go, was not burdened with chamfron or bards;
it was evident that Odard preferred this journey to sitting
thinking about it in the castle.

' Do the sledges run away downhill? ' asked Heuradys
nervously.

' No, they brake the runners with chains,' Yolande told her.
' And the men hang on with ropes, and if the slope's very
bad they take the horses away. But when the snow's like this
there shouldn't be too much slipping.'

They sat face to face under the canvas hood, nursing hot stones tied into woollen bags. Each could see little of the other except a pair of eyes.

Lake Targe lay blue beyond the snow-topped roofs and towers; ahead, the hoof-marks of yesterday's messengers led the way up the first long slope into the high Casque of Baraine.

Neither Yolande nor Heuradys knew how the fight began. They were jolted awake by the stopping of the sledge; the air seemed full of yells and curses, snow-muffled stamping of horses, and the bang and clash of steel. As they fumbled with the straps of their canopy, an arrow ripped right through it, sticking by its feathered butt in the canvas three inches from Yolande's left shoulder. It had flashed between their startled faces; Heuradys rose as she got the flap open, and Yolande found herself half-smothered by a fierce protective embrace.

'Let me see,' she mumbled, clutching in her turn. Over the rucked cloak of Heuradys she saw a steep snow-slope, dimpled with blue shadows, broken by plumed bushes or the straight sunlit boles of birches. Ahead, the middle of the little column curved out of sight under a dark covert of hollies; there the score of forest thieves had hidden above the track. They wanted food, and must have been warned which sledges carried it. They aimed to cut the convoy in two, tumble and grab as much as they could, and be off into the opposite thickets before the archers in front and rear could shoot more than a few of them down. . . .

An archer's horse carried him past a foot from Yolande's peering face. Snow seemed to smoke from a scrimmage three sledges ahead. A man sat backwards into the drift with hands up to his gashed face. Horses were plunging, and one of them gave a terrible scream. Three men came down the sunlit slope as if to round the rear of the column. Yolande felt, rather than heard, Heuradys draw her dagger; one of the slithering ruffians grinned at the two of them. An archer's mount slewed sideways between, and a mace-head swung back, almost touching the canopy. The archer's stained buff jerkin and well-polished saddle trapped an angle of glittering snow, across which his green-clad arm swept as he flung the mace. The sledge gave a great heave, and Yolande caught Heuradys with both arms to prevent her falling out. They both exclaimed as the archer toppled backwards, his steel cap hitting the runner with a full ringing smack. He was cursing down there; his horse wheeled away with a dim shape hanging on to the bridle. A skinny red-nosed apparition lurched knee-deep through the drift, swinging a spiked club low for an over-arm stroke at well-fed women who rode about in sledges.

The stroke rose only half-way. A black horse seemed to float behind the red-nosed man, and a long sword glittered under his club. A choked but dreamlike expectation of death did not prevent Yolande from wondering at the ease with which the sword passed through the ragged figure. Red nose and spiked club sought the snow together, and Diomede wrenched out the sword and looked at her with the smeared blade swinging between them.

'My lady,' he said simply, and reined round and leaped out of her range of vision.

'Open the other side,' gasped Yolande. Heuradys and she disentangled themselves, and pulled back the second flap. First they saw another steep slope, with a man lying blackly at the top of a fearful red stain. It was purple-red, not the red of blood; the man was clutching a wineskin, and it and he had been pierced by different arrows. . . .

Then a growling scrambling bundle came to a stop close to the runner on that side; two men were locked in a death-grip, and Yolande saw great brown hands beneath a staring em-purpled face that suddenly went blue-grey.

Over and behind the wrestlers appeared a grey horse. The flash of the rider's white-gold hair made Yolande want to say: *Lioncel, you've lost your hat.* Then Lioncel straightened up, and called through the din.

'He has it, man . . . you can stop squeezing.'

The ravine that had become a battlefield fell curiously quiet. Lioncel looked along it, and turned to find Yolande watching him.

'My lady,' he said. 'This is Quargis, our friend and comrade.'

The dwarf heaved himself up, smacking white powder from his belt and shoulders. He made Yolande a bow curiously courtly, considering that he was more deeply sunk in the snow than an ordinary man, and was moreover standing between the splayed legs of a corpse.

'Your servant, my lady duchess,' he rumbled, and his greenish eyes shocked Yolande, they seemed so wise and sad.

Odard came striding back from the front of the convoy. He had been unhorsed, but his battle-axe had evidently made some amends for the indignity. His anxiety for the safety of Yolande extended to that of Dom Cyril and Douce; Yolande noted with approval his pause beside their sledge. He greeted the squires with civility, thanking them for their appearance at such a useful moment. Diomede turned back to pick up the harp he had dropped when the ambush broke.

'That fortified inn is a league ahead,' Odard told Yolande. 'We can't make Pardelin tonight at the pace we're going. I've two dead men for burial. Three more are hurt, and four horses injured. We'd better stay at the village tonight. I believe the weather will hold.'

Half an hour later they moved off again, leaving one thief hanging and six more tumbled at the wayside. Dom Cyril had said a prayer for them while Odard fiddled with his charger's trappings. Yolande heard from Lioncel how he and Diomede had ridden up to the door of Philastrius.

'He leaned out of a window and told us to be off,' said Lioncel. 'He said if we hurried we'd catch you up . . . he seemed to know we wanted to. His wife is mending.'

'Our Lady be thanked,' said Yolande, and vowed a candle to mark her gratitude.

So for a second night she and Douce and Heuradys slept in all but their gowns and shoes. Dom Cyril had led the company into the tiny village church for the burial service of the two archers. When it was done he offered thanks for the preservation of the survivors from both sickness and wayside violence.

To Yolande it suddenly seemed odd to thank the Sieur God for not withdrawing a gift bestowed to glorify himself. Or if man was the sack of dung that Saint Bernard made him out to be, how did God get any glory or satisfaction out of so poor a return for his omnipotence?

Her attention shied away from heaven. Lioncel and Diomede had come again. They must stay at Pardelin for a while; Odard could not hustle them away after their sword-play in the ravine. Let blizzards blow, and snow lie thick, the better to keep them there.

Soon after noon of the next day the convoy rounded the shoulder of Siege Umbrous and followed the snow-plough through the pass. There below, like a sheet of steel dropped between the white mountains, frozen Lake Falchion gleamed dully under the yellow winter sun.

XI

FRUIT OF THUNDER

' I'M a ghost here,' thought Yolande, as she climbed stairs and faltered on thresholds in the hold of Pardelin. Also she had never been there in winter before; the silvery light on walls and ceilings added to the strangeness of her return. It irked her to have to explain the rooms and passages to Douce, so she set about doing it with courtesy and precision. Old Julian strode off to the hamlet to find a couple of women willing to work in the kitchen; archers dragged beds and chests and braziers into their appointed places, and the courtyard was loud with hoofs and brooms and chatter. When Julian came back he brought not only the women but also Dom Robert, the village priest, who was anxious to pay his respects to the duchess.

Odard presented the priest, a reserved little man with a greying beard and no need to renew his tonsure. He blessed Yolande very calmly; he and Dom Cyril eyed each other with the caution customary between Regulars and Seculars.

' I'm a ghost here,' repeated Yolande when she came to the solar. For the moment she was alone; she had arranged it that way, not wanting company at the place where she had parted from her father. Nowadays she could say *wait a few minutes*, and everybody waited.

She walked across the room, and looked out of a window at the sun, already sinking as a crimson ball in the leaden edge of the sky above Siege Fabulous at the far end of the lake. She went to the door that led down to the hall, and saw the priest still there, talking to Julian. At a sound she turned; Lioncel was standing where he had stood when she asked him to try to rescue Amarand.

But now he was much taller; the beauty and kindness of his face seemed to twist the heart in her body.

'Are you a ghost, too?' she asked him forlornly.

'If you wish it so, my lady,' he whispered. 'I'm supposed to have lost my way. When you know every inch of a place it's hard not to show it.'

'You'll have time to learn your way about,' she told him, and suddenly they both smiled. Diomede, coming quietly along the passage, looked in and saw them smiling. Yolande glanced at him and saw his face light up with more than the dim sunset-glow.

'You too, Diomede,' she said. 'Do you feel very ghostly?'

'My lady, I . . . I did until this moment. But to see you and Lioncel together here has brought my . . . brought me altogether home.'

'You saved my life yesterday,' she went on, and frowned at his quick shake of the head. Then she laughed, and went on: 'I said that as if I blamed you, didn't I? I won't hold it against you. But it's going to be hard to pretend I . . . you . . . go away now. We must have the talk we planned as soon as I can achieve it.'

Like shadows they departed, and Yolande turned back to look once more at the encrimsoned sun.

'I feel very strange,' she told it. 'As if my troubles were ending . . . but Holy Mary, I know they're only just begun. Is this the excitement they talk of that goes before the sweating sickness? How like Fate that would be . . . no, it wouldn't, Fate's got Balthasar up its sleeve for me. Any time now.'

She thought with affection of Philastrius and the wallet of so-called perfumes, which she had carried herself from Roclatour. It hung now in the great press where Alys used to guard the gowns. Kind fat Alys . . . if there were any ghosts at Pardelin, they were probably those of her friends. In fact, if she aimed to join that great company, Pardelin was the place in which to drink the *capagot*. But that meant first getting rid of everyone who might suffer for it. . . . Again, if this queer lightheadedness marked the onset of the pestilence, she might not have to screw herself up to use the Saracen potion. Lioncel and Diomede would take care of Heuradys. . . .

'They say you're thrust away and neglected,' Heuradys had

murmured as the sledge neared the castle, 'but never, I think, had any lady two more debonair swordsmen to seek her out and serve her.'

'Their service is not for long,' Yolande had replied. And now here she was, planning to end it already.

Up from the kitchen drifted an intimation of roast venison. Yolande found her mouth watering.

'I don't believe I'm going to be ill,' she told the sun and the lake and Siege Fabulous. 'I want to eat until I'm full, and drink just a little too much, and then hear Lioncel and Diomede play and sing until midnight.'

Her conscience smote her at the thought of Dame Jehane. She went to find Odard, who was in the winter parlour, emptying a brass-bound chest which had come on one of the sledges. He rose, turning a lack-lustre eye from her to the scrolls and papers and back again.

'My lord,' she asked, 'has anyone who came with us shown a sign of the sickness?'

'No one. God be praised.'

'Amen. My lord, will you mind it if I ask the young men to sing after supper? They know of your—of our great loss, and will attempt nothing but grave entertainment.'

'Eh? Oh, yes, my lady. Gramercy for your kindness. My lady Jehane, God rest her soul, would never wish us to win a battle and then fall to moping for *her*. She was always one for good company and the exchange of conversation.'

'I don't know about the exchange,' thought Yolande, and crossed herself, and left him to his papers and his loneliness.

That night she ate heartily and drank two cups of wine sparingly watered, and listened to Lioncel and Diomede as they played music and sang songs not out of place in a habitation of mourning.

'A good thing there are two of them,' she told herself suddenly. 'True Love is Leopard's Bane. It means I can't possibly fall in love with either.'

'Heuradys!'

'Yes?'

'Help me find my hunting-clothes, quick, quick, quick!'

'But you can't hunt in snow like this.'

'No, but I can go sledging. The squires are taking Douce and myself up on to Siege Umbrous. I wish you could come too; you must watch from the south-east tower, and mutter charms to finish your healing.'

'What does Dom Cyril say to a duchess who climbs mountains with strange and beautiful young men?'

'He's my confessor, pet, and knows all the sober thoughts I think are likely to please him. It was Odard, poor, man, who seemed more worried. Of course I made out it was my idea. Pull off my headdress, will you?'

'Stand still . . . there. And whose idea *was* it?'

'A very respectful squire's.'

'Which? They're both very respectful.'

'Yes . . . oh, very. Sometimes I . . . yes, those are the boots. It was de Forne . . . Heuradys!'

'What is it? I've made you sad.'

'I'm damned if I can keep it from *you*. Those two were pages here . . . the only members of my father's household to escape Turlequin's hell-dogs. They were like my brothers . . . I'm not sad . . . I love them both dearly.'

'So long as you love them *both* dearly,' said Heuradys, letting Yolande's belt dangle from her slim strong hands.

'I know all about that,' said Yolande shortly, pulling one of the soft boots over her green trunk-hose that went with the short green hunting-frock. Then she looked at her friend's bandaged ankle, and pointed to the great press.

'In there,' she told her, 'is a russet hunting-suit I could wear two years ago. See what the moths have done to it, and alter it to fit you. In a day or two you'll be sledging too.'

'I'll do that,' said Heuradys. 'I'm getting tired of being mewed up in undeserved comfort. I'd like to be upset in the snow in the arms of a debonair squire with hair like spun gold or the raven's wing.'

They smiled at each other like conspirators. They *were* conspirators, Yolande decided, as she crunched dry snow underfoot in the shadow of the gateway towers. She hoped the upflung snow-light suited her face as well as it suited Douce's. She saw Dom Cyril peering from the ramparts and waved a gloved hand at him. . . . Up and up the immaculate slopes, hand in hand with Douce, turning to wave again to the flutter of a scarf at a window in the south-east tower . . . seeing foreshortened more and more the stony snow-topped shapes of castle and hamlet and oak-tree . . . blinking ahead at the high grey blur that was Faramond's Tree. . . .

Breath that stung when drawn in and steamed when driven out, long blue shadows in the mountains, Lioncel's eyes as blue as cornflowers, Lioncel's hair straight and thick and clean-smelling like hay as she sat down behind him on the heavy sledge and put her hands on his shoulders. Douce's knees nipped her haunches; Douce was nervous. Diomede gave a grunt as he pushed off, launching her into searing delight; she hung on to Lioncel and heard herself squeal as the valley rushed up to swallow them.

Lioncel's hunting-boots swung down, first on one side and then the other, shooting up a spray of snow, altering direction in swoops which seemed to push her heart and stomach out of their proper places. Once the sledge left the ground altogether, taking a leap that ended in a glorious grounding clash and smother.

' All there? ' yelled Lioncel over his shoulder as they hurtled on again.

' All here! ' bellowed Diomede from behind. Archers and villagers cheered faintly, dragging out their own sledges. Rocks and trees heaved up and vanished, the slope flattened and brought Yolande's heart down from her throat; a braking and scraping announced that now the snow was over the bracken. . . .

Six times they retraced the course, half an hour up, two minutes down. Douce began to squeal too; when the girls changed places Diomede clasped Yolande so carefully that she ground her shoulders against him and laughed, first with pleasure and then at herself for pretending not to notice the sudden tightening of his grasp.

' *So long as I love them both dearly, like brothers.*' The

words rolled themselves up in a ball that lodged under the arch of her ribs. It was true she would have felt the same had Lioncel hugged her like that; but was it exactly how you would enjoy being held by a beloved brother?

Yolande decided that it was not, and determined that the next time she must somehow discourage so close an embrace. But the next time Diomede went in front, and it was necessary to be quite impartial. Lioncel held her not quite so tightly, but she was almost sure he used a bump to kiss her hunting-cap.

'Yolande, you *trollop*,' she said to herself. 'They'd both be horrified if they knew you were playing a kind of game with them . . . unless of course *they* are playing one too, a sad and rather silly game that can never be anything else.'

Suddenly, late that afternoon, the chance came for which they had waited. Douce's nose began to bleed; Douce retired to her bedchamber, the one formerly used by the old Dame de Chevronel. Odard was closeted with his papers; Dom Cyril had gone down to the priest's house in the village. Yolande, Lioncel, and Diomede were left together in the solar for an hour before supper. Heuradys, sewing at the russet hunting-frock, kept *cave* for them by excursions into the passage, where a pan of chestnuts sat on a brazier under a window. If Heuradys dropped a brass bowl, someone would at once begin to play the harp or lute inside.

'Now,' said Yolande, 'tell me what happened. Tell me everything.'

The fire crackled, the wind sang, the sun burned crimson again. The *chut . . . chut* of the axe of Quargis, exercising his great muscles by chopping wood in the courtyard, provided a faint relentless accompaniment to their quiet voices.

Yolande hardly spoke at all; she sat motionless, crammed against cushions in the principal chair, feeling her heart grow hot and cold and hot again. Here, almost where she now listened, her father's sword had rung as he drew it for the last time. *Never trust a Montguiscard . . .* why had he not said a little more? Perhaps he was not sure; but now she, she was sure. The faint note of steel seemed to ring once again in her ear.

'Stop!' she commanded suddenly, when Diomede's voice faltered over the news they had heard at Gax. 'Neither of you must ever again feel that you failed in your duty to my father or myself. It may be there's no remedy, but only our meeting again like this could ever bring one about. Dom Gilomar was right, the Sieur Jesu rest his soul; it would have thrown away your lives to accuse the Grand Seneschal on your evidence alone. . . .

'Now listen to me for a moment. That helmsman's name was Radomar; I saw him again very soon after . . .'

When she had told how that encounter was bent to Azo's uses, making her appear half-crazed by danger and bereavement, Lioncel spoke again from the stool where he sat with hands clasped round his knees.

'We saw him—this Radomar—yet again a fortnight ago, between Hautarroy and Roclatour. We'll tell you about that later.'

'So the chain's complete,' went on Yolande, 'and it needed all three of us to forge it. Lioncel knows it was Radomar who watched us by the lake that day, and Radomar who called himself Turlequin in the long boat. Diomede knows how I was brought ashore, without any kind of fighting, and how Radomar went with Azo to watch the hangings at the oak-tree. I know Radomar was the helmsman, and was also a captain in Azo's own service. And Heuradys comes into it here . . . her father was a boat-maker at Jarapt, who vanished about that time. Azo, who butchered his outlaw accomplices, wouldn't be likely to spare the man who secretly made his long boat for him somewhere up in the hills.'

'No, he would not,' agreed Diomede. 'What was the boat-maker's name?'

'Geraint. But how we could set about using our knowledge to damage Azo is quite another matter. And all this relates to Azo only . . . we have said nothing yet about my lord and husband Belphegor.'

Smiling at their suddenly startled faces, she stretched out both hands to screen her face from the fireglow.

'Yes, I know him by that name, too,' she assured them. 'I

want to hear all you know about him. My marriage is not . . .
I mean, it still might be annulled.'

Lioncel looked at the fire, Diomede looked out of the
window, Heuradys darned studiously, and the patient axe of
Quargis kept a beat that lagged behind that of an ordinary
pulse. Yolande let fall her hands, and spoke to the carven
leopard on the great fireplace.

' I mean never to honour the vows of this marriage,' she said.
' I will neither love nor honour nor obey the son of my father's
murderer. I know many a high marriage is mortared with
blood of relatives, especially relatives of the bride. But I had
rather kill my husband, or myself, or both of us. Or if I were
too afraid to do that, I'd rather run away with Heuradys and
become a strolling lute-player. But all that I can swear to
against Belphegor is that he killed my kitten. Now please go
on with your story.'

By leaps and bounds that story approached the sledge-trail
in the forest ravine. Yolande, exhausted but fascinated, was
watching Diomede's dark face when the bowl clashed in the
corridor. She admired the ease with which he swept the small
harp to his knee, and began softly to sing not the first but the
third verse of *Tripping-Go*. It was Dom Cyril who came in,
waving a deprecatory hand when both young men stood up.
Heuradys limped after him, carrying a platter of roasted chestnuts; he sat down by Yolande and accepted a share of the spoils.

' Dom Robert's a very worthy man,' he told her. ' I find
he studied at Hautarroy with my own nephew.'

' He'll find things quiet here, father,' said Yolande primly.

Dom Cyril was her best reminder of the maiden she was
supposed to be, and she liked him too much to begin to show
him the real workings of her mind. No doubts and few
dissatisfactions clouded the little confessions she made to him;
sometimes she thought he must find her a disappointingly
dull young duchess.

Sometimes, too, she was ashamed of hiding her absorptions
from him, but Belphegor, and Azo behind him, and the Sieur
God behind both of them, seemed subjects quite unfit for discussion with such a kind and good old man.

'A cure of souls among peasants is never very quiet,' said Dom Cyril unexpectedly. 'They are peculiarly apt to fall into snares of the Evil One. Poor creatures, he comes easily among them from deep woods and dreary mountains. But where there's a nettle the Sieur God sends a dock to heal its stings; Dom Robert tells me that a holy hermit now dwells beside the lake.'

'Whereabouts?' asked Yolande, with an interest he found gratifying.

'In a cave on the south shore, he said. Three miles or more along the water.

'Oh . . . and how does he keep himself alive?'

'Dom Robert sends him a loaf now and then. I understand he eats some meat, and the foresters have leave to visit him with scraps and umbles. The archers, too, put in now and then on their way to and from Quatrelances. And the Sieur Odard gave him leave to snare rabbits and to catch fish in the lake.'

'Ugh!' exclaimed Yolande in spite of herself.

'Why do you say that, my daughter?'

'Fish . . . from *this* lake. I shall never eat them again. Even if the stockfish gives out in Lent and I have to live on pot-herbs.'

After a pause Dom Cyril crossed himself, understanding what she meant.

That night Yolande dreamed that she rushed downhill on a sort of dolphin which whizzed across the pebbles and splashed into the lake, snapping at heads and hands of corpses that drifted half-submerged. The faces were unknown to her, but a black figure watching on the shore she knew to be that of the Grand Seneschal. The dolphin dived, and she went down with it, swirling through a green gloom. On the bottom of the lake stood Lioncel, holding out his hand to help her alight.

'You'll soon get used to it here,' he told her. 'Diomede couldn't come, because it's his turn to be Tripping-Go.'

Yolande began to cry, and woke up crying. Heuradys woke up too, and gathered her close to whisper comfort.

'It was their being parted which seemed so sad,' sobbed Yolande.

'Tch, tch, tch,' said Heuradys, stirring her pointed chin throughtfully amid the wealth of Yolande's unbound hair.

'My uncle wanted me shut away,' said Yolande, shovelling tower-top snow through a crenel so that it thumped on the frozen moat sixty feet below. 'But I doubt if even he expected such a shutting-away as this.'

'It seems to me,' said Heuradys, leaning on her great birch-broom, 'that when the snow has gone . . . you . . . that is to say *we* . . . could go too, vanishing from here never to be found again.'

Yolande turned to look at her; the frizzy hair stuck out of a blue hood half thrown back, and the eyes of Heuradys were bluer than the cloth and nearly as blue as the middle sky. Heuradys was watching the black column toiling distantly up the pass in the morning shadow of Siege Umbrous; Odard had sent back most of the men and sledges that came from Roclatour.

'You look like a very sweet witch who might fly off at any time now,' Yolande told her . 'But if you did, with me riding pillion behind you, where should we go?'

On such a glittering morning the uses of the *capagot* seemed far-off and fantastical beyond belief. Heuradys measured her beloved duchess with a gaze grown critical.

'I don't think we could go at all," she said. 'When I was dirty and shabby and wore ill-fitting clothes, I could just escape too much attention, because I'm small and can look awkward. You couldn't; you're too well-bred. Even if you dressed as a boy, and cut your hair short, and roughened your hands and dirtied every finger-nail. Unless you stained your skin, perhaps, and pretended to be some sort of foreigner. But Italians aren't liked now because of the queen's greedy relations, and Spaniards and Greeks are mistaken for Italians, and anything Saracen is likely to be stoned at sight.'

Yolande was silent, respecting experience gained on roads and fair-grounds, in streets and taverns and courtyards of merchant houses. She did not know, and would not ask, how old Heuradys might be, whether she were still a virgin, or

whether the soldier at Roclatour were the first creature whom
she had knifed.

'And once you're on the road,' went on Heuradys, stirring
her broom again, ' you find it hard to get off it again. Try
to get work in a kitchen or shop and you find yourself tangled
in all manner of lies. A strolling harpist, God save us, she'll
give the children running scabs and the menservants evil
fluxes. And of course, some of them . . . us . . . could and
would. *But* if you want . . . if you really want . . . I'll paint
you black all over and swear you're a Princess of Sheba. I'm
not trying to head you off so that I can sleep on feathers and
have supper every night in the week.'

' I knew that,' said Yolande, turning to where a bow and a
sheaf of arrows stood propped against a merlon. ' That's
partly why I'm now going to make you as good an archer as
I am. You see that silver birch standing alone? It's just a
hundred yards from the edge of the moat. That's our direction. Take off your cloak . . . that's it. Give me your left
wrist . . . you must have this bracer on it, or you'll shred your
sleeve and skin your arm. Now put on these gloves. I've
greased them with deer's suet. . . .

' This is only a lesson in the handling of the bow; you must
shoot on ground level to learn how to aim. This is how you
string it, against your foot, so. Now, take an arrow. I'll
stand behind you. . . .'

With her hands on the hands of Heuradys, and her cheek
against the frizzy hair, Yolande was suddenly happy. The
plaint of the bowstring, the whizz and flash of the long
shafts, seemed at once a fulfilment and a preparation.
Heuradys proved apt; between the turret and the silver birch
a narrow line of feathered butts soon speckled the snow of
the *esplanade*.

' We must go and gather them before it gets dark,' said
Yolande when thirty or more had flown. ' You see that stump
like a snow mushroom, over towards the boathouse tower?
That's where the cook used to practise with his choppers . . .
he used them in the fight that day . . . Heuradys! '

' Yes, what now? '

'Tell me if ever I begin to talk about Pardelin or anywhere else as poor Jehane talked about Camors.'

'You forgot I never heard her,' said Heuradys, amused. 'To me she was someone round the corner who would drive me away from you if she could. In that she was my enemy. And so was your tutor.'

'Do you think the Sieur God removed them so that we could be together?'

'No. Their deaths teach me nothing except that enemies, too, are mortal.'

'Enemies, too, are mortal . . . h'm. Look, the hunters are coming home.'

Distant figures drew near along the lakeside, one man and four horses plodding through the now. The antlers of a great stag drooped against the whiteness. Odard rode first, humped in his saddle; Yolande supposed him to be feeling desolate and relieved and ashamed.

Lioncel and Diomede rode gracefully and upright, with bows and spears slanted back behind their stirrups. Lioncel's grey horse, Diomede's black, must be part of the colour-scheme of the fabulous Chevalier Janus.

'I love them both so much,' she decided, 'that I can't love either of them at all. And they both love me . . . in a trou-badourish way, of course. They don't seem jealous of each other about me . . . should I feel offended? I don't, I only feel jealous of each of them with the other. This is a kind of coil I've never heard of; not even the silkiest Byzantine princess had it to unravel.

'Better leave it unravelled. Pretend it isn't there . . . pretend they're only sorry for you, and loyal as squires should be. Don't run the risk of casting even your shadow between them. Let dull maidenly Douce be your pattern, remembering yourself to be chained to the altar of the glory of Belphegor.'

That afternoon the squires and Quargis made a snow-man on the northern stretch of the *esplanade*. Yolande and Heuradys gathered their arrows and went to help. Douce was invited but preferred to remain with her sewing; she was embroidering a large wallet of soft Cordovan leather—for something to do, she had said when Yolande idly asked her what it was for.

The snow-man was eight feet tall; it rose up by the tree-stump, on which Diomede stood to shape a fat foolish face. For helmet they gave it a leathern bucket, for eyes two wooden pegs, and for mouth a curve of pebbles from the shore of the frozen lake. Quargis made a pile of snowballs, and soon they were bombarding the image; Yolande suddenly had the illusion that its eyes followed her movements, and that it was laughing at her.

'We must get on with those skates tonight,' said Lioncel, after testing the ice. He and Diomede were carving industriously at sheep-bones, and had promised Yolande some fashioned from the shins of the stag. Lioncel and Diomede would take great care of her . . . poor Jehane had liked to remember how she skated with the old king, but it would be better to be Yolande, skimming over the iron-grey surface hand in hand with her Gemini. . . .

She wanted to snowball them, but Heuradys and Quargis might not like to join in, and certainly could not be left out. Heuradys solved the problem with a sudden wicked ball that burst on Diomede's chin. Diomede shouted and groped for another, Quargis grinned, and Lioncel covered the grin with a well-aimed shot. In a moment they were all laughing and yelling and plastering each other with chivalry and rank forgotten in a five-cornered affray. Yolande dodged squeaking behind the snow-man; its eyes couldn't follow her there, she thought, as the world went out in a smack and a whirl of white.

'Traitress!' she gasped at Heuradys.

'It was your pink nose,' explained Heuradys, with loving cruelty. 'The pink of perfection, too beautiful to be borne, too . . . ooh!'

Heuradys sat backwards like a jointed doll. Quargis had her range, and blinded her as she spoke. Diomede darted behind her and plucked her up by the armpits.

'You're not hurt?' he demanded, remembering her injury.

'No,' said Heuradys, radiant and mischievous, clutching

his gloved hands with her own, pushing her head back against his shoulder to look up at him.

'Then you're a very sumptuous shield,' Diomede told her basely, ducking as Yolande threw at the double target.

Heuradys shrieked, and Diomede laughed, as the snowball was shattered on the slim extended throat; for the fraction of a second Yolande felt what she thought of as Byzantine. Heuradys with her queer beauty enjoying Diomede's friendly hug . . . Diomede, dark and strong and comely, bending over with Heuradys in his arms . . . Mother of God, why not, and what would it matter even if it meant more than a trick in a game?

'I'm coming to murder you, my lady,' said Lioncel cheerfully, and an oblique shot filled one side of her hood with snow. Kneeling, scrabbling for ammunition, she had another Byzantine flash, this time of dire pleasure at being threatened by Lioncel.

'Good thing Odard and Douce and Dom Cyril are all here,' she thought as Lioncel shrank craven-faced from the menace of her back-swung arm.

Next day she remembered that, too. They had sat up late making the skates, even Dom Cyril punching holes in straps under lay direction. Only Odard was not in the solar; he had an inkstain on his cheek when at length he came in for a cup of wine. In the morning Yolande slept late, and was finally roused, long after sunrise, by Heuradys, who carried two bowls of broth.

'I can't find the damsel anywhere,' said Heuradys.

There came a knock on the outer door. Heuradys put down her tray and went to see who was there.

'It's Julian,' she called. 'He has something for you.'

'Bring him in.'

The sergeant came, saluted stiffly, and handed her a sealed scroll.

'From the Sieur de Xantroy,' he said. 'He's ridden to Roclatour with the damsel and the archer Herbrand. He said I was to deliver this when he had been gone an hour.'

Yolande broke the seal and found a key taped to the thick paper. Julian and Heuradys stood silently by as she read Odard's letter.

'*Most Gracious Duchess and my very good Lady,*

God and Saint Amarand move you to forgive me that I now renounce your service: or rather, as you well know it to be, the service of my lord Grand Seneschal. I have had no liking to be almost your gaoler, but only thus might I find a home for my wife Jehane, whose soul may Our Blessed Lady have in especial care and forgiveness.

'*Yesterday, while you played in the snow, the damsel Douce, who has long comforted me with a very kind love and affection, became my wife in the church here, Dom Robert marrying us, with Julian and Dom Robert's servant Elaine as witnesses. Today we have ridden away without your knowledge, not wishing to make you accessory to our fault. Dom Cyril and Julian believe we ride to Roclatour; but I have friends in Italy, of whom I say no more, having regard to the vengeful temper of my lord Grand Seneschal.*

'*This I must tell you: I had orders to shelter at Roclatour anyone in the guise of a palmer who might give me the password Fruit of Thunder. I must then hand to him the small sealed packet which lies at the top of the brass-bound box underneath my bed. The key of the box is tied to this letter. It may be this palmer will come to Pardelin, believing me to be there. If so, you may like to give him his packet, saying that I am hunting. That would be true, as I hunt peace and contentment.*

'*I know nothing of the contents of that packet. The Grand Seneschal never put much confidence in me. In the same box are copies of all letters and reports concerning your own health and welfare, such as I sent each month to Bargreant. Also a note of such business as is handled by the steward at Roclatour. Also a list of the stores at Pardelin, and money for three months' wages for the garrison. Also the signet of Roclatour, and the personal signet, bearing a thunderbolt passing through a cloud, with which I countersealed all packets I sent to the Grand Seneschal.*

'*No one but himself expects to hear from me, and no one but I (Dom Ursus being dead) is expected to write to him concerning you. I have not reported the deaths of Dom Ursus and my lady, or the sweating sickness and our move to Pardelin. I do not know how long my lord will remain in Zurland. I have never had orders or occasion to write to my lord your husband. It rests with you to inform either or both as you please.*

'*The steward at Roclatour is honest. So is Julian. Griflet, I warn you, is a villain, suspected of priest murder on the bridge at Klingenstein.*

'*My lady Douce greets you with love, and grieves that she might not speak her own farewell. That the Holy Trinity may requite you for great courtesy and forbearance, and have you in everlasting keeping, is the prayer of your servant and well-wisher,*

Odard de Xantroy.

Given at Pardelin on the Octave of Saint Andreas in the thirteenth year of our lord King Thorismund.'

Yolande read the letter twice, giving, as she hoped, no outward sign of her astonishment. Then she looked up at the grizzled sergeant.

'Carry on as if the Sieur Odard were still here,' she bade him. 'I cannot say when he will return. The squires de Forne and de Torre will remain at present as guests; they are both good swordsmen and would help the castle guard at need. Henceforth don't send or receive any messenger without reference to me.'

'Of course, Your Grace. The Sieur de Xantroy told me that you would be your own castellan here.'

'Yes. That is all, sergeant . . . I should say, captain.'

Julian saluted again and went out, pleased with his promotion. Yolande watched him go, and then leaned back in her chair and began to laugh.

'I thought I was good at secrets,' she gasped. 'Here's what the dull and maidenly Douce has been up to. No wonder she wanted a big leathern wallet . . . no wonder Odard didn't want *me* to get the sweating sickness . . . no wonder he didn't much like her tumbling about in the snow with our heart-breaking gallants yesterday.'

She read the letter aloud and looked up at Heuradys.

'You're my only damsel now, my poppet,' she said.

Heuradys leaned over and kissed her. Yolande sat for a moment chastened by the skill with which Douce had fooled Jehane and herself.

'In the afternoons, I suppose,' she reflected, 'when Aurania and I were out riding with Griflet, and Jehane was sleeping off her woes, and Dom Ursus reviewing the morals of the town, there was time for a little quiet dalliance. So that's how Odard sustained his burden . . . and now I'll never trust anyone not to have gone to school to Dom Cupid.'

She took the little shears from her workbasket and cut the key away from the letter, looking out at the mist which hid Siege Umbrous.

'All the same it's bad weather to take your new wife riding,' she said. 'I suppose they'll go by Sanctlamine, avoiding the priory . . . and good fortune attend them, for they'll need it in this snow.'

When she was dressed and in the solar she summoned Lioncel and Diomede and Quargis; each of them in turn read Odard's farewell letter.

'Palmer Gaston passed us by, then,' Lioncel said.

'And Palmer Radomar with him,' said Diomede, reading over Lioncel's shoulder.

'The next thing,' said Yolande, 'is to open the packet. Will you bring the brass-bound box here?'

Lioncel and Diomede brought it.

'We must leave Dom Cyril out of all this,' said Yolande, thinking aloud. 'It's a good thing he's rather deaf. Where is he now?'

'Gone down to see his crony Dom Robert,' Quargis assured her.

The lock clicked, the box stood open. There at the top was a little packet, sealed with the Thunderbolt.

'If I have to run for my life,' said Yolande, looking at it,
'will you all come with me?'

'Yes,' they replied in simple chorus.

'Where to?'

'Largire, my lady,' suggested Diomede.

'We're known to come from there,' objected Lioncel.

'Ger,' said Heuradys.

Yolande considered this friendly name.

'I can't ask my kinsman to defend me from my husband,'
she decided, 'unless my husband were a traitor, or had tried
to kill me.'

She took up the packet and slit the linen cover with a pen-
knife, breaking the bright red wax to unroll a cylinder of
stiff parchment. Glued to the parchment were scraps of paper,
each bearing a name in different handwriting, some in blue
ink, some in black or brown.

'Godfrey,' read Yolande aloud. 'Boemund, Guy, Fulk,
Raoul, Jehan, Hamelin.'

'What's this?' asked Diomede. 'A muster-roll of the
First Crusade? Is there nothing else but the names?'

'Only a not very good drawing of a spray of oak with
seven acorns on it.'

'They're signatures cut from letters,' Lioncel decided.
'Whose badge is the acorns?'

'One acorn in its cup,' said Quargis, 'is the badge of the
little Duke of Honoy.'

'Fruit of thunder,' said Diomede. 'The acorn's the fruit
of the oak. The oak was the tree of Jove, the heathen god
of thunder.'

For a long moment no one said anything.

'Seven acorns, seven names,' went on Quargis thoughtfully.
'My lady duchess, I think this is a puzzle which would bear
your kinsman's scrutiny. Think of the Christian names of
the great men of Nordanay and Honoy.'

'You mean. . . .'

'Godfrey Duke of Saulte, Boemund Bishop of Belsaunt,
Fulk Marquis of Olencourt, Raoul Count of Ger, Jehan
Count of Saint-Aunay, Hamelin Bishop of Dunsberghe.

That leaves Guy . . . Guy must come from farther south. He might be the Count of Burias, lately dead. But none of these lords holds office about the little duke.'

'And here,' said Lioncel, 'the Grand Seneschal passes their names, the names they no doubt use to each other in private, to the rebel and traitor and outlaw, Gaston de Volsberghe, who fled from them twelve years ago. It seems to me we may have stumbled on some great attempted mischief.'

'It looks odd,' said Yolande. 'Quargis, you should be in a chancellery. I hope some day you'll be in mine. This paper, broken seal and all, must certainly go to Ger. But if a huge bearded palmer then appears and asks for it?'

Yolande sat back in her chair and gripped the carven arms. A curious sensation of power and excitement had come into her body. Odard had left his name and seals, Odard would never be called to account.

'It might be possible,' she said, 'to have something ready in its place.'

If Julian and the archers and servants were puzzled by Odard's continued absence they gave no sign of it as the days slid by. The snow lay firm for a week, and Christmas came near; the lake was a sheet of ice, and the guard at Quatre-lances was changed by the men's riding along the shore. Yolande saw no sense in keeping up the garrison there, except that in summer forest thieves might use the tower for shelter if it were left empty; but Odard had maintained the custom and so must she. At least it gave the archers an alter-nation of monotony, something different to grumble at; and at Quatrelances they trapped and hunted as much as they pleased. Yolande and her depleted household went to Mass in the tiny chapel, sledged and skated and threw snow about, played chess and darts and ninepins, and each night put harp and lute and hautboy to good use in the solar. Yolande withdrew to her bedchamber to practise her copyings of Odard's handwriting; she meant to keep up for a while the illusion that he was still at Pardelin. Also she pondered the curious collection of famous signatures.

Heuradys in russet hunting-frock descended with Quargis to the kitchens and set about organising Christmas cheer. One of the sledges had carried sugar and spices and choice wines; Odard had foreseen the keeping of the feast at Pardelin. Quargis became steward almost by inadvertence; the store-tallies worried old Julian, who brought them to the dwarf for advice and assistance.

But the best of those strange days were the evenings, when Yolande listened to the tales of foreign adventure told by Lioncel and Diomede. Naturally modest young men, they had lost with Janus any tendency to praise their own achievements; but they praised each other with a directness that Yolande found comical.

'Famagusta, yes,' Lioncel would say. 'That was where Diomede saved my life. He got his knee-cop between my face and the blade of a great Muslim spear. I was sprawling on the ground, tangled up in the ropes of a trebuchet we'd just rushed and put out of action.'

'I should have sprawled too,' Diomede hastened to add, 'but our chevalier propped me up with his shield from behind and sent the Muslim's head flying with his long-handled axe.'

'Talking of knee-cops,' Lioncel went on, 'the chevalier had a suit of plate with spiked elbow-cops, and except that they sometimes tore his tabards and screeched very vilely on his corselet, there was a lot to be said for them. I saw a Turk land on his back, a flying leap from a galley poop, and the chevalier gave a great backward jab with his elbow and tore the Turk wide open. He yelled and fell into the water between the ships as they swung. He dropped his silver-hilted scimitar, too, and the chevalier gave it to me.'

'Where is it now?' asked Yolande.

'Safe at Largire, my lady.'

'You'll have some wonderful treasures there.'

'One or two, at least. Diomede has a Saracen helmet inlaid with gold, taken from a corsair in a land battle near Sparta.'

'I was carried into Sparta on a shield—a wicker shield,' confessed Diomede. 'I had understood the Spartan mothers

liked to see you come in that way, but the only woman I saw
spat at me out of a window. I thought Lioncel would murder
her.'

'I can't imagine why he didn't,' Yolande found herself
saying.

'He was hurt himself,' Diomede hastened to explain. 'He
could only just sit in his saddle, with a crossbow trained on
the peasants who carried me, in case they tried to drop the
shield and run.'

'They didn't try to make you king of Argos?' she asked.

'Argos? We never went there. Oh, you mean because of
King Diomede who went to Troy. It's only a kind of village
now. I'd hate to be king of it.'

During those days, too, Yolande inspected the other contents of Odard's brassbound chest, which now lived under her
own bed.

'*My lady duchess,*' Odard had written to the Grand
Seneschal, '*hunted once this week, and was once rowed on
the lake, where she made a drawing of herons. She attends
Mass each day, and keeps good health. She is obedient and
attentive to my lady her governess. Once by permission she
visited the abbess of Saint-Marthe. I think she is losing her
desire to spend much time there. She has begun a most
exquisite banner for my lord duke's regalia of the Order of
the Bridge of Faith.*'

Yolande pulled faces as she read that letter and others. That
damned banner had been meant as a Christmas gift.

'Not that Belphegor will notice that he hasn't had one,'
she said, when her miniature council reassembled a few nights
before Christmas. 'But with the Grand Seneschal in Zurland,
and Belphegor so fully engaged at court, and the weather as
it is, we have a little time to develop the courses of deception.
Everyone here except ourselves must continue to think Odard
is at Roclatour. Everyone there must think he's here at
Pardelin.'

'Then all messages between the castles must be carried by
one of ourselves,' said Lioncel. 'And you must think as
Odard thought, my lady.'

'Yes. See, here's a letter I've written for him.'

The letter was to Griflet at Roclatour, asking for news of the sweating sickness, enquiring especially after the abbess and Aurania, and demanding to know if any more had come to light concerning the death of Dom Ursus.

'Then,' said Lioncel, when he had admired the counterfeiting of Odard's handwriting, 'one of us takes this as soon as may be.'

'There are wolves and robbers to consider,' Yolande pointed out.

'Two of us, with longbows, can risk that,' said Diomede. 'Have you decided what to do with the list of names, my lady?'

'Yes. Presume that when Azo and Belphegor and Gaston de Volsberghe are planning anything it must be a villainy. Pass the real scroll to Ger, but pass—in Odard's name—a dummy scroll to my lord duke, explaining that the palmer must have been prevented from coming to collect it.'

'A dummy?'

'Yes, with the same names, but each in a quite different hand, so that any attempt to misuse them must fail.'

'A forgery to shame all forgers?'

'A misforgery, if you like. Send it with the banner, the gift from his dutiful wife.'

'Making meanwhile all preparations to disappear from here?'

'Yes.'

That night, as she lit the bedside lantern which kept a candle burning until daylight behind thick many-coloured glass, Heuradys looked down at the dark head on the pillows they shared.

'What would happen now if my lord duke were to come here?' she asked.

Yolande stared silently at the dim jewelled light until Heuradys had extinguished the other candles and climbed into bed beside her.

'It rather depends on how many people he brings with him,' she said.

Then she told Heuradys all about the *capagot*, the *beym*, and the *adzin*.

The valley was swept by a thaw wind, and all the streams were in loud spate, when Diomede and Quargis set out for Roclatour. They had found the dwarf a coat of mail, and Diomede and he armed themselves to the teeth. Julian seemed relieved that he was not asked for an escort; six archers at Pardelin and four at Quatrelances seemed to him a miserable force if trouble of any kind arose. Yolande, sympathising with him, promised to mention the difficulty to the Sieur Odard. After supper that night, when Heuradys had played the harp and Lioncel had sung to her, Yolande asked how long it was since the squires had been separated for a night.

Lioncel thought for a moment.

'More than a year, my lady,' he decided. 'It was after the battle on the river, and before we went abroad. I was sent to take a capon to the chevalier's sister, the famous anchoress. A great thunderstorm broke, and the holy lady forbade me to ride back among the oaks, and talked to me for so long that night came on. Then she wouldn't let me start, so I slept in the stable near the anchorage.'

'What did she instruct you about?' asked Yolande softly, with a glance at Dom Cyril fast asleep in his chair.

'Almost everything,' said Lioncel, 'but most particularly about the love of men and women.'

'And was she against that?'

'Very much against it, my lady. She wanted us all to be anchorites and anchoresses.'

'And then who'd take her the capons, I wonder? But you were polite and didn't argue?'

'I was scared. I agreed except once.'

'What was it stuck in your craven gullet?'

'When she asked me to promise her never to . . . er . . . never to make love to a maiden. Or, of course, to any other woman.'

'Cautious, kind-hearted, and obstinate Lioncel!'

'Kind-hearted, my lady?'

' Yes, of course. Do you think all the kindness of love bestowed is on one side? '

' Oh. No, I suppose not.'

' And how did you slither out of that most holy and unreasonable promise? '

Yolande and Heuradys watched Lioncel with affectionate female cruelty. It was almost incredible that he should have passed through Levantine sunshine and wickedness without losing his virginity, but stranger things had been known in chivalrous young men of fastidious temper.

Lioncel's eyebrows rose in mock despair.

' You can't talk to these holy people as if they were human,' Lioncel said. ' If you tried to explain that earthly love might be as . . . as sacred and sad and healing as anything heavenly could be to *them*, they'd be horrified and talk about blasphemy. It would be like holding the Chalice of Sangreal up for them to spit into. So I . . . I took it at a different level, and said the lord king must have soldiers if we're ever to recover the Holy Sepulchre.'

A heave of indecorous mirth battered at Yolande's ribs. A fantastic picture flashed through her mind—Lioncel going from door to door of a moonlit midnight street, vanishing into one house after another, coming out and marking a little sword on the door-post before he went on. Went on, poor lamb, more and more slowly. . . .

' Lioncel! ' she whispered. ' You must name them Godfrey, Boemund, Raymond, Tancred, Robert, Baldwin . . . and send them to me to learn to write their names! But how did the holy anchoress meet your objection? '

' She said that sort of provision should be left to men of grosser temper. The chevalier, God keep him, is as frightened of her as we are, I think. He must have placated her some time by saying that Diomede and I are practically monks.'

' And, practically, are you? ' teased Yolande.

Lioncel was not embarrassed. He smiled at Heuradys and replied very sedately.

' I wish I knew how you would like that question answered, my lady.'

'With the truth, of course,' murmured Yolande, spoiling her fun a little by letting fantasy melt into moonlit Roman or Athenian probability.

'At risk of disappointing you, my lady, I think we behave as monkishly as you would have us do.'

Yolande considered the changing lights and shadows of this statement, locking her hands in her lap and staring at her rings rather than at the disastrously attractive face and throat of Lioncel.

'I think I'm answered as I deserve,' she said, with a humility as bewitching as she could make it. 'To get what one deserves is generally to be disappointed. Lioncel, you're a courtier to shame all courtiers.'

Perhaps, she reflected, it was as well Diomede would soon be back. It would be very exciting to be taken at a different level by Lioncel.

Diomede and Quargis reappeared within four days, bringing a pack-horse laden with gifts and more Christmas delicacies. The abbess was recovering, and had taken Aurania into the convent to convalesce. Two archers and three castle servants had died of the sickness. Philastrius had survived all danger, and Blanche had responded to his treatment. The pestilence was slowly abating, the deaths dropping from twenty a day to five a day within one week. There was no news from Bargreant or any other direction.

'How did Griflet receive you?' Yolande enquired.

'Rather sourly,' Diomede admitted. 'But he liked being called *captain* in every sentence.'

Zoster Adela had sent Yolande a loving greeting, and prayed for her happiness during the Christmas season.

'Happiness, what is that?' muttered Yolande, and saw Diomede's grave brown eyes flash and go blank with politeness again.

'*I* know what it is, my lady,' he whispered.

'Oh yes, unselfish service of someone who can do nothing to show how much . . . how *much* . . . she values it.'

Diomede had only bowed when he came in cloaked and

booted and spurred and muddy from his journey. Now, as she stretched out a hand, he sank on one knee, took her fingers on his wrist, and kissed them with more tenderness than respect.

'Diomede,' she sighed, and took her fingers away, appalled at the way the touch of the kiss plunged up her nerves and squeezed at her heart.

Under the midday sun was an aspen, its leafless twigs trembling although oak and beech and thorn stood still. A heavy hoar-frost had melted, and water-drops shook and flashed—diamond, ruby, emerald, sapphire, and diamond again. Yolande sat in her saddle and watched them, remembering Douce's words about dying on a sunny morning. Behind the aspen was the blue-grey lake, with Siege Perilous towering beyond. Behind Yolande were her four friends, silent on this last ride before Lioncel set out with the banner and scroll to find Belphegor.

She turned round and spoke suddenly, looking from face to attentive face.

'So far we've been successful,' she said. 'We've made a beginning of deceit and set up the ghost of Odard to help us. We've fooled two good and faithful men, Dom Cyril and Julian, and one knave, Griflet. I'm afraid of risking your lives, sometimes as afraid as this aspen seems to be, while you all seem as steady as the oaks. I carry poison now—Heuradys knows about it already—and tonight I'll give you all a share, two fatal doses. It's very quick and doesn't hurt, or so I'm told. If it did hurt a little, it would still be better than falling alive into the hands of Belphegor.'

She paused and looked at each of them again.

'And now . . . shall I give up this feud with the Montguis-cards and escape while I may out of the realm with any or all of you? I have jewels I could sell; perhaps with a harp and a lute or two we could earn our living in Italy. As comrades, not as mistress and servants, what do you say? Lioncel?'

'I say no. I want to see you ruling in Baraine.'

'Diomede?'

' I say no, too. At least try what can be done with the help of the Count of Ger.'

' Heuradys? '

' No. I follow, whatever you do, but you ask me, and I say no.'

' Quargis? '

' My lady duchess, no, by God. It may be you feel young and untried, lonely and afraid. I beg of you, go on as you have begun. I've moved at court, although mainly in the back alleys. There's one decent creature there to every six knaves or fools. I'm a man of the people, and I say: Let's have those to rule us like you, not like your husband and his father.'

' Gramercy, Quargis. I think *my* father would have liked to hear that. And none of you counsels running, so that I shall stay to see what help we can muster. If, after all, it seems hopeless, I shan't throw your lives away . . . but now we'll go ahead as we planned, and Lioncel shall start tomorrow for Hautarroy and beyond. And now he and I will show you the hidden hermitage.'

On the west side of the northern arm of the lake they came to a patch of pebbled shore that curved away under water at the base of a drum-shaped rock. With water nearly up to the horses' girths they filed round the base of the dum into a little cove where crags jutted untidily above a mass of holm-oak and hawthorn-girt boulders. In a steep gloomy little ravine full of pools and cascades they tethered their mounts beneath an overhanging scar. Lioncel stayed there on guard; Yolande led the others along a ledge of rock behind a ten-foot fall, and into a narrow gash between rocks on the farther side.

A rough natural staircase, improved here and there with small boulders, twisted out towards the lake and climbed with an overhang above it. A natural parapet, mostly more than head-high, concealed this stairway from anyone on the opposite shore of the inlet. Half-way up, on the right-hand of the way, appeared the cave-mouth; the path went on to a kind of look-out perch, and then stopped, with a sheer forty-foot drop beyond. Plainly no one could come at the cave from that side or from above.

L

'Here we are,' said Yolande, leading them into the cave.
'Dry and roomy, but no use except for a hermit who knew
how to hunt and fish and row a skiff. No gifts from the castle
came here, I warrant. Only birds and foxes seem to have used
it since I was here . . . see, I stuck this piece of holly here, and
that piece there.'

'A marvellous robbers' lair,' remarked Quargis.

'Maybe it's been that too in its time. See, the hermit, or
one of the hermits, tried his hand at carving the rock.'

Yolande pointed to where a rough cavity, elbow-high, was
dignified by a stubby cross left standing in the middle of it.
The rock had been patiently hollowed out above and around
it; there was a little depression in front of it, probably for
burning incense.

A window, too, had been pierced near the doorway; it was
curved in the thickness of the rock, as though some austere
inhabitant had denied himself the loveliness of the sunset.

The visitors climbed to the look-out place, and stared down
at the dark water and the thick grove of poplars whose tops
came near them. Hawthorns masked the top of the stairway and overhung the beetling crag thirty feet above them
again.

'A good place to starve in if you reached it alone and
wounded,' said Heuradys.

'One archer could hold it against an army as long as he
had arrows and could stay awake,' said Diomede.

'If you lit a good fire in the stairway and tipped oil down on
it, you'd have time to escape by rope from the top end,' said
Quargis.

Diomede was flat on his stomach, peering over the edge of
the parapet.

'With a rock or two on here,' he said, 'you could sink any
boat in the cove where we came in.'

'It seems to have set all your wits working,' Yolande told
them. 'Shall we provision it, and risk someone else's using
our stores, perhaps against *us*?'

'We might be very glad of it,' said Lioncel. 'Yes, my lady.
Gradually, using a boat. Oatmeal and wine and water, fire-

wood and candles and rope and oil. Bracken for bedding . . .
that can be cut nearby, and later. Now Quargis has charge
of the castle stores you can defraud yourself without old
Julian's knowing.'

That night Yolande gave each of them a share of the
capagot, pouring it into scent-flasks and inkpots of the kind
carried in belt-purses. Then, in the solar, she tried to efface
the memory of that grim little rite; taking her lute, she sang
to its accompaniment a doggerel song she had made and
entitled *Paladins in Pairs*.

> ' Mid those who temper war's alarms
> With perfect brotherhood of arms
> A foremost place I must concede
> To Lioncel and Diomede,
> In whom are found: the faith and cheer
> That Roland kept with Olivier;
> More love than kin and kith owe us,
> As Theseus show'd Pirithoüs;
> A friendship of such solid use
> As Castor had from Polydeuce;
> A bond of no less honour than
> By David shared with Jonathan.
> So rode together in the wars,
> Close comrades, Lancelot and Bors.
> Drink to my song: I wish you well,
> My Diomede, my Lioncel.'

They stood up and drank to song and singer, laughing at it
and at themselves; but in Yolande's heart the note of burlesque
grew very faint indeed.

' It's strange that the Sieur Odard stays so long away,' said
Dom Cyril twenty-four hours later.
' Yes, father,' said Yolande. ' Will you play chess? '
The castle seemed an empty place that night. Yolande was
never quite sure that she would not meet a ghost round some

corner of the keep passages. She hung a dagger to her girdle, a
thing she hardly ever did. Heuradys always carried one—
flat, with a side-curved crossbar that clasped the inside of her
forearm where it lay up her sleeve; with one lady-like movement she could pluck the hilt into her right hand. They sat
close together beside the fire in the solar.

'And the damsel Douce should be back by now,' went on the
old priest almost severely as he set out his men. 'It's not fitting
you should have so few people about you.'

'It's not for long, father,' Yolande assured him. 'As you
know, I had rebellious thoughts about deserting my friends at
Roclatour, but it seemed my duty to my husband and the duchy
to seek refuge here.'

'Yes, yes, my daughter. You have nothing to reprove
yourself with. My move, I believe.'

Heuradys attended to the wine. The wind whistled in a
battlement gutter, and clinked a chain that in the summer held
an awning in the rampart garden. When they went to bed
Yolande grabbed Heuradys and held her close; the elder girl's
quiet breathing soothed her into sleep.

Diomede without Lioncel seemed at first more of a stranger
than Lioncel without Diomede. When he and Quargis came
back they brought Balthasar's Christmas present to his duchess
—a jewelled girdle and a golden bedside bell—and these
Diomede handed over rather as if their box contained
scorpions.

Yolande was startled at the sudden silent fury he had not
meant her to see. She tossed the bell back into its nest of
feathers, and took Diomede's brown fist boldly between her
hands. The fist opened and captured several of her fingers.
Looking up at the flushed face darker than her own, she
suffered a complication of anger, misery, half-amused tenderness, and sudden reckless desire.

'If he mentions Lioncel now I shall scream,' she told herself
dizzily, but for a moment Diomede said nothing at all. He put
his other hand round her shoulders and kissed her on the
forehead and eyes and mouth. She felt the world reel away a
little and right itself again.

'Yolande, that was happiness,' Diomede whispered, and gently let go of her. They stood apart, breathing quickly, half-triumphant and half-damned.

'We mustn't do that,' said Yolande shakily, and added: '*often.*'

'My lady,' was all that Diomede replied, but the choice of words, their gratitude and reassurance, nearly flung her into his arms again. He glanced down at the gleaming gifts, and turned to pick up the gloves and steel cap he had thrown down on a bench. Nursing them, he turned at the door; the bronze pommel of his sword held a red spark for the fire and two silver sparks for the windows.

'Heuradys?' he asked, and Yolande shook her head.

'No, not about that,' she said. 'My love and trust and secrets don't always go together.'

'Or mine, now,' said Diomede sadly, and bowed to her, and went out.

The gate and armoury keys of Pardelin were kept during the day by Julian, who brought them each night to Yolande as he had formerly brought them to Odard. The other keys were with Quargis when he was there; thus it was easy to begin to move small quantities of supplies to the hidden hermitage. Diomede and Quargis rowed for exercise on days when there was no riding, and a package could easily be hidden under a cloak in the bottom of their skiff. Yolande had spare keys to the inner and outer doors of the boathouse tower; once she had conquered her aversion for that dim vaulted place she sometimes joined them in the boat. Like a princess in a story, with her squire and dwarf, she climbed amid the rocks, finding the first snowdrops, seeing the hazel bring tassel-time, hearing the missel-thrushes wake the end-song of winter.

Confusion and delight stalked her in stony Pardelin and along the misty shore of the lake. Diomede made no move, but a delicate tension persisted between them. Yolande wanted to kiss him again for not kissing her again when *he* wanted to. She fought the inclination because it seemed unfair to

him; but the fact that she was Balthasar's wife weighed not
at all.

Every day they prayed together for Lioncel's safety, timing
his journey as far as Hautarroy. Beyond there it was uncertain;
Belphegor had sent his present from Hastain, but the brief
letter that came with it gave no hint of his plans. When
Lioncel had been away for nearly three weeks, and all but the
highest streaks of snow had vanished from the mountains,
Yolande wrote another letter in Odard's name, and sent
Diomede and Quargis with it to Roclatour.

During their absence she went into the squires' bedchamber;
Diomede had locked it and given Heuradys the key. Yolande
was in search of her *History of the Kings of Neustria*, which
Lioncel had borrowed; she found it on a shelf between a steel
cap and a horn dice-box. On a lower shelf was a tray containing
songs and music. Two lines caught her eye: *Alarms, and
nightwinds rough, and bale-fires gleaming.* She pulled the
paper out, and found it to contain a poem in Diomede's
writing. The title was *Sun, Moon and Star*; she read the poem
standing in the dusk of the chilly room.

> ' *O glorious Sun,*
>   *Shine on her every going,*
> *Each dew-white morn begun*
>   *New joy bestowing.*
> *What if she love not me?*
> *This pain was meant to be.*
> *Clouded my fate, but she*
>   *The rainbow showing.*
>
> ' *O gracious Moon,*
>   *Let not your elves down-streaming*
> *Trample with silvern shoon*
>   *Her maiden dreaming.*
> *Deep is woe's root, and tough;*
> *She shall know soon enough*
> *Alarms, and night-winds rough,*
>   *And bale-fires gleaming.*

'O treacherous Star,
    With you I feign no gladness.
Green-burning, lone, and far,
    You know my madness.
Almost I trust your spite
To keep her happy quite,
Deadlier my heart to smite
    With hell's own sadness.'

'Diomede, my dear,' she said to the absent poet. 'How discreet to pretend I'm sheltered and happy and don't love you.'

She put the poem back in its place, and went and sat down by the fire in the solar, and wondered if there were really any need for hell's own sadness.

XII

BELPHEGOR'S WAY AGAIN

'DON'T go to the castle of Sabloyn alone,' said the Chevalier Janus when Lioncel found him in the monastery of Saint-Maur-in-Hautarroy. 'Even with the duke's own banner sent him by his duchess. Even with my badge in your hat. Perhaps I might say, especially with my badge in your hat.'

'Is the duke's fame so ill, sir?'

'His behaviour is ill. His fame worries a few churchmen and others who think that office and power call for virtue and dignity.'

'Among them his lady the Duchess Yolande,' said Lioncel, wishing he could tell all he knew to this eccentric paladin.

Janus, enormous in a black velvet robe patterned with white wolves *passant*, limped with a silver-headed staff across to his window-seat, and leaned on a great pile of books to peer through the stained glass.

'God aid that poor wench,' he muttered. 'But for the most part the duke's fame is matter for sniggering at court. And as you know, he's a shrewd young man. He not only scatters largesse; he pays what he owes to soldiers and craftsmen. The clothiers and armourers here in the city fall over each other to provide for him. They see their money at the month's end and swear by him in the taverns. Little they care if he roasts serfs on his country estates.'

'He saves a good deal on household expenses,' said Lioncel, with amusement in his voice. 'Bargreant's a garrison instead of a court. The clothiers there might say otherwise.'

Janus gave a rumble of agreement without looking round.

'That brings me back to my badge,' he said. 'Lioncel, I will not expose it, and yourself, to the kind of insult that might fly freely in that hold of Sabloyn. I shall ask my lord abbot here to adopt you into his household for a while, and give you a letter to his colleague the Abbot of Saint-Maur-by-Dunsberghe. Then you have a just reason first to wear the abbey badge, and secondly to pass on from Sabloyn as quickly as may be.'

'I . . . I had rather risk any . . .' began Lioncel, but the chevalier looked round at him, enjoining silence with a sea-grey eye.

'It suits me to remain here at present,' he said. 'I have now reached in my dictation the point where a certain squire, clad in nothing but his hose, jumped from a balcony on to a Turk whose dagger was a foot from my back. The squire got a scar on the face from that dagger; when I see the one I remember the other. If the squire should begin to splutter, I claim the right to distinguish between his valour and his rashness.'

Lioncel felt his face grow hot. He remembered well enough that terrified leap, the sickening jar of his landing, the Turk's howl as the Turk's arm-bone snapped under the joint weight of their down-smashed bodies.

'The abbey badge is a cross *rayonnant*,' went on Janus. 'On a cloak, this house uses the cross *azure* and the rays *or*. The Dunsberghe brethren difference it, cross *vert* and rays *argent*. It's rich and distinctive, but apt to be mistaken for the device of a military order. Which reminds me, the Prior of Saint-Jehan-in-Hautarroy is coming to supper . . .'

Lioncel first saw the castle of Sabloyn on a misty February afternoon. Behind grouped towers a dim red sunset made of them and their mound one threatening blue-grey shape. Lioncel crossed himself under his cloak, and touched the hilt of his favourite dagger, which Diomede had given to him.

Lioncel was not alone; a taciturn chevalier with the sea-horse of Elquitaine on his tabard was found to be riding to Sabloyn, and with his company of five horseman went Lioncel and a wine-merchant whose trading-vessel was undergoing repairs at Dunsberghe. With the merchant were his son and a servant, so that the cobbled street of the grey moorland village sent a great clatter of hoofs up against the ramparts.

'There I shall leave you,' said the merchant, nodding at a

bush which blackened the dusk over the doorway of a tavern ahead. 'You'll find very good wine in the castle, Master de Forne. Especially the Estragon. Don't let them give you their metheglin; say it makes you sick. It makes most of them sick, too. It's the *udromal* or hydromel of Cyprus, and you tell them you've been there. It was sent here when the Fighting Abbot had the castle—him that was killed at the king's side in the battle at Pont-de-Foy. . . .

'At Famagusta they say it was given to the *opinica*, a gryphon-like creature that laid sapphire eggs in a valley of the Lebanon; and she brought up a gnome with four arms who wrung the *udromal* out of his beard and jumped on the man with the cask, and choked him with a great sapphire, and went off in a whirl of handsprings with his feet twisting in the air and sulphurous smoke streaming out of his mouth. The *opinica* flew away, but died in mid-air and fell into the sea.'

'I must remember that,' said Lioncel, and said good-bye to the wine-merchant. As he rode up to the barbican he saw in the dusk a new white stone let into the wall above the gateway arch. On it was painted the Thunderbolt, barbed *or* on its sable ground, with the label of cadency over it, and no sign of the Leopard.

'Montguiscard pure and simple,' thought Lioncel, and grimaced in the tunnel of the barbican.

As he was led through the hall of the castle he saw a dark-faced young man, whom he recognised as Camus de Caherne, sitting at the edge of the dais, with a servant pulling off his muddy riding-boots. Camus had muddy hands, too, and he wiped them on the servant's hair, swore at the servant, and kicked him expertly under the chin with the foot that was still booted. Another servant had shoes ready; Camus stepped into them and strode away, without a glance at the crouching groaning man he had kicked, or at Lioncel and the other new-comers filing past in torchlit gloom.

Belphegor received his visitors in a tapestried council-chamber. The chevalier from Elquitaine took precedence; Lioncel waited in an anteroom where men-at-arms growled and spat. No one asked him to sit down, so he went to a table and perched himself on it, still wearing his hat, and holding his two packets with their bright seals in evidence, red wax for Odard's, purple for Yolande's.

When his turn came he marched in with the rolled banner cocked on his hip like a trumpet, and kept it in place while uncovering and bowing, as Janus had taught him to do.

'Master Lioncel de Forne, squire to the Abbot of Saint-Maur-in-Hautarroy, with letters from my lady duchess and from the Sieur de Xantroy,' said a fat major-domo with a very red nose, who might have been picked as a foil to the beauty of Belphegor.

The duke sat in a gilded chair. His angel-face was serene under a white cap, his tunic was of dark red velvet, his hose of silk of the same colour, his shoes white with a little gold serpent rearing up from each gold toe-cap. His blue eyes took Lioncel in with a remembering flicker.

'Where have I seen you before?' he asked.

Lioncel's throat was dry, but he had confronted greater lords than this one, and he answered readily enough.

'When you overthrew the Chevalier de Largire, my lord duke. I was among his attendants in the lists.'

'Yes, I remember. Why didn't Xantroy send one of his own men?'

'I understand he was afraid of the risk of passing the sweating sickness. I believe you will find his reasons in the letter.'

Belphegor stretched out his hands, and Lioncel laid the packets in them, bowing again as he stepped back. There were four other men in the room, and Lioncel knew that one of them came close behind him as he moved. Probably Belphegor had at some time sat in danger of the dagger of a shamed or maddened man.

'I thank you, Master de Forne,' said the duke, civilly enough.

Lioncel stood quite still, his spine chilling a little. The chevalier from Elquitaine was already seated near the fire; the major-domo and the fourth man, brilliant shapes in blue and green, drew a little away from their lord so that neither could read what crackled open on Belphegor's knee.

Lioncel had leisure to admire this gorgeous Peer of Neustria, who had carried captive the Franconian banners, usurped a command from the Constable, unhorsed Janus of the Silver Shield, and cuckolded the king.

'Pardelin . . . h'm,' said Belphegor impassively. Then, suddenly looking up: 'These signatures . . . what do *you* know about them?'

'Signatures, my lord duke?' repeated Lioncel, as though puzzled. 'Are not the letters signed by Her Grace and the Sieur de Xantroy?'

'The letters? Yes. Very well, no matter.'

Belphegor went on reading, and Lioncel pushed back his cloak. In spite of a cold spine he found the room warm.

Yolande had explained in the forged letter how Lioncel came to pass through Roclatour. There was amusement in the duke's face when next he glanced up.

'So the Chevalier de Largire has no present use for squires,' he said. 'I trust his broken leg entails no permanent injury.'

'I pray it won't, my lord duke. He's walking on it now.'

'Excellent. Now for my lady duchess. You saw her? She is good health?'

'Yes, my lord duke.'

'At Pardelin, hey? A dreary hold. But either there or at Roclatour I have an appointment with her this summer . . . when I can find time.'

Lioncel's fingers crisped a little in his stiff riding-gloves.

'Pardelin,' repeated Belphegor, with a crease between his godlike eyebrows. 'Oddly enough, you remind me of . . . some page or attendant there.'

Lioncel was prepared for this.

'I had a young cousin there, my lord duke, of the same name as myself. He was drowned in the lake when the outlaws seized the castle.'

'Ah, that's it, then. God rest his soul, and the souls of the Duke Engelbert and the rest. That was a great mischief. Poyntz, and you, Joscelin, hold out this banner.'

Yolande's beautiful handiwork gleamed and glowed between the fingers of the major-domo and squire. The Leopard of Baraine took precedence and had the dexter side; the sinister side was quartered for Balthasar as heir of Montguiscard. Beneath a silver label the first quarter held the red Thunderbolt on black, and the second a peacock in its pride, proper, on white. The third had six red roses on ermine, and the fourth a gold hawk-bell on blue. Belphegor sat back and regarded it with narrowed eyes and a tight-lipped smile; it would no doubt look very well in the chapel of the Order of the Bridge of Faith.

A savage volume of sound rolled up across the castle courtyards, and Lioncel recognised it as the roaring of several hungry lions.

'Be seated, de Forne,' said Belphegor graciously. 'You have time for a stoup while your bath-tub's filling.'

The wine-merchant had spoken truly; the Estragon was perfect. Later, at supper, the lean squire called Joscelin did his best to persuade Lioncel to drink metheglin. Lioncel pretended not to notice that chevaliers and other squires around him were according him that ironical interest with which men of action regard anyone whom they consider not to be a man of action.

'I never drink that stuff,' said Lioncel. 'Once was enough, at Famagusta. It raised all that had gone down before it. They remembered the Fighting Abbot's sending for it. They call it *udromal* and there's a story . . .'

'So you've been to Cyprus,' commented Joscelin, with the slightly disparaging air of one who had not had time for such a jaunt.

'With the Chevalier de Largire, I gather,' said a hook-nosed soldier opposite Lioncel.

'Yes, sir,' replied Lioncel. 'I attended him to Rome and Constantinople.'

This was agreeable to them, he noticed. If he wouldn't make a spectacle of himself with the metheglin, at least he could be somehow derided because of the overthrow of Janus.

'That coffin,' went on Hook-nose. 'Did you lug it all round the Levant with you?'

'No, sir. The Chevalier left it with his friend the Gon-
faloniere at Venice.'

'Why not the Doge?' muttered someone else, and Lioncel
heard him, and leaned forward.

'The Doge was sick, sir,' he replied courteously.

'Oh,' said the mutterer glumly, and Hook-nose grinned
across at him. Lioncel felt the weariness of a civilised creature
condemned to the company of those who live by scoring off
each other.

'Have *you* ever seen Largire cut a man in two?' asked
Joscelin.

'Not quite in two,' replied Lioncel, courteously. 'I think
all but the spine was severed. *You* would have liked to
see it.'

'Eh? Oh, yes, of course.'

'It was a corsair, in the battle of the bridge of boats. I have
seen him throw a man through a window into the Golden
Horn.'

'What for?'

'Discourtesy to a guest,' said Lioncel.

'Something of a change for you, squiring an abbot,' said
Hook-nose after a slight pause. 'The lord king is assembling a
household for the Duke of Honoy these days; you might do
worse than apply for a post in it.'

'Gramercy, sir, I'll consider doing so,' Lioncel replied.

Once Belphegor caught his eye, and raised his own goblet.
Lioncel inclined his head and responded gracefully. Soon after
that a servant came in and whispered in the duke's ear.
Belphegor frowned, and his beautiful mouth twitched down-
wards at the corners as if at bad news. Then he shrugged his
shoulders and went on talking to the chevalier from Elquitaine,
who sat beside him.

After supper there was singing by minstrels and clowning by
jesters and dwarfs. Lioncel looked for a troupe of acrobats, but
none appeared; the disappearance of Quargis might have
broken it up, he reflected.

After an hour of crude entertainment he approached the
duke and made his excuses for early retirement.

'What, ride away at dawn?' said Belphegor. 'Then you must drink a cup with me now.'

Lioncel drank standing, and bade his host good-night uncomfortably aware of some joke about him circulating behind his back.

A freckled, sly-faced page took a candle and led him to a comfortable guest-chamber. Lioncel found himself suddenly desperately sleepy.

'Strain, I suppose,' he told himself, and asked to be roused before the first light.

Nevertheless it was broad daylight when he awoke. No one had complied with his request; Joscelin came in to find him in his hose, grimly filling a basin from the great bronze ewer beside the bed.

'You were so heavily asleep it seemed a shame to waken you,' said Joscelin, and sent the page for pasties and wine.

'It means a late start,' growled Lioncel.

'As for that, my lord duke hopes you will stay for this afternoon's sport.'

'What sport is that? I'm on an errand of duty.'

Joscelin, inspecting his finger-nails, answered with elaborate carelessness.

'There's to be a fight between a man and a lion. See, here's your breakfast, with a tall soldier to see that no one else eats it.'

The page was followed into the room by an ugly-looking swordsman who overtopped Lioncel by six inches. He saluted and stood by the door as if carved of the same wood. A grotesque thought took shape in Lioncel's mind; his head felt much thicker than good Estragon should have made it, and the page was nearly grinning as he served the collation.

'Unfortunately,' went on Joscelin, 'the man who was to have fought the lion hanged himself last night in his dungeon. My lord duke wonders whether *you* would oblige him, and so uphold the honour of Saint Maur and the fame of the Silver Shield.'

'*I?*' said Lioncel, staring at him, with towel poised and hair disordered. 'What's it got to do with me?'

'Just this, that under your fine manners the duke believes you're a good fighting-man. It's true the miscreant who hanged himself could have given you inches either way, but you can have the pick of the gear in the armoury downstairs . . . but, of course, no missile weapons.'

'I can have my pick of . . . is this how strangers are treated at Sabloyn?'

'Sometimes, when they're not of importance, and if they promise good sport.'

'Take me to my lord duke.'

'He's still in bed, and . . . er . . . irritable after last night. I don't advise it, de Forne. If I were you I'd send for a priest instead.'

'You mean this fellow here is my gaoler, and I have no choice.'

'Roughly, yes. He'll take you to the armoury, and look after you.'

Lioncel finished his ablutions, and gave his face a last great towelling in case it had gone white.

'What happens if I refuse?' he asked.

'Refuse to fight? Well . . . that'll spoil the sport, but the lion won't mind.'

'I see. I suppose my last drink was drugged. Is this the same? Or would that spoil the sport, too?'

'Yes. This isn't doctored, and it's all you'll get.'

Lioncel donned his shirt and shoes, and sat down at the trestle table.

'There was one at Constantinople, too,' he said half to himself.

'One what?'

'A reptile-house.'

'It isn't a reptile-house, it's a bear-pit . . . oh, you're being bitter. Better men than you have had to do this. It was partly your name, I think . . . Lioncel and the lion's cell. Someone made a pun about it. Shall the boy bring a priest before you eat?'

'I don't think so, thank you. I should think the priests here
are not . . . I mean, their acts of consecration are probably void.'

'That's heresy, but I let it pass. I own I wouldn't like to be
you.'

'I wouldn't like to be *you*, either. And now I'll trouble you
to send this nasty child away..'

The page looked hurt, but Joscelin waved him out of the
room, and Lioncel went on: 'Does the lion always win?'

'Obviously this one has done, so far. A wolf was killed the
other day, and a bear last month, but the bear got the man
too.'

Lioncel forced himself to eat a little before he touched the
wine. The big soldier stood silently beside the door; Joscelin sat
on the bed, between Lioncel and Lioncel's sword and dagger.
Also between Lioncel and Lioncel's purse, which contained a
harmless looking ink-pot full of *capagot*.

'When the wolf was killed, was the man released?' he asked
with his mouth full.

'Of course!' said Joscelin, a little affronted. 'With a purse
of gold, too.'

'Was he robbed of the purse afterwards? Here, I mean?'

'God save us, what a mind you've got! That would have
been a villainy!'

Lioncel looked carefully at Joscelin.

'D'you know, I believe it would,' he said. 'I apologise for
suggesting it. I seem to be shocking you this morning.'

'I . . .' began Joscelin, and suddenly went red and sulky.

'Who gets my gear when I'm dead?' went on Lioncel after
a pause.

'He does,' said Joscelin, nodding at the soldier.

'Here's to the silent inheritor,' murmured Lioncel and took
a deep draught of the magnificent wine. The soldier moved
his feet, but his face remained wooden.

'What will my lord duke tell my lords the abbots?' asked
Lioncel.

'That you very chivalrously volunteered to show your skill,'
mumbled Joscelin.

Lioncel finished the pasties and sat awhile over the drink,

trying to get his mind used to what was coming upon his body. He had stood in peril of death often enough before, but usually with Paladin Janus and devoted Diomede to share it. He said a *Paternoster* and an *Ave* silently without moving his lips, and thought of Yolande, and wondered if missile weapons were barred in case a victim took a long shot at Belphegor.

Then he emptied the goblet, and got up, and put on his good fur-trimmed tunic, and combed his hair and cleaned his nails.

' Lead on to the armoury,' he said, and picked up his girdle and purse, leaving sword and dagger behind him. The coins in the purse jingled as he shook it.

' Poor pickings for corpse-robbers,' he said, and followed the soldier out.

It was obviously no good trying to run away from a lion in a bear-pit. Better be really heavily-armed, even if slow-moving. He would certainly be knocked over and pounded; it was a question of getting a jab into the creature's eye or heart.

Except, of course, that two men's doses of *capagot* could probably kill a lion.

In the armoury two gloomy-looking attendants moved round with him, showing him everything he asked to see, buckling and unbuckling patiently at his request. He chose a suit of soft leather of the kind worn under plate, and a mail shirt that came half-way down to his knees. He was most frightened of being clawed in the face or in the genitals. The tilting-helm and heavy panoply he finally selected provoked shakings of the head from his helpers.

' Fall over, you'll hardly get up,' said one in his ear.

But the helm hinged on the breast-plate, and could not be clawed round to blind him. Its breathing-holes were arranged in two round groups that gave him a fair range of vision below the level of the visor-slit. And the slit itself was well away from his eyes; a claw might tear in at it without taking his eyeballs out.

When it came to gloves Lioncel had an inspiration. He would convert his whole left arm into a wedge of steel. Mail sleeve and mitten, with a vambrace over them; over the vambrace a steel gauntlet of mail, wrapped and wired and bound at the wrist with a bandog's collar having inch-long spikes in it. . . .

A spiked buckler high up on that arm. In his right hand a battle-axe with a very broad blade. In front of his loins a short sword, easily got at. A spiked belt over the scabbard-chain, and a spiked mail collar over all . . . the Chevalier Urchin, he called himself grimly. . . .

Then, at the last minute, he would take in his left steel glove the glass inkpot with the stopper out, and try and get its contents deep into the ravening mouth. It seemed a crazy enough plan, and likely to waste the poison, but he could think of no other detail of armament.

The two custodians collected all he asked, and did what they could to help. He gave each of them a silver coin under the nose of the tall soldier, whose grim face creased a little at such an untimely dissipation of resources.

On his way back to the bedchamber, with the armour bumping and clinking in the embrace of the attendants behind him, Lioncel passed along a corridor where black-browed Camus de Caherne stood talking by a window to a gigantic priest. The Chevalier Camus turned, and so did his companion. Lioncel glanced at the churchman, whose great black beard spilled out of his hood, and wondered if it were he to whom the doomed men made their confessions.

'It's the cat's-meat procession,' said Camus lightly, and turned his back again. The bearded priest seemed faintly amused; he had a thick-lipped unclerical mouth, and had been dressed as a palmer when Lioncel had first seen him.

'Gaston de Volsberghe,' thought Lioncel dully. 'Belphegor's harbouring him, and I can't let anyone know.'

He hoped his own glare at the exile would be accepted as natural from anyone in his predicament. Gaston had the mock-signatures now—all absolutely useless if put to any test of comparison. The thought made a kind of swirl of amusement in the mist of the horror of death that was closing in on Lioncel's brain.

'How long have I now?' he asked Joscelin, when the armour was stacked by the bed.

'A couple of hours, or a little more.'

'Then will you and the soldier go over there? I want to say my prayers alone in that corner.'

'You're not going to make a confession and take the Sacraments?'

'No. I confessed and was shriven four days ago, in Hautarroy. Who's the big priest out there with Camus de Caherne?'

'Very big, with a beard? Dom Jerome. He's a foreigner, Hungarian or something.'

'He looks like it,' said Lioncel, and fished for the little crucifix he wore under his clothes. He moved away from his companions, and knelt down in the corner, and bowed his head and put his palms together, and began a confused but urgent prayer.

'Sieur God, give me a chance to kill Belphegor . . . the Duke Balthasar, I mean . . . and let it be thought my own revenge and nothing to do with anyone else. . . .

'And bless and guard the Duchess Yolande, and make and keep her name glorious, and let her remember me gladly. And if I mayn't have my chance, then please you, kill him some other way before he goes near her. Or kill *her* . . . a fall out riding, breaking her neck . . . don't let her suffer, and don't let her have to kill herself. . . .

'If you can manage it . . . I mean, if it accords with your eternal wisdom . . . let it be he who dies, and so let the Grand Seneschal's plans and power come to nothing.

'And forgive me all my sins, especially for falling in love with the duchess and for dreaming about her as I have done. Forgive my not confessing those dreams; I would rather be damned than tell them to anyone else, priest or layman. . . .

'And don't let it be so bad for Diomede without me as it would be for me without Diomede. And restore the Chevalier Janus to health and full strength, so that no one can mock him safely any more. . . .

'And grant my lord the king more sense in choice of his friends, and a prosperous and peaceful reign. . . .

'And let the lion kill me, or me kill the lion, very quickly.

Let me not cry out or lose my courage before my life. And excuse me for finding your ways so very inscrutable, so that I often don't know which of two things can more offend you . . . for instance, would it be really wrong to murder the Duke Balthasar?

'And take my soul into everlasting keeping, with the souls of my father and mother and great-uncle, for the sake of sweet Jesu and his dear Lady Mother, amen. But most of all, bless Yolande and Diomede. Amen, amen, amen.'

Lioncel turned his palms to his face and remained kneeling a little longer, thinking of the first home he scarcely remembered, of an abbey in Beltany, and of leaves whirling in a dusty gutter on the afternoon when he first realised that nothing was the same for any two people in the world. Then of Bargreant and the Duke Engelbert, and Pardelin and Yolande and Diomede and the capture of the castle. Then of Janus and Elquitaine and the glare of the Eastern Mediterranean seas and shores and cities. Then Hautarroy, and Roclatour, and Pardelin again. . . .

At length he got up and went back to his bed.

'Wake me in an hour's time,' he said, 'and send those two men to arm me.'

'Very well,' muttered Joscelin, who appeared to have lost any relish for his share in the day's entertainment.

Lioncel lay down and let the held-back terror rush on him like a wave. For a twitching trembling moment he plunged into swirls of weakness, silently bawling a protest at death itself and at such a death. Then he seemed to step ashore in a dream, and lost hold on reality. An extraordinary gust of gossiping voices reached him from a street corner in a town he had never visited.

'Oh, she's a notable poisoner, that one. First her tutor, and then her governess, and then the castellan and one of her damsels, and now she's tried it on her husband, but by God's mercy he was preserved, the valiant young duke . . .'

'There, Sieur God, you see what I mean,' thought Lioncel obscurely, and slid into a half-stunned sleep.

Waking and preparation seemed part of another dream.

One of the serving-men grunted as if he were harnessing a horse. 'Come over!' he said to a strap, and 'lie down!' to a ruckle of mail. The older one said nothing at all until the very end, when he worked the sword up and down in its sheath to make sure it moved easily, and suddenly mumbled: 'God be with you, lad.'

'If anyone took this bloody castle,' thought Lioncel, with lunatic clarity, 'these two good-natured carles would be hanged as filthy servants of a very filthy master.'

Aloud he said: 'If I should win, come and unarm me again.'

'That we will, young master,' said the younger man, and they pulled their forelocks and went away.

Lioncel paraded about the room, testing sight from his helm, feeling the weight and balance of his panoply, swinging the battle-axe, whisking out the sword. His heavily-steeled left arm was almost like another person; he wanted to talk to it. From this last eccentricity he restrained himself, but could not resist whistling a stave because of the curious sound of a whistle held in a closed helm.

Lastly he went and stood by the window, watching fluffy clouds drifting across the blue sky.

Trumpets began to sound in the castle.

'Come on,' said Joscelin miserably.

'I'm coming,' said Lioncel, and went to his purse, and then clanked out behind Joscelin, with the apparently speechless soldier following after.

The great bear-pit was rimmed with faces in two and three tiers, and a gust of laughter and applause greeted his ponderous entrance. He had the bottle of *capagot* in the leathern palm of his left glove. The stopper was out, and his thumb pressed in place of it.

The gate clanged behind him, and his steel sollerets sank firmly into the dry sand. The pit was oval, and at the far end, thirty yards away, the other gate still stood shut.

Lioncel watched it carefully as he trudged into the centre of the arena, slowly bending and raising himself to get the range of vision exact. He had no doubt that he cut a comical figure, and that most of the onlookers wanted to see him peeled and shredded and mashed and pipped like any orange in the duke's kitchen; but he felt hardly more than distaste for the down-grinning faces. Belphegor was half-way along . . . no good trying to swing the axe up at that calm seraphic head. One of the Pardelin cook's choppers, perhaps, but not the heavy axe. . . .

The castle minstrels were playing gaily somewhere up above him. Someone, in mockery or compunction, tossed a pine-frond down at his feet. He felt it crackle beneath one iron sole, and halted, moving the axe-head slowly in a gentle figure-of-eight.

'They say its breath drugs you,' he found himself muttering. 'But not with this helm on . . . not with this helm on.'

One last glance at the sky . . . a cloud up there looked like a squirrel . . . and then the music stopped. Trumpets brayed out alone, a long bloodthirsty clamour that drowned the noise of the gate opening ahead.

A great maned shape, muddier-brown than sand, slunk and paused in the sunlit gateway, with head low and eyes beginning to blaze. Snarl-wrinkles deepened, the nose heaved up, the great maw opened and opened beyond belief. A rending roar drowned the fanfare. . . .

Lioncel braced himself, left leg forward, wishing he had a spear and knowing himself too unskilled to use one properly. Yells and catcalls and piercing whistles floated for a second in his consciousness. Then there was nothing but the forward-padding lion, and his own panoply and body, with the haft of the battle-axe rough in his grip, and the sand churning a little as he flexed his right knee.

'Diomede,' said Lioncel, and lifted his huge left arm, pointing his fist at the twitching animal mask of death. The little ink-pot was hidden; polished brassart and elbow-cop had their own curves of glitter, reaching away from his shoulder. Vambrace and gauntlet beyond were almost buried in blue-brown chain mail, and beyond again gleamed the spikes of the hound's collar.

Away beyond the bulk of steel a bush-tipped tail was waving . . . huge claws, fully extended, furrowed the smooth sand. The red cavern of a mouth had shut and was opening again. Four deadly corner-fangs like white pickaxe-blades, ridged grinders ranked behind, a curling tongue like a flat flayed serpent . . . a brown chin-tuft brushing the ground . . . another roar that filled the world. . . .

The great shape rose and blotted out the sunlight. Lioncel was already whirling the axe, and flung it hard and true. The roar was twisted to a scream as he ripped out the short sword. Then he was shocked and overborne, crushed and banged and battered; great claws screeched on metal, a hot stink blasted into his helm, and he saw the lion's palate, ridged like a red tidal beach, above him.

Down on his right side and unable to use the sword, he pushed his left arm, mail and spikes and all, right into the terrible roaring chasm. Clamp, clash, grind, and wrench, and he was pulled upright and flung sideways; incredible sounds and forces surged and thrashed around and upon his tumbling body and battered steel. The spikes were well home, and blood and slaver splashed and blinded him through the visor-slit. Something ripped and rang at his middle, the buckler-edge was bent over his arm, a huge bleeding paw crashed blackly against the lower half of the helm. Then he was being dragged forwards on his knees; he suddenly remembered to shift his armoured left thumb, and was surprised to find his muscles obeying him. That arm seemed gone for good in the grinding hauling fury that had got him.

Two hammer-blows on the top of his head felled him; his left arm twisted and straightened again and slid out of its mail-wrapped gauntlet like a dagger out of its sheath. Mail and plate and spikes were left locked in the lion's gullet. The lion humped itself away and began clawing at its steel gag.

Lioncel got to his feet and tugged with his sword-hand at the remains of the buckler; the straps parted, clawed to shreds, and the spiked disc fell on the ground at his feet. The lion was shrieking now, tearing the sand and its own jaws; its

head came down, the shriek was cut off in gasps, and Lioncel
ploughed forward a stride and ran his sword-blade straight
into one tortured ghastly eye.

The lion gave a kind of thunderous mew and fell over on
its right side. It crossed its forepaws, straightened its throat,
and lay still like a cat unchallenged before a fire. Lioncel had
let go of his hilt; the sword stuck up for all to see, and the
strange new silence in his ears let him hear, as from far off, a
tumult of applause.

He stood rocking on his feet, staring down at the dead brute.
The gauntlet-rim protruded from the open jaws like some
dreadful entrail blown inside out. It was crushed to an oval
shape now, and blood ran thinly out of it.

'I believe the *capagot* did it,' said Lioncel.

He moved forward a step, and was aware of strange clank-
ings. Feeling in front of him with his left hand, he found the
overlapping taces round his loins torn apart and drooping
almost to his knees.

'I ought to be clawed to shreds,' he muttered, 'and I can't
feel anything but bruises.'

Then he bent down for a close look at unmajestic death,
and tugged his sword out, and was suddenly impelled to
stumble along and sever the tail that stuck straight out from
the flattened yellowish body.

'Just to remind me,' he said solemnly, and stooped
awkwardly to pick it up. It was warm and furry to the bare
fingers of his left hand.

He started to march slowly back to the gate, but someone
ran up to him and beat him on his armoured shoulder.

'The purse,' said a voice. 'My lord duke is waiting to
give you the purse of gold. Are you wounded?'

'Not that I know of,' said Lioncel. 'Oh, yes, the purse.'

He let himself be led to stand below the down-smiling face
of Belphegor. The purse, like a red leather sausage, fell at
his feet with a soft clink. He stuck the messy sword in the
sand, saluted, and stooped for the gift.

There was more shouting as he took it in the hand that
already held the lion's tail.

'Better keep the sword,' he thought, 'in case of any monkey-tricks.'

But he knew as he pulled the weapon out that he was too spent and shaken to defend himself any more. He followed his guide into the shadowed entry, out across a garden, and into the castle buildings.

'I hope they don't find that ink-pot!' he reflected, as the serving-men came forward to strip him of his steel. 'They might find it a spoiling of sport according to the gentle code of Sabloyn. Sieur God, I must sleep now if they cut my throat while I do so.'

'That was a good fight, lad,' muttered the older attendant. 'It was a rare trick to choke him with armour.'

'Will you get my bath ready?' he asked them. 'I don't want that evil little page about me, or that disappointed soldier either.'

The steaming bath-tent was ready by the time he was naked. The bent and twisted buckler, the clawed and bitten and ruined armour, lay in a bloodied heap, but none of the blood was Lioncel's.

Wine appeared, and he drank it, and gave each of the men a gold piece from the red purse. Then he bathed, and counted his bruises, and flung himself into bed, hardly able to open his eyes when Joscelin brought food and more wine.

'Is my lord duke angry because I spilt his lion?' he enquired.

'No, he has others,' said Joscelin. 'Come on, eat and drink this.'

'Is it poisoned?' asked Lioncel drily, and again the Montguiscard retainer went red.

'Of course not,' he growled. 'And see here, in my purse I've the paper the duke has written for you, saying how bravely you offered to fight the lion, and how skilfully you killed it.'

Lioncel began to laugh, but the smell of roast capon interrupted him.

Next morning he was roused with civility, and grinned at

by all and sundry. Another meal came to his room, and later
Belphegor sent for him.

Belphegor grinned as widely as any of his household, and
gave Lioncel a message that rounded off the adventure.

' Tell the Chevalier de Largire,' he said, ' that I pray for his
speedy recovery, and shall at any time be pleased to meet him
again in the lists. And tell the Abbot of Saint-Maur that I
grudge him his new swordsman.'

Lioncel bowed and said nothing, still expecting either not
to leave the place alive, or to be ambushed before he had gone
a mile on his way. But he reached Dunsberghe without
mishap, and delivered the letter that had been intended to
save him from any inconvenience. And when he returned to
Hautarroy he took roads that avoided Sabloyn.

Even to his squires there was no end to the oddities of
Janus of the Silver Shield. Lioncel found him sitting up in
bed embroidering a design in coloured threads on a rectangle
of soft red leather, while dictating an account of a discussion
overheard in his youth, on shipboard, between a Dominican
friar and a priest of the Greek Church.

He smiled at Lioncel, waved him to a chair, and asked
leave to finish a paragraph. Then he nodded at the solemn
young monk who was taking down his words, and went on
in a soft reflective voice, as though talking to himself.

' We were coasting before an easterly wind off a shallow
shore south of Cape Nettuno, and the priest was frightened
and a little drunk, and the friar beginning to be seasick. They
were arguing concerning symbols. The friar contended that
Saint Peter's walking on the water symbolised the undoubted
supremacy of the Lord Pope over all peoples and all churches;
for, said the friar, the waters of the inland sea symbolised the
whole sea, and the sea symbolised the world itself. Then,
asked the priest, what was symbolised by the Saint's beginning to sink? To this the friar seemed hard put for an answer,
and the priest complained that the friar made symbols as it
suited him and so darkened counsel. And, as they wrangled,
the ship ran aground on a sandbank, and they fell down and

rolled along the deck in each other's arms. And when we had
got the ship afloat again, by all moving to the stern with such
gear as we could drag and carry, I told these two that their
fall was a true symbol, the word coming from the Greek and
meaning ' thrown together '; for they had been thrown
together half the length of the ship. This made them very
angry, as though I had ruined the word for them by uncovering so simple a meaning. But I do not doubt they soon buried
its simplicity in a thicket of disputed definitions.'

Janus dismissed his amanuensis, who seemed to Lioncel to
have followed the words but not their meaning; for on his way
out he suddenly faltered, as though perceiving a doctrinal
sandbank under his own spiritual keel.

' And now come over here,' said Janus, ' and tell me what
you found at Sabloyn.'

His fine strong face grew graver and pinker as the recital
proceeded. He laid down his embroidery and linked his hands
over it; a sapphire, set in silver filigree, shone on one great
finger, its sparkle changing as the hand became a fist.

' By God's Monday,' rumbled Janus at length, ' I'll take up
that challenge in due time.'

Lioncel was silent for a moment, wondering if he had done
wisely. Then he took a very old bull by the horns.

' May I ask you now, sir,' he began, ' what the Lord Prior
of Sanctlamine, God rest his soul, told you when Diomede
and I first took refuge in your service? '

' Yes, why not? He told me that Diomede and yourself
were in danger, through no fault of your own, so long as Azo
de Montguiscard ruled in Baraine. I took that to mean you
had stumbled on some secret discreditable to him who is now
Grand Seneschal. And I gathered that you had escaped the
massacre at Pardelin by being at that time on a visit to
Sanctlamine. But I was asked not to enquire, and I have not
enquired.'

' For which we remain grateful, sir. Can you tell me something else? Has any news reached you of the late queen's
treasure? '

' No, except that Burias bequeathed it to our lord the king.

A tantalising bequest, for no one can tell him where it's to be found. Burias himself had not found out.'

'Was there jealously between the Count of Burias and the Duke of Baraine?'

'Yes. It was said that Burias might have replaced the duke as prime favourite. But that I doubt; if the Grand Seneschal carries through this marriage project as the king would have it, I think we may see him chancellor of the realm. Short of accidents, the Montguiscards, allied with the queen's party, will govern the kingdom through the king for some time to come.'

XIII

'MY DIOMEDE, MY LIONCEL'

ON an evening of blurred cloud and shifting glooms, when the wind sighed in the bare trees and the snow-streaked mountains seemed crowding forward to threaten the castle and the lake, Yolande and Diomede kissed each other again.

They had climbed to the westward tower-top together, with a lantern which Diomede left burning in the stairhead. He stood respectfully away from his duchess, mindful of the sentinel on the highest turret behind them.

'I wish Lioncel would come back,' said Yolande, glancing up at the pass that carried the track from Roclatour.

'No need to worry yet, my lady,' Diomede assured her, but his voice belied his words, and she turned to look at him.

'You're as anxious as I am,' she told him. 'Or more anxious, because you know more of the real danger. And when he comes back it's your turn again . . . your turn to be Tripping-Go.'

'My turn to be *what*, my lady?'

'Tripping-Go. Don't look so startled.'

She told him about the dream of the dolphin, and he smiled rather grimly.

'I woke up crying because Lioncel and you were parted,' she confessed. 'But it's I who part you . . . that is, these journeys. . . .'

Diomede made a little open-handed gesture as though flicking something over the battlements.

'I set no store by dreams,' he said. 'By my own dreams, I mean. They're a jumble with no sense or comfort . . . for more than a moment. They're savage and distorted and queer, so that I'm a stranger in them. I've seen myself with my head off. . . .'

'Diomede!'

'And I've fought battles against empty helmets on legs. And I've sat again in the oak tree there, with all the hanged men laughing at me and Saracens setting the tree on fire.'

'They're not *all* cruel and bloody, are they?'

'Saints, no. I wander a great deal, round corners in places I've never been to but seem to know in the dream. I revisit them, too. I lose Lioncel and find him again, doing things he oughtn't to do and wouldn't do, so that I'm terrified something will happen to him. . . .'

'What things?'

'Hiding treasure, or finding it. Eating meat in Lent. Wearing gloves in church. Steering a ship on dry land. Riding a unicorn. . . .'

'Why shouldn't he do that?'

'I don't know, but in the dream it seemed a fearful crime. And then I have lonely dreams when I'm not looking for anything. I come out of the edge of a wood to what seems the world's end . . . rather like this evening here.'

He turned to look along the sombre lake, so that his hood quite hid his face from her. Yolande spoke a thought aloud.

'So long as you find Lioncel again all's well, I suppose.'

'It's the best thing there is, except. . . .'

'Except what?'

'Except you, of course,' he said simply.

'Do . . . do I walk in your dreams too?'

'Yes, my lady.'

'With elves down-streaming from a gracious moon? Diomede, don't be angry. I read your lovely poem, almost by accident. It's mean to plague you with questions you're too honest to answer with lies.'

'I'm not angry,' he muttered, 'or very honest, either.'

'Neither am I. It's getting dark. Take me downstairs.'

Silently he moved, picked up the lantern, and preceded her down the winding stair. She latched the turret door behind her with one hand, and dropped the hand to her skirt for safety on the narrow stone tread. The other she held out to Diomede, and he went carefully ahead, holding her fingers gently at the height of his shoulder. In the passage at the stair-foot he paused and raised the lantern so that they saw each other's face clearly. Yolande put her free hand up to his smooth dark cheek and chin.

'Why are we so sad?' she whispered. 'The end of the world might come tonight. No, I'm not teasing you. Nor am I frightened of . . . anything. Nor have I need to be. The *capagot* is not my only powerful and useful medicine. I belong to myself, not to those damned Montguiscards . . . but it's not hatred or spite of them that makes me stand here like this. You know that, don't you?'

Diomede put the lantern down and crushed her in his arms, kissing her blindly so that she gasped and clung to him in a melting enchantment.

'Everything I should say is taken from me,' he murmured, 'except that I love you beyond all telling, and that you've broken my sadness for ever, and that there's nothing I wouldn't do for you . . . or *to* you.'

Yolande laughed in her throat, provoking a new rain of kisses.

'Azo arranged this very well,' she breathed. 'And now you must let me go, and we must be rather solemn again.'

'Until . . . ?'

'Yes, until.'

'Will Heuradys be jealous of me?'

'Of *you*? I don't think so. She might be jealous of *me*.'

'Yolande . . . what nonsense!'

'Why? I'm sure she loves you a little, and you love her a little, don't you?'

'Yes, of course. She loves you so much, and she'd tear the eyes out of anyone who hurt you.'

'O Diomede . . . now we must go. Pick up that lantern while there's any sense left in me.'

Yolande went to her bedchamber, changed her heavy cloak for a light one, stared at herself in her silver mirror, shaped her mouth as if for kisses, picked up her ivory comb and whispered to the little golden lizard that dragged his tail along the back of it, and finally opened the wallet that held the

wooden case of liquids. She unstoppered the violet perfume
called Memory of Doves, and took a thoughtful sniff, staring
fixedly at the green *ezd* or *adzin*.

Heuradys came in and saw her, and knew as if by witchcraft. Her pale pointed face grew elfin; she crossed the room
and picked up Yolande's hand that held the silver stopper.

'Back to my truckle-bed,' she said, and brushed the hand
against her cheek.

'I think . . .' began Yolande uncertainly.

'You don't need to think, my treasure. You've thought too
much and too long. Don't worry, Dom Cyril won't notice;
it's only Dom Cupid and sinful me that know such signs
when we see them.'

'Such signs as what?'

'A look that passes through yourself. Or a blank look that
knows everything, like a flower's gazing at the sun.'

Before supper Heuradys brought wine into the solar. Dom
Cyril was setting out the chessmen, with grunts and ivory
rattlings. Diomede, warming his hands at the fire, saw
Heuradys take Yolande's goblet and bring it across to him.

'Why, Heuradys,' he began, puzzled, but she smiled at
him and closed his fingers round the stem of the goblet.

'My name tonight is Brangwain,' she whispered.

Brangwain was the lady who served the magic potion to
Tristram and Yseult. Diomede drank first to Yolande and
then to Heuradys.

Supper seemed a long meal to those who shared it with Dom
Cyril, and Diomede's chess afterwards was much less than
brilliant. Dom Cyril chuckled as he worked havoc; Heuradys
smiled as she bit her threads, and Yolande read a page of the
History of the Kings of Neustria three times without making
any sense of it. Outside in the Pardelin woods an owl called
repeatedly.

'The bird of wisdom,' thought Yolande. 'You're too late,
little counsellor. A prophesy of owls perhaps, but a memory
of doves.'

When Julian brought her the castle keys she poured out his
cup of wine herself, and he drank to her health and repose.

M

'The night's clearing, my lady duchess,' he told her with soldierly pride, as though he had cleared it himself. 'If it keeps dry for three or four days we'll have hunting weather again.'

For Diomede the stony passage was full of lonely magic; his candle trembled to a rising wind that seemed to sing for him. In the antechamber the steam of the bath-tub curled between the curtains of its tent; he shivered as he came to the tub, and shivered again when he left it and donned his cloak to stand at the inner door. Heuradys opened at his knock; her smile was a benediction as she stood aside for him to enter and went out behind him.

The stained-glass lantern was turned so that its shutter shadowed the great bed, but firelight slid and flickered on blue and silver hangings and on the welcoming cream-gold arms and breasts of Yolande of Baraine. Beneath the canopy of purple silk she took to herself the love and worship and tenderness and beauty of Diomede. Golden leopards on the curtains guarded the joy and pain, the raptures and trances and surrenders, of their sovereign leopardess.

Petulant voices of the night-wind gathered round the keep of Pardelin; from the hearth came the mutter and flap of flames and the rustle of crumbled ash. Once, waking to well-being, Yolande discovered that she was thirsty, and writhed in her lover's arms to reach the wine beside the bed. Diomede awoke too, and tightened his grasp of her.

'It's real, then,' he whispered. 'I dreamed I was walking beside the lake and thinking I'd dreamed of this . . . and this . . . and this.'

'If you hold me so tightly you'll make me spill it,' she told him warningly, and sure enough the cup tilted, and Yolande squeaked softly as drops splashed and ran redly down her shoulder and breast.

'This is how the old gods drank it,' said Diomede, lifting a drowsy greedy mouth.

Before he left her he suddenly caught her face between his hands and pleaded with her.

'Beloved, don't let Lioncel know. I think he might be hurt.'

'Why should he be hurt?'

'I think he loves you in a . . . in a holier way.'

'And would he be disappointed in me?'

'I don't know. He might blame *me*.'

'Would he quarrel with you?'

'Maybe. It would be a one-sided quarrel. I should never fight him. You'd . . . you'd not want me to, would you?'

'No, you're right, I shouldn't. Diomede, we're caught in a coil. Of course I won't tell him. Dear love, I'm glad *your* love is like my own and not so holy. But Diomede!'

'Yes?'

'Do you talk in your sleep?'

'I don't know. Do I?'

'I don't know either . . . you didn't sleep much, and you put me to sleep so deeply.'

'This is a kind of sacrament the good priests don't know about,' he said, and kissed her gently, and pulled on his cloak and went away into the windy darkness of the morning. She heard him exchange a greeting with Heuradys as he passed the truckle-bed in the antechamber. Then the outer door closed, and she was alone with her new awareness.

She yawned and stretched her body in utter contentment, pondering, as though from outside it, the danger and folly and pleasure of being a wicked young woman. God and Azo and Belphegor were now more than ever on the same side. Dom Cyril, Saints uphold him, must now be, more than ever, deceived. And Lioncel, dear Lioncel . . . he must be deceived too. When he came back she must be especially kind to him.

'Lioncel,' she cried, when, after three strange happy days, she clutched his hands in welcome. 'Lioncel, *what* have you round your hat?'

'A lion's tail, my lady.'

'*What?* Why?'

'To prove to myself I wasn't dreaming when I cut it off the dead lion. But my lord duke gave me a kind of a warrant which you shall read presently. And Gaston's there in disguise.'

'Lioncel . . . do you mean . . . oh, come in quickly and tell me. I'm so happy to see you. We'd begun to be ghastly brave about you. Quargis has taken the bath-tub to your room. Here's Heuradys with a homecoming-cup. When will the duke. . . .'

'He spoke of the summer, my lady.'

'And the sweating sickness in Roclatour?'

'Ended. Griflet expects you . . . and the Sieur de Xantroy.'

'We'll give Odard the gout, then. Here comes Dom Cyril. Tell me about it later.'

That night, when his story was ended, Yolande begged a hair from the tail of the lion and reinforced with it the link binding her agate talisman to her gold neck-chain.

'Philastrius said it would bring me vigour and success,' she told him. 'Tomorrow I write to the Count of Ger.'

'My lord Count and very good cousin,' (she wrote), *'Very heartily I commend myself to you, sending the tablets you gave me on the night of the interrupted feast in the castle of Bargreant.*

'The bearer, Diomede de Torre, is my discreet and resolute friend, and very loyal servant. He wears the badge of the Chevalier de Largire for reasons he will himself explain.

'My lord, he will speak three tokens to you concerning the tablets. First, of my hands. Second, of the square you drew in the wax, which I have smoothed out. Third, of your estates. Only you and I, and now he, know what we said about these things. If the messenger makes any mistake, he is not Diomede de Torre, but some other who impersonates him.

'Having proved his identity, believe everything he tells you. He speaks with my authority, and will bring me an exact reply.

'My lord, by the fame of those whose ancient blood we share, help me to vengeance for my father foully slain here, and for sacrilege and murder done on the persons of his chaplain and faithful servants, who died trying to protect me.

'*As for my husband, I mean to break my marriage with him. He consorts with the traitor Gaston de Volsberghe; in the guise of a demon he murdered the Count of Burias; and for his many infamous cruelties he is well-named Belphegor, Peer of Hell.*

'*Your cousin and friend and servant, who prays for you,*
Yolande.'

She sat for a while looking at the tablets, at the dagger with its cornelian boar of Burias for pommel, and at the parchment with the signatures and the drawing of acorns.

The sound of voices and horsehoofs drifted in at the windows. She got up and looked out; Lioncel and Diomede were riding into the sunlit woods.

'They should have hawks and hounds,' she reflected. 'They should be leading men-at-arms or standing guard in the king's corridors. Instead they're risking everything by running errands for a crazy girl. Lioncel was nearly killed by the lion. Diomede's going to Ger, and I can't have him while Lioncel's here, and I don't want them parted, and True Love is Leopard's Bane, and . . . Philastrius, I need your skill again. Some dark body-stain, and more of the *capagot*, the *beym*, and the *adzin*.

'But Diomede, my darling, in all my heart there's not one scrap of shame or regret or remorse.'

She turned back to her table, caught up the dagger, and struck it into the wood, letting go so that the hilt quivered to the trembling of the blade. The doll Amarand stood blandly by, and presently, out of his scented inside, Yolande took the privy seal of Baraine.

Next day again, just after dawn, Diomede came on her alone in the passage near her bedchamber door. Catching her in his arms, he held her close for a moment, in pride and torment and thankfulness that found her dumb and nearly weeping. Their formal leave-taking an hour later was restrained almost to the point of coldness.

'These winter journeys are an imposition,' she said, as he bent over her fingers.

'Not in your service, my lady duchess,' said Diomede, haughtily.

Lioncel and Quargis escorted him to Roclatour. At the castle there, Diomede gave Griflet one of Yolande's notes purporting to come from Odard.

'How long's he going to stay in that hole?' growled Griflet, who read with some difficulty, despising all arts aside from war and the hunting of women and animals.

'He was very afflicted by the death of his lady,' said Diomede, smoothly. 'This gout I ascribe to melancholy rather than to Christmas cheer.'

Griflet glowered, resenting the confidence placed in these travelled and musical squires; but they treated him with such respect that he liked to walk with them beyond the barbican, so that townspeople should see the trim salutes they gave him.

They let him assume that Diomede was bound for Haut-arroy and Sabloyn, but when he offered an escort, Diomede gracefully declined it.

Actually, as he was going north, his way would lie among villages, with abbey guesthouses in plenty, and castles if he preferred their hospitality.

They went to bed early, leaving Griflet playing ninepins in the chamber of parade with his cronies among the younger burghers. These townsmen liked to lounge in at the castle gate, with a nod and a password to the archers on duty; if discipline seemed lacking its absence contributed to their self-importance.

'I wish I were coming with you,' said Lioncel, looking out at the crescent moon as it settled among the lakeland hills.

'So do I,' said Diomede.

'In one way,' went on Lioncel, slowly closing the window-shutters, 'I don't want this sword-of-Damocles life to stop, but I came back with my heart in my mouth, wondering if she and you were safe. I expect you'll do the same.'

'So do I,' said Diomede.

'And I hope to God my lady isn't misjudging the Count of Ger. Mind you take no risks beyond the first few miles alone.'

'My natural timidity already asserts itself.'

Lioncel laughed, not realising how much his own presence steadied Diomede in action.

The dawn was drizzly, and the eye of the sergeant at the north gate sardonic, as he saluted the outgoing squire. Roclatour boasted no suburbs; leafless woods, trimmed back from the roadside, stood as if watching the solitary rider on his powerful black horse. Diomede drew the hood of his storm-cloak up over his steel cap, and took the loaded crossbow out of its canvas case, keeping it dry and ready beneath the thick frieze.

He was nervous, and irritated with himself, knowing his nervousness rooted in a lively sense of sin. He had told Yolande the truth when he said she had broken his sadness for ever; the stolen joy they had shared was too sacred and sweet for him to set it in any balance; but the Sieur God might not look at it like that. He would have liked to thank God for it, but that would have seemed an impertinence. If the chance came again he would take it; if not, he meant to guard the memory without bitterness.

Innocent Lioncel, not he, had been called upon to face the lion. What had Destiny (call it that) in store for guilty Diomede? And for Yolande, too, whose equal guilt—for she would scorn to take less than half the blame—would, if it were known, seem so enormous?

The drizzle and the sighing wind offered no comfortable answer. Diomede turned and looked at the already dim shape of the castle, with the misted edges of the Casque of Baraine frowning behind and to westward of it.

'We'll see what can be done,' he said, knowing the Count of Ger to be famous for justice and fair dealing, and hence unlikely to send a guest to earn his supper in a bear-pit.

A rocky height stood up ahead, with a village in front of it. There the road forked, going westward to Hautarroy, or northward to the frontier of Baraine and into Nordanay beyond. Arable land pushed back the woods and moorland; lambs bleated in stone folds, rooks drifted among gaunt elms,

and smoke rose from thatched roofs behind cut haystacks and
thick thorn hedges. A peasant laden with brushwood stood
by a farmyard gate to watch horse and rider splash past him.

'You don't carry very good weather with you, soldier,' he
called, with red face wrinkled in a grin.

Diomede waved in answer; he would have liked to say
grandly: '*No, but I carry the fate of Baraine.*'

In a market town that afternoon he found wool-merchants
going north to visit the great sheep-rearing abbeys; for three
days he rode in their slow company. At Glion, first city of
Nordanay, he sought the provost and showed him the letter
given him by the Chevalier Janus, establishing his identity
and requesting any assistance proper to a messenger on his
lawful occasions.

'You're in luck, Master de Torre,' the provost told him.
'The count isn't at Ger; he kept Christmas at Marckmont, his
little hold in the marshes, and last week he was still there,
although his household's gone north again. He's built a
causeway two leagues long that carries a new road eastward
from Marckmont to Var, thirty miles north of here. Start
early tomorrow and you'll make it in daylight.'

An east wind raced over the reeds and furrowed the wide
wastes of water when Diomede passed the arches of the
fortalice of Var and rode out upon the new causeway. The
hold of Marckmont he could not yet see, for woods masked
the distant shore, but tall cressets on the fortalice ramparts
showed that signals could be exchanged from there.

The sun was low in the south-west, and red and white sails
of boats slid far off in the misty reaches; when Diomede had
ridden a mile or more a wild swan flew across his way, its
great wings making a *whong-whong-whong* as they beat
darkly against the yellow sky. Twice he passed turreted
guard-houses standing locked and empty in pairs beside the
parapeted causeway. Each tower had winding-gear on its top,
so that boats could be slung on to, or across, the road. On the
other, older causeway, which reached northward from the

castle, Raoul of Ger had turned back Gaston de Volsberghe's army during the great insurrection; plainly he meant to be able to check another here if need arose.

From the first village on the far side Diomede saw the four squat towers of Marckmont, still a couple of leagues away across inlets and woods and ploughland. Windmills whirled their sails steadily, as if all were well with life; prosperous-looking peasants were felling trees by the roadside, and at a second, larger village, a crowd of squealing children bowled hoops along a flagged path by the church. Two men-at-arms with gold swans on their tabards touched their bright steel caps as the black horse cantered past them at a tavern door.

'You are to speak three tokens,' said Raoul of Ger, looking up from silent scrutiny of Yolande's letter.

'Yes, my lord count. First, of my lady's hands: they were scratched by the kitten my lord duke threw to his hounds. Second, of the square; it was the Square of Saturn, you told her, adding up to fifteen all ways. Third, of your estates; they were estates in Queranay, and you said that your way to them might lie through Bargreant, or Roclatour, or Pardelin.'

'So. This letter speaks well of you. Take a drink of wine, and begin.'

Diomede glanced at the gaunt dark man sitting beside the count.

'This is Hubriton, my secretary,' said Raoul of Ger. 'He will make notes for me. You may speak as if we were alone.'

Diomede began.

The count sat almost motionless, except that he sometimes plucked slowly at the point of his light brown beard. His eyes, and the gems of three rings on his fingers, reflected the lights of the candelabrum set in front of the secretary. While Diomede talked the fire crackled, the wind moaned, and the quill squeaked. Afterglow faded beyond the window-glass. The cedar-wood tablets stood open at the count's elbow; the black gerfalcon seemed to float in its bright yellow shield.

'And only the five of you know these things?' asked Raoul of Ger at one point.

'Yes, my lord count.'

'Go on.'

A little later he interrupted again.

'The Duchess Yolande is in touch with no one at Bargreant?'

'No one, my lord count.'

'There may be members of her late father's household there, dismissed or lowered in status, who might be expected to prefer her return as sole ruler?'

'I hope so, my lord count, but I don't know. None of us knows.'

'You have never been there? No. Go on again.'

When, at length, Diomede had said his say, Raoul of Ger sat silent, holding the dagger adorned with the little cornelian boar of Burias. He slid the blade half out and back again, looking at the parchment of true signatures, and Yolande's copy of the substituted group that had gone in its place to Sabloyn, and the letter of Janus commending Diomede, and a list made by Quargis of Belphegor's chief captains and agents. Diomede made of his face a mask; a hunting-horn, blown far away, seemed almost to accuse him of bringing strife into this pleasant peaceful place.

Then Raoul of Ger spoke again.

'It seems . . . unwise to incur the enmity of the Duchess Yolande. And by the same token, advisable to keep her friendship. How old is she now, Master de Torre?'

'She will be seventeen in June, my lord count.'

'Then at any time she may be driven to hide herself from her husband.'

'Yes, my lord count. If she cannot escape I believe she will kill herself, and, if possible, the duke as well.'

Again a silence. Diomede rose to his feet, moved aside so that the table was no longer between them, and sank pleadingly, on one knee, with a ring of his spurs and a rattle of his scabbard.

'My lord count, save her from that fiend of hell. If you

cannot or will not, she sends you this last message, *that for the sake of the people of the duchy she is glad that you will be Duke of Baraine.*'

Raoul of Ger smiled and laid down the dagger.

'Put that down, Hubriton,' he said. 'Master de Torre, I shall keep my promise to help my lady duchess. If need be she can take refuge here, but that we will discuss later. Get up and refresh yourself.'

He paused and looked down at his signature among the others, and went on.

'Hubriton, how the devil did this come into the hands of the Grand Seneschal?'

'Probably from the Bishop of Bargreant, my lord.'

'By Our Lady, that's it! I wrote to him about . . . what was it?'

'His request that a cousin of his might have the next vacancy among your chaplains,' said the secretary drily.

'Yes, I remember now. Make a note: who and where are the kinsmen of the Lord Bishop of Bargreant? Master de Torre, I can tell you this: the Grand Seneschal has arranged the betrothal of the Duke of Honoy and the Princess of Zurland. In May the little princess will come by sea to Ger. In June the duke and she will be married at Hautarroy. Among the lords appointed to meet her at the coast is the Duke of Baraine.'

'Yes, my lord count.'

The count rang his table-bell, and a page stepped silently into the room.

'Adelard, attend Master de Torre.'

Diomede bowed, and as he went out heard Raoul of Ger speak to Hubriton.

'A letter to the Count of Saint-Aunay, under private seal. *Nino, meet me at once in Belsaunt at the palace of my lord bishop. . . .*'

When Diomede had received and digested his return messages, he was escorted by six buff-coated archers to within sight of the towers of Roclatour.

'You've been mighty quick,' said Griflet gloomily.

'Only to Hautarroy and back,' said Diomede, and repeated the new of the coming marriage of the king's son and the movements of the Montguiscards.

'Time our duke came for *his* duchess,' said Griflet, not without malice.

'High time,' agreed Diomede, with baffling alacrity. 'She's tired of being shut away there. She speaks of sending for the damsel Aurania soon. Lioncel and I only stay to oblige the Sieur de Xantroy. It's the last place anyone would go to for choice.'

Apart from Yolande's messengers, indeed, there was nothing to link Pardelin with the world outside the valley; the villagers were strangers with no kinsmen anywhere near, and if Dom Cyril and Dom Robert were scandalised by Yolande's isolation, they accepted it as imposed upon her, and Dom Cyril asked no more questions.

And so, assisted by wild weather, the ghost of Odard continued to hover somewhere in air between the castles of Roclatour and Pardelin. It recovered from gout, had a fall out hunting, wrote letters with Yolande's quill, and even sent for the Roclatour accounts—but not for the clerk, which greatly relieved that unadventurous worthy.

Yolande and her squires spent a couple of days inspecting pay-rolls and lists of stores and purchases. There were payments to millers and arrow-makers and armourers, to saddlers and chandlers and carters, to men who kept the forest and controlled the village granges. There was a fee to Philastrius for setting a broken arm, and to a fisherman for saving a castle groom who had fallen into the lake. And there were fees to the hangman and his fellows who had burnt the three witches.

When she had signed Odard's name, accepting the balanced accounts, and had banged the seal of the clouded thunderbolt into a splash of red wax, Yolande gave a great puff of relief and pushed the feather of her goose-quill down by the dainty bowed nape of Heuradys.

Heuradys gave a wriggle of pleasure and went on with her

sewing. Yolande sat admiring her self-contained and rather melancholy beauty.

'I suppose I'm making it very hard for you to marry and have a home,' went on Yolande.

'Some nest in a town,' said Heuradys, 'with a murmuration of neighbours, and a husband of regular habits to keep the cradle full for me, and beyond his snoring the wind in the roof, to mock me with the nights when I sang songs with my duchess.'

'A wicked duchess.'

'A duchess who doesn't snore, at least. Shall I promise to flit some day without a sound, like Damsel Douce?'

'Don't do that,' said Yolande, suddenly depressed. 'And now I've reminded myself of Aurania; I can't leave her at Saint-Marthe for ever. Nothing goes right with my household . . . I believe poor Dom Cyril will have to take to his bed with that cough and the weakness in his legs.'

Dom Cyril fell ill, as she expected, and Quargis nursed him with help from the rest of them. This meant that Dom Robert came daily into the castle, often taking his meals with them, able closely to observe this now most unsuitably-constructed household. But the fictitious Odard still haunted the board, and Yolande assumed a distant air, talking chiefly of days at Bargreant, trying to keep down the 'I, I, I,' which recalled Jehane at Roclatour.

When Dom Robert said Mass she had everybody attend it but the men asleep or on duty, and the kitchen folk who prepared remedies against the chill of the tiny chapel.

But in Yolande's heart was a savage joy in her secret love of Diomede, an almost insane delight in the awakening of that year's spring, and a faint recurrent thrill like that of trumpets—the far-away but friendly trumpets of Ger.

The problem of Aurania solved itself by violence. In the early afternoon of a sunny, windy April day, the war-horn bellowed on the keep and set the conspirators arming themselves and running and striding to prearranged duties and positions.

Everyone was living in hunting gear. Yolande darted to her bedchamber to collect wallets containing Amarand and her perfumes. Heuradys had the harp and lute in their cases almost before the horn was silent. Lioncel raced up to the turret to enquire what the sentinel had seen; Diomede went to the stable and had five horses saddled, thereafter waiting near the postern, of which he had a key. Quargis trotted along to the boathouse tower, waiting by a lancet window on the floor above the boats for a signal from one of the windows in the solar.

'Two horsemen, sir,' said the sentinel archer.

'Riding fast?'

'Not specially, sir. See, at the bend there.'

Lioncel peered from under his palm, and thought that one of the two looked like a woman.

'Give us another blow if any more appear,' he said.

'Right, sir,' said the archer.

Lioncel descended, gave the news, and rode out to meet the visitors.

They proved to be Griflet and Aurania, he in half-armour, she in a horned headdress and a russet riding-cloak. They might have been a chevalier with the damsel rescued from distress in some tale of the Round Table.

They might have been, but they were not; Aurania stared at Lioncel as if she were half-crazy, and Griflet's grim square-jawed face wore a kind of defiant leer.

'You've never come alone?' asked Lioncel, unceremoniously, with his hat off and his white-gold hair flying in the wind.

'I sent the escort back from Herindal,' said Griflet. 'Is the Sieur de Xantroy in the castle?'

'He's out riding,' said Lioncel. 'My lady duchess will be waiting to see you. Dom Cyril's ill in bed.'

'And Douce?' asked Aurania hoarsely.

'I think she is well,' said Lioncel, smoothly, and wheeled his mount to ride beside them up to the gate of the castle.

Diomede had dodged up to the ramparts and in at a second-floor entrance. Heuradys signalled to Quargis that he was wanted. Yolande sat by the fire and waited, twisting a ring on her finger, then folding her hands to keep them still.

Footsteps in the passage. Diomede opening the door. Aurania almost swooping in, to fall on her knees beside Yolande. Behind her Griflet, Lioncel, and the mystified Julian. Last of all, by another door, Quargis, unostentatiously carrying his crossbow.

'My lady duchess,' muttered Aurania, pressing Yolande's hands to her face. 'My lady, may I talk to you alone?'

'Why, Aurania,' began Yolande, acknowledging with a nod the almost exaggerated bow of Griflet. 'What's amiss? What are you doing here?'

'You . . . you sent for me, my lady!'

'I understood Master de Torre to say I was to bring her here,' said Griflet.

'I said my lady duchess spoke of sending for the damsel,' said Diomede. 'No more than that.'

He looked Griflet steadily in the eye.

'Let me see you alone, my lady,' begged Aurania again.

Griflet looked down at Yolande.

'She'll tell you a lot of lies,' he said scornfully.

'Lies what about, captain?'

'I ask to see the Sieur de Xantroy,' Griflet replied, as if losing his temper.

'Answer my question, captain,' said Yolande.

'This woman . . .' he began, but Aurania interrupted him. Twisting herself upright on her knees, she swung half round to point at Griflet, clinging to Yolande's fingers with her other hand.

'That man,' she cried hoarsely, 'that wild hog in armour there, raped me last night in the inn at the village high up in the hills. His men were drunk below, singing and stamping and yelling. The inn folk were scared, and there was no one to hear or help me. And something I haven't told him I now tell you: round his neck he wears a gold medal with emblems on it, a dove, a fish, a peacock, a torch. *Dom Ursus wore that medal the last time I saw it!*'

'What, round his neck in bed?' jeered Griflet. 'My lady

duchess, this young woman's never been right in her head since Dom Ursus died. . . .'

'You deny the charge?' asked Yolande.

'Of course I do. I showed her the medal at supper. It's my own, and always has been.'

'*And he has a forked scar on his right hip!*' screamed Aurania, hiding her face in Yolande's lap.

'Did you show her that at supper too?' asked Yolande, looking up at him.

'I demand to see the Sieur de Xantroy . . .' began Griflet again.

'Captain Julian, arrest him,' said Yolande. 'Give up your weapons, Griflet.'

'This is a plot,' said Griflet, moving slightly so that he stood against the wall. 'Julian, stand back.'

'This is Pardelin,' said Yolande coldly, 'not Klingenstein.'

Griflet gave a growl and ripped out his sword. Julian, Lioncel and Diomede followed suit, but a deep note from the crossbow forestalled any crossing of steel. There was a queer metallic slap; Griflet hiccoughed, dropped his sword, gave at the knees, and crashed sideways into the rushes.

The sword-hilt struck the foot of Heuradys, who had leapt between him and Yolande with her dagger bright in her hand.

'He's dead,' said Julian, and crossed himself.

'Drawing steel on Her Grace,' said Lioncel.

Yolande stood up, addressing Julian.

'He resisted arrest on charges of sacrilege, murder, and rape,' she said. 'Outside this room, captain, it was sacrilege and murder only . . . you understand?'

'Yes, my lady.'

'Lay his body in the hawksheds, set a guard over it, and send for Dom Robert. But first, give me his purse.'

Julian unclasped Griflet's sword-belt and pulled the purse away from it. Yolande emptied the contents on the table. Among the coins and dice were two keys, a cloak-clasp, and a great gold ring with a rock-crystal skull on it. Absolute silence reigned in the solar until Yolande spoke again.

'I thought that might be found,' she said. 'He couldn't part with it at Roclatour, and he's been nowhere else but here since he killed Dom Ursus. Gramercy to you, Quargis.'

She led Aurania away, put her on her own bed, and gave her wine to drink while Heuradys prepared the bed in the chamber last used by Douce. While Aurania drank she watched her, marvelling sadly at their differing fortunes of the flesh.

'He knew you and Dom Ursus were lovers?' she asked softly.

'He only guessed . . . my lady, *you* knew all the time?'

'Not all the time . . . no, Douce didn't give you away.'

'Then . . . when you gave me the draught . . .'

'Yes.'

'Then, my lady, in the name of God, can you not . . .'

'Yes, it happens that I can. You shall have another draught. On one condition.'

'Anything, my lady, anything.'

'Just this. Go back to the convent for the present. Only the abbess shall know what has happened, and she will accept it as due reason. About the draught she will know nothing. And now, this. Odard de Xantroy . . .'

Aurania's beautiful blue eyes grew wide as she listened. Very eagerly Aurania grasped Yolande's little gold cross to swear an oath of silence. Then she lay back on the pillows and stared at Yolande again.

'Last time I saw you,' she said, 'you were turning into the great lady they didn't want you to be. Now you *are* a great lady, and I'm frightened of you . . . but I trust you. Mayn't I stay here after all?'

'No. I shan't forget you, Aurania. I shall hope to have you with me again, but not just now.'

When Yolande gave her the ring with the skull on it, Aurania cried a good deal.

'You . . . you don't seem to blame me at all!' she sobbed, almost accusingly.

'It's not my place to judge you,' said Yolande. 'I judge nothing but meanness and cruelty.'

'Nothing but those!' exclaimed Aurania, as though appalled at this new interpretation of justice.

In consideration of his crimes, real and suppositious, Griflet was buried on the north side of the church, without benefit of clergy. Lioncel and Diomede escorted Aurania back to Roclatour, with a letter giving the steward charge of the castle, where burghers would no longer play ninepins on the swept boards of the chamber of parade.

Snow was quite gone from the mountains, and the three riders made the twelve leagues in a day. Their conversation was disjointed; the squires did not like to leave Aurania out of it, and Aurania was watching for any trace of scorn, disapproval, or amusement.

'This Heuradys,' she said suddenly, once. 'What made my lady take her out of the straw like that?'

'A kind heart, I expect,' replied Diomede. 'But the damsel's brave and faithful and accomplished. Griflet would have had to put his sword through her to reach my lady duchess.'

'H'm, yes, I suppose so. But *Heuradys* ... what a heathen name.'

'Like Her Grace's and your own.'

'*What?*'

'They're all three from the Greek to begin with. Eurydice, Iolanthe, Ourania.'

'Ourania ... what does it mean?'

'Heavenly.'

'Oh! And Douce?'

'From the Latin *dulcis*, sweet.'

'What a lot you know, Master Diomede ... but of course you've travelled in the East.'

Aurania fell silent for a while. She was interested in Byzantine splendours as they related to women whom she could envy or despise, but it was hard to ask questions which would not sooner or later confront her with discomfort because of her own situation. Slavery, and Turkish harems, and Eastern vices generally, were not easy to discuss with two grave young men.

'Master Diomede,' she began at length. 'Why does my lady send me away like this?'

'Probably to spare you trouble.'

'But .... what's the point of it? Why does she live such a

mean life, with no proper attendance. No women of . . . of standing, I mean. Anyone not knowing her . . . and you, of course . . . might think it a scandal.'

'It's her pleasure, damsel, and that's the end of it for us.'

'Another thing . . . why do you wear the Silver Wolf and serve the Golden Leopard? '

'The Chevalier de Largire is in retreat,' said Diomede.

'From what I hear of my lord duke, *he's* not in retreat, or likely to approve of her living thus at Pardelin.'

'No doubt all will be arranged,' said Diomede easily.

When they approached the village of Herindal it was Lioncel and he who felt embarrassed, but Aurania summoned a nonchalance which blossomed into bravado as the wine went round.

'Which of you is it? ' she asked suddenly, over the rim of her goblet.

'Is what? ' asked Lioncel, puzzled.

'What do you mean? ' asked Diomede, who knew perfectly well.

Aurania lost confidence under the cold double scrutiny.

'No matter,' she said sulkily. 'I've no right to ask. I've no right to anything.'

'You have,' Lioncel told her, patting her beautiful hand. 'You're a friend of my lady duchess and we're proud to serve you.'

Aurania looked at him with two large tears escaping from her long eyelashes.

'I'm making a fool of myself,' she whispered. 'You're both very kind. I shall pray for my lady and you too, and for her quick return to Roclatour.'

May sunshine dried the flanks of the mountains, and Lioncel led Yolande and Heuradys and Diomede on long riding expeditions around the lake. In the space of three weeks they climbed all five of the Sieges, except that Lioncel and Diomede went alone to the summit of Siege Perilous.

Those were great days, with the water a jewel in the sunshine, and the Talon of Baraine spiked and blue along the western skyline. From Siege Gracious they counted the northern mountains of the province, that overlooked the Marshes of Marckmont; from Siege Orgulous they saw the first hills of Queranay blotted out by rain. From the top of Siege Fabulous they saw nothing at all, for a cloud shut down as they reached the circle of standing stones, and they took their food and wine on the altar and crowned Yolande with a spray of rowan-leaves which she wore all the way home and hung up beside her mirror.

On the way up Siege Umbrous they paused by Faramond's Tree to drink of the stream above the fall and look down on Pardelin.

Heuradys, told how the great hawthorn got its name, patted the limb from which the mercenary captain was hanged over the dark ravine.

' I expect she led him on,' said Heuradys, ' thinking life dull and herself safe and clever.'

' Mercenary captains,' said Lioncel, ' don't need leading on.'

Yolande thought of Aurania and looked at Lioncel. Her own life was neither dull nor very safe, and she and Diomede were clever enough to keep their physical love a secret from Lioncel; but Lioncel had begun to take an unconscious revenge on her. Without ceasing to want Diomede, she now wanted Lioncel as well.

' Out-byzantining the Byzantines,' she called it in her own mind. She was amused and slightly shocked to find no sense of piled-up iniquity darkening her awareness There was only a sweet throbbing determination, as natural as the song of a stream or the burrowing of a bee in a flower.

She withdrew her thoughtful gaze from Lioncel's calm, pure profile, and let it slide over Diomede's smooth brown neck. Just out of sight there, she knew, under the thick dark curls, was a tiny mole in the shape of the moon a quarter past the full. The Sieur Decrescent, she called it, and invented dire adventures for him, which Diomede threatened to set to music.

' You female Turk,' she said to herself, and looked away at the hills beyond Quatrelances. ' But supposing you could make Lioncel as happy as you make Diomede? '

She half-dreamed, half-schemed contentedly all morning, while now one squire and now the other gave her a hand over the rocks and through the deep heather. On the summit of the mountain they built a cairn, and saw an eagle soar from her eyrie on the face of a distant crag.

Heuradys exclaimed in delight, turning so quickly to watch that she all but fell off a boulder. Lioncel caught her and held her safe; a spectral horseman seemed to glide up to the ramparts of Yolande's heart.

'Get back to hell,' Yolande bade him. 'I'm wicked enough without you to follow me.'

She took up a sharp piece of stone and scratched a Greek cross deeply on a flat surface of rock. At the end of each arm she marked an initial.

'Y, D, H, L,' read Diomede over her shoulder. 'That'll puzzle some poor shepherd one of these days.'

'He'll think it sorcery.'

'It is sorcery. The best I ever heard of. Lioncel, Heuradys, we're all joined in an enchantment.'

'Lock your hands,' said Yolande, when they stood around her. 'Each take hold of someone else's wrist. Now, hands against the cross.'

The four brown fists assembled in a square.

'Siege Umbrous,' said Yolande clearly, 'and Spirits of the Mountains of Baraine, lock us in our love for each other and strengthen us in those purposes which we cannot discuss with Heaven. Yolande who honours you asks this.'

'And Diomede.'

'And Heuradys.'

'And Lioncel.

They they let go, looking a little queerly at each other, and picked up their cloaks and bows and started down the mountain.

Algidus, the hermit on the south shore, was a thin, worried-looking creature, with greying hair and a stoop and prominent hazel eyes that flickered and darted their gaze about as if their owner were continually birds'-nesting. His voice was nasal but sonorous; and he was said to dislike the very sight of women.

Yolande and Heuradys took him a chicken and some candles; Lioncel handed him these gifts, while the girls drew rein some yards away, with cloaks about them to muffle all disturbing contours.

' Are you content with the gauds and follies, the wretched solace of this life? ' boomed the hermit.

' No, brother,' said Yolande.

' You know that you're heaps of corruption, food for worms, sacks of dung? '

' We're as God made us, brother,' said Yolande amicably.

' No, no, no! ' roared the hermit. ' Sister duchess, you're misled by vanity, and snared with comfortable folly in the net of the Evil One who delights in deception and destruction! '

He dodged into his abode—half-cave, half-freestone hut— with the chicken and the candles, and came out clutching a rough cross of the kind given in pictures to Saint Jehan Baptist. Holding this up, and planting himself a dozen paces away from Yolande's stirrup, he pointed a lean finger at her and tried to extend to her the state of half-pleasurable terror which was wearing away his own wits and body.

Yolande listened for a quarter of an hour, crossing herself from time to time, and trying to keep hold of a thread of discourse.

Nowhere in this man's religion appeared any peace or dignity. The world was a part of hell, or a cranny between hell and heaven, in which the soul was stuck for a season, its front half writhing in ecstasy, its hinder parts bouncing in torment. Strains of celestial music and bawlings of praise clashed with shrieks of the damned and bangings of infernal anvils. No matter which power might win in this game of pull-Maker, pull-devil, it seemed certain the soul of Algidus would emerge something like a singed dishclout.

' Brother Algidus,' said Yolande at length, ' are you telling us that the wickedness of man is greater than the goodness of the Sieur God? '

The hermit made a desperate sound like *Wah!* Turning and

diving into his cell, he slammed the rope-hinged door behind him. A psalm began to thunder out, the seventy-fourth, demanding to know why God's anger was aroused against the sheep of his pasture. Yolande wiped her forehead and led her little cavalcade away.

'If Algidus were to poke his head out of the cave now, what would you do?' asked Yolande, treading cautiously the rough stairway to the hidden hermitage on the other side of the lake.

'I should hide behind you,' said Lioncel.

'That would do you no good, for I should scream and jump into the water.'

Diomede was Tripping-Go, and Heuradys was tending Dom Cyril, and Quargis was superintending the unloading of firewood in the castle courtyard. Lioncel had rowed Yolande round Isle of Cats and into the north inlet. It was a calm spring afternoon, and the westering sunlight struck in long rays through oaks and poplars of a side ravine on the inlet shore.

'Poor soul,' went on Lioncel. 'But he makes less misery there than he would by a church or in a cloister.'

'Weren't you a little frightened?' asked Yolande. 'I was, though I pretended not to be.'

'No, my lady. He brings ridicule on what he tries to explain.'

'Yes. And I suppose the lion made even more noise.'

Lioncel laughed, and spread his cloak against the foot of the overhanging cliff, right at the top of the winding path. They sat down and looked out across the steel-blue and green-brown water; the place and hour were very still, except that poplar and aspen leaves flickered to a breath that moved no others.

'There might be nobody else alive,' whispered Yolande, unbuckling the chin-strap of her hunting-cap, and shaking forward over her shoulders the thick black plaits of her hair.

Lioncel took off his bycocked hat, with its jay's feather caught in by the brooch of the silver wolf. The neck of his green tunic was square-cut and low, and his white shirt open at the throat, showing sunburned skin as delicate as a girl's. Yolande shut her eyes.

' Lioncel,' she exclaimed, half-mischievous, half-sad.

' Yes, my lady? '

' Did anyone ever tell you your face is like an angel's? '

' Well . . . yes.'

' Tell me . . . who was she? '

Yolande's eyes were wide open again. Lioncel looked at her with a sort of rueful adoration.

' It wasn't a she. It was Messer Baldassare della Chiava, at Florence. He pestered me into letting him paint me.'

' As an angel, you mean? '

' Yes. The second from the left in his picture of Our Lady and the Infant Jesu, done for the Cardinal Bevilacqua. The Cardinal's there, too, kneeling, with three chins. I never dared tell anyone, except of course Diomede.'

' What did he say? '

' He said he was glad someone else had noticed it, because he'd always hoped we should be killed together, and then he could get into heaven on the strength of my face.'

' Dear, wicked, frowning Diomede. *He* looks more like a faun. It's partly your frownlessness that makes you look angelic. As well as being good, of course. But now I'm being rude.'

' No. But . . . *good*! '

Lioncel tossed a pebble over the edge of the cliff, and from some near tree-top a blackbird flew away chattering. Then all was still again.

' What was it Quargis called Belphegor? The Angel of the Peacock! I suppose he *is* beautiful . . . like the tigers and the great striped snake the king keeps at Hautarroy.'

' Shall we go, my lady? ' asked Lioncel gently.

' No, not yet. I've been silly as well as rude. You don't like my talking about my husband . . . I think I was doing it to prove to myself that I know I shouldn't be so happy as I am here at this moment.'

' My lady! '

' Of course, I *could* be a little happier.'

' How? ' asked Lioncel, so softly she only just heard him.

' If you could forget that I have a husband, that I'm a duchess, with duties and castles and all the damned rest of it.'

'If you weren't, you wouldn't be here with me,' said Lioncel, who had gone white and still.

'Very well. Suppose I'm not. This is another Yolande who's here with you. An elf-woman if you like, born in a Green Mound. Something to terrify Algidus. . . .'

'Something to terrify me,' said Lioncel, and took her in his arms and kissed her. . . .

Presently, with his lips on her throat and the white-gold hair half-blinding her, she whispered that it would be quite warm in the mouth of the cave. Only the late sun saw them seal their tender love for each other. Lioncel was clumsier than Diomede, and shyer, but Yolande was not shy. She had supposed it impossible to find such joy twice over.

After a while, as they lay still, hearing only each other's heartbeat, with perhaps the bark of a fox or the faint splash of a leaping fish, Yolande laughed.

'What is it?' murmured Lioncel, pulling closer the cloak he had drawn over them.

'Something Belphegor said when he came to Pardelin. He hoped our pages there would not prove too ladylike.'

Lioncel laughed too, and then grew very solemn.

'Yolande.'

'Yes?'

'Don't tell Diomede. I think it might hurt him.'

'Do you? Of course I won't tell him. Come to me tonight, won't you? Heuradys won't tell either.'

'O my lovely lady . . . look, the evening star, Venus, blessing us as we honour her. It's time we left this happy place to the scandalised ghosts of the old hermits.'

Their skiff stole out into the light of afterglow. Yolande trailed a hand in the water and sang as she neared Pardelin.

XIV

YOLANDE'S WAY

'JULIAN, I'm going to Roclatour,' said Yolande one day at the end of May. 'I shall be gone perhaps a week . . . what? Yes, perhaps the Sieur Odard will come back with me.'

Actually she was not going to Roclatour at all; the Tripping-Goes had brought from there old clothing and a body-stain and lutes less ornamental than Yolande's in the castle. The four comrades were going to venture out among the villages along the road to Hautarroy.

This meant leaving all but one of their horses in a forester's hut high up in the hills. The forester, bribed with gold and the promise of more gold, accepted the sortie as a great joke and promised to feed and water the animals.

Grooms blinked when the scrubbiest palfrey was ordered for Heuradys; the palfrey was to carry the lutes and stormcloaks and food and wine, or anyone who tired on the steeps of the north-east corner of the Casque. All these were concealed in the cave, and the first day was spent in climbing the pass and doubling back along the heights to come down to the hermitage and re-equip the expedition.

Quargis, left in the castle, had condemned the sortie as crazy; but it was against all likelihood that any message should come to the castle in their absence, for all the might and grandeur of Neustria was now in or converging on Hautarroy.

'Except the poor neglected Duchess of Baraine,' said Yolande, with her hands on the shoulders of Quargis. 'I must have practice, you know. I mustn't give my fellow-minstrels away.'

To the horror of the squires, she cut her hair short to the shoulders like a page's. It appeared that they had overlooked this obvious necessity.

Julian, too, shook his head, but the climbing and riding had accustomed him to ducal whimsies, and he was glad to keep the garrison intact. The garrison itself would soon be a problem, for at the end of June it was due for replacement and duty elsewhere; but the end of June was a month away, and the summer clouds cast grateful shadows on rocks and heather and bracken of the pass as the four walked their horses up the first steep slopes towards it. . . .

Lioncel and Diomede changed their clothes at the foot of the hermitage stairway. Yolande stripped in the cave, and Heuradys painted as much of her as prudence dictated. By midday they were leading the palfrey along high sheep-tracks north of Siege Gracious.

'Dame, let my young brother stay here with you, will you? He's got a croak in his throat and can't sing; no use his coming to the convent with us. Give him some supper and a drink or two with this, and keep the rest.'

Diomede slid a silver coin into the hand of the innkeeper's fat wife, who revolved by a steaming cook-pot and nodded and winked good-naturedly at Yolande.

Yolande had remembered that in the convent was a nun who had helped to nurse her at Roclatour. So the others went alone to sing to the good sisters, leaving her bunched on a settle near the fire in the smoky village tavern.

Composed enough, if a little forlorn, she accepted black bread and a rib of pork and a helping of cheese so harsh that it made her gums ache. There was also a cup of second-best wine, and the come-and-go of village custom to entertain her.

This was the third night out from Pardelin; to Yolande it no longer seemed inevitable that the quarrelsome country voices would lead up to fisticuffs and stabbings. Seed-corn, waggon-wheels, hedging and ditching, someone dead and heriot to be found, someone else married at the point of a pitchfork, the miller (God rot him) to be paid, the convent baliff (fiend fly off with his soul in a sack) to be satisfied about the cutting of a dog's claws. . . .

'Drink up,' advised the innkeeper's wife, sitting down beside

Yolande. 'How's trade? That's a good nag you've got . . .
it's what we mostly judge by. Strapping lads your brother and
his friend. They stand so straight you'd think they'd been
soldiers. The little boy looks sulky. You'll be for the midsummer fairs in the plain?'

'Ay, that's where we're going,' said Yolande, roughening
her voice.

'Not so many of your kind round this year,' said the woman.
'They're all huddling at Hautarroy like flies on a cow-pat. I
wish them a merrier outcome than when our little duchess was
married. D'you remember that?'

'Ay, I heard about it.'

'I've scarcely heard of her since. Some say she's a bit of a
dotterel, like. And the young duke's not been near her yet;
keeping too many other men's wives warm at court, they say.
But there, it's part of the curse of the castles. All the castle
folk are crazy, or go crazy in the end.'

'Do they?' asked Yolande.

'Ay, that they do. Sitting up there, idle and greedy, watching
serfs' bottoms up-ended in the fields. With a pack of archers
and suchlike to fight each other. Protecting the country, they
call it; it's them the country needs protecting against. Mostly
what we see of them is bottoms and all, bumping up and down
in the saddles instead of stopping to spend a coin.'

'But the Grand Seneschal rules right, doesn't he?' asked
Yolande innocently.

'Nobody rules right, except a wife that rules her husband.
The Grand Seneschal's taxes are as hard to pay as anyone else's.
Oh, ay, he won a great battle, and got us a new duke, but by
all accounts that lad isn't one you'd want on your doorstep.'

'Why, what does he do?'

'Nay, there's tales about him . . . he must be madder than
the nightmare's groom that goes to bite the moon for a pasty.'

'I reckon it's just tales, isn't it? How do they know, if he's
never been near?'

'He's got a castle up in the hills, near the king's town of
Hastain. There's a torture-chamber there, the finest in the
kingdom. I know a woman whose husband's cousin supplies

that castle with lime. They use a lot of lime, in a tower where they put the bodies when he's finished with 'em. All screwed out of shape they are, or flayed, or nailed together. People who'd done nothing to him or anyone else . . . poor devils who never asked nothing but to get blind drunk six times a year. He just wants to see how near you can get to killing without finishing it. And how people break down into beasts and betray each other. What he'll be like when he does come, God only knows.'

'This is good wine,' said Yolande, a little faintly.

'One more, then. Your brother mustn't come back and find you pitching folk out of the tavern.'

During the next four days the wanderers sang in a castle hall and in the yards of two taverns, helped a waggoner haul his waggon out of a slough, saw a man hanged for stabbing his brother, and found crows tearing the bodies of a dead woman and her dead new-born baby in a wood. Driving the crows away, they buried the poor bodies and said prayers over the grave. That night they spent on heather in the lee of a crag; near midnight, under a half-grown moon, Lioncel awoke the others by shooting with his great crossbow at something that came near their fire and crashed away into darkness and silence.

The next evening again found them back at Pardelin. Mist and moonlight wrapped the place in unforgettable beauty. The squires rowed Yolande and Heuradys down the enchanted lake.

'It's like some night at Camelot,' said Yolande dreamily, 'except that King Arthur's ladies weren't sore from scrubbing brown stain off their noses.'

In mid-lake Lioncel and Diomede shipped their oars, and Heuradys took the lute and sang.

> '*There is a vale of wonder,*
> *Between the silent fells,*
> *Where dark-brow'd Florimunda*
> *Rides out with silver bells*
> *And weaves strange spells.*

' *The hawthorn turns to greet her,*
    The pine awakes from dream,
And sharply to entreat her
    Beside the dashing stream
      The curlew scream.

' *And I, who follow after*
    While valley folk can see,
Shall share her secret laughter
    When, riding knee to knee
      She sings with me.

' *Alone of all who dwell there*
    She reads the carven rocks;
Her sorceries compel there
    A company that mocks
      The dawn-shrill cocks.

' *And I, who hold her bridle*
    While the blue candles flare,
Know all my prayers are idle,
    Know all the doom we dare,
      And do not care.

' *For many a rose-red morning*
    When all the rout has gone
My love in her adorning
    Lets fall her jewelled zone
      For me alone.

' *So on a night of thunder*
    Great demons, I foretell,
Will strangle Florimunda,
    And bear her soul to hell,
      And mine as well.'

' And they lived happily ever after,' said Diomede softly, and everybody laughed.

Then Lioncel sang *Green Mounds*, and Yolande sang the song that so upset Dom Ursus, and Diomede sang *Excalibur* and *Eglantine,* as on the far-off day when Yolande and he waited for Lioncel and the wild strawberries. Lastly they all sang together to the dip and flash of the oars.

Yolande determined that some night soon she would swim by moonlight.

Five days later when Diomede was at Roclatour, Lioncel slipped into her hand a scroll with a new poem on it. There was no title; it needed none. Yolande sat in the rampart garden and read it, with pigeons floating and flapping and cooing around the corner turret where they lived.

> ' *Against a golden west*
> *The poplar leaves are stirring;*
> *Headlong, with wings whirring,*
> *A blackbird seeks her nest.*
> *Far off are tower and town,*
> *Envy and greed and snarling;*
> *My joy, my brown darling,*
> *Do off your green gown.*
>
> ' *No one may discover us*
> *Here on the hidden sward;*
> *The downward path is barr'd,*
> *The cliff hangs over us.*
> *So gain'd some gentle hermit*
> *Escape from harsh mankind*
> *Nor guess'd our love would find*
> *A like sweet permit.*
>
> ' *If any fiend assail'd him*
> *In shape so firm and fine,*
> *I know not, heart of mine,*
> *How sanctity avail'd him.*
> *Nor may your lover wonder*
> *The wanton wind should lift*
> *The edges of your shift*
> *To kiss what glows under.*

' Enchantment to behold,
Triumphant in surrender,
Brown body strong and tender,
Blue veins amid the gold.
Here no denials are,
And over all the sweetness,
The madness, the completeness,
A purple cloud-bar
And a blazing silver star.'

Yolande read the poem three times, kissed it, and went to lock it away with her other treasures. That night Lioncel rowed her out alone.

The moon was nearing the full now, and again the night was misty though warm. The little tent was up in the boat; Yolande had intended to swim in a linen tunic caught up like a loin-cloth, but when she saw the moon slide in beauty behind tall pine-crests she exclaimed impatiently and let the last of her clothing fall around her feet. Her head was bare, and to keep her shortened hair out of her eyes she wore as a fillet a broad red ribbon with a silver star pinned in front of it.

Lioncel said her name quietly as she stepped from between the curtains. She stood upright, cream-gold in the moonlight, arms at her sides, with palms turned forward a little, giving her loveliness gladly to his grave worship. Then she sprang over-board, straightening her knees, vanishing with a neat splash, leaving the boat shuddering at the heart of a thousand points of watery glitter.

Her dark head split the surface again, her smooth arms and shoulders glimmered among the ripples, and Lioncel leaned on his oars entranced, only beginning to row again when she called to him to keep pace with her.

For perhaps a hundred yards she swam parallel with the shore; then she turned and laid a hand on the gunwale, point-ing with the other.

' I'm going to see what that white thing is,' she said. ' Pull in a little, will you? See, there, under the trees.'

' I think you'd better not,' he began, but already she had

slipped away and was heading a pointed shoreward ripple.
Lioncel paddled to keep her in sight, swinging the boat into
the shadow of a tall island rock about twenty yards from the
water's edge. Yolande was already erect, striding through the
the shallows; her body moved in the moonlight like that of a
heathen water-goddess. Mountains, trees, and lake seemed
enchanted; Lioncel saw the flash of her smile as she turned to
call over her shoulder. His heart was near to breaking under
the strain of perfection.

'Music, Chevalier Lioncelot!'

Groping for the lute, he found himself trying to play the
crossbow.

'It's a stag's head, mightily-antlered,' she called. 'He was a
great hart of ten. I'm going to take it . . . no, better not, the
forester'll think some poor devil of a serf has stolen it.'

Lioncel found the lute and began to play softly. Yolande
moved among the trees, with shadows sliding and checking
like kisses all over her body. She lifted the bony relic by its
antlers, and dropped it again quickly. . . .

A husky howl split the music-haunted hush and echoed up
against a crag at the foot of Siege Orgulous .

'Avaunt, avaunt, avaunt, fiend!' yelled the hermit Algidus,
bouncing out of the shadowy thickets with both arms raised
and eyes starting out of his head. 'Back to hell, back to hell,
in nomine Patris, Filii, et Spiritus Sancti, amen!'

'Go away,' said Yolande crossly. She had caught up the
skull again, screening herself a little. Skipping sideways into
the water, she backed and then stood her ground, ankle-deep
and scowling. Lioncel had snatched up the crossbow and all
but pulled the trigger; then he had grasped an oar and thrust
it deep to keep the boat still.

'Get you behind me, Satan!' screeched Algidus. 'You're
sent to tempt me into mortal sin . . . I spit on your filthy allure-
ments . . . I command you to obedience . . . I conjure you,
return to the shape of your beastliness!'

'If you want me behind you, turn round, you fool, and go
away!' she shouted in exasperation. Lioncel was splashing
shore now, with her cloak held out. Algidus, jumping up and

N

down, suddenly stopped bellowing and gasped; then he gave a
great groan, as though the dreadful truth had dawned on
him.

All his hermit's life, no doubt, he had longed for such a
distinction—a fiend disguised as a naked woman, sent to test
his sanctity. And now . . . a night walk in the teeth of evil
magic from the waxing moon . . . insidious music of the powers
of air . . . a fiend sufficient for Saint Anthony's own studied
inattention, surprised in the act of changing his shape from
that of a horned stag . . . perfect proof that modest Algidus held
rank as an enemy of the Enemy . . . and then something had
gone wrong, and he couldn't even see what the hosts of hell
should most rely upon for his destruction.

' Go home! ' growled Lioncel in a fury, flinging the cloak
round Yolande's shoulders, and gripping an antler by one
great tine to swing the skull away from her. The stag had
died when his antlers were coming to their term; the horn
cracked across at the root, and the skull splashed in the shallow
water. Algidus jumped and stood gibbering, and Lioncel
swore and threw the antler at him.

Foiled of one glory, Algidus fell on his knees and swiped at
another, a crown of martyrdom. But the antler only buffeted
his shoulder and glanced off into the bushes. He let out a yell,
clasped his hands over his head, and was still noisily adjusting
the matter with heaven when Lioncel dropped Yolande on the
cushions of the boat and climbed in to fend off and escape.

Two hundred yards away Yolande stopped towelling herself
to laugh. Lioncel was grim for a few more yards, and then
collapsed on his oars.

' Rout of Lioncelot and the Lady of the Lake,' he gasped.
' Sanctity sufficiently availed *him*. He's stopped yowling now.
He'll have started off home with the skull, working up a
seemly version of his encounter with the Adversary.'

He rowed across the lake and into the shadow of rocks on the
opposite shore.

' If anyone was awake within a league they must have heard
him,' said Yolande. ' He's brave, to wander about so far from
his cell.'

'Not brave,' said Lioncel. 'Immune from fear. Poor carle, how his eyes stuck out! I suppose there's a moral somewhere . . . brr!'

'You're cold,' said Yolande remorsefully, but presently they were both quite warm again.

Diomede brought back a letter addressed to Odard at Roclatour. It had been dropped by a courier riding from Hautarroy to Jarapt; and it bore the seal of Baraine. It said that the duke was coming to Roclatour with seven in his company, and wanted his duchess there to meet him.

'There's even a letter to me enclosed,' Yolande told her friends. 'Dated at Hautarroy five days ago . . . that's two days before the wedding.'

'*Most Excellent Duchess and my Lady Wife, lovingly I commend myself to you. Concerning the duty we owe to the duchy, be ready at Roclatour on the day of Saint Barnabas. I shall stay for a night or two only, and then make haste to Jarapt. Your loving master and dutiful servant, Balthasar.*

'*Have a personable woman at hand for Camus. For the rest, six women of the town will serve.*'

No one spoke for a moment.

'I wonder what sends him to Jarapt,' said Yolande, laying down the letter. 'No matter, these are our marching orders. We must carry enough food and drink to keep us out of taverns . . . and that reminds me, not for any ransom will I leave behind my little keg of *beym*. It may yet put a Council of Baraine to sleep and give me a chance to govern.'

On that last day at Pardelin Yolande wandered through the castle from the boathouse tower to the rampart garden, now watching through window or archery-slit the sunlight of leafy June and the quiver of heat on the mountain ranges, now turning to look at dust and cobwebs, or at the long scratches on the stones in the passage where her father had died fighting.

When she came to the garden itself she heard a curious resonant rattling sound; Lioncel and Diomede sprang up from a bench when they found her watching them.

' I'm the only duchess,' she said, ' who ever found her whole army playing dice on one drum. What are you staking? '

' The other provinces of Neustria, my lady,' said Lioncel ruefully. ' I've only Arroy and Nordanay left. Diomede's had the luck.'

' Let me join in with Baraine,' she said, and sat down between them. Whether they cheated or not to arrive at the result, she won the whole kingdom from them in quite a short time.

' Where did you find the drum? ' she asked, and Lioncel answered.

' In the old armoury,' he said. ' There was a mouldy snake-skin there too, for repairing it I suppose, and a heap of antlers, and some caltrops, and a thumbscrew, and this white wand for a steward, and that rusty little mace.'

' Antlers,' said Diomede. ' Quargis was telling me our hermit's had a visit, or visitation, from a horned fiend that came up out of the lake, and turned into a beautiful maiden. But he exorcised it back into its proper shape and fought it, and tore one of its antlers off, and has it there to show.'

' Wonders will never cease,' said Lioncel.

Yolande picked up the white wand and held it out to Diomede.

' I've just won a kingdom,' she said, ' and I need a Lord High Steward.'

Diomede bowed and kissed her hand. She turned on Lioncel with the mace.

' And a Lord High Constable,' she told him, putting it into his hand. Lioncel fell on one knee and kissed her fingers.

' If only Belphegor were here,' she reflected, ' I could give him *two* fine pairs of antlers.'

She looked through the window into the dusty room.

' Antlers,' she said aloud to herself, and turned away and took an arm of each of her lovers. The moment was perfect in its way, for they were all three sharing the ancient joke, although Lioncel and Diomede each had only half of it.

Yolande thought of that little conceit later, when supper was laying and the sentinel's horn brought everybody's head up.

Lioncel darted out upon the twilit ramparts; the archer on duty pointed to a sail bearing along the lake.

'It's the old barge they keep at Quatrelances, sir,' the archer called to Julian, who was down in the courtyard.

Diomede armed and corseleted, Yolande and Heuradys in their morrow's hunting-gear, Quargis with his crossbow tucked under one arm and the boathouse tower keys in his hand, waited in the solar. Lioncel came in a second time, and now his face was white.

'Eight in the boat,' he said. 'They're going to beach it, I think, instead of coming in to the tower. We've about ten minutes.'

Yolande put her hand on the little keg of *beym*.

'If it's Belphegor and his party,' she said stonily, 'can we put the castle, his men and ours, asleep with this? Have them all in the hall, to drink a health to this auspicious night? All but ourselves, that is Heuradys and I, with Diomede as . . .'

'As steward,' said Diomede, taking the white wand up from a window-sill, 'He might remember my name. I am now Taurus de Taure, appointed by Odard de Xantroy.'

'Yes. Lioncel and Quargis must hide. I must have a word with Julian, and meet the duke myself. Plead for a private supper in the solar here, Camus and he and I. Heuradys to serve us. Diomede carves. Lioncel and Quargis take the nearest cask of Estragon, let out a good couple of jugsfull and put in the *beym*, and let Julian have it in charge on a table in the hall. . . .'

Their quiet voices whipped the plot into desperate shape.

'Dom Cyril?'

'Quargis gives him a draught, and locks him in for his safety.'

'The cooks and all must go into the hall for that toast. . . .'

'Everyone but the man on the turret and the man at the gate.'

'I'll take them each a separate cup.'

'The women must go back to the village.'

'The villagers must be kept out—not enough food, we'll say.'

'Then we must somehow separate my lady and Heuradys from Belphegor and Camus.'

'Get them alone in the courtyard with all the doors locked.'

'And then . . . and then . . . '

It was Belphegor, surely enough, with Camus de Caherne and six tall reckless-looking soldiers. When the boat grounded Yolande was standing alone under the portcullis, with the keys of the castle in her hands. A star winked at her from between Sieges Perilous and Orgulous. She had put on some of the perfume called Memory of Doves, and a sweat of terror brought it strongly up to her nostrils. . . . Villagers were scurrying up to form a group at a respectful distance. She knew most of them now by name, but they were always too much awed for her to consider them as possible supporters. . . .

She had made a confession to Dom Cyril earlier in the day, a sad little confession of trifles. And now she was probably going to die unshriven of a load of deadly sin. And she was unrepentant, even commending herself to the Sieur Jesu and His Mother, thanking them for the love and comfort she had had from her friends, begging them to look after those friends if they could not protect her any more.

Belphegor had taken off his helmet; his golden hair gleamed in the twilight, his tread was spurred and crisp and terrible on the pebbled shore. He might have been one of the great soldier-saints—Michael, Dionysius, Joris—except that the slight lift at the outer corners of his eyes brought an ambiguous note of blankness or intensity into his expression. Their irises were the sovereign blue of Sigurd's when he slew the dragon.

'Why, Yolande, you've grown into a beauty,' he said, his voice deeper than she remembered. His right hand caught hers to his mouth, and came up to tilt her chin. A triumphant greedy kiss flattened her lips against her teeth.

'My lord,' she got out hoarsely, 'I render you the keys of your castle. You're very welcome here, but we had no time to prepare . . .'

'Ha! What matter? I remembered how the message came about Drogo Boqueron, and thought I'd have another look at this lost lonely place. Our horses will follow tomorrow. Find-

ing you here has saved time . . . there's great doings to tell
you. Where's Odard de Xantroy?'

'My lady Jehane died, and he married one of my damsels
secretly and ran away with her . . . last week.'

'What? That stick of melancholy!' cried Balthasar with
a shout of laughter. 'Camus, come here: de Xantroy's shot the
moon with a wench!'

The tall dark chevalier bowed in his turn over her hand.
The life he shared with the duke had not been kind to his round
dark face.

'It's left me with a very scanty household,' she went on,
offering her fingers to Belphegor once again. 'My father confessor is sick, and I have only one damsel, and a squire to act
as steward, and Captain Julian to command the garrison.'

Her husband took her hand, and she led him into the castle.
Villagers and servants cheered, Heuradys curtseyed, Diomede
bowed with his white wand well to the fore, Julian saluted with
four archers presenting swords behind him.

'I gave your Quatrelances men a scare, captain,' said the duke
jovially. 'But they were inside their tower and all set to break
our teeth by the time we reached it.'

The serving-men had wine on trays, and Belphegor handed
a cup to Yolande. His blue eyes twinkled as he touched the
breast of his shield-embroidered tabard. Golden Leopard and
red Thunderbolt appeared side by side on their fields of purple
and black. He leaned aside and spoke in her ear.

'Here's to my impalement of a leopardess!' he said.

At this crude but heraldic jest Yolande summoned a stiff
smile. The newcomers shouted and drank to her, and she led
Belphegor into the hall.

'My lord,' she said, looking up into his bronzed and godlike
face, 'you won't mind my giving them a cask of Estragon
here tonight?'

'Why, no, who could grudge it? I'm getting more than
Estragon. Is that little piece game for Camus?'

'Oh, yes, my lord. But will you and he sup with me in the
solar? We can come to the hall for a toast or two . . . I'm still
a little shy, my lord. . . .'

'Hey? Very well, but we'll soon put an end to shyness. We'll eat where you like so long as all the wine isn't in here too.'

'There's plenty for the castle, my lord, but I'm shutting the village people out, for we were expecting to move tomorrow and our food is short. They can have an ox to roast tomorrow. . . .'

'Yes, yes, have it as you like. Is there a page to take my helmet?'

'No, my lord. The steward, Master Taurus, will attend you to the bath.'

Diomede bowed again and led the way upstairs.

'Who are you?' demanded Belphegor, clanking after him into the chamber where the great tub steamed.

'Taurus de Taure, my lord, of Zoriot in Beltany. Shall I help you unarm? The boys are only grooms.'

'No. How long have you been here?'

'Six months, my lord. My family and the Sieur de Xantroy's were neighbours when I was a child.'

'Well, Taurus de Taure, I don't much like your face, or being attended by a steward with a corselet and a sword.'

'I'll change my clothing, my lord duke. We stood to arms, not knowing it was Your Grace who came.'

'And find someone to clean this armour properly.'

'Yes, my lord duke.'

'And now get out, and send two of my men up with my saddle-bags.'

'Yes, my lord duke.'

Diomede bowed himself out, found the men, and went to change into a black robe furred with grey. He clasped a chain of Largire silver round his waist, and swung from it a purse and dagger to match. In the purse was his share of the *capagot*; he looked at the vial oddly before putting it there.

There were tiny beads of moisture on his forehead as he combed his hair at his little steel mirror.

Yolande and Heuradys had worked miracles of speed; their horned headdresses glistened in the solar when

Diomede returned to it. Yolande was in crimson and gold, Heuradys in green and silver; except that they both wore their own thick eyebrows they could have passed muster in any provincial city.

They were squeezing each other's hands beneath the level of the table. Hearing the duke approach, Diomede signalled in the goose and the capons; the frightened serving-men darted upstairs with silver covers. Diomede began to carve, his face like doom; Heuradys rose and stood behind Yolande's chair, and the postponed marriage-feast was ready.

The duke came in, in sky-blue, with Camus in particolour of violet and tawny. Both wore jewelled sword-belts, and jewels encrusted the hilts of their swords and daggers.

'Dom Cyril blesses the bread from afar,' said Yolande. 'He prays for you and begs you to visit him tomorrow.'

'Eh? Oh, yes. We'll have some more to confess by then.'

'Heuradys, serve my lord. Tell me, my lord, all about the wedding. Is the little princess very beautiful?'

'It was a fitting progress, and a very gay wedding. The princess is a square little wench, red in the cheeks, with black eyes slanted and a little staring, and a mouth like a raspberry split across. She's only eight, of course, and may improve. I thought the Duke of Honoy had a fright when he first saw her. Her clothes were so stiff with jewels, she looked like a doll.'

'Our Lady comfort her, so far from home,' said Yolande compassionately.

'Eh? Yes, of course, amen. But what I wanted to tell you about is a great plot that's come to light . . . a plot to kill the king. . . .'

'My lord!'

'Yes, kill the king and seize the queen and the newly-wedded children, and set up rule in the boy-king's name, by a group of the northern lords who've lost some of their power and places.'

'My lord!' exclaimed Yolande again, and started and laughed as a roaring cheer came up from the hall.

'They're drinking our healths, my lord,' she said. 'We'll go down later. Tell me about this dreadful plot.'

'Not only the king was to be killed,' went on Belphegor, through a mouthful of goose. 'My sweet cousin and wife, you were to be made a widow. My father, Elquitaine, Ahun, and the Chancellor were all to be quitted of mortal troubles. There were our names in a list, with the signatures of our would-be takers-off, and six acorns on a spray in token of their league. The acorn is the badge of Honoy.'

'But who were these villainous lords?'

'Saulte the displaced chancellor, Olencourt the Constable whose castellany of Montenair the king gave to me, Ger who's been jealous of my father since Arionbel, Saint-Aunay who's Ger's upstart crony, and a couple of bishops of poor family who still ought to have known better.'

'But my lord, it was found out and broken?'

'A trusty captain of my father's, a man called Radomar, intercepted a message going from Saulte to the Constable. We were all to be arrested last night. Instead, it's the others who'll be arrested.'

The sentinel's horn gave a split kind of bellow. Lioncel was not so skilful as the archers. A vague uproar swelled and died and swelled again in the hall. Yolande needed no artifice to look startled.

'Steward,' she said, 'go and see what that means.'

Diomede laid down his carvers, picked up his wand, and glided out.

'I don't think you'll find that you'll need that young man much longer,' said Belphegor after a drink.

'There was no one else,' Yolande explained. 'He's rather glum, but I think he caught that from Odard de Xantroy.'

'Maybe he did. I suppose this isn't Odard come back, pursued by his new wife?'

A faint banging and shouting drifted up from below. Diomede reappeared, looking worried.

'My lord duke, a messenger from Roclatour. He wants to speak with you at once. May we have the keys to let him in?'

'One messenger?'

'Yes, my lord duke. Badged with the Leopard.'

'Here you are.'

The keys were thrown at rather than to Diomede, but he caught them and slipped out.

'Were you expecting a messenger, my lord?' asked Yolande brightly.

'No,' said Belphegor, and champed for a moment. Camus reached a long arm behind Yolande's chair, and pinched Heuradys, who gave him a sideways smile.

Diomede came padding upstairs again, still very anxious.

'My lord duke, he's wounded,' he said.

'What's that?'

'He's wounded and can't come up; he's lying in the guard-room. They could hardly get him off his horse. He says he must speak to you yourself. He's bleeding, my lord.'

'God damn all bleeding messengers!' said Belphegor irritably. 'Come on, Camus, let's see what it's all about.'

'My lord, the poor man,' twittered Yolande. 'Shall I bring bandages and water?'

'Yes, do,' said her husband. 'And hurry up about it.'

'This way, if it please you, my lord duke,' purred Diomede, holding a lighted taper.

'It doesn't please me at all, you maggot,' said Belphegor. 'Lead on.'

Diomede descended a turret stair, crossed a little stone lobby half-full of fire-logs, and paused with his back to the in-swung door, holding the taper for the duke's emergence.

Then he moved out into the cobbled courtyard, where only a torch or two burned in high wall-brackets. There was a confused sound from the hall; its windows were high, and their lit rank patterned the dark wall on the opposite side of the enclosure.

Diomede swallowed, and gestured towards the blackness of the gateway arch, where a strip of light fell obliquely from the guard-room doorway.

'Julian's in there with him, my lord duke. Shall I wait to light my lady duchess down the stair?'

'Huh? Yes, I suppose so.'

'This way, my lord duke,' said Lioncel from inside the guardroom.

As the magnificent figure came under the gateway arch Lioncel slammed the guardroom door and bolted it.

A startled shout from the duke went up with the answering clang of the other door. Camus de Caherne spun on his heel, but Diomede had slipped back inside, and Quargis, standing among logs against the wall behind the door, had two bolts shot before the weight of the swearing Camus thudded against the iron-scrolled oak.

'Open up, you dung-faced ape!' roared Camus, flashing his sword-point in at the archery-slit on one side of the doorway.

Diomede stood breathing deeply, holding up the taper. Quargis chuckled, picked up a faggot, and beat the bright steel out into the darkness.

'Camus!' he said. 'Camus! Go and tell Belphegor that a thousand good curses have come home to roost!'

The angry chevalier outside snarled something in reply, but it was lost in the rending crash of the dropped portcullis.

That crash was what Yolande first heard as she carried a torch out on to the rampart walk thirty feet above the cobbles. The walk was doubly-parapeted, joining the second floor of the keep with the outer rampart walk. Below her on the left was the lobby door, with Camus stamping and swearing beside it; farther away to the right, Belphegor emerged from the blackness of the gateway. At sight of her both men stood still, sword in hand, staring upwards.

'Is this a joke, my crimson lily?' asked the duke, as if prepared to find it one.

'No, my lord,' said Yolande. 'It's a trap, and you're the rats in the trap.'

'If you try to throw your dagger I shoot you in the back,' said Lioncel from the parapet of the gate-tower above Belphegor.

The duke looked up and backed to the wall. With three graceful bounds Camus skipped to his side.

'And if you try it from there, *my lord duke*,' said Diomede, now on the lowest keep ramparts and level with Yolande, 'if you try it from there I shoot you in the belly.'

Belphegor's battle voice thundered out, fearless and magnificent.

'*Hamo! Constantine! Flambard! To me! Montguiscard! A Montguiscard!*'

The resonances climbed their stone shell and died in the calm summer night. Yolande's torch spluttered, and she held it down and away a little. Heuradys, with an arrow nocked on her bowstring, stood close to the keep door of the walk.

'No use, my lord,' said Yolande. 'Your men and all the castle people are drugged in honour of this merry occasion. All the doors are locked against you, there's no place where an arrow cannot find you, and all the ghosts of the people you've tormented are come out of that tower at Sabloyn to watch you die.'

'Listen, my duchess, my duckling,' said Belphegor almost amicably. 'I don't know who your friends are, except the maggoty steward and that little whore up there, but if you drop the castle keys they can all go free, and I'll even spare you the spanking you deserve.'

'Listen to me again, Belphegor,' said Yolande steadily. 'Your father set the outlaws on to kill my father here. The boat from which I was saved, as they called it, was made by this damsel's father in secret. Your father then no doubt had him killed, as he had the outlaws killed when they had taken the castle. Do you remember the two pages who served us the night we first met? You thought they might prove too ladylike. Both of them escaped, both of them are here, both of them served the Chevalier de Largire . . . and neither of them's a lady.'

'Hey there, my lord,' said Lioncel, leaning out at a crenel. 'We met at Sabloyn too, but then it was you looked down and I looked up. Lioncel's my name, and I killed your lion instead of going as gobbets into the lion's cell.'

'And what has the other gentleman against me?' asked the duke, pointing with his sword at Diomede.

'What any gentleman has against you,' replied Diomede coldly. 'The sickening mean bloody soul of a hyena behind your *bel figor*.'

'Your steward has a turn of phrase, my lady,' said the duke. 'Tell me, is there anyone else in this league?'

'Yes, there's Quargis,' said the dwarf harshly, through the slit by the lobby door.

'Quargis?' repeated the duke.

'Yes, Quargis, whom you called a hump-backed ordure, and sent to be killed because he knew too much. Quargis who knows you wear mail under your satin, and can see you talking out of the side of your mouth to cut-throat Camus. Quargis who kept *cave* while you cuckolded the king, and watched you kill Guy of Burias in the churchyard at Maradette.'

'You saw that, clever Quargis?' said Belphegor mockingly. 'Is this all your array, my lady?'

'Yes. It will serve your turn. Do you think it too few?'

'No. I was remembering how many hooks there are on a certain wall at Sabloyn. There's just enough for your friends to hang on to get a good view of what'll happen to *you*.'

'Tell me what you mean to do to me,' said Yolande, sticking her torch in a socket and shading her eyes to get a better sight of the smiling mask of rage and wickedness below.

Belphegor told her, his self-control cracking towards the end, so that he finished by screaming and cutting shapes in the air with his jewelled sword. Yolande listened, her mind attentive, her body twitching here and there. Politely she forbore to call on the Sieur Jesu, who suffered on Calvary that the soul of Balthasar de Montguiscard might be saved among the rest.

'*And you'll still be alive!*' yelled the nonpareil of Neustria, with foam on his curled-back lips and a glaze of confused lusts in his eyes.

Yolande pushed the spike of her crossbow out over the edge of the merlon against which she leaned.

'Wipe your mouth, slaverer,' she said, 'and listen to me.

Your plot's known. The names on that scroll under the acorns are forged. Saulte and Ger and the rest can prove them nothing like their own. *I* wrote those names that have fooled you and your friends. There were seven acorns at first, and seven names, were there not? The king knows by now how you planned to deceive him, and how you killed Burias and plotted with Gaston de Volsberghe. I think your thunderbolt is broken . . . and one last jog to your memory, Belphegor. *Do you remember my kitten?* '

Her husband stood as if rooted to the spot, staring up at her vengeful face. Diomede's crossbow rasped on stone, the horn tip of the longbow of Heuradys glistened in the torchlight. Lioncel grunted, shifting a lump of lead sewn into sacking to make it a handier missile. Quargis had gone from behind his door, and was carrying torches round the rampart walk, lighting them and setting them here and there to show up dark corners. Camus de Caherne was watching him, and Diomede was watching the faint gleam of the whites of the eyes of Camus.

Yolande picked up her crossbow.

'*It was very foolish of you,*' she said, '*to kill my kitten.*'

She loosed off at his throat and missed by an inch; he shrank against the wall and bounded away, the bolt skidding in front of him. Lioncel's lead weight jarred the cobblestones just behind the heel of forward-leaping Camus, who yelled as Diomede's bolt tore his left thigh above the knee.

Two such powerful athletes could have got on the stable roof by swarming up the wooden pipe that led rain-water into a horse-trough, but that Quargis waited for that attempt, and nailed Belphegor's gem-ringed hand to the gutter as it came over. The other hunters were following Quargis round the ramparts; Diomede was dimly aware of noise outside the gate.

'Villagers wondering what's happening,' he thought, and dismissed the matter.

Belphegor had wrenched his shattered hand out of the gutter, and with calm ferocity continued to climb, boosted by Camus below him. Horses, frightened by the noise, stamped and fidgeted in the stable; from the far side of the courtyard Lioncel shot Camus in one arm just as Diomede put a bolt through both of Belphegor's cheeks.

Belphegor, still silent, dropped the sword from between his teeth, stretched his neck, and fell backwards, taking Camus with him into a kicking heap on the dunghill. Two torches gave light there; crossbows and longbow hummed and spat, finishing what they had begun. At such range the best mail was not proof against archery.

Once the disfigured Belphegor struggled up, swinging his sword at Lioncel on the rampart wall above him, but Lioncel parried the steel with his crossbow, and it rang sweetly back on stone. Belphegor shook his fist in the air and said something that sounded like 'Cowards!'

'This isn't a fight, it's an execution,' said Yolande, although he could not hear. She was reloading without knowing she did it; the last bolt she used sank up to its feathers in Belphegor's back.

He arched over and fell flat and lay still. Camus was already prone, a bristle of bolts and arrows. Lioncel strode back to the gateway towers to fetch the keys. . . .

Five minutes later he was holding a torch over the sprawling corpses. Quargis picked up one of the jewelled swords and looked at Yolande.

'Let there be no mistake, my lady,' said Diomede hoarsely. 'Take his head to Ger . . . we shall have to leave his body. Hippocras should serve. There's some in the cellar.'

'Very well,' said Yolande, wearily, and nodded at Quargis. 'And Diomede, will you go to the gate and tell the villagers there's been a little disagreement but all is remedied now?'

Before dawn the party left with its two packhorses, one of them carrying the transfixed and gruesome head in pickle. Diomede waited behind the rest, and after a while rode down to the priest's house, taking the keys of the castle, with various orders to be read to Julian when he should come out of his drugged sleep in the castle hall.

On the pink tonsure of old Dom Cyril Yolande had

dropped an affectionate kiss, knowing that Dom Robert
would look after him. And so for an hour or more the castle
was garrisoned entirely by the priest in his bed and the men
tumbled about—one on a turret, one in a guadroom, the rest
on benches and rushes in the hall. Quargis had gone in there
with his dagger, and nobody asked him what he did.

Diomede, leaving the priest's house, saluted the full moon
as she sank behind Siege Fabulous, and watched the silver
gleam die on the topmost turret of Pardelin and on the mast
and spar whence Lioncel had removed Yolande's banner.

Passing beneath the great oak tree, he saluted that too;
life could not help but be different now, and it might be long
before he saw this corner of the province again.

He tried to recapture the moon by hastening up the road to
the pass, but the shape of the distant mountain defeated him,
spreading shadow far ahead. When he overtook the others the
five of them sat for a moment looking silently down on the
lake.

'You are all witnesses,' said Yolande abruptly, 'that I was
never alone with my husband or taken by him as his wife.'

Half an hour later they left the eastward track and struck
northward across dew-wet heather in the first paleness of
dawn.

Wild rumours were shaking along the road from Hautarroy.
Great lords were arrested, someone had tried to stab the king,
the Grand Seneschal had saved the king, the Constable had
fled the kingdom, the little Duke of Honoy was poisoned, the
Count of Ger had run off with the queen, and a woman called
Jacquerelle had had a fit in the nave of Saint Andreas, and
had spoken a remarkable rime that a clerk had the wit to take
down in his tablets.

Soon to be seen a new queen,
A queen from the East with an angry beast;
From a moorland and a dour land, but not a poor land,
After Honoy bringing joy to Hautarroy.

'No one's allowed to repeat it,' said Lioncel, who had
brought the rime back from a tavern. 'So everybody has it by

heart already. Some people say it's *annoy*, not *Honoy*, but
the mischief's done, and anyway it is as good as promises the
king hasn't long to live. They've bundled the prophetess into
a convent in case she obliges again.'

'The angry beast is the Bear of Zurland, of course,' said
Diomede.

'Or the Grand Seneschal,' said Yolande, flippant with
weariness.

They raced the rumours to Var, and found themselves in an
armed camp. Their password *Saturn* let them on to the causeway, and under the wings of wild swans in the village called
Cremalvay they met the swan banner of Marckmont, this time
floating beside the black gerfalcon of Ger.

Everyone fell back as Yolande met the Count Raoul and the
swarthy straight-nosed man whom she guessed to be the Count
of Saint-Aunay.

'You must call him Nino,' said the Count Raoul as he made
them known to one another.

The honey-coloured eyes of the Tuscan twinkled as he bent
over her hand.

'You'd better neither of you call *me* anything until you
hear what's in that little tub,' said Yolande grimly.

When she had told them there was a moment's silence,
broken only by the crowing of a cock and the creaking of a
windmill's sails beyond the village.

The two counts were in full armour except for velvet
bonnets, which both held in their hands. They and their great
destriers, one dappled and one black, towered up on either side
of Yolande's sturdy Tancred. Raoul of Ger cleared his
throat.

'That's saved a lot of trouble,' he said.

'We used a sack on a similar occasion,' said the Count of
Saint-Aunay reminiscently.

'Come, cousin, there's news to exchange,' went on the
Count Raoul, reining round and gesturing to the chevaliers
and squires who had followed him.

So, in a chasm of steel and horseflesh, Yolande rode to the

castle of Marckmont and heard what had happened at Hautarroy.

'The plot was to show us jealous and afraid, scheming to kill the king,' said Raoul. 'Saulte had lost the chancellery. If Olencourt were no longer Constable, and I no longer Warden of the Coast March, our group would consist of men ruling only for a few leagues around our various castles. . . .

'So much for motive. Now to kill the king and leave the little duke in the hands of the queen's party would advance us nothing, so all its notables were to be arrested or made away with. *I*, if you please, was to kidnap the queen and bring her here as a prisoner. . . .'

'Lioncel heard in a tavern that you'd run away with her,' said Yolande.

'Yes? Do they say the poor little Princess of Zurland—the Duchess of Honoy—has two heads and eats raw meat?'

'They're saying it's prophesied she'll very soon be queen herself,' murmured Yolande.

'You've heard that too? Cousin, you're a Peer of Baraine. Your friends are very few and evidently very faithful, but this is for you alone.'

Yolande felt the first chill end of the iron wedge of state secrecy.

'It shall be so,' she said.

The Count of Saint-Aunay made some gesture which increased the distance between the three of them and the chevalier who rode with Heuradys immediately behind. The Castle of Marckmont glowed sombrely in the rich light of the June evening; to westward, beyond the many-coloured meres, the blue horizon was dimly shaped by the Uplands of Honoy.

'None of us,' said Raoul of Ger, 'could speak to the king without some of our enemies standing by. So we had to find someone who could. He was sailing a boat on a monastery pond. . . .'

'Janus of the Silver Shield!'

'The same. For us he was Janus of the Silver Ship; he'd sent a wonderful galleon as a wedding-present to the little duke. Young Réné asked questions; in no time he was lying in the silver coffin, with the two-faced silver helm on his stomach, and the chevalier playing to him on the silver harp. . . .

'Now at court the name of Janus was something of a jest among popinjays who could none of them have lifted his battle-axe. The king was ensnared by young Réné into visiting the monastery.'

'What brought Janus in on our side?' ·

'Partly old comradeship of Pont-de-Foy; partly chivalry, a word not very well understood except by such as Janus. Partly the obstinate loyalty of your two squires, to whom the king has commanded me to give the accolade at once.'

'I was going to ask for that,' said Yolande joyfully. 'You were saying, my lord. . . .'

'And since Janus is human like the rest of us, I think he was also influenced by an overthrow in the lists, and an insult connected with one of the aforesaid squires and a lion.'

'I want to see the Chevalier Janus.'

'No doubt you will before long. Unlike you, the king expected to find a valiant but whimsical trifler. He found a student of war and history, a poet, and a collector of rare and curious jewels and statuary. But of course Elquitaine was there, and Ahun, and the Chancellor. Janus got the king alone by telling him of a particular statue which the little duke should not be allowed to see. And once alone, he asked for a private audience to read some of his memoirs to the king. . . .

'After that he had to restrain His Majesty, who as you know has red hair and a violent temper, from riding off to the Chapel of the Order of the Bridge of Faith instantly to compare the names on the Roll with the names in the copy of your mock forgery. . . .

'But the king's aware of his own hastiness, and when Janus offered him a goblet of rare Venetian glass to dash down on the tiles to ease his temper, he laughed and agreed to wait to see in what shape the mock signatures would reach him. . . .

'They reached him in due form a week later, six signatures instead of seven, under the acorn spray.'

' Belphegor told me about that.'

' So the king had to believe us, and gave us a secret audience together in the archbishop's palace. The wedding took place, the banquets and jousts began, and the king made Janus a palace marshal for the period of the festivities. So that Janus emerged in splendour from his long obscurity; and he had charge of the archers of the guard on the night of the breaking of the plot. . . .

' But just as the Montguiscards reckoned without their duchess, so we, all of us, reckoned without the queen. You know she was insanely in love with your . . . with the Duke of Baraine? '

' In love, yes, I suppose so. Insanely, no, I didn't know. Call him Belphegor.'

' She was very passionate. . . .'

' *Was*, my lord? '

' Yes, poor lady. She had coughed blood all winter, and had fancies that must be assuaged. And the duke seems to have treated her as he treated no other woman. Most of all she was afraid of his finding in *you* a happiness of the kind not common in courts. She would have done anything to keep him away from you. The king and she usually paid no attention to each other's love affairs, but it's said it was she who persuaded him to send Belphegor among those who were to meet the little princess.'

' She sent him away from herself so long as it also kept him away from me? '

' Yes. Now the plot, being largely the Grand Seneschal's, had another plot within it. That was to kill the king indeed, and let us bear the blame. And the Grand Seneschal had taken care to visit the little duke each evening at about the time he went to bed, so that when the stabbings were done, and the king's body and our bodies were strewn about in proper order, the Grand Seneschal should appear leading by the hand the new king. . . .

' And apparently Elquitaine too was to be killed, leaving the Grand Seneschal supreme in the kingdom. But all this grandeur of his was nothing unless his son could enjoy it, and

it was plain there would be some butchery that night. So like
a careful father he arranged that Belphegor should be elsewhere . . . ensuring the succession of Baraine on the way, but
actually sent to secure the old queen's treasure.'

' So *that* was what really brought Belphegor into
Baraine! '

' Yes. The Montguiscards were stealing a march on their
ally Gaston de Volsberghe.'

' My lord, how did all this come out? '

' Radomar. We have him safe in irons. He's as vain as the
silliest wench. His hand was in everything, and he's proud to
show it there.'

' Oh,' said Yolande, and thought of the heave of the long
boat as it rammed the barge. Then the Count Raoul spoke
again.

' The queen in a great rage, being I think half-drunk, and
having coughed blood that day, refused to admit the Grand
Seneschal to see the little duke, unless he brought Belphegor
with him. She had missed Belphegor, and accused Azo of
keeping him from her. So Azo was scratching his head outside a slammed door when the plot broke and Janus and the
archers began arresting the men who expected to see us
arrested. . . .'

' And he escaped? '

' Yes, by boat. All this, of course, was on Isle Royal in the
middle of the river. He'll be at Bargreant by now.'

' Did you get the others? '

' Yes. Gaston and all. Azo must have hoped to rejoin
Belphegor at Bargreant . . . Yolande, it'll break him.'

' I hope so. I'll send him Belphegor's head. And I think I
shall take a new motto: *Frango Fulmen*. But the queen, my
lord, what happened to the queen? '

' She died that night of rage, and exhaustion, and loss of
blood.'

' Jesu and Our Lady have mercy on her soul,' said Yolande
crossing herself. ' I see her truth of Belphegor was stranger
than mine. And what happens now? '

' The king has outlawed the Grand Seneschal from Arroy

and the northern provinces, but only you can dismiss him and outlaw him from Baraine.'

Yolande looked up at the fine ivory-brown face with its high cheekbones and proud but merciful eyes.

'Raoul,' she said, 'I have two squires and a dwarf to enforce all my bidding.'

'No. You have me, and Nino here, with five thousand men by the time we reach your frontier. The king has bidden us take great care of so loyal and redoubtable a Peer of Neustria. The Constable is moving from Hautarroy with five thousand more. He'll be below the Talon of Baraine by the time we're at Glion.'

'But I don't want to lead or send armies against my own people.'

'The king, and we, know that. No one moves across your frontiers without your invitation. We're in touch with a dozen barons and chevaliers of the province. Belphegor's death will . . . er . . . persuade many more as to where their loyalty lies.'

'Their loyalty. Yes. Raoul, how do you keep your good name?'

'Such as it is, by remembering a time when I was treated like a serf. By never taking bribes or arguing with bullies, or hushing up an infamy done by a man with six cows against a woman with two. By keeping my soldiers in order, and paying my debts, I suppose. But largely also by luck; more largely, by having good friends, Nino and a few others. Possibly by being very fond of my lady and our children.'

'That recipe I shall remember,' said Yolande, slowly. 'And tonight, my lords, I'll ask you both to help me with my proclamation.'

In the proclamation Yolande gave notice that Azo de Montguiscard was dismissed from his post of Grand Seneschal, and outlawed for his great crimes, thereafter detailed. His household and his war captains were outlawed also, and any man found wearing his device one day after the issue of the proclamation.

But to Azo himself she wrote very briefly on a square scrap of vellum:

Azo Giscardi Montis: Numquid pax potest esse Zambri, qui interfecit dominum suum?

Jolanda Baraniae Dux.

' What peace can Zambri have, who slew his master? ' she repeated, and the Chevalier Lioncel de Forne tacked the vellum down on top of the little tub, and the Chevalier Diomede de Torre splashed purple wax over the skin and the wood, and Yolande pressed into the yielding lump the privy seal of Baraine.

XV

A QUEEN FROM THE EAST

GREY clouds scurried over the green heather, tarns shone blue and white and grey again, rowans swayed and gorse shuddered and bracken was furrowed beneath the crags. A grey stone hamlet crouched in a wide dip where a pack-horse bridge went over a stream; crouch it well might, for the north bank was Nordanay and the south bank Baraine, and at either edge of the dip long lines of lances hedged the sky.

To the north Gold Puss held pride of place, with the black Gerfalcon of Ger on one side, and the black Cross-crosslet and Golden Ram of Saint-Aunay on the other. To the south the Thunderbolt of Montguiscard strained in solitary fury.

Azo had left the duchy in turmoil behind him, mounting every man he could arm, stealing every horse he could find, so that his army snowballed northwards with three times as many chargers as men and a vast number of lesser beasts, some of them laden with loot of churches and town chests and armouries. Like locusts they ate up the meadows and haystacks along the main roads; and no one could muster a force to follow with any speed.

With the Franconian frontier only a few leagues to the east of him, Azo meant to break out of Baraine; but first he had a score to settle with the slayer of his darling son. . . .

And so to a stuttering of trumpets a multicoloured torrent of horseflesh was driven through gaps in his line to surge down the slope and into the shallow stream-bed and up the opposite incline towards the yellow and black-and-white lines of Ger and Saint-Aunay.

Lowered lances kept them away from Ger's line, but Azo's mounted archers began to range with far-shot arrows; an occasional scream in the whirling mass proclaimed a hit.

Azo wanted confusion and a mask between the opposing forces.

Two such captains as Ger and he had naturally sent out flanking-parties and patrols; these began to meet and skirmish over a wide stretch of moorland. Savage ambushes and onfalls, sudden encounters in pine-clumps and gorse-thickets, gradually drew a tangle of battle closer around the ordered fronts.

Some of the horses in Ger's lines were becoming restive; a few, infected by the stamping fright of the unsaddled rout ahead, broke formation and tried to bolt. Yolande wished that Lioncel would not get right in her way, and then realised that arrows were beginning to flicker and fall near. The sky was growing dark, and thunder rumbled on the left.

' He's massing a wedge,' said Raoul of Ger to Jehan of Saint-Aunay.

' Flank archers in front then, and flank lances close on the centre? '

' Yes.'

A trumpet tore complicated patterns of sound out of the air near Yolande's right ear.

' You may have to ride back a little,' said Saint-Aunay quietly from her other side.

Lightning glared beyond him as he spoke, and a nearer rumble shook the sky, stabbed by a new quivering uproar of Montguiscard trumpets across the way.

' Of course the thunder would come to help *him*,' Yolande found herself thinking.

Then she saw Diomede's steel-gloved hand slide out to take her bridle; Raoul of Ger had given to each of her new chevaliers a suit of plate complete. Lioncel was still partly in front, but over the crupper of his grey destrier she saw an extraordinary sight; hundreds of mounted Montguiscard archers let fly a converging volley slap into the mass of frightened animals milling around in the stream bed immediately below the banners.

Yolande gasped at the hideous outburst of animal agony; dozens of the beasts were down and kicking and splashing in the water, and with a great heave to left and right the rest began plunging and crowding away.

Down the opposite slope came the black tongue of the drumming charge, with the Thunderbolt in its midst. As it came a double sleet of archery frayed it at the edges; horses and men whirled out and fell, but the tongue continued to reach up over the crest; it kept shape, mass and direction, driving straight towards her.

In front the steel and yellow had thickened to twice its bulk; lightning glittered on great hedges of metal, and suddenly the whole bulk was leaning and sliding away downhill. A bump and rattle of thunder drowned the long steady roar of ' Ger! ', but the roar outlasted the rattle, and ran into a multiple crash of onset a hundred yards from where Yolande and her escorting party waited.

Yolande blinked at the lightning, put a hand on Diomede's sword-hilt, remembered herself lying in bed and pitying men who had to fight, and saw the yellow waves below bending uphill again in the middle. The three banners were there in line, with the Thunderbolt thrusting blackly below.

Lioncel made a gesture with upraised sword, and Diomede pulled Tancred round. Yolande found Heuradys close behind her, grimly watching the struggle. Quargis, perched on his roan gelding, felt for the crossbow by his stirrup and wheeled to cover her other side.

In front were six archers of Ger, now riding slowly in line away from her. Amid a great racket of thunder Yolande realised that black-coated men had somehow appeared in a gully twenty yards away. The yellow coats slid between with a shout.

Diomede checked Tancred and thrust him past two thick thorn-bushes, pulling Yolande out of the saddle to stand her behind a six-foot boulder. Then he unslung his shield—blue, with a white turret on it—and slipped the strap over her head.

' Keep it up,' he said quietly. ' They're throwing heavy stones.'

Then he shut his visor and sat a moment, and suddenly pulled his black horse off to her left.

Lioncel appeared on her right, swinging his shield into place. The dazzle of its wavy red and white was charged with a sable hunting-horn. A big stone hit it silently . . . that was because the thunder was bellowing. Lioncel twitched his visor down and swung forward out of her sight. . . .

A man in a torn black tabard flapped up from nowhere, heaving a guisarme sideways; Diomede was suddenly behind him, cutting him down with calm precision. . . .

A fearful flash drove Yolande to her knees under the shield. When she opened her eyes again Quargis was shepherding Heuradys round the edge of the rock, taking up his stand beyond her with his crossbow at the ready. Beyond him reappeared Lioncel, dismounted and shouting, but his words were lost in the thunder.

Yolande poked shield and head round the rock to see what was happening. Heuradys pulled her back, Lioncel disappeared again, Quargis suddenly tossed up the bow, shot a bolt, and began to reload.

Yolande stood obstinately up, shield over her head. Lioncel and Diomede, both dismounted now, were standing together on a nearby boulder, bright in their full armour, slamming away at figures beyond them. A man in yellow shouted and pointed; Yolande turned, and a stone flew past her head. Then she saw, against the near-black sky over the closest crest of all, a great silvery-armoured figure on a great cream-white destrier, couching a white lance with pennon of cloth of silver, his silvered steel of helm and shield and chamfron blazing back the purple-white of lightning overhead.

Behind him were other figures in black-and-white, in green, in crimson; Yolande laughed amid the thunder, and turned to look again at her lovers. Something flew over the rim of the lowered shield and hit her hard between the eyes.

She awoke in a poor rough bed in a village tavern, with Heuradys bathing her bruised forehead, and Quargis sitting crying quietly at her other side. The village street was loud with the hoofs of rounded-up riderless horses. Taking in the grief of Quargis, she framed a dreadful question.

'Which of them is dead?' she whispered.

'Both,' said Heuradys, and her tears, too, ran, for the first time that Yolande could remember.

'How?'

'A flash of lightning. Just after you were stunned. The enemy were already running.'

'Oh . . . oh, then I can't take my new motto.'

'What was that, my heart's darling?' asked Heuradys chokingly.

'*Frango Fulmen*, I break the Thunderbolt. The thunderbolt's had the best of it.'

She put a hand over her eyes.

'I hope they've told each other now, and forgiven me,' she thought. 'I hope they laughed. Diomede wanted them to die together. It's the Sieur God who doesn't forgive me.'

She took her hand away, and laid it on the big clenched fist of the dwarf.

'What about the Grand Seneschal?' she asked.

'Captured,' muttered Quargis. 'His men are routed or slaughtered or taken.'

'Have you got *their* shields for me?'

'Yes, my lady, I have their shields.'

'Quargis, I'll bury them both at Bargreant, near the great tomb I'm going to build for my father.'

'My lord of Ger will be coming presently,' said Heuradys, 'and with him, I think, the Chevalier de Largire.'

'Comb my hair,' said Yolande, and put her other hand up to the wet cheek of Heuradys.

When Raoul of Ger came in alone she held out her arms like a child, and he flung a cloak across the cold steel of his armour so that she might lie against his shoulder and forget that she was the triumphant Duchess of Baraine.

The collar of the Order of the Bridge of Faith was a magnificent affair, each link a rose of gold and garnets; the pendant was a little golden bridge, across which a golden destrier bore a golden chevalier whose shield and crest and banner were of rubies.

Raoul of Ger had brought it to her at Pardelin, together with a friendly letter from the king.

'You must sign the Roll when we get to Hautarroy,' said Raoul, when he had arranged the collar on her shoulders. 'See, here's the list of chevaliers; each of us is given a copy of it.'

Yolande unrolled the parchment and glanced at the names, of which the first was *Torismundus rex* and the last *Jolanda, Baraniae dux*.

The Latin sonorities boomed in her mind. *Godricus Savultiae dux,* Chancellor again. *Falcasius Olenticuriae marchio*, the Constable, who had hanged Uncle Azo at Bargreant for all Baraine to see. *Radulfus, Hierrae comes*, who stood silently beside her. *Janus, Argyriae eques*, whom she and the Count Raoul had persuaded to become her new Grand Seneschal. Her father's name was there, and Drogo's, with the crosses that marked the honourable dead. And last of all before her own were the names of the two Montguiscards, each with a red ink line drawn firmly through it.

Jolanda, Baraniae dux.

Yolande sighed, laid down the list, and took Raoul of Ger by the arm.

'Come up on to the keep,' she said, and led him out to the ramparts.

It was the time of afterglow, and no wind stirred the iron-grey and silver-grey, the rose and blue and saffron of the lake. Clouds were high and still; the mountains lifted their rocky summits towards the first stars. The confusion of crags and screes, of heather and bracken and gorse and pine, stooped sombrely to the greenwood along the twilit shore.

'Raoul,' began Yolande abruptly, 'how long before they begin to worry me to marry again?'

'Why?'

'I don't want to marry again. At least, not yet. I know it was said Azo made haste in case you wanted me for Lothair. You don't, do you? Or if you do . . . if you want *him* to be a duke I must tell you this. Lioncel and Diomede were both my lovers, neither knowing about the other, and nothing,

nothing, will ever make me sorry or ashamed because of it.'

Raoul of Ger put his arm around her.

'Don't think any more about Lothair,' he said. 'I hope he'll marry Nino's daughter. And he will be a duke some day; the king's going to make me Duke of Nordanay.'

Yolande embarked upon a little speech of congratulation. He thanked her absently.

'As to your own marriage,' he said, 'I know the king has taken some thought concerning it.'

'Already?'

'Already.'

'O damnation! Raoul, who is it this time?'

'The king is also concerned . . . worried . . . about that prophecy.'

'Mad Jacquerelle's, you mean? It wasn't very clever.'

'Can you repeat it?'

'Yes:

Soon to be seen a new queen,
A queen from the east with an angry beast,
From a moorland and a dour land but not a poor land,
After Honoy bringing joy to Hautarroy.'

'That's it. But the king prefers " after annoy " to " after Honoy ".'

'What difference does it make? Has it set him against his poor little daughter-in-law?'

'No, he seems fond of her, and he's certainly very fond of Réné. The fact is, he appears to have found another reading.'

'But it's very plain. The rimes with Zurland, and the angry beast from the East. . . .'

'Cousin, coming east from Hautarroy you don't *have* to fetch up on the shore of the Baltic Sea.'

Yolande raised her head and followed his glance at Gold Puss magnificent above and behind them.

She stiffened in his friendly grasp, and presently summoned a curt laugh.

' By the bones of Saint Amarand,' she swore, ' I should never have thought of that.'

The mountains of Baraine stood dreaming in the twilight, indifferent to the amused dismay of their once-shy Leopardess.

' Think of it soon,' advised Raoul of Ger. ' No matter what you told me just now, it will make for a cleaner air at court, and for peace and strength in the kingdom.'

Yolande stood silent for a long moment, holding the count's hand close against her side, wondering, beginning to scheme against grief and loneliness and absurdity.

' From here,' she said calmly at length, ' you can see why it's called Lake Falchion.'

THE NEWCASTLE MYTHOLOGY LIBRARY

———— Book One
M-030-5
$4.95

CELTIC MYTH AND LEGEND, by Charles Squire.
Admirers of Evangeline Walton, Kenneth Morris, Katherine Kurtz, and Lloyd Alexander will find this massive 500-page compendium of Celtic mythology an essential guide to the gods, heroes, giants, and other legendary figures of early Gaelic and Welsh lore. Copiously illustrated.

———— Book Two
M-038-0
$4.95

THE ROMANCE OF CHIVALRY, by A. R. Hope Moncrieff.
Moncrieff covers all the legends from the wondrous Age of Chivalry, including the stories of Arthur, Charlemagne, Roland and Oliver, Huon of Bordeaux, Ogier the Dane, Sir Grey-steel, Amadis of Gaul, Esplandian, and many of the other great heroes and villains so celibrated in medieval tale and lore. Nearly 450 pages of text, with numerous illustrations.

———— Book Three
M-042-9
$3.95

TALES OF ATLANTIS AND THE ENCHANTED ISLANDS, by Thomas Wentworth Higginson.
Plato's classic tale of lost Atlantis has given birth to scores of colorful and mysterious legends of the Enchanted Islands of the Atlantic, a fascinating body of folklore in which myth and magic mix tantalizingly with scraps of facts from ancient explorers. Here is a unique collection of tales dealing with strange Atlantic islands, some wholly imaginary, some persisting on mariners' charts well into the 19th century.

OTHER TALES OF THE FANTASTIC

———— P-005-4
$2.45

GHOSTS I HAVE MET, by John Kendrick Bangs.
Bangs was one of the earliest writers to introduce humor into the fantasy story, in such classic compendiums as A HOUSE-BOAT ON THE STYX, in which various famous characters from history return from the grave to comment on contemporary customs and mores. GHOSTS I HAVE MET takes a hilarious peek at those off-beat spooks who just won't stay put in their graves. With an introduction by Douglas Menville.

———— X-028-3
$2.95

THE QUEST OF THE GOLDEN STAIRS, by Arthur Edward Waite.
The Land of Faërie is old beyond the measure of man, and its people are tired of kings who rule without end. The gods promise that a new hero will someday come. That hero is Starbeam, a Prince of the royal house, who is sent upon a quest to find the golden stairs stretching into the heavens, and through them his betrothed, the beautiful Cynthia. An allegory filled with magic and enchantment.

———— X-032-1
$2.95

ENTER DR. NIKOLA! by Guy Boothby (Dr. Nikola, Book One).
A curious Chinese token is the key to Nikola's ambitions, and Nikola will have it, whatever the cost. And if Wetherell refuses to sell, perhaps a suitable trade can be arranged: Wetherell's beautiful daughter for the strangely-inscribed token. Only Richard Hatteras can foil the Doctor's nefarious schemes, but Hatteras is being held captive in Port Said, and Nikola has already fled with the girl to the South Seas. Can anyone stop Doctor Nikola?

———— X-034-8
$2.95

DR. NIKOLA RETURNS, by Guy Boothby (Dr. Nikola, Book Two).
In his second exciting adventure, Nikola infiltrates a mysterious Chinese sect to gain the secrets of eternal life. With his new assistant, he penetrates the deepest regions of hidden Tibet, where he convinces the princes that he is the newest member of their ruling triumvirate. As the installation begins, the real priest appears, and Nikola is unmasked. The lamas sit in judgment, and their verdict is death!

NEWCASTLE ASTROLOGY CLASSICS

———— P-014-3
$3.75

AN INTRODUCTION TO ASTROLOGY, by William Lilly.
William Lilly was one of the most renowned astrologers in English history. He wrote and published many early texts on the subject, cast horoscopes for King Charles I, and predicted the great fire of London in 1666 so accurately that he was suspected of complicity in the conflagration. This book, which remains one of the most comprehensive books ever written on the subject, was first published in 1647; the Newcastle edition is reprinted from the 1852 version edited by the well-known 19th century astrologer, Zadkiel.

———— P-018-6
$2.95

PRACTICAL ASTROLOGY, by Comte C. de Saint-Germain.
Saint-Germain, a pseudonym of Edgar de Valcourt-Vermont, published a number of books on astrology, hypnotism, and palmistry (including his classic text, THE PRACTICE OF PALMISTRY, also available in a Newcastle edition). PRACTICAL ASTROLOGY examines the basics of astrological principles, and presents a clear, easy-to-understand method for casting horoscopes. Saint-Germain also examines the relationship between astrology and the tarot.

———— T-026-7
$4.95

THE ARCANA OF ASTROLOGY, by William J. Simmonite.
Originally published as THE COMPLETE ARCANA OF ASTRAL PHILOSOPHY, this fascinating text presents, clearly and logically, the fundamentals of astrology, with questions and problems to help the reader absorb the material. Crammed with tables, diagrams, and illustrations, here's a book as relevant to today's astrologers as it was when first published nearly a century ago.

———— P-031-3
$2.95

ASTROLOGY AND THE TAROT, by A.E. Thierens.
Dr. Thierens offers a clear, concise explanation of the Tarot, both the Lesser and the Greater Arcana, and sets forth for the first time a carefully-worked-out system of correspondences between the Tarot and astrology.

———— P-035-6
$3.95

ASTROLOGY: ITS TECHNIQUES AND ETHICS, by C. Aq. Libra.
Originally published in the Netherlands, this important occult work has long been unavailable to those interested in the role of the stars in man's spiritual evolution. Libra covers the following topics: the laws of karma and reincarnation, calculation of the horoscope, the progressive horoscope, the zodiac of the head, astrology and medicine, proportions in the cosmos in nature and art, and astrology and the Bible.

———— P-039-9
$4.95

ASTROLOGY AND ITS PRACTICAL APPLICATION, by Else Parker.
This classic study of astro-psychology illustrates the practical value of astrology in everyday life. A. E. Thierens, author of ASTROLOGY AND THE TAROT (also available in a Newcastle edition) called it "of great value for its insights." First American edition.

NEWCASTLE ARCANA

VICTOR H. LINDLAHR HEALTH BOOKS

_____ H-004-6   YOU ARE WHAT YOU EAT.
$2.95   Lindlahr's classic revelation of diet and nutrition
tells how to balance one's meals, where to find
vitamins and minerals in natural foods, how to
prepare dishes without destroying nutritional content, and much more. Includes complete nutritional tables for all fruits and vegetables.

_____ D-011-9   THE LINDLAHR VITAMIN COOKBOOK.
$2.95   Fresh foods contain all the vitamins and nutrients
needed by the human body. The key to preserv-
ing these essential constituents lies in the proper
preparation of meals and dishes. Complete with
vitamin balance charts and recipes.

_____ H-015-1   EAT AND REDUCE!
$2.95   Diet the Lindlahr way, as America's leading nutri-
tionist outlines a safe and healthy method of
getting rid of extra pounds without endangering
one's health. Includes diet plans and calorie
tables.

_____ H-017-8   THE NATURAL WAY TO HEALTH.
$2.95   Here is Dr. Lindlahr's own story of his research into
the natural values of organically grown foods. The
secret of good health lies in living a balanced and
sane life, and eating natural foods. Lindlahr anti-
cipited much of today's findings in food research.

_____ H-040-2   VICTOR LINDLAHR'S 7-DAY REDUCING DIET.
$2.95   The author of YOU ARE WHAT YOU EAT presents
a practical, down-to-earth reducing plan that will
get the reader's weight down to where it should
be—and keep it that way. Here are 201 tasty and
imaginative recipes, plus a helpful question-and-
answer section, calorie counters, and many important food facts.

OTHER HEALTH BOOKS

_____ H-016-X   ROMANY REMEDIES AND RECIPES,
$2.25   by Gipsy Petulengro.
Petulengro's book is a classic compilation of Gypsy
health foods and herbal medicines, painstakingly
uncovered by trial-and-error over many centuries
of wandering the countrysides of Europe and
America. Profusely illustrated.

_____ H-021-6   VIEWPOINT ON NUTRITION, by Arnold Pike.
$2.95   Dr. Pike provides nutritional highlights from his
television show, including interviews with Gaylord
Hauser, Linus Pauling, Eddie Albert, Julie Harris,
and many others. An original Newcastle publication.

NEWCASTLE SELF-ENRICHMENT BOOKS

_____ S-000-3   FORTUNATE STRANGERS,
$2.95   by Cornelius Beukenkamp, Jr.
Dr. Beukenkamp's work is a pioneering study of
psychology and group psychotherapy that has
justly been regarded as a classic book in its field.
"An interesting demonstration—and documenta-
tion—of this method in the words of the partici-
pants." —The Kirkus Review. Reprinted from the
Rinehart edition.

_____ S-002-X   LOVE, HATE, FEAR, ANGER, AND OTHER
$2.95   LIVELY EMOTIONS, by June Callwood.
Recently excerpted in the Reader's Digest, this
Doubleday reprint studies the human emotions,
and shows how they master, or are mastered by,
the individual.

_____ G-006-2   THE IMPORTANCE OF FEELING INFERIOR,
$2.95   by Marie Beynon Ray.
Ray shows how one's feelings of inferiority can be
used to propel the individual to greater heights
of achievement, and to guide each person to a
richer, more productive life. Originally published
by Harper & Row.

_____ G-009-7   THE CONQUEST OF FEAR, by Basil King.
$2.95   Inspired by the author's blindness, this reprint of
the Doubleday edition provides a practical guide
to overcoming the fears each person must face
in their everyday life.

_____ W-013-5   THE ORIGINS OF POPULAR SUPERSTITIONS
$2.95   AND CUSTOMS, by T. Sharper Knowlson.
Knowlson's fascinating account of the follies of
human belief includes sections on amulets,
charms, divining rods, drinking customs, dreams
and omens, crystal gazing, lucky stars, vampires,
and much more. Complete with index.

_____ W-022-4   MARRIAGE COUNSELING: FACT OR FALLACY?,
$2.95   by Jerold R. Kuhn.
Dr. Kuhn provides a scholarly and timely treatment of a current topic, as drawn from actual
case histories at the American Institute of Family
Relations. The situations include minor communi-
cation problems, incompatibility, sexual disfunc-
tion, and money worries. An original Newcastle
publication.

_____ G-036-4   YOUR HANDWRITING AND WHAT IT MEANS,
$2.95   by William Leslie French.
An uncomplicated survey of the techniques of
handwriting analysis, and how it can be used to
reveal hidden character traits in oneself and
others. Many signatures of noted personalities
included.